Postcards
from the
Cove

Jennifer Bardsley

BOOKS BY JENNIFER BARDSLEY

Postcards

from the

Cove

JENNIFER BARDSLEY

bookouture

Published by Bookouture in 2024

An imprint of Storyfire Ltd.
Carmelite House
50 Victoria Embankment
London EC4Y 0DZ

www.bookouture.com

ISBN: 978-1-83790-536-2
eBook ISBN: 978-1-83790-532-4

To my sister, Diane Williams, and our joint belief in the motto "it's better with bacon."

ONE

New Year's Day should be bright and full of promise, but instead of enjoying a brisk morning walk along the windswept beaches of Sand Dollar Cove and then brunching with friends, Hannah was stuck indoors and freezing. As much as she loved wearing her dad's old down coat, it had lost its fluff over the years, and wasn't that warm anymore. But Hannah clung to the coat, like she clung to the notion that this year would be different. With enough hard work and determination, the American dream would finally come through for her. *It had to.* Hannah had spent all twenty-four years and eleven months of her life believing that responsibility was the path to happiness. She thought that her father had believed that too.

Hannah zipped up the coat and stared at the mountain of junk that had accumulated in Strawberry Cottage. As the assistant general manager of Seaside Resort, holidays on the calendar meant another day of work for her. Strawberry Cottage was once the grandest accommodation on the property, but was now scheduled for demolition that summer because of a cracked foundation. They'd been using it as an extra storage facility ever since the city inspector had issued the cottage's death warrant three years ago. The heater was broken and the whole room bore a musty odor.

"This is Nick's fault," Hannah grumbled to herself as she sorted through half-used tins of paint. "Just because he's the head maintenance man doesn't mean he can commandeer any building he wants."

The architect was coming the next morning and needed to see the cottage properly. Right now, the pile of garbage sitting in the middle of the room was an enormous distraction. Hannah moved a box of aging ceiling paint to the porch and then came back for a load of broken porcelain tiles. She paused as she crossed the threshold, sad for what the cottage had become.

Hannah took out her phone and texted Nick. *Where are you? There's a pile of junk here that you need to take to the dumpster.*

I'll get there when I get there, he replied a minute later.

Nick's totally unprofessional response didn't surprise Hannah. Since he was poker buddies with Herman, the general manager, Nick got away with shoddy workmanship and a poor attitude.

Fuming, but trying to remain calm, Hannah texted Nick back. *The architect will be here tomorrow. Strawberry Cottage needs to be cleared today. Before you go home.*

Like I said, Nick answered. *I'll get there when I get there.*

Hannah raked her fingers through her long brown hair and looked up at the stained ceiling, feeling exasperated. She thought about calling Herman—calling him because her boss didn't know how to text—but knew it was pointless. Herman would back his buddy up. It was up to her to get this job done. She couldn't count on anyone to help her.

Wind from a passing storm rattled the cottage windows, and the lights flickered. The foghorn sang in the distance as Hannah worked through the debris. Most days, the foghorn blew every three minutes, which was a constant complaint the resort received on Yelp. Those were the reviews that annoyed Hannah the most because there was nothing she could do to fix them, unless she could conjure a magic wand that would add triple-paned windows to every cottage on the property.

Hannah pushed rolls of linoleum onto the porch, and heaved an old, cracked dresser outside. It was raining now, and the wet weather soaked the growing pile of debris. But that was Nick's problem, not Hannah's. If he'd come when he had said he would, things wouldn't be a soggy mess.

"It's looking a lot better," she said to herself, as she cleared more floor space. A second later, something wiggled behind a cardboard box.

Hannah screamed when she saw a squiggly tail. She looked around for a weapon, but all she found was a broken umbrella.

"I don't want any trouble," Hannah declared in a fierce tone, as if that might make the invader disappear. Hannah poked at the box where the wiggling had come from, but nothing happened. "This isn't Olympic National Park, this is Sand Dollar Cove." Hannah banged the tip of the umbrella against the cardboard. "We love wildlife, but not indoors."

When nothing more happened, Hannah straightened her spine, still keeping her death grip on the umbrella. Maybe she'd been imagining things. But no! A rat streaked across the floor and into a hole in the wall.

"Gross!" Hannah screeched, realizing that everything she'd touched might have been covered with rodent droppings. Letting go of the umbrella, she ran over to the kitchenette to wash her hands in scalding hot water. Enough was enough. She'd march into the maintenance shed and drag Nick out by the ears if she had to. Since there wasn't any towel to dry her hands, Hannah walked over to a pile of old linens on the bed and used them instead. When she stood, her arm brushed against a stained lampshade and the wire poking out of the frame ripped across her sleeve.

"Dad's coat!" Hannah cried. Feathers shot out and floated to the ground. This couldn't be happening. She slapped her hand over her elbow to stop the destruction, and then bent down to collect the loose feathers with her free hand.

This was the worst, the absolute worst way to begin the new year. Hannah wasn't crying. She would never cry. The tears sprouting were from dust, that was all. She took a deep breath to steady herself and did what she always did in the face of heart-break; she called her grandma.

Cheryl picked up on the second ring. "Hi, sweet girl, what's up?"

"Dad's coat got ripped." Hannah looked at the tiny pile of feathers in front of her. "I'm here cleaning Strawberry Cottage, and since the heater's kaput, I put on Dad's coat. It caught on something and now the sleeve's ruined, and it's all my fault."

"It's not your fault," Cheryl said in a calm tone. "It was an accident."

"But Gran—"

"It's a coat, Hannah, it's not your dad. Max would understand."

"I know, but..."

"Bring it home and I'll see if Patti can fix it the next time I go to the senior center. She's a whiz when it comes to sewing. I can barely thread a needle."

"Do you think it can be saved?" Hannah looked at her arm and carefully pulled her hand away from the torn blue fabric. A few more feathers floated down.

"Probably. But if it can't be saved, you could wear that new coat Mary got you last year for your birthday. You know she picked up extra shifts at the coffee stand to afford it."

"I've worn it a few times." It wasn't that Hannah didn't appreciate her sister's generosity; it was that every time she wore Max's coat, it felt like her dad was still with her. "I'll look for a box so I can gather all the feathers. Patti might need them."

"Or she can repair it with new feathers," Cheryl suggested. "That might be better."

"No. These feathers will work." Hannah refused to lose one ounce of this connection to her father. "I'm sure of it." She scanned the room, looking for a container. "I just wish my New Year's Day hadn't started off so badly."

"Remember what I always say. A bad day in Sand Dollar Cove is better than a great day in Seattle."

"Thanks, Gran. Are you and Ferdinand doing okay?" The senior center was closed for the holiday, so Cheryl was home with the cat while Hannah and Mary worked.

"He's sitting on my lap watching *Miss Marple* with me."

"That's good. I'll be home in time to heat up some leftovers for dinner."

"Drive safe, and I'll see you then," said Cheryl. "Love you."

"Love you, too." Hannah slipped her phone in the back pocket of her pants and searched for a feather receptacle. A few minutes later she found a plastic bag that would work, and she carefully plucked every last feather she could find and sealed it inside. She was putting the bag into her purse when a reflection of light caught her attention.

There, in the corner, underneath the end table, sat an ornately carved mahogany box. Curious, because she'd never seen a box like this in any of the cottages before, Hannah stooped down and picked it up.

A thick layer of dust covered the outside of the box, but once Hannah blew away the dirt, she could see a rhododendron flower carved on the top. One of the former guests must have left it. Feeling slightly guilty, like she was invading their privacy, Hannah pried the lid open. She reasoned she had to. Otherwise, how would she find out who the owners were so she could return it to them? Seaside Resort *always* tried to return lost belongings to guests. Over the years they'd mailed a wide assortment of things: bathrobes, cell phones,

eyeglasses, and even dentures, but never anything as interesting as this.

Inside the box was a glass jar with a blue ribbon tied around
the rim. Dried sand dollars—flat sea urchins with flower-shaped
markings at their centers—rested in white sand next to postcards. Hannah unscrewed the lid. When she opened the jar, she
caught a faint whiff of the ocean. She pinched a postcard and
carefully removed it from the container. It showed a vintage
picture of Strawberry Cottage, nestled on its cliff overlooking
the sea. Hannah turned the postcard over to see what was
written on the back and found another photo. This picture was
a stylized map of Washington State with a sand dollar and a
sailboat drawn next to a dot on the map.

Visit Sand Dollar Cove, said the headline. *The Riviera of the
West.*

An old memory, from the deep recesses of Hannah's mind,
pinged her attention. She was holding Max's hand. Her mom
stood next to her, cradling baby Mary. They stood in the lobby
of Seaside Resort waiting for Cheryl to get off work so they
could take her to dinner. Hannah had seen these postcards a
long time ago, in the sales rack of the lobby. But that must have
been ages ago. Max had died when she was five years old.
Seaside Resort hadn't sold souvenirs like these in decades.

But what grabbed Hannah's attention the most was that
Frank Sinatra had signed the card, addressing it to "Joe from
Connecticut." There was his autograph underneath the sailboat, clear as day. Not only that, but there was a third piece of
paper in the jar. Instead of a postcard, it was a thick piece of
cardstock with cursive writing that was difficult to decipher.
Hannah brought it closer to the light.

Dearest One,

They say love makes people do foolish things. Perhaps that's why I've held onto this for all these years. Love has made me keep it. Love has made me hide it. Love is prompting me to bring it back to you. I still believe in our happily ever after. Together we can return this to the sea.

Always yours,

Joe

What was this about? Who was Joe from Connecticut, and why had he left the jar for someone to find? Strawberry Cottage had been decommissioned three years ago. Maybe she'd be able to find him in the guest records if she had a moment to look. She should return the box, if possible. That Frank Sinatra autograph might be valuable.

It wasn't until a few hours later, after she'd guilt-tripped Nick into actually doing his job for once and finishing the cleanup work on the cottage, that Hannah finally had time to pull up the old records on the cottage.

She stood at the front desk of the lobby waiting to assist guests. But since it was 2 p.m. and check-in time wasn't until four, she usually used this quiet time to catch up on administration duties like creating schedules, reordering toner for the printer, and updating the resort's Facebook page.

Hannah opened the spreadsheet with the Strawberry Cottage records and searched for any entry that mentioned a man named Joe, or the state of Connecticut. She scrolled through hundreds of entries for Washington, Oregon, Idaho, Montana, and British Columbia—the Olympic Peninsula was a popular destination for the Pacific Northwest—but couldn't find any mention of Connecticut until she spotted a registration from 2004. That was an awfully long time ago. But there was his name, Joe Smith, clear as day. Since it was the only guest who'd visited from Connecticut, Hannah printed out an address label with his name on it, packed the ornately carved box into cardboard, and left it for the mail carrier to pick up tomorrow. She didn't know if the address they had on file for him was still in use, but she hoped for the best.

On her way back to the reception area she helped herself to a steaming mug of coffee from the beverage station in the lobby and added a generous helping of cream. Wrapping her hands around the mug to warm them, Hannah stared through the floor-to-ceiling windows at the churning waves and silver sky. She thought about the box and the glass jar with the note inside it.

Would she ever have a love like that? Or even the thrill of going to a concert and having a famous person sign their autograph? *Probably not.* Sometimes her life felt small, consumed by work, and caring for her grandma and sister. Romance and recreation never made it onto her to-do list. Occasionally her heart yearned for something more. Adventure! A great love! But responsibility was the only security Hannah had. If she stayed on track... If she worked hard... If she focused on small, measurable dreams she could actually achieve, she'd be safe. Grandiose plans destroyed lives.

A bad day in Sand Dollar Cove is better than a great day in Seattle, she repeated to herself. Sometimes she needed that reminder, too. The front door opened, and Hannah turned to welcome the first guests of the new year.

TWO

Four months later, adventure and romance finally walked through Hannah's front door—or the front door of Seaside Resort, that is. After the wellness director abruptly quit, they had hired Guy Barret, who was not only well qualified for the position but also so... *dreamy*. There was no other word for him, and it flustered Hannah to admit it. Six feet tall with dark blond hair and blue eyes, Guy had a kind demeanor that calmed a person, which made him a perfect fit for working with guests who were nervous about accessing the resort's fitness and wellness program. Not only that, but Guy had graduated from Dartmouth and spoke three languages: English, Spanish, and French, plus a smattering of Italian. It had said so on his application and Hannah had no reason to doubt it, because every conversation they'd had together proved that he was highly intelligent.

Hannah felt bad for Lark, their head housekeeper, who had been dating the former wellness director, but as far as she was concerned, Guy moving to Sand Dollar Cove was an improvement for everyone. The only problem was that Hannah turned into an especially businesslike version of herself whenever she was around him. Her flirting skills were rusted into place. She'd never fallen for a co-worker before, and to complicate matters, Hannah might become his boss in a few months' time. Herman had announced his retirement and was recommending that Blanchet Maison, the corporation that owned the resort, appoint her as the new general manager. Would it be appropriate for a boss to date an employee? Hannah didn't think so. Still, that didn't stop her from swooning every time she saw him.

Today was Saturday, April 27th, and Hannah was inventorying the supplies in the health and wellness studio. She tried to focus on her clipboard and checklists, but it was hard not to eavesdrop on Guy and the two guests from Seattle whom he was training as part of the brand-new "Two Weeks to Fitness" package he'd introduced.

"Way to go, Mrs. Dario, you're doing great. Keep those arms moving." Guy smiled encouragingly. "Your triceps will thank you tomorrow." He stood between them and the workout mirrors.

"Why is this so hard?" Mrs. Dario, who was in her early seventies, sweated profusely. She had on black slacks and a Seaside Resort T-shirt she must have purchased in the gift shop. Multiple rings adorned her manicured hands. "I'm not even using weights."

"Keep at it, Elena," said her friend, who worked out next to her. "You'll get there." Mrs. Sanchez pumped her arms as if the three-pound weights she held were light as feathers.

"That's right, Mrs. Dario." Guy touched her elbow, adjusting her form. "After a few weeks of body-weight reps you'll be ready for soup cans."

"Soup cans?" Mrs. Dario raised her eyebrows. "You're kidding me."

"He's serious," said Mrs. Sanchez. "Soup cans are the next step." She wore form-fitting leggings and a tank top that showed off her toned arms. A gold necklace glistened around her throat.

"Yes," said Guy. "Once the soup cans become too easy, you can graduate to one-pound weights."

Mrs. Dario pumped her triceps. "I wish I could bring you home with me, Guy. I haven't gotten this much exercise since taking dance lessons for my *quinceañera*."

Hannah wished she could bring Guy home with her, too, but that might be awkward since she lived with her grandma and sister... She made a note on her clipboard and kept working. The next line on her checklist was counting the packs of disinfectant wipes.

"You don't need Guy," said Mrs. Sanchez. "Just start coming to the SilverSneakers class I go to three days a week."

"Those classes must work," said Guy, "because your range of motion is seriously impressive."

Mrs. Sanchez stood straight and flexed her biceps. "Use it or lose it, that's what my SilverSneakers instructor says."

"Stop showing off, Brenda," said Mrs. Dario. "You look like an advertisement for Ensure."

"I'll take that as a compliment." Mrs. Sanchez switched into shoulder presses even though Guy hadn't given that cue yet.

"Great job with those triceps extensions, Mrs. Dario," said Guy. "Let's move into shoulder presses, like Mrs. Sanchez is showing. Lift your arms up above your head but keep your shoulders down and away from your ears." He watched carefully as Mrs. Dario gave it a go. "That's right. You got it."

"I feel like I'm doing semaphore," said Mrs. Dario. "Quick, Brenda, what am I saying?"

"You're saying, 'Thank you for telling Carlos and me about Seaside Resort. This was just what I needed to get my blood pressure under control.'"

Yes! Hannah thought. *That's exactly what we want. Word-of-mouth advertising.* After only three months on the job, Guy was already making an impact.

"I said all that with my arms?" Mrs. Dario laughed. "I

thought I was waving spy planes onto a secret airstrip in the middle of the Cold War."

"You read too many historical romance novels," said Mrs. Sanchez.

"That's impossible," said Guy. "There can never be such a thing as too much reading, or too much romance."

Hannah's heart fluttered. *Guy enjoyed reading?* She loved books, too. The Sand Dollar Cove library wasn't large, but it could request books from across Grays Harbor County, and Hannah frequently used that benefit. Just because she didn't have the time, money, or courage to travel, didn't mean she couldn't enjoy reading about other people's adventures. She was her father's daughter, after all. When poor eyesight had thwarted Max's dreams of a military career, he'd taken a job as an independent contractor and worked all over the world.

"You love reading?" Mrs. Dario held the back of her hand to her forehead and pretended to swoon. "Be still my heart! I knew I wanted to take you home with me."

You and me both, thought Hannah.

"Stop flirting with our trainer," said Mrs. Sanchez. "Maybe I don't want to take you with me to SilverSneakers, after all. You might embarrass me."

"I bet you'd have a blast," said Guy. "Exercising is always better with friends. If you take one thing away from our time together, that's what I want you to remember. Once you find a workout buddy, exercising will always be fun. Intramural sports at college taught me that."

"Look at you with your Brad Pitt face and your Dr. Phil wise advice." Mrs. Dario fanned her face with her fingertips. "I fall more in love with you each day."

"There you go, flirting again." Mrs. Sanchez shot her friend a look.

I wish Mrs. Dario could teach me some lessons, thought Hannah. She couldn't remember *how* to flirt.

"Why don't we all rest for a moment and have a sip of water?" Guy handed them both fresh towels. He glanced over at Hannah and grinned conspiratorially.

Guy was grinning at her? What was she supposed to do? Grin back? Hannah hid behind her clipboard.

"Thanks." Mrs. Dario wiped her forehead and smeared a streak of makeup off. "I'm sweating like an ice cream carton on a hot day."

"That's the best part of working out." Mrs. Sanchez blotted her face with the towel. "It detoxes your pores."

"How am I supposed to know what workouts to do when I get home to Seattle next week?" Mrs. Dario asked.

"I'll write it all down for you," said Guy. "I promise. A thirty-minute walk, plus ten minutes of strength exercise, and five minutes of stretching. Start with three times a week and build from there. Or take Mrs. Sanchez up on her offer for that SilverSneakers class. That would be good, too."

"Maybe..." Mrs. Dario unscrewed the cap to her water bottle.

"We'll go shopping beforehand and buy you some new outfits," said Mrs. Sanchez.

"I do love shopping." Mrs. Dario sipped her water. "How about I work up to the soup cans first, and then we talk about it?"

"That sounds like a wonderful goal," said Guy. "Right, Mrs. Sanchez?"

"Agreed." Mrs. Sanchez nodded. "I really think you'd have fun once you got there, Elena."

"What's been your favorite part of your vacation so far?" Guy asked.

Hannah was curious about that, too. It was one of her standard questions. It was a simple way to keep the conversation moving, but it also gave her insight into what guests appreciated about Seaside Resort, and what they might like to see improved.

"Oh gosh, it's hard to pick just one thing," said Mrs. Dario.

"This 'Two Weeks to Fitness' program has been great," said Mrs. Sanchez. "An hour of personal training every morning followed up by a spa treatment in the afternoon is hard to beat."

"If it weren't for the spa treatments, I might not have signed up for this," said Mrs. Dario. "But I agree with Brenda. It's only been two days so far, but this has been one of my favorite parts of the trip."

"I'm glad to hear it," said Guy. "I'm not involved with the esthetician side of things, of course, but I love helping clients build simple exercise regimens they can take with them when they go home." He moved his shoulder in an odd way that Hannah wondered about, but then she reminded herself that she was there to check inventory, not check Guy out.

"The hiking, whale watching, and beachcombing has also been fun," said Mrs. Sanchez.

"All this fresh sea air has been so good for me." Mrs. Dario beamed. "Wait until I tell my cardiologist how much my blood pressure has improved. I'm sure our morning workouts have played a big part in that."

"I'm just glad that you took the first step." Mrs. Sanchez patted her friend's back. "I'd hug you, but I'm all sweaty."

"I don't mind." Mrs. Dario opened her arms and the two women embraced.

Hannah jotted a note on her clipboard and moved on to counting water jugs. She'd campaigned for Herman to approve the purchase of a built-in bottled water dispenser, but he'd nixed that idea as being "too trendy."

"Okay, you two," said Guy. "The workout isn't over yet. Let's end with Drinking Bird, just like we did yesterday. Balance on the front part of your feet, extend your arms, and push your booty back."

"I haven't had a booty in fifty years," Mrs. Dario said, giggling.

"I'm sure Carlos would disagree with that." Mrs. Sanchez executed the Drinking Bird posture with the precision of a yogi. "Do you think he and Vicente caught anything out on their charter this morning?"

"Probably. Carlos is bummed that they missed halibut season, but they made up for it yesterday with albacore tuna." Mrs. Dario looked up at Guy. "Do you fish?"

"No, I'm a vegetarian."

"A vegetarian?" Mrs. Dario gasped.

Hannah's ears perked. She hadn't realized that about Guy either.

"It's not like he told you he was a Martian, Elena," said Mrs. Sanchez. "Calm down."

"Great job with Drinking Bird," said Guy, who was clearly trying to keep them on task. "Let's stretch those muscles out, and then we can be done for today." He pulled out three mats and carefully arranged them on the floor. "Do you remember how to do the hamstring stretch we did yesterday?"

Mrs. Dario nodded. "Sure do." When she sat down on the mat, she groaned. "Ooof. My knees aren't what they used to be."

"That's okay." Guy offered his arm for support. "Take your time."

"Thanks," said Mrs. Dario. "You're such a love to help me like this without making me feel a million years old."

"My pleasure." Guy turned to help Mrs. Sanchez, but she was already on the mat and doing a runner's lunge. Guy sat between them and stretched out his leg. "Reach for your right toe, Mrs. Dario, but not to the point that it hurts. Stretching shouldn't be painful."

"Here goes nothing." Mrs. Dario leaned forward until she brushed her fingertips to the middle of her shin.

"Nice job, Elena," said Mrs. Sanchez. She looked at Guy. "I've thought about being vegetarian before but could never commit. How long has it been since you ate meat?"

"I've been a vegetarian ever since my dad took me deer hunting in the Adirondacks. I was twelve at the time and—" Guy shuddered. "My father was so proud of my first kill, but all I could think about was the way the deer's eyelashes fluttered closed as her blood seeped into the ground."

Wow, thought Hannah. *That must have been awful.* She opened the first-aid kit and began counting bandages.

"I came home from the hunt," Guy continued, "and told my parents that from then on, I was a vegetarian."

"How'd they take it?" Mrs. Dario asked.

"Not so well," Guy admitted.

"Did you learn to cook your own meals?" Mrs. Dario asked. "Carlos is a mess in the kitchen, but I taught both of my sons to cook. It's a good thing too, because while I love my daughters-in-law to death, both of them are too busy with their careers to have time to make dinner."

"No, that wasn't really an option for me," said Guy.

"Why not?" Mrs. Dario asked.

"Well..." Guy scratched his head. "Before I tell you that, let's lay on our backs and roll out our ankles."

"Sure thing," said Mrs. Dario. "You know I love being horizontal with you."

Hannah giggled, despite herself, and then covered her mouth with her hand. From the corner of her eye, she caught Guy looking at her, his eyes twinkling. Blushing, Hannah picked up the tube of Neosporin from the first-aid kit and turned it over, inspecting the expiration date.

"Elena, for the last time," Mrs. Sanchez exclaimed with an exasperated tone. "Stop flirting with our instructor."

"He's the one who told me what to do with my booty just now," said Mrs. Dario.

Guy laughed. "Back to why I didn't learn to cook as a teenager. I wasn't allowed in the kitchen. Once I graduated from college and was living in my apartment, I took classes at a local vegetarian restaurant, and now I'm pretty good in the kitchen."

"I bet," said Mrs. Dario. "But where do you shop? Driving up to the resort, we only passed one grocery store."

"That's right," said Mrs. Sanchez. "How can Sand Dollar Cove survive with only one grocery store?"

"It's a challenge, especially with all the remote workers moving to town." Guy lifted himself up onto his elbows. "But Hannah could tell you more about the town than I can, since I just moved here."

"What?" Hannah asked, startled to be mentioned by name.

"How many people live in Sand Dollar Cove?" Guy asked.

"Oh." Hannah stood straight. "Well, around five thousand people live here full time, but like you said, remote workers are arriving every day, which is really changing things."

"How many restaurants are there?" Mrs. Dario asked.

That was a simple question for Hannah to answer. "In town there's the T Bone Bluff and a McDonald's. That's not including the restaurant we have here at Seaside Resort, of course. Jasmine, our head chef at The Summer Wind, sources our food from local farms and gets the rest from restaurant supply deliveries."

"I've been extraordinarily impressed with the food here," said Mrs. Sanchez. "That chocolate torte we had for dessert last night was incredible."

"I'm glad to hear it," said Hannah.

"We should order that again tonight," said Mrs. Dario. "With an extra scoop of the raspberry gelato. It made me think a bit of the chocolate-coffee body scrub on the spa menu. Maybe I'll get that treatment this afternoon."

"That sounds good," said Mrs. Sanchez. "But today I'm going for the deep tissue massage."

"Tell us more about Sand Dollar Cove," said Mrs. Dario. "How did it come to be?"

Hannah put down her clipboard so she could give the guests her full attention. "It's an interesting story, really. At least, *I* think it's interesting." She shrugged. "I'm biased, because my great-grandfather was involved. In the 1960s a developer from Las Vegas swooped in, with the dream of making Sand Dollar Cove the trendiest vacation town on the West Coast. He bought vast amounts of land from a cattle rancher, and then recruited construction workers like my great-grandpa to create a Pacific Northwest riviera. Seaside Resort was the crown jewel, but there were also thousands of vacation homes spread out around town, next to human-engineered canals that led to the ocean."

"That's what those canals are from?" Mrs. Sanchez asked. "I was wondering if they were natural."

"Nope." Hannah shook her head. "Not natural. They were man-made. The idea was that homeowners could sail from their own private dock to the harbor. Originally, the homes sold quickly, especially once the developer started chartering planes from Hollywood and bringing in celebrities to boost publicity. The T Bone Bluff even had its own bandstand."

"Like, for concerts?" Guy asked.

Hannah nodded. "And dinner dancing. Sand Dollar Cove real estate was white-hot, and rumors that Washington State might legalize gambling added fuel to the flames. But then in the late 1970s, the boom went bust when Washington State's grand jury cracked down on gambling. By the time inflation rattled the country in the early 1980s, the place looked like a ghost town. That was right around when the international hotel conglomerate, Blanchet Maison, purchased Seaside Resort for half of what it was previously worth."

She tried to hide the bitterness from her tone, but it was difficult. Seaside Resort had been slowly fading ever since. The briny air caused the exteriors to deteriorate with remarkable speed, and Blanchet Maison never reinvested sufficient funds into refurbishment. "My grandma worked here for fifty years as head of housekeeping, so this place is like a second home to me."

"What do you mean?" Mrs. Sanchez asked. "Did you live in one of the cottages, or something?"

"I wish, but no," said Hannah. "My grandma brought me and my sister to work with her all the time. Some of my happiest memories are of climbing the trees and peeking through the cottage curtains, imagining that I was one of the lucky guests."

"A happy childhood is important," said Mrs. Sanchez. "I'm glad your grandma was able to bring you with her to work."

"I agree," said Mrs. Dario. "I wish we had more affordable childcare in this country. It's awful out there."

A timer dinged. "That means it's time to stretch," said Guy. He looked at Hannah. "Not to interrupt you, though."

"Of course not. I need to finish my inventory." Hannah looked down at her clipboard.

"Let's move on to a figure-four stretch," Guy told the women. "Put your right ankle over your left thigh, and then gently bring your left leg upward so you feel the stretch in the side of your right hip."

Mrs. Dario let out a deep breath. "This feels great. I wish I could have convinced Carlos to skip one day of fishing so he could join us."

"Not me," said Mrs. Sanchez. "Vicente needs to be out on the water with nothing to do but wait for a bite. That type of forced relaxation is good for him."

"It would bore the hell out of me, that's for sure," said Mrs. Dario. "Every time I've gone fishing with Carlos he's been annoyed with me for talking too much."

"I'm shocked," said Mrs. Sanchez. "Completely shocked."

"If it wasn't for me, you wouldn't know half the gossip in Ballard," said Mrs. Dario.

"That's true," Mrs. Sanchez admitted. She glanced at Guy. "This one keeps me in the loop."

"I bet." Guy grinned.

"Should we switch to the other leg now?" Mrs. Dario asked.

"Yup. Good instincts. See?" Guy gave her a thumbs up. "You've learned so much already. You'll do great once you're exercising at home."

"My goal is to get Carlos to join me, because goodness knows it would be beneficial for him to up his step count." Mrs. Dario made a figure four with her left leg. "Do your parents exercise, too?"

"My parents?" Guy asked.

Hannah was curious about them, too. Guy rarely mentioned his folks back home. The only thing she knew was that he'd grown up in New York.

"Yeah," said Mrs. Dario. "Your folks."

"I bet with a son like you they're in great shape," said Mrs. Sanchez.

"Um..." Guy stood and picked up his mat.

"Are they athletes, too?" Mrs. Dario prompted.

"My dad skis and my mom does Pilates." Guy put his mat away.

"Sounds swanky." Mrs. Dario wiggled her eyebrows. "Do they live around here?"

"No. They live in New York. That's where I'm from."

"New York, eh?" Mrs. Dario took a break from stretching and leaned back on her hands. "I've always wanted to go to New York to see the shows, but Carlos doesn't like to do anything that requires wearing a tie. That's why this vacation has been perfect. He can be out on the water, and I can check out the cute shops downtown and then come back and soak in the hot tub."

"I'd go to the shows with you," said Mrs. Sanchez. "I love Broadway. Maybe we should book a girls' trip together."

"Really, Brenda?"

"Absolutely. Let's do it."

"Where should we stay?" Mrs. Dario looked at Guy. "Do you have any suggestions?"

"Ah..." Guy reached down to help them up. "Why don't we stand and move on to shoulder rolls to finish our stretching?" The two ladies rose to their feet with Guy's help.

Mrs. Sanchez immediately began rolling her shoulders back. "How about the flagship Blanchet Maison? I heard that's lovely."

Hannah groaned quietly. Blanchet Maison properties were always lovely, unless you were part of their "Local Flavors" division like Seaside Resort. Those properties were treated like second-class citizens.

"Oooh." Mrs. Dario clapped her hands together. "Now you're talking. But it's pricey, right?"

"Yes, but we'll split the cost, so that'll help." Mrs. Sanchez looked at Guy. "What do you think? Have you been there?"

"Yes, I've seen the place." Guy nodded. "It has a great location, close to Central Park." Another timer dinged on Guy's desk. "Please continue stretching, ladies, but I need to go. I have another client arriving in ten minutes."

Hannah checked her watch. She was due at the front desk soon.

"Oh gosh," said Mrs. Sanchez. "We better scoot if we're going to clean up for lunch."

"I don't know what you're talking about." Mrs. Dario swiped her sweat towel across her face and a streak of foundation smeared off. "I'm as fresh as a daisy."

Laughing, both women waved goodbye and walked out of the gym. As Hannah watched them leave, nervousness paralyzed her. Now she was alone with Guy. She jammed her pen into the clamp of her clipboard and warped into business mode. "Well," she said in a prim tone, "I better be off, too, or I'll miss my shift at the front desk."

Guy looked at her. "Did I catch you grinning back there

when Mrs. Dario and Mrs. Sanchez were giving me a hard time?"

"Me?" Hannah pressed her hand to her chart. "I would never laugh at our guests."

"Of course not. You're a serious professional who rarely cracks a smile—"

"I wouldn't go as far as that in describing me," Hannah interrupted.

"I wasn't finished with my description." Guy cleared his throat. "Hannah Turner, serious professional who rarely cracks a smile, but when she does, it's like sunshine basking you in a vitamin D glow."

Was Guy teasing her? Hannah wasn't sure, but she thought he might be. Perhaps he was getting her back for eavesdropping. If so, she wasn't going to take it. "Does that line usually work on people?" she asked pertly. "Because I'm not sure it's working for me. See you later."

Clipboard in hand, Hannah marched out of the wellness studio and into the brisk spring air, which did little to cool off the heat she felt in her burning cheeks.

THREE

On the short walk to the lobby for her shift on reception, Hannah's phone rang.

"Hey, sis, what's up? I only have a couple minutes to chat because I'm on my way to the front desk."

"It's Aidan!" Mary's excitement was contagious, even over the phone. "I think he's going to propose!"

"Really? But you're too young to get married."

"I am not, I'm twenty-two—the same age Mom was when she married Dad."

And look how well that turned out, Hannah wanted to say, but knew that bashing Kelly wouldn't be helpful. "What I meant to say is... that's great. After all these years of dating. How exciting for you."

"I know, right? We've been together ever since I came back from Hollywood."

After she'd graduated from high school, Mary had packed her suitcase and taken the bus to LA, hoping to become an actress. She'd immediately found work as a Starbucks barista, but had never signed with an agent or landed a paid acting job. But she had performed in community theater, which is where she'd become enamored with set design. Now she was finishing two years of interior design coursework at the local community college.

"When does Aidan come home?" Hannah asked.

"Next month, on May 31st. He's working in a small town in Kansas right now. They are desperate for traveling nurses, and he's making a ton of money."

"That's good, because I'm guessing you have expensive taste in engagement rings." Hannah picked up a piece of litter on the path and held onto it until she came to the nearest trash can.

"If you're going to wear something for the rest of your life it needs to be perfect. Which is where you come in."

"Huh?"

"If Aidan calls you to ask your opinion about what ring to buy me, this is what you should say."

"Okay," Hannah prompted, when Mary didn't continue.

"I'm waiting for you to get a notepad. Do you have one?"

"No, I'm outside. Hang on a second." She hurried through the back door of the lobby, tossed the litter into a wastebasket, rushed to the printer station, and took a piece of paper from the tray. "Okay," Hannah said as she loaded up her clipboard. "Shoot."

"White gold, or platinum. But not yellow gold, and definitely not rose gold, because that's too trendy. I'd like a pear-shaped solitaire, not round, and I'm okay with a white sapphire instead of a diamond, because I'd rather have the bling. And also conflict diamonds—gross. There's just too much risk of that."

"Blingy pears with no conflict," Hannah repeated. "Got it."

"Are you being serious right now? Because I can't tell, and this is important."

"White gold or platinum, pear-shaped, white sapphires okay but no conflict diamonds," Hannah read from her notes.

She might be terrible at flirting with Guy, but when it came to teasing her sister, she was a pro. "What's your ring size?"

"Six point five."

"I'm writing that down."

"This is big, Hannah, really big. Aidan proposing, I mean."

"I know, sweetie."

"His parents are rich. They have a waterfront view."

"Of a canal, not the beach," Hannah clarified. "There's a difference."

"Still, their house is huge. And I've always thought that Aidan's parents didn't think I was good enough."

"Of course you're good enough," Hannah said, feeling insulted on her sister's behalf. "You're smart, beautiful, talented, and despite your flashy taste in jewelry, really down-to-earth. They would be lucky to have you as a daughter-in-law. In fact, I don't think they deserve you." Hannah didn't think Aidan deserved Mary either, but it wasn't her place to say so. Aidan didn't call Mary when he said he would, and when he was in town, he usually arrived late to pick her up for dates. Hannah couldn't tell if Aidan was flaky, inconsiderate, or both. But Mary seemed happy, and that was all that mattered. "What possible reason could Aidan's parents have for not liking you?"

"Because the whole town knows about Mom being an alcoholic and moving to Aberdeen."

"Gran's worth two of Mom, and everybody knows it." It was true; Cheryl's reputation was spotless. Everyone who had grown up in Sand Dollar Cove loved her. Kelly, on the other hand, was never spoken kindly of at all.

"It's not only Mom," said Mary. "Aidan's mentioned Dad, and how he died, and his folks wonder if depression runs in our family."

Hannah took a sharp breath. "That's not fair."

"It might not be fair, but it's a cloud hanging over us. It's hung over us our whole lives."

"There's no record of Dad having depression. The insurance company suggested it was reactionary trauma related to horrific things he'd witnessed overseas."

Twenty years ago, their father had returned from working as a private contractor in Afghanistan, where he'd spent over a year building schools for girls. Hannah had been four years old, and carried a smattering of happy memories from that time. Max lifting her up on his shoulders so she could see the Fourth of July parade. Max helping her fly a kite on the beach and showing her how to position the string just right. Max holding her hand as they walked into the donut shop. But then, a few weeks after her fifth birthday, right before he was due to return to Afghanistan, Max drove his truck off Blackfish Point and into the Pacific Ocean. The insurance company ruled it a suicide and refused to pay out on his life insurance policy. Unable to cope with the loss of her husband, Kelly had turned to alcohol. Eventually, Cheryl had stepped in and gained custody of her granddaughters.

"Dad's death involved mitigating circumstances," said Hannah. "We'll never know what was going through his mind that day, and if it was related to mental health, then he deserves compassion, not judgment. Mental illness is a disease."

"That's what I told Aidan."

"Good. Stick up for yourself, and for Dad." Hannah didn't like that Aidan had made Mary feel bad about this. She wanted to say more, but she saw Herman enter his office. She didn't want him to catch her being late. Hannah was never late. Tardiness triggered her. "Mary, I'll see you when I get home. I'm needed at the front desk."

"Love you."

"Love you, too." Hannah ended the call, stuck her phone in her pocket, and headed toward the lobby. "Happy Saturday," she said as she passed Herman's door. "I thought you were taking today off."

"I was." Herman frowned as he picked up his coffee mug. He wore gray slacks and a mustard-colored flannel shirt with a moth hole at the elbow. "But that was before Nancy insisted I clean the rain gutters."

"I see," Hannah said, trying to be careful what she said about Nancy, whom she adored. Herman's wife was brilliant. Hannah had learned that in high school, when Nancy had offered to help proofread her college applications. Mary had thought it impossible that anyone who loved home perms could be clever, but as it turned out, Nancy was equal parts clever and generous. Not only did she offer suggestions to help punch up Hannah's application essay, she also helped Cheryl fill out the financial aid application.

"I told her it didn't make sense to climb up on the ladder in the middle of a sprinkle, but you know Nancy and her schedules." Herman's furry eyebrows knit together.

"She's definitely efficient," said Hannah, noting one of the things she admired about her.

"Anyhow, I'm going to sit here and look through RV catalogues. Forty-three days and counting until I retire."

"That's right. Any news on when Blanchet Maison will make the announcement about your replacement?"

"Hopefully soon. I raved about you. It should be a rubber stamp, I think, although they did mention something about needing to consider outside candidates."

"What?" Hannah asked, panic shooting through her.

"Everyone at corporate is a moron. I wouldn't let those numbskulls from Blanchet Maison worry you. I'm not retiring until you get the job."

The tension building in her shoulders eased slightly. "I hope so. Thanks for putting my name forward."

"Of course. You know Nancy and I are rooting for you." Herman set down his coffee mug. "Always."

"Thanks, boss. Have fun plotting your retirement."

Hannah quickened her step as she entered the lobby to take over the front desk for Will, who worked part-time because he was taking classes at Grays Harbor State to become a marine biologist. A member of the Squamish People, he had shiny black hair which he wore loose at his shoulders.

"Right on time, as usual." Will closed his textbook. "It's been slow today because of the rain, but we have a bunch of people scheduled to check in this afternoon."

"I saw that in the reservation system." Hannah took her place at the desk and turned on her computer. "What are you studying?"

"Kelp. I have a test later this week that's worth thirty percent of my grade. My friends asked me to go out tonight, but I'm hitting the books instead." Will sighed. "I can't wait until I graduate."

Hannah chuckled. "I remember those days. Good luck."

"Thanks." Will turned off his computer. "I'll see you tomorrow." He put on his raincoat and left.

Hannah logged into the system and checked the room turnover stats. Lark's housekeeping team was excellent, but if they happened to be short-staffed because of someone calling in sick, hitting the 4 p.m. check-in time could be tricky. Today it appeared everything was in order, though. Since the arrival rush hadn't started yet, Hannah caught up on email. Then she clicked over to the national news to catch up on headlines.

An article about a disgraced hedge fund manager from Connecticut caught her attention. She didn't care about the dirty world of high finance, but the mention of Connecticut reminded her of that box she'd mailed off at the beginning of the year. The one that had the jar in it with the postcards. Had the delivery gone through? Hannah couldn't remember.

She opened her email again and searched for the tracking number. Once she clicked on it, she saw that, yes, the package had been delivered on January 11th. That was it, she figured. She'd never find out any more information beyond that.

Scrolling over to Yelp, Hannah clicked on the Seaside Resort account to see if there were any fresh reviews. A new one caught her attention claiming that the service was great, but that Mermaid's Grotto was shabby. Hannah gritted her teeth, knowing that the reviewer had been right. Mermaid's Grotto wasn't scheduled for renovation until next year.

She looked around the dimly lit lobby. There was so much she wanted to do to this place to bring it back to its former glory, starting with replacing the fluorescent tube lights above the front door. Hopefully Blanchet Maison would approve her promotion soon, and give her the leeway she required to make Seaside Resort shine. It had been irresponsible of them to let it deteriorate like this. That's what irked Hannah the most. Blanchet Maison had squandered the opportunity to polish Seaside Resort like the jewel it once was—like the jewel it could still be. She looked down at the keyboard, and as she did so, her gaze drifted to the scar on her wrist. Her focus glued to the silvery line. Irresponsibility always made Hannah think of her mom.

When Max had died, he'd left Kelly with a house, two kids, a modest savings account, and a life insurance policy. Even though the insurance failed to pay out, Kelly had still had plenty of opportunity to provide a decent life for her daughters. She could have sold the house and bought something cheaper, or rented out the spare bedroom to earn extra cash. She could have taken a job in housekeeping with Cheryl and brought her daughters to work with her. She could have hired a lawyer and sued the insurance company for payment. But Kelly didn't do any of those things.

Hannah stared at the computer screen and scrolled through Yelp listings, trying to calm herself down, but it was difficult, especially now that she was thinking about the dumb things

Kelly did. Losing the house still hurt to this day. If her mother had only had one ounce of responsibility, things might have been different.

Mary didn't remember anything about their old home, but Hannah did. She remembered Max hanging the piñata for her fifth birthday on a tree in the front yard. She remembered the black and white tile in the bathroom that was shaped like hearts. But apparently, Kelly didn't make one mortgage payment after Max died and so—poof! There went the house.

And why didn't Kelly pay the mortgage bill? That was the worst part. Kelly had taken the savings account and blown it on a Corvette. The sports car only had two seat belts. There was no room for Mary's car seat or Hannah's booster. What type of mom did that? A bad mom, that's what.

Kelly's irresponsibility had nearly killed her daughters. Thinking of it now, Hannah simmered with rage. But no, she wouldn't picture the accident. She couldn't. Hannah was here, at work, in front of her computer. She didn't need to relive past trauma; she could study the resort's Yelp reviews instead. That would be much better for her soul.

Only now Hannah couldn't focus on the screen, not when she was thinking about the rest of it.

After the bank had repossessed their house, they'd moved to a series of apartments, one after another, because Kelly had a bad habit of not paying bills. By then her alcoholism had started, and...

No! What good would it do to let the bad memory replay in her imagination like a horror movie? But Hannah was unable to stop the memories from coming. She gripped the scar on her wrist from when Kelly drank half a bottle of rum and crashed the Corvette. Hannah had been six years old and Mary was only three. The first responders had said it was a miracle that they had survived. The terror of that event lived with her to this day.

Hannah shuddered and used the calming presence of the space around her to sweep away her fear. The lobby might be shabby-looking, but it offered comfort.

Thank goodness for Cheryl, and thank goodness for Seaside Resort. Her grandma never failed her and neither did this property.

Even when a window cracked. Even when a crabby customer complained about scratchy towels. Even when the wind howled and chased guests up from the beach. Even then, this place meant safety.

Seaside Resort had provided sanctuary during the roughest part of her life, when she and Mary were frightened children and Cheryl had promised they'd be safe here, drawing chalk on the sidewalk and jumping rope underneath the cedars. Seaside Resort was knit into her heart. Now, it was up to Hannah to preserve it. Nobody could love this place more than her.

FOUR

A couple of days later, Hannah's Monday morning was off to a lousy start. Between unclogging a toilet at Starfish Cottage, assisting a guest who'd woken up ill at Dolphin House, and discovering that the curtain rod at Maple Manor had ripped off the wall, her day had been rough. But it was her lunch break now, and Hannah intended to use all sixty minutes of it to recharge. She filled her mug with coffee from the bar in the lobby, and went through the hallway to the back room where the printer station, staff refrigerator, and a mismatched collection of old furniture sufficed as the employee break area. Lark was already there, sitting on a lumpy sofa, and slurping noodles.

"How's it going?" Lark asked.

"Not good." Hannah sat down next to her and opened her lunch bag. She had a day-old muffin that Mary had brought from the coffee stand where she worked, an apple, and string cheese. "How about you?"

"Still recovering from the incident at Dolphin House." Lark turned up her nose. "I'm washing the bedding in hot water with extra bleach, but that might not be enough to save it. There was puke everywhere."

"Oh boy." Hannah looked at her muffin, no longer as hungry as she once was.

The back door opened and Guy entered, his blond hair gleaming in the fluorescent light. He was holding a book, and Hannah strained her eyes to see what he was reading. An autobiography of Rosemary Clooney? Wasn't she the actress from *White Christmas* with Bing Crosby that came on television every December? Hannah had no idea that he was into celebrity memoirs.

"Hey, neighbor," said Guy. "I see you've helped yourself to the Pad Thai I made last night."

"What?" Hannah asked.

"He means me." Lark finished slurping. "Guy lives three doors down from me in the same apartment building."

"And apparently I shouldn't have given her the spare key in case I locked myself out," Guy said with a good-natured smile. He opened the refrigerator and removed a glass container.

"I was returning the travel mug I'd borrowed." Lark spun her plastic fork around in the bowl. "The only thing in my fridge is a half-empty jar of sauerkraut that my ex-girlfriend left, and a block of moldy cheese. It was either steal your leftovers or wait in the drive-thru line at McDonald's, but rumor has it the ice cream machine broke again."

Guy popped his lunch into the microwave. "Or you could go to the grocery store and buy the ingredients to prepare that tofu stir-fry I taught you how to make last week."

"Coulda. Shoulda. Woulda." Lark dug her fork into the food. "Besides, if it weren't for me, you'd still be making enough food to feed a family of five and then tossing the extra out."

"What?" Hannah asked. Food waste was a big no-no in her house, where every bit of thriftiness counted.

"I didn't know any better," Guy said sheepishly. He held up the lid to his Pyrex. "But now I've bought storage containers.

I've followed all of Lark's instructions, and instead of cooking seven nights a week, I'm down to three."

"You're welcome," said Lark.

"I didn't say thank you," said Guy. "Yeah, I'm saving money, but now I have nothing to do on my non-cooking nights. I love reading books on my balcony, but there are only so many celebrity memoirs I can check out from the library without feeling weird." He showed them the cover of the Rosemary Clooney book.

"I didn't know you were so interested in Hollywood," said Hannah, who adored old movies.

"I'm not." Guy glanced at the microwave and then back at her. "But since the Sand Dollar Cove library only has two rooms, and one of them is for kids... The adult section only has beach reads and celebrity biographies... Somehow that's translated into me getting sucked into reading one memoir after another. This one on Rosemary Clooney is really juicy. She was George Clooney's aunt."

"You know you can request books from any library in Grays Harbor County, right?" Hannah asked. "That's what I do. I like historical fiction."

"Me too," Guy said, right as the microwave beeped. "Thanks for the tip. I'll try that."

"Is that the rice and beans that doesn't have rice in it?" Lark asked. "I can smell the lemon flavor."

"Quinoa." Guy scratched the back of his neck. "It's a quinoa bowl."

"Whatever it's called, it was delicious," said Lark. "Since I started eating with you, I've lost ten pounds. If I lose any more, this peony might look like a butterfly." She pointed to the tattoo on her biceps. "My arms are shrinking."

"Uh... sorry about that." Guy sat down in an armchair with a stain on the back.

"Don't apologize. I'm thrilled." Lark waved her elbows back and forth. "Look at this. My bat wings are melting away."

Hannah felt a tinge of envy for the easy banter Lark and Guy shared. She knew Lark only dated women and wasn't interested in Guy romantically, but that didn't curb Hannah's jealousy. She wished she could chat so easily with Guy, instead of clamming up.

Guy loaded up a bite of quinoa onto his fork. "I've always thought vegetables had magic powers. Do you think my balcony gets enough sunlight to grow tomatoes?"

"I don't know," said Lark. "When I was little, my mom always had a tomato plant growing in front of our trailer, but it was hit or miss if we got ripe ones."

"I thought tomatoes were easy to grow?" Guy asked.

"Not in Washington, at least not west of the Cascades," said Hannah. "My grandma grows them on our front porch. She has some going right now that are little babies."

"And you both grew up in Sand Dollar Cove, right?" Guy asked.

Hannah nodded. "I've lived here all my life. Gran used to have Lark's job as head of housekeeping."

"Cheryl's a legend," said Lark. "I was born and raised here, too."

"Where'd your mom work again?" Hannah asked. "I forget."

"At the Lumberjack." Lark wiped her mouth with a napkin. "She was a cocktail waitress. You'd never believe it looking at her now, but back in the 1980s she was quite the hottie. Here, I think there's a picture on my phone."

"I've never heard of the Lumberjack," said Guy.

Lark scrolled through her camera roll. "It's closed now. The Lumberjack was on its way out when my mom began working there in the early 1980s."

"That's right when our little boom town went bust," Hannah explained. "Sand Dollar Cove sprouted practically overnight in the 1960s, like we were a gold-mining town in a western, and then—"

"Poof!" Lark interrupted. "The economy tanked and all the money left."

"That was the 'bust' part, I take it?" Guy asked.

"Yeah," said Lark. "It was really hard on restaurants. There was another place called the Jet Set that hung on there for a while and didn't close until I was ten years old. That was in 1999. Their last event was a Y2K party on New Year's." Lark leaned forward and shoved her phone in front of Guy's face. "There. That's my mom now at her condo in Florida." She swiped the screen. "And this is my mom and me when I was two years old. See how pretty she was?"

"A knockout," said Guy. "She kind of looked like you do now, only without the tattoos."

"Or the arm flaps." Lark wiggled her loose skin.

Hannah hadn't known Karen well, but remembered seeing her around town. She was memorable because she drove a yellow Volkswagen Cabriolet convertible.

"Did anyone exciting ever perform at the Lumberjack?" Guy pointed to his library book with his thumb. "Rosemary Clooney, perhaps?"

"I still don't know who that is," said Lark.

"George Clooney's aunt," said Hannah. "Guy already mentioned that."

"Oh," said Lark. "That's right. Well, I'm not sure if she ever visited here, but lots of famous people came to town."

"Even Sinatra," Hannah said, remembering the autographed postcard she'd found at Strawberry Cottage.

"Wow." Guy raised his eyebrows. "Old Blue Eyes himself."

Hannah nodded. "This used to be an 'it' place, like Washington's version of Ibiza."

Lark put her empty bowl on the end table and began rubbing her forearm, kneading her knuckles into the flesh.

"Are you okay?" Hannah asked.

Lark switched to the other arm. "Yeah. It's just my tendonitis bugging me. Hazards of being a housekeeper."

"What did your doctor say?" Guy asked with concern.

Lark scoffed. "Doctor? I haven't seen a doctor since I went to the ER two years ago with a badly sprained ankle. That put me out of work for over a month, and I'm still making payments on the medical bills."

"Oh. I'm sorry." Guy's forehead crinkled. "I'm obviously not your doctor, but have you tried wearing arm braces? You can buy them at the pharmacy. In the meantime, try this." Guy held out his arm and gently bent his fingers down, pressing on the knuckles with the opposite hand. "Stretches can help, but your best bet is to get those arm braces and at least wear them at night while you sleep, if not at work, too."

Lark imitated the stretch and her eyes widened. "Ah. That does feel a little bit better."

"How do you know so much about this stuff?" Hannah asked.

"Oh... um..." Guy squinted for a second. "I knew a few people who had tendonitis after I graduated from college. One was a young mom with a three-month-old baby. Her tendonitis was so bad she couldn't push the stroller or a grocery cart. But after she wore the braces for six weeks, the pain went away. Although, apparently, it was annoying to change diapers because she had to take the braces off each time."

Lark leaned back in her chair. "A mom with a baby? Are you sure this wasn't an old girlfriend? Do you have a secret child you haven't told me about?"

Guy laughed. "No, it was just a woman in New York that I knew. There was another person I met who had tendonitis from typing on his laptop computer while sitting on the couch instead of at his desk, which would have better ergonomics.

Once he changed his habits and bought a better keyboard and mouse, his tendonitis improved."

"Interesting." Hannah opened her string cheese.

"In fact," Guy continued, "Lark, if you can analyze your daily habits, there might be something you're doing at work repeatedly that's making your pain worse. If you can identify what that is, or how to accomplish the task differently, your pain might get better."

Lark rolled out her wrist. "Okay, I'm going to have to start calling you Dr. Guy from now on, because you seem to know a lot about this."

"Not really." Guy shrugged modestly. "It would still be good for you to have your own doctor. Is there a free clinic? Or what about the Affordable Care Act?"

"I have one of those plans," said Lark. "But the office visits are still super expensive. I'll stop by the drugstore and buy those braces you were talking about. That's a good idea." She brought her bowl to the sink.

"You need to be doing less housework, not more," said Hannah, feeling guilty that her employee was suffering. "I'll wash that for you in a bit."

"It's not a big deal." Lark added suds to the bowl and rinsed it out. "Besides, I need to give it back to Mr. Vegetarian over here." She dried it with a towel and brought it over to Guy. "There's something wrong with the back of your neck," she said, peering down at him.

"What?" Guy asked.

"Your neck. There's a red patch of skin. A hive, or something."

Guy felt the back of his neck and his fingers brushed against his collar. "I better go look in the mirror." He hurried to the staff bathroom and closed the door.

"Maybe it's an allergic reaction to fake rice," said Lark.

"Quinoa," Hannah corrected. She'd eaten it before at The

Summer Wind. Her friend Jasmine, the resort's head chef, often served it as a side dish.

"Quinoa. Whatever. It's good, but it would have been better with bacon."

"I think you might be right about an allergic reaction," said Hannah.

"Yeah, that looked like a hive to me. I'll go see if we have anything to help." Lark walked over to the printer station and took the first-aid kit down from the shelf. "There we go," she said a minute later. "Benadryl."

When Guy returned from the bathroom, Lark held out the box of antihistamines. "Maybe you should take that, in case you're having an allergic reaction."

"Now who's playing doctor?" Guy asked.

"You want it, or what?" Lark waved the box.

Guy held out his hand. "Couldn't hurt."

"I prefer to think of myself as a pharmacist." Lark passed him the allergy medicine. "I should get going, because the Dolphin House quilt is probably ready for the dryer now... or the dumpster. Thanks for lunch."

"Thanks for the company." Guy popped a pill into his mouth. Then he turned his attention to Hannah.

Feeling her stomach flip-flop under the intensity of his gaze, Hannah almost choked on her muffin.

"I love hearing you talk about Sand Dollar Cove history," Guy said as he sank onto the sofa next to her. "Even if Rosemary Clooney never showed up."

"She might have." Hannah brushed crumbs off her mouth. "I'll ask Gran."

"One of the best parts of working here is the rich history this place has." Guy tapped his foot against the ground. "And the nature, of course. I've spent so much time running on the beach that I haven't been able to explore Olympic National Park yet, but I know it's there waiting for me."

"Better visit it soon before the tourists swarm." Hannah crumpled her cheese stick wrapper and put it into her lunch sack. "At least Olympic National Park isn't as crowded as Mount Rainier."

"That's another place I want to visit, but it's a drive, right?"

Hannah nodded. "About three hours. We used to go there for picnics until my grandma's osteoporosis got so bad that car trips became miserable for her."

"I didn't know that your grandmother had osteoporosis. I'm sorry."

"That's what finally forced her to retire." Hannah sighed. Cheryl probably would have worked forever if she could have. It wasn't in her nature to relax and take it easy.

"There's this one place that I really want to go that I've heard a local mention, and that I haven't found yet. I wonder if you could tell me where it is?"

"Sure." Hannah shrugged. "Probably."

"Rhododendron Lane. Have you heard of it?"

"Yeah. That's only a ten-minute walk from here. We don't have it marked on the resort map though, because it's so close to a cliff that it's an insurance liability. But it's really pretty, especially now when they are blooming."

"It sounds stunning. I don't suppose you'd have time to show me, would you?" Guy asked hopefully.

Hannah wasn't sure that taking Guy to one of the most romantic vista points in Sand Dollar Cove was a wise idea, but then again, as a brand-new employee, he deserved to know every nuance of the property. She checked her watch and looked up at him, trying to keep her demeanor as professional as possible. "Sure. I still have thirty minutes left of my lunch break. Let me grab my coat."

FIVE

"Does it bother you that people can drive their cars on the beach?" Guy asked.

"Not really," said Hannah. "I've never known any different." They walked along a path that skirted the cliff's edge. Down below the Pacific Ocean crashed against the shore. But even from that high vantage point, they could see vehicles drive up and down the sand.

"Cars on the beach was the first thing I noticed about this place." Guy stuffed his hands in his pockets. "Most of the beaches I've visited in the past have been protected."

"What about horses? Do they bother you, too?"

"Only when I accidentally run through manure. But that hasn't happened in a while because now I keep a lookout."

Hannah laughed. "My high school boyfriend worked at the stable his family owned, so I got to ride all the time for free." That was the simple way of putting things, but the complex version was that the only time Hannah had felt truly at ease was freshman and sophomore year when she'd dated Rob.

Hannah had fallen for Rob hard, and for a while it had seemed like they'd beaten the odds and would be the rare high school romance that turned into forever. But Rob was two years older than Hannah. He went off to Gonzaga during Hannah's Junior year. When he came home at winter break, he dumped her. He'd met someone else. Now that "someone else" was his wife and the mother of his baby. Thankfully, he lived in Seattle, so at least Hannah didn't have to see him around. Her heartbreak had healed, but the burn was still there. Hannah had dated a few men since then but had never fallen in love. She had a hard time trusting people.

Hannah zipped up her dad's old coat against the icy wind. Patti had done such a good job mending it that you could no longer see the tear. "Back to the car thing though, you're right that out-of-towners think it's unusual. In my mind that's something we could capitalize on."

"How?" Guy asked.

"Already we have to-go lunchboxes available from The Summer Wind. Jasmine does a great job with those. But we could attract day-trippers from Tacoma, Olympia, and Seattle if we offered a "car date escape." At least, that's what I would call it—I haven't quite settled on a name yet. The pitch could be driving to Sand Dollar Cove for a day trip from the city, picking up a gourmet picnic at The Summer Wind, driving onto the beach for some fun, and then perhaps returning to Seaside Resort for a massage or facial before the drive home."

"Like a day trip vacation." Guy paused for a moment and looked out at the water. "That has potential. Maybe you could even advertise it on a travel site like Expedia."

"Exactly! That's what I told Herman, too, but he didn't think we had the capacity to serve clients beyond our registered guests, and he has a point. Jasmine's had trouble keeping dishwashers because we don't pay enough to match the rising rental market." Which was a whole other problem facing Sand Dollar Cove right now, especially with the influx of remote workers and their big-tech job paychecks gobbling up affordable housing. Hannah felt grateful that the house she, Cheryl, and Mary rented wasn't too expensive.

They were approaching the path to Rhododendron Lane now, only it was overgrown with blackberry vines. That was on purpose. Hannah had instructed the landscaping crew to let those brambles grow to keep guests away from the old trail.

"Here we are," she said. "But this is really important. You can't tell anyone else that this trail still exists. It used to be a lot safer, but a few years ago a big storm came through and there's been erosion. Now it's too much of a liability to allow guests to find it."

"The secret's safe with me," said Guy, his blue eyes the same color as the ocean below. His blond hair looked extra light in the sunshine, even with the cloud clover. The only thing about him that wasn't picture-perfect was the red hive popping up on his neck. The Benadryl must not have kicked in yet.

"Okay, here we go." Hannah picked her foot up as high as it would go and stepped over the patch of vines. "It's a good thing we're both wearing long pants, because these Himalayan blackberries have thorns. In a month or two, they'll be so big that the trail will be completely impassable." She felt a sticker hook into her slacks and wiggled her leg to escape the thorn. Before she moved any further, Hannah removed her coat, bundled it up, and carried it on top of her head.

"What are you doing?" Guy asked.

"Trying to keep my coat safe from blackberry thorns."

"Do you want me to hold it for you? I'm taller."

Hannah paused mid-step and considered Guy's offer. Could she trust him? "It belonged to my dad," she said. "He wore it in high school, that's why it fits me."

"I promise I'll be careful with it."

"Okay." Hannah took a deep breath and handed it over. Guy was right. He *was* taller than her. With him holding her coat the blackberries wouldn't come close. "Thanks."

Guy lifted the puffy bundle above his head. "I didn't know this would be such an adventure." He scrambled over the vines to follow her.

"That's a recent development. It didn't use to be like this. Five, ten, fifteen years ago, this was a popular make-out spot." Hannah remembered times she'd spent here with Rob and pushed the bittersweet memories away.

They were past the blackberries now, and Guy gave her back the coat. Hannah stuffed her arms into the sleeves and instantly felt warmer. Had her dad ever visited Rhododendron Lane wearing this coat? Probably. The thought made her smile, as if Max was there too, watching over her, like an invisible protector.

"Wow!" Guy said, as the rhododendrons came into sight. Pink, purple, red, yellow, and peach, the trees budded like a rainbow, arching together to form a tunnel that framed a stunning view of the ocean. The blossoms hadn't fully developed, but you could see more than a hint of the glory to come. "This is spectacular."

"It is, isn't it?" Hannah smiled, happy that a big-city New Yorker like Guy was impressed by one of her favorite places in Sand Dollar Cove. "My great-grandpa knew the landscape designer. It was some hotshot from Seattle who didn't get along with Kara Lee Paul, the architect of Seaside Resort. He didn't think a woman should tell him what to do. But I mean, come on. You can't plant things willy-nilly without taking the buildings into consideration. Otherwise you have things like that magnolia tree growing so close to Strawberry Cottage making a colossal mess, and this, a path leading directly to the edge of a cliff."

They could see the edge now. A crumbling bit of earth that was slipping into the Pacific. Hannah held back, not progressing past the halfway mark of the rhododendrons. Creeping forward was too much of a risk. Waterlogged cliffs were known to collapse. Washington State mudslides could kill.

"It seems like there should be a gazebo here." Guy stopped next to her, standing by her side and not moving an inch further.

"Exactly. There was going to be a gazebo, but that turned into what's now The Summer Wind restaurant pavilion. Really this path should have led to that, which would have been amazing."

"Why did the landscaper make plans before the architect finished the building designs?"

"That's a good question. I don't know the details of that, but I bet my grandma would."

"If the Blanchet Maison insurance team saw this, they'd probably flip out. It's literally an attractive nuisance."

Hannah bristled at the word nuisance. "Fifty-year-old rhododendrons aren't nuisances. These were bushes once, and now they're trees. These rhodies are extremely valuable."

"I misspoke." Guy turned and looked at her. "I'm sorry. I didn't mean to insult your trees."

"They're not *my* trees. Technically, they belong to Seaside Resort, which belongs to Blanchet Maison. But really, this spot belongs to everyone who loves Sand Dollar Cove."

"What I meant, but worded really poorly, is that as beautiful as this place is, it's a huge insurance liability. Someone could get hurt—or even lose their life. There should be a guardrail, or something."

"A guardrail would only offer a false sense of protection. We have no idea what this cliff is capable of."

"Well, Blanchet Maison should find out, right? They could send out geologists to survey what's going on, and then they could post guardrails at the appropriate points as well as 'enter at your own risk' signs to reduce liability."

"Blanchet Maison would never pay for that. We're part of

the Local Flavors division, which is basically their version of an afterthought. They only remember us when our franchise fees are due, or when we need final approval on a new hire." *Or a promotion*, Hannah thought with a pinch of nervousness.

"It sounds like you don't like them very much."

"It's not that I don't like them. I don't respect them. There's a difference. Blanchet Maison is like an absentee overlord. We're the thirteen colonies and they're King George."

"Why do they own Seaside Resort then, if they don't take an active interest in it?"

"Beats me." But that wasn't true, exactly. Hannah had thought about it a lot. "Seaside Resort was owned by one of the original developers from Las Vegas for a long time. But then in 1980, when the boom went bust—"

"You locals talk about the boom going bust quite a lot, I've noticed."

"Because it was a big freaking deal. Anyhow, when the boom went bust, Blanchet Maison swooped in like a vulture and bought us for a rock-bottom price. Then they've been leeching money from us ever since. It's the major reason things are so run-down around here. If we could take the money we send them in franchise fees every year and reinvest that into infrastructure, we could become one of the premier resorts on the West Coast." *Instead of a sad has-been*, she added privately, because it felt so disloyal.

"Why doesn't corporate help you out more, do you think?"

"Because the Blanchets are idiots, that's why." As soon as she'd said it, Hannah realized she'd let her ire get the better of her professionalism. "Idiot's a strong word."

Guy chuckled. "At least you didn't say assholes."

"I might have been too harsh just now. Guido Blanchet III, the president, who goes by Gabe, is really only known for competing in the Olympics. Every time someone from corporate comes to visit, we have to put his picture up real quick, to show off his bronze medal. Then the son, Guido Blanchet IV, has nothing to do with the company at all except to enjoy an unearned seat on the board. He was in some sort of Twitter disaster a while ago. That was hilarious."

Guy winced. "Twitter can be a cesspool."

"True, but this was his own fault. He showed up to a board meeting on Zoom with a bunny filter over his face. It was such a PR nightmare that the stock price tanked."

"Wow... I guess I can see why you said idiot."

"Like I said, I shouldn't have said idiot. Guido Blanchet II, who went by Gabriel—bunny guy's grandfather—must have been smart. He's the one who built up the empire. But he died last year, and that caused the stock to tank too."

"Maybe they don't have the money to reinvest into Seaside Resort?"

"I doubt it. The Blanchets are billionaires. Probably everyone on the board makes more than all of us here at Seaside Resort combined." Hannah looked down at her watch. "Shoot. I love being outside, but it's time to head back. I have a shift at the front desk."

"Thanks for bringing me out here," he said as they turned back.

"My pleasure. I love seeing the rhodies in bloom." She looked up at Guy. "But here, I've been blathering on about company politics and haven't let you get a word in edgewise. Tell me more about yourself. Why'd you move out here? I know you said in your interview that you wanted to escape the big city, but why Sand Dollar Cove? How'd you find us?"

"That's a long story." Guy's broad shoulders slumped for a minute before he straightened them. They started the walk back to work. "I felt trapped in New York. People talk about it being an urban jungle, and that's true to a certain extent. For a while I was happy. I made friends with my doorman, and I had my favorite haunts. The delicatessen where the pickles had extra snap. The newsstand where the owner always stocked my favorite type of gum. My boss at work was great, and there were so many good vegetarian restaurants. I could eat out every night at a different place."

"That sounds expensive."

"Yeah. That's why I learned to cook."

"Good plan." The icy wind stung Hannah's cheeks. They were at the brambly entrance to the lane now, and the blackberries seemed to have multiplied. "Do you mind?" Hannah asked as she unzipped her coat again.

"Of course not." Guy carefully lifted the garment so it would be safe. "Does your dad live nearby?"

Hannah looked out at the water. "No. He died a few months before I started kindergarten." She hopped gingerly over the vines.

"I'm sorry to hear that." Guy leapt after her. "Here you go." He helped her into her coat like a gentleman. "Is that why your grandmother brought you to work with her?"

Hannah nodded but didn't elaborate further. She was grateful when Guy changed the subject.

"Back to why I left New York," he said as she zipped up her coat. "The thing I didn't like about city life was that it felt like the people around me were so focused on performance and reputation that I was always one "gotcha" moment away from total humiliation. And that also meant that nobody was looking out for me but me."

"Gosh," said Hannah. "That's sounds like a dog-eat-dog way of living."

"Right. And that wore me down." Guy raised his hand like he was pitching a baseball. "So I threw a dart at the map. I didn't know where I was going but I knew I couldn't stay in New York anymore. At first the dart landed in Canada, but I figured dealing with immigration issues would be too much of a headache. I walked my fingers down the paper and reached

Washington State. After that, it was only a matter of looking up personal trainer jobs that might match my skill set."

"And now you're here," said Hannah, feeling lucky that fate had brought them together. She immediately discounted that thought. They weren't *together* together; Guy was her co-worker, nothing more. Still, he seemed like an asset that Seaside Resort could be proud of. "What do you think of Sand Dollar Cove so far?"

"It's freezing cold. I didn't expect life on the beach to be so windy."

Hannah laughed, as the foghorn crooned in the distance. "It'll warm up in summer. But yeah, Washington State beaches aren't like Hawaii, that's for sure." Not that she'd ever been to Hawaii. Wouldn't that be nice, to zip off to someplace sunny? *Sounds risky*, she told herself a second later. *You're safer here.*

Guy tempered his long strides to match her shorter ones. "Aside from the weather," he said, "I'm really impressed. I've only lived here three months and I already know my neighbors. The grocery clerks chat with me. When I go into town, there's always an easy place to park. And the air..." He took a deep breath. "It's so clean out here."

"It is..." Hannah said cautiously. "And it always used to be. But you haven't been here for wildfire season yet. That's a sad thing that's been happening to the Pacific Northwest in recent years. Once the forests in British Columbia burn, or the woods on the other side of the Puget Sound..." Hannah shuddered. "There can be a haze that looks like we're trapped in a dystopian sci-fi novel. Olympic National Forest is usually safe, though. It helps that we have rainforests, I think."

"That blows my mind that there are rainforests in Washington."

"Have you been to the Hoh Rain Forest?" Hannah asked, mentioning a popular destination in Olympic National Park.

"Not yet."

"It's incredible. Moss hangs down like fabric off the trees. When you look at it from a distance, you think it's going to be soft and moist, but often it looks soft, but is actually crunchy. Just make sure you bring bug spray when you visit, because the mosquitoes will eat you alive if you're there in summer. If you visited right now, you'd be fine, though, because it's too cold for the bloodsuckers."

"I'd love to go there someday. Could I convince you to take me?" Guy's blue eyes flashed at her with a hopeful expression. "It seems like you have the insider knowledge."

Was Guy asking her on a date, or to be his unpaid tourist guide? Hannah wasn't sure. Still, her heart flip-flopped with the possibility. "That would be fun," she said noncommittally. They were at the path that forked to the lobby and wellness studio now.

"Thanks for taking me to see Rhododendron Lane." Guy tilted his head to the side and smiled at her warmly. "I promise I won't tell anyone about it, unless those jerks from Blanchet Maison show up. In that case I'll demand that they invest millions of dollars into shoring up the cliff and adding safety precautions."

Hannah snorted. "Good luck with that."

When she headed back to the lobby, there was a slight skip to her step that she prayed Guy didn't notice. But it was like her feet had minds of their own. Hannah's spirit felt so light, she practically floated.

SIX

"Save Ferdinand!" Mary cried. "He's drowning!"

Hannah jumped off her sofa bed and raced to the bedroom Mary shared with Cheryl. It was the middle of the night, the day after her lovely walk with Guy to Rhododendron Lane. Her sleep-addled brain told her it was impossible for her cat to drown in the middle of their one-bedroom rental, yet there Ferdinand was, balanced precariously on a laundry basket, floating in a deluge of water. Hannah waded into the flood and picked him up. Ferdinand clawed her arms by way of a thank you.

"Oh my goodness!" Hannah surveyed the chaos. "What happened?"

"It's that blasted shower." Cheryl pointed at the wall between the bedroom and shower. "We told the landlord it was leaking but he wouldn't listen."

"I can't stop it." Mary had both hands above her head pressed firmly against a gaping hole in the wall. Water streamed down her blonde hair and wallboard particles speckled her face. "It's like Niagara Falls in here."

"What a disaster!" Hannah plopped Ferdinand on the bed where he'd be safe.

"Let me get the spare towels," Cheryl said as she tried to rise from her chair. Eighty-two years old, she slept in a reclining chair because it was too difficult for her to lay flat with her osteoporosis.

"You stay put, Gran," said Hannah. "Mary and I can manage."

"But I want to help," Cheryl protested.

Hannah pointed to the cat. "You watch Ferdinand so he doesn't run out the door and get lost. Again." Their cat was a natural-born escape artist. But he was good company for Cheryl, especially when Mary was on campus or at the barista stand and Hannah was at work.

"I can do more than cat-sit," said Cheryl. "Hand me my phone and I'll call the landlord this instant."

"Good idea. Send him some pictures while you're at it." Hannah collected her grandmother's phone off the nightstand and handed it to her.

"Damn Seattleites, robbing us blind," Cheryl muttered.

"Can you make the water stop?" Mary asked. "It just keeps coming."

"Right." Hannah slogged through the water in her wool socks. "I'll go find the shut-off valve."

"We have a shut-off switch?" Mary asked.

"A shut-off *valve*, and yes, it's outside." Hannah wasn't surprised that Mary didn't know this. Her sister was strong on creativity but weak when it came to practical detail. Hannah knew that instead of having an easy turnoff valve like modern building codes required, their rental was a plumbing disaster waiting to happen. In order to turn off the water, Hannah needed a wrench, a flashlight, and occasionally, a miracle. Cheryl used to manage these things for them, but now it was too difficult for her to move.

Hannah pulled on her rubber boots and her father's coat. She grabbed the rusty toolbox they kept underneath the sink and headed out into the night. Wind whipped her chestnut-brown hair across her cheeks and the scent of the Pacific Ocean kissed her nose. Trudging across the gravel driveway, Hannah cursed their greedy landlord for not hiring the plumber to upgrade their leaky pipes. Then she felt ashamed of herself for not being able to afford someplace safer to live. She wished she could have come up with the extra housing money somehow. Perhaps she could have borrowed from a shady payday lender, or sold one of her kidneys on the black market. Anything would have been better than the terrified look on her grandma's face as water gushed around her.

Hannah knelt on the ground at the end of the driveway and winced as gravel bit into her knees. She lifted the utilities cover and set it aside. As she shined the flashlight into the cavity, she heard a hissing sound coming from a corroded-looking pipe.

"Here goes nothing," Hannah muttered as she wrenched the valve to the right. The hissing sound stopped.

Hannah looked over her shoulder and back at the house. She could see Cheryl's potted plants on the porch; the baby tomatoes leaning against their cages. For all its faults, the crummy rental was home. The three of them had lived there together ever since Cheryl gained custody of the girls eighteen years ago, when Hannah was seven and Mary was four. It was Cheryl who brushed Hannah's hair each night and made her and Mary say their prayers before bedtime. It was Cheryl who had attended parent–teacher conferences and hung their report cards on the refrigerator—straight As for Hannah, and a mixture of As, Bs, and the occasional C+ for Mary. It was Cheryl who had encouraged Hannah to earn her business degree at Grays Harbor State University. Now the safe home her grandma had made for them was destroyed. Hannah needed to fix things pronto.

She lugged the cover over the utility compartment and hurried back to the house. As soon as Hannah crossed the threshold, she was relieved to see that the spray of water had abated. The water seeped across the living room carpet, but at least it was no longer rising. "Gran?" she called. "Mary? Are you okay?"

"We're fine." Mary poked her head out of the bedroom. As soon as the sisters locked eyes, Mary shot Hannah a look. A sisterly glance that telepathically said: everything is *not* fine. "We need to get Gran into some dry clothes. She's all wet."

"Here." Hannah rushed to the plastic box on top of the cabinet where she kept her own belongings. "I have a sweatshirt and yoga pants that might work."

"Gran, in leggings?" Mary raised her eyebrows. "Tonight gets weirder and weirder."

"It's going to be fine." Hannah handed the clothes to Mary. "We'll get through this together, like we always do." Ferdinand mewed from the bedroom, and through the cracked door, Hannah saw Cheryl's hands cover her face and her shoulders shake with sobs. "It's going to be okay, Gran," Hannah called out. "Mary will get you into some warm clothes, and I'll clean up the water." She pushed the bedroom door open wider and a stream of water flowed from one room to another.

"That's right," Mary said with false brightness. "Hannah will call the renter's insurance company first thing tomorrow."

Now it was Hannah's turn to shoot her sister a telepathic look. She shook her head ever so slightly. They didn't have renter's insurance anymore, not after the premium had gone up.

"What did the landlord say?" Mary asked.

"He wouldn't pick up the phone," Cheryl wailed. "It went to an answering service who took down a message but wouldn't promise to help."

"I'll call the landlord again tomorrow," said Hannah. "Hell, I'll call the Red Cross if I have to. But right now, I'm going to sop up this water." Squaring her shoulders, Hannah was about to flick on the living room floor lamp when she thought better of it. Electricity and water did not go together. She glanced up nervously at the overhead light and wondered if it was safe. Maybe she should turn off the power to the house? Was that possible? Hannah didn't know how to do that. "Best not to turn on anything electrical," she told Mary, who was doing well enough in her interior design courses at college, but was not so astute in common sense terms.

"Good thinking." Mary wiped tears away with the sleeve of her nightshirt. "Come on, Gran. Let's get you into these dry clothes."

Hannah took a deep breath before she tackled the cleanup. She found a cooking pot in the kitchen and headed to the bathroom, using it to scoop up water and dump it in the sink. A one-woman bucket brigade, she quickly dealt with most of the water pooling around the tiled floor. Her boots squished on the soggy bath mat.

"What can I do to help?" Mary asked, a few minutes later.

"Um..." Hannah wasn't exactly sure of the best course of action to take, but she was a whiz at improvising. "Let's open the windows to increase airflow, and then use towels and blankets to suck up the water." She walked into the hallway and opened the linen closet.

"There aren't enough towels in the world to clean up this mess." Mary blew a puff of bangs out of her eyes.

"I know, but we have to try." Hannah handed her a blanket.

"I can't use this one." Mary flashed her an indignant look. "This was my final project for my textile class last semester. I wove the cotton myself and hemstitched the satin edge."

"I'm not trying to ruin your precious blanket. I'm trying to save everything else we own."

"I'm helping, too." Mary grabbed a beach towel with the Seaside Resort logo. "Don't act like I'm not."

"Sorry. I didn't mean to snap." Hannah clutched her coat tighter and zipped it shut. Then, getting down on her hands and knees, she began sopping up water from the carpet. "I'm worried about Gran," Hannah whispered. "She'll catch pneumonia if we can't get this place dried out."

"I'm not sure if you, me, and all the towels in Sand Dollar Cove would be enough to dry out this flood." Mary looked at the clock on the mantel. "It's two a.m. That only gives us six hours before I have to be on campus. It's my portfolio review with my advisor, the best interior designer in Grays Harbor County. If she likes my work, she could recommend me to her Airbnb clients after graduation this June."

"That would be awesome, and I'm sure she'll love your designs. But I have to be at work by nine. That doesn't give us long to make this place habitable again."

Mary scooped up a quilt from the sofa bed and pressed it onto the soggy carpet. "Can't you take the day off, since we're in crisis mode?"

"That's not possible." Hannah opened the window by the front door. "It'll look bad if I skip work now. I'm on the cusp of getting that promotion. If Herman makes me general manager, we'll have so much money that we can start a savings account and maybe even travel to Seattle for the weekend, like you've been talking about."

"And see the Seattle Art Museum and the Center for Architecture and Design?"

"Yes. Whatever you want." Hannah opened the next window.

"But who would look after Gran? She can't handle a long car ride, and you know how she hates Seattle."

"We'll figure something out." Hannah partially collapsed the hide-a-bed, grateful that other than the feet, it hadn't gotten wet.

"I can't imagine them not promoting you." Mary folded her

towel in half and pressed it against the carpet. "You know more about Seaside Resort than anyone."

"Anyone except for Gran, that is."

"Gran led the housekeeping staff. You know how to organize the business side of things. The reservations, the staffing issues, the advertising, and everything."

"Herman mentioned something about needing to consider outside candidates, and I'm really nervous." Hannah picked up an area rug and dragged it out onto the porch.

"Herman won't give the job to an outsider," Mary said, after Hannah had come back inside. "Besides, you graduated summa cum laude from Grays Harbor State. You're the smartest person I know."

"Thanks, but nothing is a given, especially since I just barely turned twenty-five." Hannah picked up a towel and went to work drying the carpet beside Mary.

"Age is just a number."

"I hope the executives at corporate headquarters see it that way." Hannah wrung out a towel in the sink before using it to sop up more water.

"I think that if Herman recommends you, they won't say no. You've done great things as assistant manager, including bringing the staffing levels back to normal. How's the new personal trainer doing, by the way?"

"Guy Barret?" *The hunk. The charmer. The only employee at Seaside Resort that could fluster her.*

"Yeah."

"Fine, I guess," said Hannah. "Everyone seems to love him." *But not her. It was a crush, that was all.* "I told you what happened yesterday, right?" Hannah asked.

"No. What?"

"A guest rolled up in a BMW and Guy got into a ten-minute conversation with him about trim options and engine power. I couldn't follow half of it." Hannah repositioned her towel. "But that's the type of panache we need if we are going to bring in guests able to spend at a higher price point."

"The one time I saw him I thought he looked liked Ryan Reynolds."

Hannah wrung out a rag. "I don't see the resemblance." *Except that she did.* Hannah punched the towel to soak up more water. "But back to me dealing with our staffing level situation, you're right. If it had been up to Herman, those open job positions never would have been filled. Maybe that will help me get the promotion. I hope Blanchet Maison agrees."

"You mean the money-grubbing oligarchs?" Mary sat back on her heels and paused for a second. "They've never even been to Seaside Resort. What do they know?"

"I'm not sure, but..." Hannah squeezed out her towel over the kitchen sink and glanced around. Their rental looked like a hurricane had hit it. "I hope I get that promotion. The increased salary would really help."

"I can drop out." Mary clutched the edge of a soggy towel. "I could up my hours at the coffee stand to full time, and help pay the bills." Her sister's offer was sincere, but Hannah could hear Mary's hesitancy. "Or I could ask Aidan for money. He might float me a loan."

"I would never ask you to do that. You only have a few more months to go, and you shouldn't be asking your boyfriend for money."

"My almost-fiancé." Mary pinched two fingers together. "Aidan's *this* close to proposing. I can sense it."

"That's great, but I'm more excited about your graduation this summer." Hannah collected a pair of shoes off the floor and put them on a table where they could dry out. Mary was already working hard to finish her degree and study for the National Council for Interior Design qualification exam at the same time. "I'm enormously proud of you for earning your degree, and Gran is, too."

"But—"

"Stop worrying so much. I've got our finances under control. Your interior design career will be amazing even though your Hollywood dreams fell through. I won't let you down. Now, you deal with the living room and I'll go finish in the bathroom." Hannah rushed to the hall closet, grabbed the last two towels, and wiped down the walls of the bathroom.

She'd put on a brave face for Mary just now, but the truth was, their financial situation was more precarious than ever. Her job as assistant manager at Seaside Resort paid okay, but not well enough to handle unforeseen expenses like this one. Experts said that responsible adults should maintain a three-month emergency fund. Hannah had responsibility oozing out of every pore, but she lived paycheck to paycheck. When she needed to buy clothes, she thrifted. When she was sick, she searched WebMD. Vacations to her meant having two days off in a row.

She didn't usually mind her frugal existence. Hannah was grateful for all she had. Besides, who needed fancy vacations when they already lived in one of the most beautiful places on earth? People came from all over the world to visit Sand Dollar Cove, and Hannah was happy to welcome them. But the stress of eking out their meager existence was hard to bear, especially knowing that Cheryl was suffering.

The hole in the shower wall was so big she could see straight through to the bedroom, where Cheryl lay awkwardly on the bed with Ferdinand curled by her feet. Her recliner must have been wet, otherwise she wouldn't be on the mattress. In the dim light Hannah could see Cheryl wince in pain. What would they do if they had to move out? Rental prices had skyrocketed all over Sand Dollar Cove as the small town flooded with remote workers and tech money retirees. What had formerly been affordable housing had turned into Airbnbs. Hannah and Mary could couch-surf with friends until they found something suitable, but Cheryl couldn't do that. No, her grandma needed three things to survive: her granddaughters, her recliner, and her cable TV. Normally Hannah would have considered cable an unnecessary expense, but watching what she called "her shows" was the only thing that helped Cheryl cope with chronic pain.

"This towel's done for," Hannah muttered, as she wrung it out over the sink. After it was as dry as possible, she mopped the floor with it, knowing she would have to throw it away after. A chill blasted in through the open door, making her shiver.

"Everything important is off the carpet now," called Mary.

"Great work!" Hannah hollered back.

The strenuous effort was making her thirsty, so she picked up the mug she kept next to her toothbrush and turned on the faucet, forgetting that she'd shut off the water. There were a few drops, but nothing more. "Shoot!" Hannah turned off the faucet, ashamed at being flustered. Looking up at the mirror, she paused for a second. Her father's coat swallowed her slight frame. Chestnut hair streamed down her back and her brown eyes had dark circles under them. She looked like a twenty-five-year-old orphan waif. Which she was. Tears filled her eyes, but she didn't have time for self-pity. Hannah mustered her courage and lifted her chin. "It's going to be okay," she whispered to her reflection. "I'll get the promotion at work, I'll start earning more money, and we'll find a safer place to live." Easy-peasy.

Only nothing was easy in Hannah Turner's world. Sand Dollar Cove was a blissful place where travelers came to relax and enjoy life. But even if Hannah had been offered the opportunity to pause for a moment and relax, she wouldn't know how. Tension was the only thing holding her together.

SEVEN

"Whoa! What happened to you?" Lark asked. The housekeeper appraised Hannah from head to toe. "You're all sweaty and..." She waved her hand under her nose. "You don't smell that great." They were in the laundry room in front of a giant pile of fresh towels waiting to be folded.

"I know." Hannah cringed. "Sorry that I stink. Is it okay if I take a quick shower in Sunscape Cottage if I clean up after myself? I don't think anyone is staying there right now."

"I'd say yes, except a couple from Arizona checked in late last night. The shower in Strawberry Cottage still works though, if you don't mind rodent droppings. It's a good thing it'll be razed soon." Lark handed her a towel. "Why didn't you shower at home? Was the hot water out again?"

"Even worse. The pipe burst. Half of what we own is now destroyed. I called the landlord five times this morning, and he finally called me back while I was on the way here. My car doesn't have Bluetooth, so I had to pull over to the side of the road. I was so upset I was shaking, and didn't want to talk and drive."

"Yikes! Here, take two towels." Lark handed her a freshly

folded one, and then turned around and grabbed her some toiletries as well.

"The landlord said that the plumber was coming out right away."

"That's good."

"Is it?" Hannah hugged the towels closer. "Even if he can fix the pipes, what about mildew? The whole place flooded."

"I'm so sorry, Hannah."

"Thanks. I need to hurry too, or I'll be late for my meeting with Herman."

"A nice shower will make things better." Lark rubbed her elbows for a few seconds before folding more towels.

"Hopefully so."

"And don't let your landlord screw you over. He should find emergency housing for you for at least the number of nights that you've paid forward in rent."

"What happens after that?" Hannah couldn't keep the panic from her voice. "I canceled our renter's insurance because it was too expensive."

"It's always too expensive." Lark sighed as she folded the next towel. "But who knows? Maybe it'll turn out to be an easy cleanup and you won't have to move out."

"Maybe." Hannah tried to keep hope afloat, but in the harsh light of day, that was difficult. She'd dropped Cheryl off at the senior center this morning, and Ferdinand was in his carrier at home so that he wouldn't run away with the landlord, the plumber, or anyone else who came into the apartment. Mary had promised she'd come home to let him out as soon as she could get away from campus.

"Chin up, Hannah." Lark patted her back. "This is Sand Dollar Cove. Nobody here is going to let you, Cheryl, or Mary become homeless."

"It doesn't feel like Sand Dollar Cove anymore," said

Hannah. "Almost everyone I knew growing up has moved away. The town's packed with newcomers now."

"There's still a lot of us old-timers left," said Lark. "We'll start a GoFundMe if we have to."

"Gran would be so embarrassed. She doesn't even like to accept help getting out of her recliner."

"Your grandma likes her independence, alright. I still remember my first day working here when Cheryl was training me. She told me that the best part of working on the house-cleaning staff is that you got to take a dirty room and show it who was boss. Cheryl said the great thing about cleaning toilets was that they never talked back to you. She reigned supreme in every room." Lark grinned. "Your grandma was the living embodiment of 'hashtag bosslife.'"

Hannah smiled. "That sounds like Gran, alright." She clutched the towels closer. "I better go wash up before I stink out your freshly cleaned laundry."

"Good luck with your landlord."

Hannah frowned. "I'm going to need it."

Walking into the bright sunlight made her feel slightly better. Pacific Northwest Aprils were known for gray skies and unpredictable weather, but today was sunny. As Hannah walked through the twisty paths that connected one cottage to the next, she felt the calming presence of the resort wash over her. Flowers bloomed in the gardens along each side of the path, and bird feeders attracted multiple species. Hannah heard a hummingbird before she saw it. It whizzed past her ear and hovered near a fuchsia to feed.

If only Gran hadn't sold her house to pay for my dad to go to college, Hannah mused, like she'd done countless times before. She was proud of Max for graduating from the University of Washington with a degree in civil engineering, of course, but if Cheryl still owned her house, it would be worth close to a million dollars by now. Like all cycles, Sand Dollar Cove's white-hot real estate market had returned, leaving the Turner women in the cold.

Seeing Strawberry Cottage made her sad, knowing that it would be torn down on July 1st. She used her master key to open the front door, and one whiff of the musty air reminded her how dilapidated the cottage had become. The remaining couch was ripped, the mattress sagged, and the kitchenette had a sprung mousetrap on the counter—with the decomposing remains of a rodent caught under its hammer.

Stylistically the place was a disaster, too. Now that all the junk was gone, it was easier to see that. Turquoise shag carpet and peachy walls reminded her of a different era. This was the cottage that Liza Minnelli had stayed in when she visited Seaside Resort in the early 1970s. There was an autographed picture of her on the wall, next to another one with Elizabeth Taylor, and Dennis Quaid. Cheryl joked that she had vacuumed up enough cocaine out of the carpets to stock a New York City nightclub. Those days were long gone, of course, because Hollywood types never visited Seaside Resort anymore. But Hannah was proud of how, under her stewardship, they had successfully marketed to baby boomers with money to burn. Families with young children came too, especially now that there was a kids' club on the weekends in July and August.

Hannah checked her watch. She had twenty minutes before her meeting with Herman. That was barely enough time to shower and blow-dry her thick hair. Dropping her things on the bamboo table, Hannah hopped into the mildewed shower and was grateful when the hot water turned on after a minute. The refurbished cottages had tankless water heaters, but this one didn't. A little while later she was dressed in her best, most professional outfit: form-fitting slacks and a Ralph Lauren blazer a guest had left behind three years ago. It had languished in the lost and found for six months until Herman gave her permission to keep it.

Normally she wasn't nervous about any meetings with Herman. Her boss was practically her honorary uncle. When Cheryl had been completely unable to teach Hannah how to parallel-park, it had been Herman who had come to the rescue. Hannah credited her exceptional parallel-parking skills to Herman's patient instructions as she practiced maneuvering his behemoth of a Buick in front of the hardware store on Main Street again and again. "Turn on your blinker and stay calm," he'd say. "You got this." But today she felt on edge, both because of the flood and her not-yet-official promotion.

Hannah locked the door to Strawberry Cottage behind her. "Take a deep breath," she told herself, and she repeated Herman's encouraging words from days past. "You got this." She took a moment to drink in the view. From the doorstep she could see all parts of the cove, including the still-functioning lighthouse on a peninsula of rock, out in the distance. It was so sunny today that the foghorn didn't sound. All Hannah could hear were the peep of chirping birds and the roll of the ocean.

Shoulders back, head held high, and heart full of hope, Hannah walked down the path until she reached the main lodge. Two of Guy's training clients were filling up their water bottles from a glass dispenser next to the complimentary coffee station.

"Hello, Mrs. Sanchez and Mrs. Dario." Hannah waved. "Are you enjoying your stay?"

"We sure are," said Mrs. Sanchez. "Just got back from a walk. I'm so glad I convinced Elena and her husband to come here."

"Same," said Mrs. Dario. "I love this place. Even the water tastes good." She sniffed her water bottle before screwing on the lid. "It must be the strawberry and mint they add."

"I'm glad you like it," said Hannah. "And Mrs. Sanchez, I'm so happy you and your husband came back to visit us with friends. We appreciate the word-of-mouth referrals."

"I appreciated the resort credit." Mrs. Sanchez shrugged. "Of course, my husband blew it all on his first day of deep-sea fishing, but it was still nice to receive."

"Until we have to drive home with three coolers of fish on dry ice." Mrs. Dario shook her head. "Why can't Carlos and Vicente take up hiking instead?"

"Vicente used to hike, you know," said Mrs. Sanchez. "But his back gives him too many problems now."

"Has he seen our massage therapist?" Hannah asked. "Maybe that would help."

"I wish he would," said Mrs. Sanchez. "But Vicente refuses to do anything but pop Advil."

Energy quickened over Hannah. From the corner of her eye, she saw Guy cross the lobby. It was like there was a silk ribbon tied between them that vibrated whenever Guy was near. *Did he feel the connection too?* The pull was so strong that it made her heart beat harder, as if every cell in her body had ignited.

"Have a wonderful day," Hannah said to the guests, focusing her attention on them, and not Guy. "Please ring the front desk if you need anything, and they'll text me."

"We're going to need an Escalade full of dry ice next week for all the fish our husbands have caught, but aside from that, I think we're good," said Mrs. Sanchez.

"I hate fish," Mrs. Dario muttered. "There. I said it. My plan is to host a big party with my relatives and give it all away."

Hannah scooted past them and nodded to the clerks at the front desk. Her phone rang. Looking down at the screen, Hannah saw that it was her landlord. Shoot! What should she do now? She needed to take this call, but she couldn't risk torpedoing her chances for the promotion. Hannah tapped her screen, and the call went to voice mail. Then she quickly texted the landlord. *In a meeting. Will call back in an hour.*

Moisture Mitigators are drying the walls now, her landlord texted back. *The water won't turn back on for at least two weeks until the plumber can get us on his schedule. I'll refund you $682 for this month's rent.*

Hannah's heart sank. This was the worst possible news. When she called back in an hour, she'd let the landlord have it. He should put them up in a hotel! The returned rent wouldn't cover three nights of hotel living, let alone two weeks. Hannah noted the time on her phone. She *hoped* she could call back in an hour. She had no idea how long this meeting would last. Herman had a tendency to ramble.

After opening the door, Hannah stepped into Herman's cramped office and was startled to see that Guy was there too, wearing a Seaside Resort polo shirt, khaki shorts, and clean white sneakers. Why was Guy at the meeting? The chair he sat in squeaked annoyingly. Hannah kept a neutral expression, and settled in the remaining chair, sitting primly with both hands folded on her knees.

"Both of you are right on time, like always." Herman rapped his knuckles on the desk. "Punctuality is essential in this business. Guests don't like to be kept waiting, and neither do I. One reason it's been a pleasure working with both of you is that you are always on time."

"Thanks, boss," said Guy.

"Yes, thank you," Hannah echoed. Instead of thinking about Guy, whose presence took up the entire room, she let her eyes drift momentarily to the wood-paneled walls and ceiling that was textured like popcorn. The general manager's office was the only room in the main lodge that hadn't been redecorated fifteen years ago. The wallpaper, desk, and drapes were original to the 1960s. Herman said it made little sense to spend money on a room that guests wouldn't see. Hannah disagreed, because guests did occasionally enter Herman's office, especially when lodging a complaint (like about the foghorn noise). In Hannah's opinion, Seaside Resort should emote peaceful confidence, not decay.

Peaceful confidence, she told herself. It didn't matter whether Guy sat next to her, or if Mary was right and he was a dead ringer for Ryan Reynolds. She wouldn't let him rattle her.

"Here's the thing," said Herman. "Apparently Blanchet Maison is doing this big reorg, and they want fresh ideas for the future. I brought you two in here because you're both smart as whips. Hannah practically grew up on the resort property, and Guy has that fancy Ivy League diploma."

"Uh, thanks," said Guy. "But I'm brand-new, so I don't know what I'll be able to contribute."

"A fresh look, that's what," said Herman. "What you might not know, though is that Hannah is being considered for promotion to general manager after I retire in six weeks. But the corporate fellows at Blanchet Maison won't let me go ahead and appoint her."

As soon as Herman said that, Hannah felt crushed. She forced every tiny muscle in her face to hold still so she wouldn't show one ounce of disappointment.

Herman continued. "Blanchet Maison has posted the position internally, and I've been hitting the delete button on all of those applications."

"Really?" Guy asked.

Herman drew his furry eyebrows together. "Yes, really. Seaside Resort is a Sand Dollar Cove institution. We can't hand over the keys to an outsider."

"Yes, but Blanchet Maison is an international brand," said Guy. "They have some of the best hotels in the world. Surely some of their candidates—"

"Would be better than me?" Hannah squeaked. She cursed her voice for betraying her. "I mean," she said, in a lower tone. "What are you implying? That I'm not cut out for the job?" *Maybe Guy wasn't her friend after all.*

"No, of course not." Guy scratched his arm. "Just that Blanchet Maison is a well-oiled machine. They have their procedures in place for a reason."

"Oh, so you're a Blanchet Maison expert, are you?" Herman asked.

"I never claimed to be an expert about anything," said Guy. "I think Hannah would be great for the job. She knows all the employees, has great customer service skills, and is always responsive whenever I have a question."

"That's what I think, too." Herman nodded.

Hannah's hands hurt, and when she looked down to see what was wrong, she realized she was squeezing the armrests of her chair so tightly that her knuckles were white. Loosening her grip, she tried to relax.

"You're doing a great job too, Guy," said Herman. "Right, Hannah?" He looked at her.

Right, boss. That's what her brain told her to say, but Hannah was still irked. "Guests say wonderful things about your health and wellness program all the time." She thought about Mrs. Sanchez's remarks. "Lots of people have enjoyed your fitness program so much that they are booking return trips before they leave."

"Excellent." Herman smiled. "And great details for me to jot down, too." He scribbled into a notebook and didn't look up.

What's going on? Hannah wondered. What did Guy have to do with her promotion?

Herman put down his pen. "I had a talk with the HR lady last Friday, and she flat-out told me I couldn't appoint Hannah to be my replacement unless I'd proven that I'd given an equally qualified alternative fair consideration. She suggested half a dozen internal candidates from other properties that I'd already rejected."

Hannah's heart sank. This was it. This was why Herman

had called Guy into their meeting. She wasn't going to get the job, after all.

"But we can't have some unknown corporate type come in here and make Seaside Resort into something it's not," said Herman. "The general manager who replaces me needs to be the right person. Which is where you come in, Guy." Herman removed his eyeglasses and wiped them on the hem of his shirt.

Hannah leaned forward ever so slightly. What the heck? Guy wasn't general manager material. He'd only worked here for three months.

"It was Nancy's idea." Herman put his glasses back on. "She came up with the entire plan."

"What plan?" Hannah asked. *Nancy had betrayed her, too?*

"I'm going to tell corporate that the two of you are in the running for the promotion," said Herman. "I need to provide them with data that shows I've carefully considered both of you for the job."

"What?" Guy asked.

"Guy couldn't run a hotel," Hannah said, before she could help herself.

"I could," Guy said.

"How?" she asked. "You didn't mention any experience in hospitality on your job application."

"I don't need Guy to run Seaside Resort," said Herman. "I just need to pick his brain for ideas that I can write down to prove that I gave him fair consideration for the role."

"While not giving me fair consideration," said Guy. "Because of nepotism."

"Not nepotism," said Hannah. "I've earned this promotion with hard work and experience."

Guy lifted his palms in the air. "I'm not judging. People get jobs for all sorts of reasons in this world."

"All sorts of reasons that include my college degree, and my ten years of experience working at Seaside Resort from the ground up," said Hannah. "I worked here twenty hours a week even when I attended college."

"That's right." Herman nodded. "Ask anyone in Sand Dollar Cove and they'll tell you that a Turner is the right person for this job."

Hannah cringed. Herman wasn't helping her anti-nepotism case.

Guy raised his eyebrows. "I'm happy to help with this ruse. One thing I hope you know about me is that I'm a team player." He bent toward Herman's desk. "What do you need from me to help show New York that Hannah's the right person for this job?"

Hannah felt a puff of relief when Guy said that. She didn't know why he was willing to help. Maybe what he said about being a team player was true. Or maybe he wanted her to double his salary as soon as she got the promotion. Time would tell.

"Here's what we're going to do." Herman's chair squeaked. "Right now, I'm giving you a chance to pitch me your vision of what Seaside Resort should be like in one, five, and ten years. I'm recording your answers, if that's all right with you."

"Sure," said Hannah.

"Yes, that's fine," said Guy.

"Good." Herman flashed a thumbs up. "Now, this recording isn't the end of it. In one week, I want you to come back here with one of those fancy presentations they show at the city council meetings. You know, the ones with the pictures and graphs and stuff."

"You mean a PowerPoint presentation?" Hannah asked.

"Is that what they're called?" Herman asked.

Hannah nodded.

"Yes, then a PowerPoint presentation. I'll use that in my recommendation to Blanchet Maison on who should get the promotion."

"Do you want me to do a good job with my presentations, or blow them on purpose?" Guy asked.

"Good question," said Herman. "Hannah? What do you think?"

Feeling put on the spot, Hannah chose honesty. "Do your best," she said. "It's true that you've only worked here for three months and don't have prior experience in the hospitality industry, but you probably have ideas on how this place could be better. It behooves us to hear them if we're serious about improving our bottom line. And I am serious—I want to return Seaside Resort to its former glory."

"With Frank Sinatra and everything?" Guy asked, with a peculiar look in his eye.

"I was thinking Michael Bublé," said Hannah. "Since he's still alive."

Guy laughed. "Good point."

"Let me just get my tape recorder ready." Herman set an ancient cassette player on his desk.

"Where did you get that?" Guy asked. *"Back to the Future?"*

"Nancy had it in our coat closet." Herman put in a fresh tape. "You never know when one of these things will come in handy."

"You could also use your phone," Hannah suggested.

"Really?" Herman pulled out his Jitterbug.

"Uh... never mind," said Hannah. "I'm not sure that one has a record feature."

"I don't need my phone to do anything but call people," said Herman.

"Who goes first on the pitch?" Guy asked.

Herman shrugged. "I hadn't thought about it."

"How about we flip a coin?" Hannah suggested.

"Works for me." Herman reached into his pocket and pulled out a quarter. "You choose, Hannah, heads or tails."

"Heads," she said without thinking. Herman flipped the quarter and it landed tail side up.

"Looks like Guy goes first," said Herman. "You've got five minutes." He pressed a button on the cassette player. "Starting now."

Hannah had planned to use this time to think about her own response, except that when Guy launched into his pitch, she was so mesmerized by what he said that she didn't plan her own spiel. How was he able to come up with such articulate ideas so fast? He practically pulled them out of thin air.

"There are hotels all over the Pacific Coast, but what sets Seaside Resort apart is our cottage model as well as the unique amenities we offer guests." Guy sat straight, both feet now planted firmly on the ground. "Since I've taken over as activities director, our programming revenue has gone up one hundred and eighty percent. I believe that by focusing on activity packages, we can become a travel destination for visitors from across America, instead of a regional draw for residents along the Pacific Coast. One year from now I'd like to add a heated indoor-outdoor saltwater pool that can be used year-round. Many of our guests are older, and adding water fitness to our list of amenities is important.

"I'd also like to hire a naturalist from the community college to come lead special themed weeks on bird-watching, clam digging, and whale watching. We can reach out to The Mountaineers, and see if they'd be willing to partner with us. We'd offer their members discounts in exchange for them advertising our programs.

"Five years from now, I'd like Seaside Resort to double the number of wheelchair-friendly cottages we offer. I'd like us to have a physical therapist on staff, so that guests can come here to heal from injuries. The baby boomer generation is aging, and accommodating their changing needs is important. Ten years from now, I'd like Seaside Resort to be the premier health resort in the Pacific Northwest. Like the Miraval resorts in Arizona, Texas, and Massachusetts, I want it to be a place where guests come not just for a vacation, but for a life-changing experience that transforms their entire outlook on living."

"Who's going to afford that?" Hannah blurted, pivoting to defense mode. *How the heck was Guy's pitch so good?* "I've done my research. I know what resorts like Miraval charge. And they're adults-only. Are you saying families shouldn't be allowed to come to Seaside? What about the kids' club I just got going? It's been really successful."

"Easy there, killer." Herman chuckled. "I didn't say anything about rebuttals. Let me start my stopwatch, and you'll get your say."

Hannah's temper boiled, but when she spoke, her voice was clear. She refused to let Guy's impressive response rattle her.

"The best thing Seaside Resort has to offer is scenic beauty, and our overarching goal should be to respect nature," Hannah said. "When Kara Lee Paul designed the property in the early 1960s, her goal was to bring modern, indoor-outdoor spaces to the Pacific Northwest. She wanted the cottages to be affordable, easy to maintain, and to blend into the view. That's why the original siding of the buildings was stained wood. Twelve months from now, I'd like to give the whole resort a facelift and return to the original palette. Scrape off the paint and let the wood siding glow. The main lodge especially needs to be upgraded. Right now, we're leaving the impression of a facility that has seen better days."

"I don't know if that's true," said Herman. "We replace the carpets every ten years, and building and grounds touch up the paint all the time."

Hannah shot him a look. "You said no rebuttals."

Herman held up his hands. "That's right, I did. You may continue."

"Restoring the interiors to their original mid-century

modern glory will improve our Yelp and TripAdvisor ratings, which I constantly monitor. It's true that Guy's work in programming has garnished positive reviews, but I believe cosmetic improvements will impact our ratings so much that Triple A will bump us up from three stars to four, increasing our prospective revenue by three hundred percent. But back to Mother Nature. My five-year plan would have solar panels on every roof so that all of our energy was renewable. I'd like to quadruple our EV charging stations so that we can be prepared for the future's increase in electric vehicles.

"Guy's idea about partnering with The Mountaineers and naturalists is good, but I've lived here my whole life. My last boyfriend was a Mountaineer. Half of them are self-proclaimed 'dirtbag climbers.' They don't want luxury accommodation; they want lodge-style dormitories that are cheap places to crash. Surfers and fishermen often want the same thing. That's why I suggest tearing down the storage shed by the back parking lot and turning it into a bunkhouse so that we can accommodate guests at a lower price point." She looked deliberately at Guy. "It shouldn't just be rich people who come here."

Turning her gaze back to Herman, she continued. "My ten-year plan would see Seaside Resort becoming—"

Buzz. Buzz. Buzz.

Her phone rang, interrupting her. "Sorry about that." Hannah looked down at the screen, intending to silence it. "Oh, no. It's the senior center. They might be calling about Gran."

"Go ahead and take it," said Herman. "You can finish your last nine seconds when you're done."

"Thanks for understanding." Hannah accepted the call as she rose to her feet.

"Hi, Hannah, this is Keith from the senior center."

"Hi, Keith. Is my grandma okay?" Hannah opened the door to exit Herman's office, anxious to escape. Keith spoke so loudly that Herman and Guy could probably hear what he said.

"Cheryl is fine, but is it true that you three are homeless?"

"What?" Herman barked.

Hannah looked over her shoulder at him and winced. "Not homeless, exactly," she said. "At least, not yet." She closed the door behind her and made a beeline to the broom closet. There, in the dim fluorescent light, with her back to the door, she finished the conversation as quickly as possible. "I'm in the middle of an important meeting, Keith, can I call you back?"

"What's more important than knowing where your grandma will sleep tonight?" Keith said accusingly. His tone reminded Hannah of his father, who had been her math teacher back in high school.

"I won't let Gran become homeless!" Hannah said, feeling put on the spot.

"Sorry, I didn't mean to sound like I was attacking you. It's just that Cheryl said all of her things are ruined."

"Hopefully not everything." Hannah bit her bottom lip for a second. "I'm not exactly sure what's salvageable. We haven't had a chance to check."

"I'm sorry I have to ask this, but do you or do you not have a safe place for your grandmother to sleep tonight?"

Hannah squeezed her eyes shut, unsure of what to say. "I haven't thought that far," she admitted. Tears dotted her cheeks. This day was too much.

"I have access to a limited number of hotel vouchers I can offer you," Keith said. "I wish I had more, but it'll be enough for three nights at the Motel 6 on Harbor Drive. Do you want me to call them and hold you a room?"

"Yes, please." Hannah felt a lump in her throat the size of a golf ball. Her eyes blurred with tears. "We would be grateful. Thank you so much, and I absolutely will repay you as soon as I can. Right now, I'm in crisis mode."

"Cheryl is a valuable member of our senior community and we want her to be safe, as I know you do, too. The waitlist for

Section 8 housing is incredibly long right now, but I can make some calls and get your name on the list if that would be helpful."

"Thank you, but we don't qualify." Hannah felt ashamed to admit that she'd investigated that option. "I earn $280 a month too much for us to get services."

"I see. Well, I'll keep my eye on the community board for new rentals. What's your budget?"

"Fourteen hundred a month, maybe fifteen if we stretch it."

"I'll be looking," said Keith. "Keep me in the loop, okay? I'm here to support Cheryl in any way I can."

"Thank you." Hannah said goodbye and patted her wet cheeks with a Kleenex she'd found in the pocket of her blazer. When she stood it shocked her to see that she wasn't alone; Guy was standing by the entrance, eavesdropping. His muscled frame leaned against the doorjamb. He must have overheard every word she said.

"What are you doing spying on me?" She jumped to her feet. "How dare you listen to my private conversation!"

Guy held up his hands like he was trying to calm a wild horse.

"I didn't mean to eavesdrop. I came here to get a bottle of WD40 for those squeaky chairs in Herman's office."

"Yeah, right." Hannah brushed past him as she stormed out of the closet.

"I'm not the enemy. I'm trying to help."

"I know. But why was your pitch so good?"

"Because you said for it to be good! I gave you my best."

"That wasn't your best," said Hannah. "That was a pitch you had, like, zero seconds to come up with. If you'd actually had time to think about it, like I have, your plan would probably be even better. You're making it harder for me to get this promotion, not easier."

"Wait." He grabbed the fabric of her blazer and tugged. "What was that you said back there about being homeless?"

"Not homeless. I said *not*."

"What's going on?"

"I don't see how it's any of your business, but since gossip spreads so fast around here I might as well tell you. Our house flooded last night. The landlord says we have to be out for at least two weeks."

"That's awful," Guy said with concern. "Where will you go?"

Hannah squared her shoulders. "To the Motel 6. We have vouchers."

"Please let me know if there's anything I can do to help."

"Thanks," Hannah said, turning away and figuring it was a hollow offer. She was already worrying about what would happen when the vouchers ran out.

EIGHT

When her phone rang at 5 a.m. the next morning, Hannah was so exhausted that she almost didn't answer it. The bed she shared with Mary at the Motel 6 felt like it had rocks in it. But she answered the phone on the third ring, hoping it was the landlord with the all-clear to return home. *That* was wishful thinking. As soon as she wiped the sleep out of her eyes, Hannah remembered that it would be at least a couple of weeks before the rental would have plumbing.

Hannah slid her feet into her sneakers and grabbed the down coat. "Hello?" Swiping a keycard off the dresser, she slipped outside onto the patio and closed the door behind her so she wouldn't wake Cheryl and Mary. "Hannah Turner," she added groggily.

"Hi, Hannah, it's Aidan."

Mary's boyfriend? What was he doing calling this early? "Is everything okay? What's the matter?"

"What? Oh, damn. I forgot about the time difference. I just got off a shift at the hospital and figured you'd be up by now. I've been awake the past twelve hours."

"You're in Kansas, right?"

"Yeah. In Hutchinson. There was a nursing shortage, so they called us in. I have a sweet Airbnb that's only a few blocks away."

"That's good. That must cut down on your commute." Hannah yawned. "Look, I don't want to rush you, but the sun won't be up for a couple of hours here and I'd like to go back to bed, if I could."

"Sorry about that. I'll be quick. I wanted your advice on engagement rings."

Hallelujah! Hannah cheered for her sister. Mary had been right about Aidan proposing. Her sister would be so excited. Cheryl, too. The Turner women were due for happy news. "I've got lots of advice about rings," Hannah said quickly. "Mary and I have talked about them and she has great taste."

"She does, doesn't she? I've always admired that about Mary. I'm glad she gave you ideas, too, because it wouldn't be right to call her directly and ask her about this."

Boy, was Aidan old-fashioned. It wouldn't surprise Hannah if he called Cheryl next and asked permission for Mary's hand.

"What type of ring do you think Mary would suggest?" Aidan asked.

It was a good thing that Mary had given her detailed notes on this subject. "Pear-shaped." Hannah snuggled into the coat. "White gold or platinum. *Not* yellow gold, and definitely not rose gold. Mary loves bling, so the bigger the stone the better, but she's okay with white sapphires. She'd rather have two carats of lab-created white sapphire than half a carat of natural diamond."

"I thought sapphires were blue," said Aidan. "Mary thinks a blue engagement ring would be nice?"

"Not blue. *White.* A white sapphire."

"I didn't know they came in white, but I guess you can grow anything in a lab these days. Even meat. I treated a farmer a few days ago who was really pissed off about alternative meat products. He wouldn't shut up about them. That, and nut milk. He said neither should be in the butcher or dairy aisles."

This rambling conversation at five in the morning was exactly what Hannah disliked about Aidan, although she'd never tell Mary that. He had no consideration for other people's feelings. First, he was too careless to check the time zone, then he woke her up before dawn, and now he was wasting her time blabbing about something when she could be sleeping in bed. "Is there anything else you need?" she asked curtly. "It's freezing here."

"Oh. Sorry about that. Is it okay if I text you some pictures later when I'm at the jewelry store?"

"Sure. You have my number. Happy shopping."

"Thanks."

Hannah hung up, turned the sound off on her phone, and went inside. She climbed into bed, and scooted next to Mary, back-to-back, for warmth. Then she closed her eyes, intending to doze off. But sleep wouldn't come. The conversation with Aidan left her too wound up with excitement for Mary—and unease about her own future. Hannah was happy that Mary was getting what she wanted. But where did that leave Hannah and Cheryl? They'd be stuck where they always were, struggling to make ends meet. And instead of Mary being there by her side, able to assist with Cheryl as their grandmother's osteoporosis became worse, it would be all up to Hannah. What if Aidan whisked Mary off someplace and moved out of town? What if that traveling nurse's job in Hutchinson was so promising that Aidan brought Mary to Kansas? Hannah squeezed her eyes shut and wished for sleep to soothe her, but all that came were silently falling tears.

A few hours later, after dropping Cheryl off at the senior center, Hannah did something she rarely did: she helped herself to the breakfast buffet at The Summer Wind. Employees weren't supposed to eat in the restaurant, but Hannah was so wiped out that she needed the energy. At least, that's what Jasmine said when Hannah came into the kitchen to ask if there were leftover pastries. Hannah and Jasmine had been friends ever since middle school when they'd been assigned to the same group project in history. This morning Jasmine took one look at her and gasped.

"No offense, but you've got bags under your eyes that are bigger that Walla Walla onions." Jasmine opened the dishwasher and took out a clean mug. She filled it to the brim with percolated coffee and gave it to Hannah. "Drink up, and tell me what happened. Is this about your house flood?"

Hannah didn't normally drink coffee black, but she was too tired to ask for milk. "Yes, and no." She sighed, and leaned against the wall by the counter where Jasmine was chopping zucchini. "We have two more nights at the Motel 6, and then I don't know what will happen after that." Hannah's fingernails pressed moon-shaped divots into the tender flesh of her palm.

"But you can move back into your house eventually, right?"

"I think so," Hannah said uncertainly. "I called the landlord an hour ago, and he hasn't called me back."

"I always thought that house was sketchy. The walls are paper-thin."

"Yeah. Whenever it frosts outside, we need expensive space heaters to keep warm. And the drapes are so decrepit you have to pull the cord to the left, and then to the right, and then to the left again to make them open." The tension in Hannah's neck felt like it would break her.

"What if you use this as an opportunity to find something better?" Jasmine asked, as she whacked a zucchini.

Hannah shook her head. "I've been looking, but everything's out of our price range."

"Rent's nuts around here. You could move in with me and

my boyfriend. We'll sleep in the living room and you three can have the bedroom until you're back in your old place."

"Thanks for the offer, but I can't inconvenience you like that."

"Sure you could. Now, tell me why you're so tired."

"Mary's boyfriend Aidan woke me up at five a.m. asking what type of engagement ring she'd like when he proposes."

"That's great for Mary, but why did the doofus have to call so dang early?"

Hannah shrugged and took another sip of java. "Beats me. Do you have any leftover pastries? Gran's eating at the senior center, but I didn't have time to stop and grab a bite."

"And you think I'll feed you day-old Danish?" Jasmine snorted and chopped the squash in front of her angrily. "No can do. You're going to walk into the dining room, pick up a warm plate, and gorge on my absolutely amazing breakfast buffet. Seriously, I outdid myself today. Wait until you see the frittata. Make sure you load up on protein because you need the extra energy."

"But employees aren't supposed to—"

"Look like the walking dead," Jasmine interrupted. "Now scoot."

"I realize I look bad, but I didn't know I looked *that* bad."

"I have some concealer you can borrow when you're done," Jasmine called after her.

Hannah walked out the back door of the kitchen and entered through The Summer Wind's main entrance. The restaurant boasted one of the best views in the whole resort. Floor-to-ceiling windows wrapped around the front, and the terraced dining room allowed people sitting in the back row of tables a view of the ocean that was almost as good as the diners got who sat next to the glass.

After picking up a plate, Hannah entered the buffet line, her stomach growling. She added blueberry ricotta pancakes with lemon butter, raspberry compote, crisp strips of bacon, a helping of veggie frittata, and two poached tomatoes to her plate. Then she piled on a wedge of brie and prosciutto, and refilled her coffee mug before heading to an open table.

"Hopefully you have a second stomach," said a voice from the table next to her. Hannah looked over and saw Mrs. Sanchez grinning at her.

"That's what I forgot to pack," said Mrs. Dario, who sat across from her friend. "My second stomach."

"You'll know for next time, Brenda," Mrs. Sanchez said with a laugh.

"Everything looked so good," Hannah explained. "I don't normally eat this much."

"You'll get no judgment from us," said Mrs. Sanchez. She picked up her plate, her champagne glass, and a pitcher of mimosa and sat over at Hannah's table. Mrs. Dario followed.

"So, what do you know about Guy?" Mrs. Dario asked, wiggling her eyebrows. "We want to know all the details."

"There are no details." Hannah sliced into her pancakes. "At least, none that I can share. He's my co-worker."

"Very proper of you to say," said Mrs. Sanchez. "You definitely don't want to get in trouble with HR."

Mrs. Dario tilted her head to the side. "But you could tell us if Guy has a girlfriend, right?"

"Or a boyfriend?" Mrs. Sanchez added.

"I don't know." Hannah tried to change the subject. "It's not really any of my business what he does in his spare time."

"I would love to know what Guy does in his spare time," said Mrs. Dario. "If I was thirty years younger and not married..."

"Same." Mrs. Sanchez clasped her hands together. "Guy's dreamy. Even when he's sweaty."

"Especially when he's sweaty." Mrs. Dario giggled.

Privately, Hannah had to agree. She blushed and cut into

her frittata, thinking about a sunny day a couple of weeks ago when she'd been walking down to the beach and he'd run past her, not wearing his shirt. It was a miracle her eyes hadn't popped out of their sockets.

"Hannah?" Mrs. Sanchez prodded. "Are you okay?"

"What?" Hannah gulped, not realizing she'd become lost in thought.

"I asked you if you knew if Guy liked pets," said Mrs. Dario.

"Oh, uh... I don't know exactly. Why?"

"Because my daughter's a veterinarian," said Mrs. Sanchez.

"*And* she's single." Mrs. Dario rapped her fingernails on the table. "Brenda doesn't like to admit it, but I'm an expert matchmaker."

"That's not true! I'll admit it." Mrs. Sanchez sipped from her mimosa. "You introduced me to Vicente, after all."

"And fifteen years later, you're still in love."

"Eighteen years." Mrs. Sanchez lifted her mimosa to toast. "We've been married for fifteen, but dated for three."

"I'll drink to that." Mrs. Dario clinked her champagne glass against her friend's.

Relieved that they were no longer talking about Guy, Hannah worked at keeping this new line of discussion flowing. "How'd you meet? Did Mrs. Dario set you up on a blind date?"

"I'm much too slick for that. I invited them both for a back-yard barbecue." Mrs. Dario refilled her glass from the pitcher of mimosa on the table. "Want some?" she asked Hannah.

"No, thanks. I'm headed to work."

"Gotcha." Mrs. Dario put the pitcher down.

"I'd been single so long that I figured that was it for me. I couldn't handle dating another loser," said Mrs. Sanchez.

"Only luckily for you, Vicente wasn't a loser." Mrs. Dario beamed.

"No." Mrs. Sanchez smiled. "He was a true gentleman. Brought me flowers on our first date. Made me dinner on our second. Vicente had all my grandkids' names memorized by our third. That impressed me."

"How many grandchildren do you have?" Hannah asked.

"Nine."

"Show her the pictures," said Mrs. Dario.

"I would, but I don't have my purse with me. I paid for breakfast with my room number." Mrs. Sanchez held up her fingers, flashing numbers. "I have three kids and seven grand-children, and then Vicente has a son and a daughter with another two grandkids. That makes nine grandchildren to spoil, which is the best part of retirement."

"Stop bragging." Mrs. Dario frowned. "You're breaking my heart."

"Oh Elena, I'm sorry." Mrs. Sanchez reached forward and patted her friend on the hand. "I didn't mean to carry on like that."

Mrs. Dario slumped over, and Hannah instantly became concerned. "Are you okay?" she asked, worried they needed the defibrillator machine.

Mrs. Dario sat up. "Physically, yes, emotionally, no. Both of my sons have been married for years and neither of them has children."

"I blame your daughters-in-law," said Mrs. Sanchez. "One of them is a horse nut and the other travels so much for work that it's no wonder they don't have kids yet. She's never home long enough for them to get things done."

"I love my daughters-in-law and I'm proud of both of them." Mrs. Sanchez straightened her posture. "But you're right about their busy schedules." She turned her attention to Hannah. "What about your schedule? Are you dating anyone?"

"Me?" Hannah blotted her mouth with the cloth napkin. "No, not at the moment."

"A-ha!" Mrs. Dario exclaimed. "See, Brenda? I was right. She's single."

"Is it that obvious?" Hannah asked, feeling bedraggled. Maybe she should take Jasmine up on her offer of concealer. She cleared her throat. "I'm not sure what my love life, or lack of one, has to do with anything." That seemed more polite than saying "it's none of your business."

"It has everything to do with everything," said Mrs. Sanchez. "A sweet woman like you deserves to be happy." She looked at Mrs. Dario. "Maybe Elena could set you up with Guy."

"He's my co-worker. That wouldn't be appropriate." Hannah didn't like where this was going. *Or did she?*

Mrs. Dario picked up an empty water glass on the table, filled it with mimosa, and handed it to Hannah. "True love is always appropriate."

Hannah pushed the glass away. "Thanks for the drink, but I'm on duty in ten minutes."

"I remember," said Mrs. Dario.

"She remembers everything," said Mrs. Sanchez. "Like how Guy mentioned majoring in biology at Dartmouth."

"He didn't so much mention it, as I dragged it out of him." Mrs. Dario smiled, like she was pleased with herself. "We were talking about Seattle and I asked him if he ever visited the city. He said he'd had enough of city life and wanted to live in a small town like Sand Dollar Cove where neighbors cared for each other."

Hannah took a small sip of mimosa, just to be polite. "That sounds like Guy," she said, as she recalled their conversation on the walk to Rhododendron Lane.

"Community support is *so* important." Mrs. Sanchez adjusted the clasp of her gold necklace. "*Mi familia* live in Texas, and my first husband ran off on me. The school district paid okay, but as a single mom raising three kids, it was difficult." She shot a grateful look to Mrs. Dario. "That's how I met Elena. She ran an at-home daycare that was a lifesaver."

Mrs. Dario nodded. "For twenty-one years. I was licensed, too. At first it was so I could stay home with my boys and earn a little extra money, but there was such a need in my community for daycare that it just sort of exploded."

"Elena's being modest, but she helped a lot of people," said Mrs. Sanchez. "Not just the children in her care, but also the parents like me who relied on her, and the employees who needed jobs."

"That's impressive," said Hannah. "Thank you for sharing with me." But the conversation led to a new crop of worries. Even if she found stable housing... even if she met prince charming... how would she afford daycare someday?

"Have you and Guy ever eaten brunch together here?" Mrs. Dario asked. She glanced sideways at Mrs. Sanchez.

"Maybe with a romantic view at one of the tables by the windows?" Mrs. Sanchez fluttered her eyelashes.

"No." Hannah put her fork down. "Employees don't usually eat here. Today was an exception for me."

"Maybe you work out together?" Mrs. Dario asked.

"Like gym buddies," Mrs. Sanchez added. "You're both in great shape."

"No," Hannah shook her head. "I'm not nearly as fit as Guy."

"But you've noticed how fit he is, have you?" Mrs. Sanchez winked at Mrs. Dario.

"No. I mean, I didn't mean it that way," Hannah sputtered. "I don't comment on my co-workers' appearances."

"Probably wise in this day and age," said Mrs. Sanchez. "Everyone sues everyone."

"Not that Guy would sue you," said Mrs. Dario. "He would never. But he might say yes if you asked him out."

"I don't need to be set up with my co-worker," Hannah said firmly. "That would be inappropriate."

"Co-workers date each other all the time," said Mrs. Dario.

"That's how my youngest son met his wife. It's called a strategic alliance."

Hannah's phone rang, saving herself from the discussion. "Excuse me. I need to take this. It's from my landlord." Hannah dashed away from their table and hurried out the door. "Hello?" she said, as soon as she was outside.

"Hi, Hannah, I'm glad I caught you," he said. "I felt this was important to say over the phone and not by text."

"What?" The sun shone brightly, but Hannah had goosebumps.

"I'm rebuilding the house."

"You are? How?" Hannah walked over to the edge of the observation deck and held onto to the railing for support.

"By tearing it down first."

"I don't understand." Hannah's knuckles turned white. "How can you do that when my family lives there?"

"Ah... that's the thing," he said slowly. "You won't live there anymore."

"But we have a lease. A year's lease that has eight more months on it."

"And the contract says it can be broken due to a catastrophic occurrence, like this one. Look, Hannah, I'm sorry about what this means. I've been renting to Cheryl for years, and when you and Mary signed on to the lease too, I was happy to continue working with all of you. This is a business decision, nothing more. I'm giving you the $682 I owe you for the remaining rent this week, plus your deposit of $1,200. Since I'm a generous person, I'm rounding up that amount to $2,000. You're welcome."

"I didn't say thank you."

"Goodbye, Hannah. Tell Cheryl I said hi." The landlord hung up the phone.

"Shit!" Hannah exclaimed, even though she rarely swore. "Shit! Shit! Shit!"

"Is everything alright?" asked a voice behind her.

Hannah turned and saw Mrs. Dario and Mrs. Sanchez looking at her with concern. She wasn't sure which woman had addressed her. "Just a little housing drama, that's all." Hannah forced a smile. "Enjoy your day at Seaside Resort." She raced away before they could respond.

NINE

"What are you going to do?" Lark asked. It was later that day, and Hannah was in the break room eating a quick lunch of instant noodles before heading back to work.

"I have no idea," Hannah answered honestly, since she and Lark were the only people in the room. "We have two more nights' worth of vouchers left at the Motel 6, and then..." She covered her face with her hands, not wanting Lark to see the emotion written there.

"Maybe you could stay at the motel longer until you find new digs?"

Hannah took her hands away. "But how would we afford that? The spring season has started, and the rates have already gone up."

"Let's think of something else then." Lark massaged her forearm. "Tent camping at the state park?"

"Gran could never manage that with her bad back."

"She could stay with me. You and Mary could camp and Cheryl and Ferdinand could be my temporary roommates."

Hannah felt trickles of tears slip down her cheeks, but she blinked them away. *Tears get you nowhere*, she told herself.

Don't cry. Instead, she focused on the generosity of Lark's offer. "We're lucky to have friends like you, and thank you, but..." She took a deep breath. "Your apartment has stairs but no elevator, right?"

Lark nodded. "I didn't think of that. Can Cheryl...?" Lark tiptoed her fingers like they were climbing.

Hannah shook her head. "She needs something accessible for wheelchair users, like with a ramp or elevator."

"Oh, boy." Lark leaned back into her chair. "This is a tough one."

"What's going on?" Guy asked, as he came into the staffroom holding a container of what looked to be homemade food.

"Hannah's practically homeless, that's what," Lark answered.

"Lark!" Hannah shot her a look. It was horrible enough being in this situation, without being embarrassed in front of Guy as well.

Guy looked at her with concern. "I thought you said you had hotel vouchers?"

"*Motel* vouchers," Lark corrected. "And they run out after tomorrow night."

"Our landlord is tearing down our house to rebuild a McMansion," Hannah added. "At least, I'm assuming he's building something hideous like that."

"That's awful." Guy put his food into the microwave. "I'm sorry to hear that. Have you had any luck finding a new apartment?"

Hannah shook her head. "I haven't had a chance to look yet. Right now, I'm trying to figure out our temporary housing situation."

"What if we posted a GoFundMe account to raise money for you to stay at the Motel 6 as long as you needed?" Lark suggested.

"I'm not sure the Motel 6 would have room for us much longer. The spring break crowd has prebooked all the rooms. But I appreciate the thought." The deeper truth was that Hannah didn't want to accept charity like that, not from friends, and certainly not from strangers. Self-reliance was her cornerstone. If she couldn't take care of herself and her family, then what had she become? Hannah looked down at the silvery scar along her wrist. Helpless, that's what.

Helpless like when she was six years old and Mary was three. They'd been watching TV in their dirty apartment, sitting on a couch that stank. Mary had been crying all morning. Both girls were hungry and had finished the half-empty box of Cheerios Kelly had offered them for dinner the night before. Hannah had wanted desperately to help her sister stop crying, so she'd poked their mom's shoulder until Kelly woke up from her stupor, and then...

But Hannah wouldn't think of that now. She pushed away at the memory. Hannah was grown up now, with her own car, her own bank account—small as it was—and a college degree. *I'll work hard and things will improve,* she told herself. *I just need to keep at it.*

"I think there's a vacancy in the apartment building next to ours," Guy said. "Isn't there?" he looked at Lark for confirmation.

"It's a third-floor unit," said Lark. "At least, that's what the sign out front says. But Cheryl can't handle stairs."

"We need a ground-floor apartment or a place with an elevator," Hannah confirmed.

"Gotcha." The microwave beeped and Guy removed his lunch. The delicious aroma of garlic and tomatoes filled the room. He sat down next to them. "What about you apply to the Blanchet Maison employee assistance fund?"

Hannah and Lark burst out laughing.

"Oh yeah," Lark snickered. "Great idea."

"I'll get right on it," Hannah said with a chuckle.

"What's so funny?" Guy asked.

Lark looked at him like he was stupid. "There is no employee assistance fund."

"Yes there is," said Guy. "I saw it on the Blanchet Maison website."

"Well, if the Blanchets have it on their website, then it must be true." Hannah wiped a tear out of her eyes, she'd been laughing so hard.

"I don't understand." Guy speared a tomato with his fork. "They wouldn't lie about something like that."

"Except that they would." Hannah placed her bowl of noodles on the table. "It could be that a fund exists, minimal as it will be. But over the years we've had dozens of employees apply to it, for reasons like cancer treatments, house fires, injuries, and even help with adoption fees."

"I applied to it once when I needed to take extra time off to recover from pneumonia." Lark thumped her chest. "It got into my lungs and—wow. I could barely get out of bed."

"And the fund didn't help you?" Guy's forehead creased into furrows.

Lark shook her head. "Nope. Me, and everyone else, got the same form letter back. Something about how we were valued members of the Blanchet Maison global family, and an employee relations liaison would get back to us shortly." Lark frowned. "That really got my hopes up, but they ghosted me."

"Along with everyone else who applied," said Hannah. "I wish the IRS would audit them. If Blanchet Maison is taking a tax deduction on that supposed program, then that's criminal."

"Whoa." Guy pushed a stray lock of hair off his forehead. "I had no idea they were so untrustworthy."

"Scummy, is how I'd put it." Lark sat up straight. "Hey, I've got a wild idea. It's probably stupid, but maybe it would work."

"No idea is stupid at this point." Hannah picked up her noodle bowl again. "What are you thinking?"

"Strawberry Cottage." Lark clapped her hands together. "It's gross, but it's available."

Hannah jerked back her head. "What?" Lark had been right; that idea *was* stupid. "Employees can't stay in cottages for free."

"Why not?" Lark asked. "Nobody's living there."

"I thought Strawberry Cottage was unsafe," Guy said.

"There's a crack in the foundation, making it a poor choice for refurbishment," said Hannah. "And because of that, we've put money into updating the other cottages instead. But it's not about to fall down on its own anytime soon... I hope."

"It's a huge mess at this point," said Lark. "But technically livable." She looked at Hannah. "It's not being torn down until later this summer, right?"

"On July first," Hannah confirmed.

"I think Lark's on to something," Guy said. "You're a valued employee. Your grandmother worked here for decades. This is something the company owes you."

"Owes me?" Hannah raised her eyebrows. "I doubt the corporate oligarchs at Blanchet Maison think they owe me anything."

"But we wouldn't have to tell them, would we?" Lark asked. "Just clear it with Herman first. I'm sure he'll say yes."

"Hmm..." Hannah tapped her chin. "Maybe. It would only be temporary. Mary and I could push Gran up the path in her wheelchair. Once she got to the cottage she could walk on her own. We would need to add a portable shower bench though."

Guy's blue eyes were full of concern. "Osteoporosis can be a hard condition to manage."

"My gran manages just fine." Hannah's spine stiffened.

"But you like my idea then?" Lark smiled hopefully. "About moving into Strawberry Cottage?"

"I do. Very much." Hannah put down her noodle bowl and threw her arms around Lark, giving her a big hug. "Thank you. Now we just need Herman to agree to it."

"Agree to what?" Herman asked, as he walked into the room holding a stack of RV brochures.

Hannah pulled away from Lark and looked at her boss. "Would it be okay if my gran, sister, and I moved into Strawberry Cottage for a little bit while we search for a new apartment? Our landlord's tearing down our house."

"Sure." Herman rubbed his chin. "That's better than Nancy's idea of turning my poker room over to you. I wasn't sure where we'd put the table. It's hand-carved mahogany, and really heavy."

Knowing that Nancy had been thinking of her warmed Hannah's heart. "That would have been really kind of both of you," she said. "But if you think it's okay for us to use Strawberry Cottage for a while, that might be a perfect solution."

"I agree," said Herman. "Just make sure you give Nick a chance to kill the rats first."

"Kill the rats?" Guy asked.

"I'll probably want to spend a few days disinfecting the place, too," Hannah said. "With extra bleach."

"I can help with that," said Guy.

"And I'll rustle you up some bedding and towels," said Lark.

Hannah felt the tension in her neck and shoulders ease for the first time in days. "Thank you," she said. "This means a lot to me."

It did, too. *I'm not helpless.* Hannah ran her fingertip over the scar. *I'm safe here.* Once again, Seaside Resort was offering her shelter when she needed it the most.

TEN

"I always wanted to stay in one of the cottages." Mary clasped her hands together, an expression of pure glee on her face. "Especially knowing that Gran's dad helped build them."

"This is only temporary. They're tearing it down in July." Hannah took the key out of her pocket. "And it won't be the typical Seaside Resort experience, either." It was Wednesday night, and the two sisters were standing on the porch of Strawberry Cottage, ready to work. Cheryl was at the Motel 6 with Ferdinand, watching her shows. "There is so much work to be done before we move in on Saturday. Every second counts."

"Thank goodness Keith came through with extra vouchers so we didn't have to rush out of the Motel 6 so fast."

"Yeah. I don't know where he found them, but they are a huge help." Hannah stuck the key in the door but didn't turn it yet. She needed to make sure Mary understood certain facts first. "This is the deal. Nick from building and grounds said we need to get rid of everything that's made of fabric." She wrinkled her nose. "Because of mice droppings."

"Mice!" Mary shrieked. "You didn't tell me rodents were involved."

"Shhh!" Hannah pressed a finger to her lips. "Keep your voice down or the guests will hear you."

"There were never mice when Gran was in charge of housekeeping. I thought you said Lark was a great replacement."

"She *is* great. It's not Lark's fault." Hannah chewed her thumbnail for a second, uncertain how much to share. She didn't want to freak her sister out, but Mary deserved to understand their new reality. "Do you see that magnolia tree there?"

"Yes." Mary smiled. "I remember climbing on it when I was little and Gran used to bring me to work with her. She said it was over fifty years old."

"Yes. Well..." Hannah massaged her temple. "I used to love climbing on it, too. The thing is, rats were crawling up the branches onto the roof, and finding their way inside the cottage through the exhaust vent for the heater. They chewed right through the wire mesh that was supposed to protect it."

"Rats!" Mary held up her hands. "Wait a second, you said mice."

"And I also said to keep your voice down." Hannah folded her arms. "Nick has assured me that the rodent mitigation team shored up all the openings and that the building is now pest-free. However, just to be safe, everything with fabric needs to be removed from the cottage, and the remaining surfaces need to be thoroughly disinfected, so we don't get sick."

"Can't we just stay in the hotel until we find a new house? Or I could call up Aidan and beg him to talk his parents into letting us stay at their house. They have a guest room."

"Gran would never want to impose on them like that. And we need to save all our money for first and last month's rent on our new place. This is our best option." Hannah squared her shoulders and put on a brave face. "Besides, I thought you might enjoy the ultimate design challenge." She unlocked the door and swung it open. "You'll be working with a blank slate."

"This is not a design challenge. The only way to fix this is demolition." Mary held her nose as she walked into the cottage.

"Stop being dramatic. And let go of your nose. It doesn't smell at all. Well, not that much, anyway." Hannah crossed the shag carpet and opened up the front windows to let in fresh air. The foghorn sounded in the distance. "Nick said he'd send a crew up to take away the mattress and couch, but it's up to us to haul away the drapes, linens, and carpet."

Mary picked up a corner of the faded turquoise quilt on the bed and let it drop unceremoniously. A cloud of dust billowed up, making her sneeze. "Are you sure there aren't bedbugs?"

"Nick is taking away the mattress, so you don't need to worry about it." Hannah pulled a chair from the kitchenette over to the windows and began removing the drapes. Cobwebs covered the thick velvet fabric.

"If there's no mattress, where will we sleep?"

"I haven't thought that far. Are you just going to stand there, or are you going to help? I can't do everything myself."

Mary glared at her. "Who picked up Gran from the senior center today and brought her to the hotel? Who did seven loads of laundry between classes, and fended off creepy advances from an old man wearing a bad toupee at the laundromat? Who brought you a turkey sandwich for dinner?"

"It's not like I was doing nothing all day." Hannah yanked on the drapes. "I was at work."

"Yeah, well, I was working too, even though it was my day off from the coffee stand." Mary bundled the quilt into a ball. "A little appreciation goes a long way. You should remember that, considering you might become general manager of this place."

Hannah wiped dust out of her eyes. "Look, I'm sorry. I didn't mean to sound ungrateful. I didn't get much sleep last night, and with everything going on, I'm not at my best."

"Gran's groaning kept you up, too?"

Hannah nodded. "I feel so bad for her. I don't know which is a worse position for her osteoporosis—trying to lie flat on the bed, or sitting upright in her wheelchair."

"That was a good idea you had, going out to the lobby for extra pillows. Once she was propped up at an angle, she finally fell asleep."

"Yeah. That seemed to help." Hannah dragged the drapes out of the cottage and left them on the front porch.

It felt weird how their situation had reversed. Cheryl had provided stability and support ever since Hannah and Mary were little. Now, their roles had flipped. Hannah wasn't sure if Mary felt the full weight of the responsibility of caring for their grandma. Hopefully not. She wanted her sister to enjoy being twenty-two. But that seemed hard to do given the present circumstances.

"Back to the mattress question, where are we going to sleep once we move in here?" Mary added the bedding to the pile outside.

"You and I could sleep on the floor if we have to. Or we could buy a cheap air mattress at Walmart. But I don't know about Gran. Her recliner was soaked. I don't think it's salvageable."

"I'll look in the Sand Dollar Cove Buy Nothing group. We might get a lot of the things we need that way." Mary coughed into her elbow. "I wonder if we should wear masks? It's probably not good for us to breathe all this junk into our lungs."

"Good idea." Hannah unzipped her purse, which was sitting on the kitchenette table. "I have some in here."

Once they had masked up, the sisters went back to work, carrying out all the towels from the bathroom, scrubbing the floor with bleach, and then moving on to the kitchen, where they disinfected the small refrigerator. They wiped down the inside walls with the bleach solution too, and watched the turquoise wallpaper fade to a pale blue. Everything they touched was covered with a thick layer of grime. Some surfaces bore an unexplained stickiness that was extra disgusting. An hour and a half later, the cottage looked a lot better, except Nick and his team still hadn't showed up to haul away the mattress and couch.

"I'll text him." Hannah tapped on her phone. "Nick said he'd be here by now." Him not showing up yet was annoying, and was giving her flashbacks of New Year's Day, when she'd had to clear out the garbage by herself.

Hi Nick, this is Hannah, she texted. *We're ready for you to take away the couch and mattress.* After a few minutes of him not responding, she tried again. *You said you'd take away the mattress and couch in Strawberry Cottage. We're ready for you.* She added a smiley face to soften her request, and then felt dumb about it. Herman wouldn't have added an emoji. Hannah waited two more minutes before she sent one more text. *See you soon. Thanks for coming.*

Feeling frustrated, Hannah slipped her phone into her back pocket. She couldn't let Nick's tardiness impede their progress. "How about we haul the junk on the front porch down to the dumpsters, and I'll stop by the building and grounds workshop on our way back?" she asked Mary.

"I have to go out in public like this?" Mary wiped sweat off her forehead with her hand and left a smear of dirt.

"Fine. I'll do it." Hannah removed her mask. "If you clean the windows."

"Deal." Mary reached for the Windex.

Hannah went out to the porch and picked up a ginormous load of soiled fabric. Her arms were so full that she could barely see where she was going and almost bumped into Mr. and Mrs. Dario, who were on their way to dinner.

"What have you got there?" Mrs. Dario asked. She wore a flowing dress with a wide belt that cinched at the waist. "It looks like you killed a couch."

"Not yet." Hannah sighed. "I still need to move that out of the guest cottage I'm refurbishing." That seemed like an easier explanation than describing why she was moving in.

"Elena, isn't that the same fabric that was in your *abuela*'s living room?"

"That's where I recognized it from." Mrs. Dario kissed her husband on the cheek. "I forget how smart you are."

"I have my moments." He held her hand as they walked down the path to the restaurant.

Hannah went to the dumpster behind the lodge and then walked up a side path to the building and grounds workshop. She knocked on the door as hard as she could, but nobody answered. Checking her phone again, she was peeved to see that Nick still hadn't responded. She tried calling him as she walked back to Strawberry Cottage.

"Hey there, Hannah," he said, answering on the third ring. "What's up—oh wait! Shoot. I said I'd help you with that couch situation, right?"

"Right." Hannah said through clenched teeth.

"Totally slipped my mind. It's poker night, and Herman's hosting. You know how Nancy loves to make hors d'oeuvres. She's spoiling us rotten."

"Hi, Hannah," Herman called over the line.

"Hi, boss." Hannah paused for a second and looked out at the ocean, trying to cool her simmering irritation before it bubbled into a boil. "Okay, by some miracle is there anyone else from the building and grounds staff working tonight?" She knew that was a long shot, since most of them clocked out at five.

"No, but I'll be there first thing in the morning."

That didn't help Hannah much. By tomorrow morning she'd be back at work and Mary would be on campus.

"Okay. Um... I'll figure something out." Hannah walked toward the cottage. "Say hi to Nancy for me." She scooped up the second load of soiled fabric and brought it to the dumpster without telling Mary the disappointing news. Hannah needed time to process it herself. Then she got the third load, and the fourth. She was just walking away from the dumpster for the last time when she felt a flutter like a light breeze kiss her skin. Turning, she saw Guy headed toward her. The fading daylight glowed around him, accenting his blond hair and tanned skin. *Act normal,* Hannah told herself. But it was too late. She already had the jitters.

"Hey, Hannah, I heard you needed help moving a couch." Guy raked his fingers through his beach-blond hair.

"Did Nick call you?" Hannah thought maybe the old codger had made up for his mistake by passing the buck to Guy.

"Nick? No, I bumped into Mrs. Dario and she said you needed help."

"Oh. That was nice of her." Hannah realized how desperate and disgustingly filthy she must look for Mrs. Dario to tell Guy that she needed help. *She was a hot mess.* Great. Just great. "Disgusting" and "filthy" were two adjectives that she did *not* want to be, around Guy. But desperate times... Hannah lifted her chin and spoke clearly. "Nick said he'd help clear out the mattress and couch from Strawberry Cottage, but he flaked on me. Now my sister and I can't finish cleaning because those are in the way. We were hoping to tear out the carpet before we went back to the motel tonight."

"All in one night? That's a lot of work for two people."

"It was supposed to be three people, because Nick said he'd be here, but..."

"Nick being as reliable as ever, eh?"

Hannah shared the one and only conspiratorial glance she'd ever exchanged with Guy. Was this for real? Had they both confessed to their mutual disapproval of Nick's job performance? "Exactly," she said. "He and Herman are playing poker."

"Wouldn't want to disturb that." Guy put his hands into his pockets. "Herman asked me to join, but I thought the buy-in was too high."

"Herman invited you to his club, but not me?" Hurt pinched Hannah's pride. She'd worked for Herman since high school, yet he'd extended her an invitation. "I mean, how much was the buy-in? It sounds like it would be too steep for me, anyway." *Maybe that was why he hadn't included her.*

"Five hundred dollars."

"For a poker game? Yikes!"

"I thought it was hefty, too, especially considering I don't like poker." Guy waved his hand toward the cottage. "I'll move the mattress and couch for you."

"You will?" Hope fluttered in Hannah's chest. "It might be a three-person job."

"We'll see. I have a dolly I keep in the gym for moving weights equipment. I'll go get that and meet you up there."

"Are you sure you don't mind?"

"It's either this or go home and eat leftovers."

Leftovers sounded good to Hannah. That turkey sandwich Mary had brought her hadn't quite filled her up. "Thank you," she said with feeling. "I really appreciate it." As soon as he was gone, she rushed back to the cottage and flung open the door. "Reinforcements are coming."

Mary sprayed disinfectant on the table. "You found the elusive Nick?"

"No. He's gone, but Guy is coming to help."

"No way! But I look like a hag, and all the towels are gone. I can't even wash up." Mary took off her mask and raced to the bathroom.

"It's just Guy," Hannah called after her. "Why'd you want to clean up for him?"

Behind her someone cleared his throat.

Hannah whirled around and saw Guy standing at the

threshold, gripping the handle of an orange and black dolly. "How'd you get here so fast?" she demanded.

"I jogged," he admitted sheepishly. "You seemed like you were under a time crunch."

"We are." Mary poked her freshly washed face out of the bathroom. The hemline of her shirt was damp from where she must have used it as an impromptu towel. "Thank you so much for coming to our rescue like this."

"I'm glad to be of service." Guy surveyed the room. "Shall I start with the bed?"

"Might as well." Hannah walked to the headboard and helped him shove the mattress off the frame. When they tipped it upright, something squeaked. A dozen pink bodies the size of index fingers fell to the ground, along with shredded mattress fiber.

"Rats!" Mary screamed. She jumped onto the bamboo table.

Hannah froze, especially when she saw where several of the baby rodents had landed—on her shoes. "Oh my goodness. Oh my goodness. Oh my goodness!" She kicked out her foot and watched in horror as squirming bodies flew off in the opposite direction.

"Way to go, Blanchet Maison," Guy muttered. "Rats in the mattress."

"They could be mice," Hannah said in a voice that was an octave too high.

After balancing the mattress against the wall, Guy peered into the torn part of the mattress where the nest was. "No, that's definitely a mama rat. Does anyone have a container?" he asked, not taking his eyes off the largest rodent. "I'll bring them to the woods where they can be safe."

"Um..." Hannah looked around. The only thing she saw that qualified was the trash can. She picked it up and handed it to him. Was Guy really going to *rescue* the rats instead of kill them?

"I can't look!" Mary covered her eyes from her perch on top of the table.

But Hannah couldn't look away. She watched as Guy picked up the mother rat by its tail and dropped it gently into the trash.

"Here you go, little lady," he said soothingly. Then he collected the babies Hannah had kicked across the floor.

She was so focused on Guy that it wasn't until she felt a tickle over her left foot that she glanced down and saw another rat scramble over her toes. "Guy!" she shrieked. "Help!"

He calmly picked it up and placed it in the can, before collecting the rest of the vermin, too. Guy cradled the wastebasket. "I'll be right back," he said, before exiting the cottage.

"Is it safe to look?" Mary asked.

Hannah scanned the carpet. "Yes, I think so." She hurried to the sink and scrubbed her hands in hot water. The hope she'd been clinging to ever since Lark suggested that Strawberry Cottage could be her family's temporary home evaporated with the steam. Her safe place to stay had become a rat farm.

"Do you think there are any more?" Mary slowly uncovered her face, but didn't come down from the table.

"I don't know." Hannah turned off the water. "Could be." She looked up at her sister. "Stop being a drama queen and get off the table. They were just rats. Some people love rats. I've heard they make great pets." *Just not sleeping inches from your pillow...* Hannah pushed that thought aside. "Guy must have saved them for a reason."

"Because he's deranged." Mary stepped off the table. "Do you know how many diseases those things might have been carrying?" She spun around. "Where's my mask? I'm putting it back on."

"That might be a good idea," Hannah admitted. She reached into her back pocket where she'd stashed it on her trips to the dumpster and put her mask on, too.

"Ah. Masked up, I see." Guy entered by the front door. "Probably a wise idea, considering hantavirus."

"What's that?" Mary asked.

"A disease spread through rodent droppings." Guy inspected the mattress as if he was looking for more nests. "I think we got them all, but when you see one rat there can often be twenty." He went to the sink and washed his hands thoroughly.

Hannah unzipped her purse and found an extra mask for Guy. She handed it to him. "How'd you learn so much about rats?"

"I'm a New Yorker." Guy put on his mask and slid the mattress toward the door. "I'll bring this to the dumpster."

"You can't bring it all the way there on your own." Hannah rushed to help, but Guy waved her away.

"Don't worry. I've got the dolly. I'll be back for the couch in a jiff."

"Thank you." Hannah stood at the threshold and watched him go for a few seconds before turning to face the room. The first thing she saw was the box spring. Was it her imagination, or was part of it moving? She waited for Guy before investigating.

When he came back, he took one look at the box spring and pounded an ashtray against an undulating spot in the corner a few times. "Wolf spiders," he said with a shiver. "I love mammals, but creepy-crawly things freak me out." He dragged the box spring away without further comment. Hannah was impressed. She wished she could be that stoic around rodents and spiders. She also felt embarrassed that Guy was doing the dirty work, while she stood around like a helpless female—which she certainly wasn't.

"Mary, where's the bleach?" Hannah asked. She would make sure they disinfected the bedframe from top to bottom. In fact, she'd already sprayed the headboard when Guy returned.

"What are you doing?" he asked.

"Cleaning." Hannah squirted the bottle.

"What if there are bedbugs?" Guy scratched the back of his neck.

"What?" Mary shrieked.

Hannah looked over her shoulder and glared at her sister. "Stop with your hysterics. It's embarrassing." She turned her attention to Guy. "Do you really think there could be bedbugs?"

"I don't know." His forehead crinkled in a way that made him look more like Ryan Gosling than Ryan Reynolds.

Ryan Gosling, but with blonder hair, Hannah mused. Was Guy's hair lighter? It must have been from running on the beach in the sun.

"Hannah," he asked. "What do you think?"

"About what?" she asked, still thinking about his sun-kissed hair.

"The chances of bedbugs. You're the hospitality expert."

"Oh." She leaned back on her heels. "Well, we've only had two cottages come down with bedbugs since I've worked here, and they were both nightmares to treat. But... um..." She adjusted her mask, feeling overwhelmed. "Between the rats, and the carpets, and..." Hannah sighed, unable to complete her thoughts.

"We don't have a new mattress to put on the bedframe anyway," said Mary. "And that headboard is ugly. Let's get rid of it all and have a blank slate, like you said. That'll make it easier to remove the carpet, too."

"Okay." Hannah put down the bleach and stood. "That makes sense to me." She looked apologetically at Guy. "Mary and I can probably handle moving this. You've already sacrificed enough of your evening to help us."

"I don't mind." Guy walked to the other side of the headboard. "I'll handle this side and you two can get the other. Once it's positioned on the dolly, I can roll it down to the dumpster myself."

"Maybe we could get a hide-a-bed, or a daybed." Mary lifted the footboard. "Then it could be a studio apartment."

They couldn't afford new furniture. If there had been some way that the bedframe could have accommodated an air mattress, Hannah would have thought twice about keeping it, but it was so old that it looked more likely to pop an air mattress than support one.

"Here we are," said Guy, once they were closer to the dolly.

"How is this going to work?" Hannah asked. She didn't see how something so huge and unwieldy could balance.

"I put the mattress on its side to carry it away." Guy lifted the metal frame and wedged it onto the dolly's bars. "But... hmm... This might take two people to support it."

"You go," said Mary. "I want to take a picture of the carpet before we rip it out, for my portfolio."

"Your portfolio?" Guy removed his mask.

"I'm in design school." Mary took out her phone. "Now that the rats are gone, I'm actually becoming excited about this project."

"Don't get too excited." Hannah pulled down her mask too. "New furniture isn't in the budget and this is only temporary, remember."

Mary swept her hand toward the sea. "With a view like that you don't need a budget for a place to be magical." She spun on her heel and headed back inside.

"Less photography and more bleach!" Hannah called after her. She frowned. Left to her own devices, her sister might spend the whole evening crafting the perfect Instagram post.

"So," said Guy as he rolled the unwieldy side of the dolly down the twisty path. "You follow a budget then?"

"Yeah," said Hannah, taken aback by the odd question. "Of course. But as much as Mary would like to hope otherwise, buying a new suite of furniture isn't in it, especially not when we'll need to come up with first and last month's rent to move into a new place."

"That's why I always set aside some of each paycheck for emergencies. A financial planner taught me that trick."

"It must be nice to have room in your budget to do that." Hannah readjusted her grip on the bedframe. She reminded herself that since Guy was doing them a huge favor, she shouldn't bite his head off for mansplaining.

"Pay yourself first. That's another tip the planner taught me. Don't spend money on anything frivolous until you've sent money to your savings account."

Hannah let go of her end of the bedframe, and it wobbled precariously. "Do you think I'm an idiot who doesn't know how savings accounts work?"

"What?" Guy steadied the dolly. "Well..."

"You think I'm blowing my paycheck at the casinos? Or getting my nails done, or buying designer purses?" Hot tears misted her eyes, but Hannah blinked them away. "My grandma's disabled and receives minimal social security. I'm paying Mary's tuition bill in full, so she doesn't have to go up to her eyeballs in student loan debt. Maybe I should get a second job, but then who would take care of Gran in the evening when Mary's at her part-time job? Huh?"

"I just thought—"

"That I was too stupid to budget? I'm not stupid, I'm just barely scraping by. Correlation does not equal causation."

"My apologies." Guy's tan face paled in the twilight. "I shouldn't have made assumptions."

"Damn right." Hannah grabbed onto the bedframe. "Let's roll this to the dumpster and then you can go."

"I don't mind helping. The carpet might be hard to take—"

"Thanks, but Mary and I can manage. Like we always have," Hannah added with an edge to her voice.

She didn't say another word to him until they reached the dumpster. It took both of them to heave the bedframe into it.

"Thanks for your help," Hannah said curtly. "I appreciate it." She spun on her heel and marched away, only to hear Guy's footsteps and the rattle of the dolly behind her. "You don't need to follow me," she said, without looking back. "We don't need any more help."

"I'm not following you. I'm returning the dolly to the wellness center where it belongs."

"Oh."

"But I'm not sure you and Mary don't need my help. It seems to me that—"

"That what?" Hannah whirled around. "We're too stupid to budget, too weak to rip out carpet, and too helpless to—"

"Why, look who's here!" exclaimed a voice. It was Mrs. Sanchez, along with her husband and the Darios. The two couples walked up the path from the restaurant. Mrs. Sanchez wore a black tunic and red leggings. A thick gold necklace lay across her chest and matching earrings dangled next to her silver-streaked hair. Her husband, who was wearing a Hawaiian shirt and khaki slacks, stood beside her, holding her hand. "We were just talking about you two," she said.

"You were?" Hannah pulled down her shirt and finger-combed her hair. She didn't need a mirror to tell her she looked like a hurricane had hit her.

"That's right, we were," said Mrs. Dario. "I was just telling Carlos that he should take a day off from fishing so he could come to our personal training class with Guy."

Carlos, who had a considerable beer gut hanging over his jeans, grunted. "And I told Elena that I couldn't miss a day on the water after all the trouble Hannah went to, to arrange our daily charter boats." He tipped an imaginary hat to her. "Best salmon fishing of my life, outside of Alaska."

"Glad to hear it." Hannah smiled, feeling a little bit of confidence return.

"Come on," said Mrs. Sanchez. "Let's go, so Guy and Hannah can get on with whatever they intended to do with that dolly."

"Or *on* the dolly," said Mrs. Dario.

"Elena!" Mrs. Sanchez giggled. "Why do you have to be so crude?"

"Because that's the way I like her." Mr. Dario patted his wife on the bottom.

"Have fun with that dolly." Mrs. Dario winked, before they walked away.

Hannah felt her cheeks blush deep red. "See you tomorrow," she told Guy. Her feet moved so fast as she walked away, she practically flew.

ELEVEN

Humiliation stung Hannah like rubbing alcohol on a skinned knee. She couldn't believe the nerve of Guy, insinuating that she was irresponsible about money. As if she was in dire straits by choice! As if she could go back in time and make decisions that would have prevented it. And yes, maybe hindsight had proven that canceling the renter's insurance was a bad idea, but what else would she have needed to give up to afford it? Her grandma's cable? Gas money? Public transportation in Sand Dollar Cove was spotty, and if she'd cut cable, then Cheryl would be stuck in her recliner each weekend when the senior center was closed, with nothing to distract her from her pain.

At least her work at Seaside Resort made Hannah feel proud. The rest of her life might be in shambles, but she was good at her job. Hannah knew every housekeeper by name. She was friends with the landscaping crew. She pitched in and helped alongside them when they were short-staffed. Hannah wasn't afraid to roll up her sleeves and weed a flower bed, or scrub a toilet, if needed. She saw each employee as an integral part of Seaside Resort.

Hannah stood at the reception desk available to help guests, but also updating the resort's social media channels. Their highly curated Instagram feed was all Hannah's doing. Herman didn't do social media at all. The good thing about his lack of interest was that Hannah had free rein to do whatever she wanted. She had started the account from scratch two years ago, and had built up a follower count of 7,300 through creativity and determination. The bad thing about Herman's lack of interest was that he still thought social media was a waste of time. It wasn't until Blanchet Maison did a marketing audit that he agreed to let Hannah start the Instagram feed in the first place.

At that moment, Hannah was between guests. Since there wasn't a line at reception, she could concentrate on the post she was writing. It was an eye-catching picture of the restaurant's soup of the day, with a sunset view behind it.

"Whatcha working on?" Herman asked, as he walked down the hall from his office. "That Point Power presentation I asked for?"

"Not at the moment." Hannah hit *post* and put down her phone. "But I'm excited for you to see my PowerPoint presentation as soon as I finish it." *Or start it,* she thought to herself. She'd been so busy with the flood and the move that she hadn't been able to work on her presentation yet. "I was just updating Insta. My last post got three hundred hearts and two dozen comments."

"Proof that people will waste time on anything, I guess." Herman shook his head. "Don't people have better things to do than that scroll-amabob?" He spun his index finger around in circles.

"I guess not. But free advertising is good for business. Which is why I think we should offer a special coupon code now, for fall. It could be a flash sale that we post on our accounts, but that's only good for twenty-four hours."

Herman shoved his hand into his pocket. "A flash sale?"

"Targeting our November vacancy rate, which is historically higher than we'd like."

"Might as well try it." Herman shrugged. "But only twenty percent off. This isn't a hostel."

"Twenty-five percent would bring in more guests, who would then eat at The Summer Wind and book activity packages." Hannah caught the eye of a guest who was entering the lobby and smiled. She needed to wrap up this conversation fast, because the guest probably needed assistance. "The extra five percent off wouldn't cost us much, but could pay back in folds."

"Let me think about it."

"That's fine. I'll create some mock-up ad copy and show you soon." Hannah nodded to Herman before she greeted the guest. It was a mom wearing leggings and a hoodie, with a fleece vest.

"Help," said the mom. "Please tell me you have sand toys because we already lost ours."

"No worries, Mrs. Leary. We've got you covered." Hannah pointed to the gift shop display area. "There are some for sale right over there."

"Thanks so much." Mrs. Leary was about to walk over to the merchandise when her son tugged at her hoodie.

"I gotta go potty," he said. The curly-haired tyke hopped from one foot to the other.

"You do?" Mrs. Leary looked down at him. "Thanks for telling me." She grabbed his hand, and they raced to the lobby restroom. But they didn't get there in time.

"Mom!" the boy cried. "The pee is coming out!"

Hannah saw a small puddle on the floor. She picked up the cleaning bucket she kept behind the front desk and went to help.

"I am so sorry." Mrs. Leary reached in her purse and pulled out a pack of wet wipes, which she used to help Hannah clean. "He's potty training right now, and it's been a struggle."

"It's not a big deal," said Hannah. "Accidents happen." She

looked at the young guest. "Your name's Jason, right?" He nodded. "Good job telling your mom that you needed to use the potty."

"But I'm wet," Jason whimpered.

"That's okay." Mrs. Leary hugged him. "Let's go to our room and get you cleaned up."

A few minutes after Hannah said goodbye to Mrs. Leary and Jason, a steady stream of front desk calls kept her busy until her lunch break. By the time she got around to working on her PowerPoint presentation, she was sitting in the kitchen of The Summer Wind eating a sandwich that Jasmine had set aside for her. It was ham on rye, Hannah's second favorite. Her favorite was Dungeness crab salad. Jasmine added chopped celery and homemade mayonnaise to the mixture, which made it extra delicious. The ham on rye was good, too, especially with slices of Jasmine's homemade pickles.

"I don't understand why you have to make a PowerPoint." Jasmine looked over Hannah's shoulder at the screen. Her dark hair was tied back in a knot and she wore a clean white apron. "You've worked here since you were fifteen. Nobody cares about this place more than you."

"I don't know about that. Apparently Herman needs to prove to corporate that he's considered other candidates, and since Guy has that fancy degree from Dartmouth, he's now up for the job, too."

"Why didn't he choose me?" Jasmine asked. "I know how to run a business. I have a vested interest in Seaside Resort being successful. I don't want to be general manager, but I could have faked it better than Guy."

Privately, Hannah was unsure about that. Guy had done a damn good job of faking it in Herman's office the other day. He almost had her convinced that he really wanted the job. "You would have been a brilliant choice," she said. "I don't know why Herman didn't consider you."

"It could be sexism." Jasmine pulled out a chair and sat down, bringing a big bowl of green beans with her. She snapped off the ends one by one.

"You think Herman picked Guy because he's a man?" Hannah thought about the poker club. Maybe that's why she hadn't been invited...

Jasmine shrugged. "It wouldn't be the first time. Remember how he almost passed me over for the head chef position because he said I was less experienced than the other candidate?"

Hannah rolled her eyes. "That's right! Thank goodness I was on the interview team. No way could a Taco Truck owner from Sequim compare to your culinary school background."

"Yeah, but I'm not the son of one of his poker buddies, so..." A timer rang and Jasmine hopped to her feet. "Those are the baguettes. Don't work too hard, okay?"

"Me? Work too hard?"

Jasmine pointed at her. "There's more to life than work."

Hannah nodded and looked back at her screen. It was easy for Jasmine to lecture her about not working too hard. Jasmine's dad retired from the navy after twenty years and opened his own deep-sea fishing charter boat business. Her mom stayed at home and packed gourmet lunches for all three kids. That's probably where Jasmine gained her appreciation for fine cuisine. But Hannah hadn't grown up with that type of security. Cheryl did what she could, of course, but money had always been tight.

Hannah finished two slides of her PowerPoint before her lunch break ended. She stashed her computer into her messenger bag and headed outside. From the deck of The Summer Wind Hannah could see all the way to the horizon. She scanned the ocean, looking for whales. She'd seen them before, their spouts of water shooting up, or their breach as they crashed against the water. But today all she saw was an expanse of blue, and gray clouds swirling above, threatening rain. When she got to the lobby, she would turn the gas fireplace on and double-check that the complimentary resort umbrellas were stocked by the front door. That's where she was headed when she ran into Guy holding a coffee drink in each hand.

"This is for you." He passed her a cup. "It's a mocha."

"You brought me a mocha?" Hannah's fingers curled around the paper cupholder, absorbing the warmth.

"To apologize." Guy's blue eyes gazed at her. "I'm an idiot. I'm sorry I was a jerk to you last night."

Wow, thought Hannah. *I can't believe he's apologizing.* "You weren't a jerk," she said. "You helped us deal with those..." She looked to the left and right to make sure there were no guests who could overhear their conversation. "Rats."

"Yeah, but I also said some things I regret." Guy rubbed his shoulder for a moment before dropping his hand. "I made assumptions that were unfair, and for that, I'm sorry."

Hannah wasn't quite ready to forgive him, but he was her co-worker and she couldn't afford to be rude. Plus, the mocha smelled delicious, and she could really use a jolt of caffeine right now. "Apology accepted," she said with all the dignity she could muster.

"How's Strawberry Cottage coming along? Do you need any more help?"

"No. Mary and I have it under control." They didn't, in fact, but she wouldn't tell Guy that.

"What about the carpet?" Guy asked. "That's probably contaminated."

"I know," Hannah said, fighting the tone of irritation in her voice. "Mary and I are going to rip it out tonight and bleach the floorboards." They wouldn't have time to pull up all the tacks or scrape away glue, but they could do that after they'd moved in. Sure, it would be inconvenient, but convenience wasn't something they could afford.

"I don't have plans tonight. I could come help."

"Thanks, but we got it."

"I know you do, but I'd like to help anyway."

"Why?"

"Why?" Guy echoed.

"Yes, why?" Alarm bells were going off inside Hannah's head. Why was Guy being so nice all of a sudden? They had a cordial relationship, suitable for co-workers, but volunteering for unpaid manual labor was something else altogether. "Is this about the promotion?" she asked. "Are you trying to prove something to Herman?"

"No, of course not." Guy widened his stance. "I don't even want the promotion. I was just trying to be helpful, that's it."

Maybe he's interested in Mary and doesn't know that she's about to get engaged, Hannah thought. Her sister was gorgeous, after all. Jealousy pricked her heart. *He's not that handsome or smart or charming,* she told herself. *I don't feel anything for Guy at all.* "Well—" she said.

"Mary mentioned something about painting a stencil on the floor. The sooner you get the carpet out of there, the quicker she can get to work."

Suspicions confirmed, Hannah narrowed her eyes at Guy as she considered whether he was good enough for her sister. Begrudgingly, she had to admit that he was. Hannah sighed and blew a puff of hair out of her eyes. "Fine. We appreciate the help." Hannah thought that the conversation was over, but when she walked toward the main lodge, Guy followed her.

"What you said Tuesday in Herman's office about the architect of the resort was really interesting. What was her name again?"

"Kara Lee Paul. She was one of only a handful of women to graduate from the University of Washington's school of Architecture in the 1940s."

"Is she famous?"

"She should be. I mean, she would probably be a household name if she were a man. People compared her to Frank Lloyd Wright."

"Wow. I had no idea." Guy waved to a guest in the distance and beamed a megawatt smile. "What else do you know about her?"

Hannah stopped in her tracks. "Are you trying to steal my idea?"

"What? No."

But his innocent expression didn't fool Hannah. "You are. I thought you said you didn't want the promotion."

"I don't. I'm just curious about Seaside Resort history. That's it."

"Oh." Hannah puzzled on that for a moment. "Why?"

"Why do I like history? I just do. This is a fascinating place."

Hannah couldn't argue with him there. "Okay, well, if you're interested in learning more about Kara Lee Paul, you can drive by her Octagon House the next time you head to the city. There's also archives about her at the University of Washington."

"Fascinating." Guy zipped up his raincoat.

"So, what are you going to do your presentation to Herman about?" Hannah asked.

"Now who's trying to steal ideas?" Guy elbowed her gently and grinned.

"That came out wrong. Sorry."

"You already know my focus. It's on health and rehabilitation."

The reasonable part of her brain told her that was true. But it was hard to think clearly about anything while staring into Guy's blue eyes. He smelled good, too, like he'd stepped out of an Irish Spring commercial. If she wasn't careful, his handsome demeanor would mesmerize her again like when he'd first arrived. The last thing she needed to add to her plate was a silly crush.

"I'm on your side," Guy said. "I hope you get the promotion."

"Technically, you're my competition."

"I'm your co-worker, and hopefully your friend. No matter what happens, we'll still need to work with each other."

"We're not friends. We're co-workers, nothing more."

"Co-workers, then. Fine."

"Okay then."

"Why can't we be friends?"

"What?"

Guy stuffed his hands in his pockets. "Why don't you like me? What did I do that was so wrong, aside from my stupid suggestions about budgeting last night? Did I offend you before that?"

Why didn't she like him? Hannah felt put on the spot. Worse, she didn't have a socially acceptable answer to give. If anything, she liked him too much, despite last night's mansplaining. Her heart went pitter-patter every time he entered the room. But she couldn't very well say *that*. Instead, she blurted out the first thing she could think of that came to mind. "You hold up the checkout line at the front desk."

"I don't work at the front desk."

"I know. I mean..." *Dang, her heart was pitter-pattering again.* "Sometimes when I'm checking guests out and you walk through the lodge, you chat with them and that slows down the process."

"I was trying to be friendly, so that when they go home they'll leave a positive review."

"Why would they do that when it took them twice as long to settle their bill?" Hannah asked, even though that technically wasn't fair.

"Have people left negative reviews about the checkout process?"

"No," Hannah admitted.

"But they've left positive ones about the health and wellness program, right?"

Begrudgingly, Hannah nodded her head. She didn't add that some reviewers mentioned Guy's Two Weeks to Fitness program as being the best part of their visit.

"So is there really a problem then?" Guy asked.

"Not with the reviews," Hannah said. "But interfering with my checkout procedures wastes my time."

"I'll try to avoid that in the future."

"Thanks." Hannah begged her heart to stop pounding so fast. Every nerve in her body was on alert, from the confrontation, but also from her undeniable attraction to Guy. Raindrops fell from the sky, softly cascading all around, but Hannah didn't notice at first because she was marveling at the square shape of Guy's jawline, and how his teeth were even straighter when up close. Forget Irish Spring—he could be from a Colgate commercial. If she kissed him, would he taste like mint?

"What are you staring at?" Guy rubbed his chin. "Did I get coffee on me?"

"No." Hannah quickly looked away. "I was just noticing how straight your teeth are."

"Three years of braces and one year of headgear will do that."

"Headgear?" Hannah glanced back up. "I thought that wasn't used anymore."

"Only in extreme cases." Guy checked his watch. "Gotta go. I have clients coming in five minutes." Taking long strides, he walked down the path to the wellness center.

Hannah pulled the hood of her coat up and watched him go. *Mary must have made quite the impression on him*, she thought to herself. The jealousy she felt irked her. The last thing she needed in her life was more competition. But then, when she was *not* admiring Guy's well-shaped backside, he turned a corner and she saw something peeking out of his raincoat pocket. Something flat, and rectangular-shaped, with large type across the top.

Was that a vintage postcard? Weird. Where did Guy find one of those? Hannah hadn't seen one like that in ages.

TWELVE

A couple of days later Hannah was doing her biannual check of the smoke detector batteries, and happened to be in the wellness studio at the exact same time Guy was training Mrs. Dario and Mrs. Sanchez. She dragged her stepstool to the first detector.

"Do you want some help with that?" Guy pointed behind him to the weights area where Mrs. Sanchez and Mrs. Dario were at the machines. "I'll be done with my clients in fifteen minutes, and then I could lend you a hand."

"No need, but thanks." Hannah looked up at the ceiling, searching for the red flash of light. "I promise to stay out of your way, though."

"They seem to all be in working order, but don't quote me on that."

"Don't worry, I won't." Hannah smiled innocently. "Just go about your business and forget I'm here."

"Will do." Guy walked over to the cable machines.

Hannah popped her stepstool next to Guy's desk. Then she set the package of batteries on top of the blotter next to a cup full of ballpoint pens, a stack of liability release waivers, and a dog-eared copy of a running magazine.

"Five pounds?" Mrs. Sanchez exclaimed from the cable machine. "Give me fifteen, I can take it."

"Um... that's quite a lot," said Guy. "How about we try eight, and see how that goes first?"

Hannah glanced over to see what was happening.

Mrs. Sanchez pushed up her sweatband where it had slipped down her forehead. "Are you saying that because I'm seventy-two? Because I assure you, I can handle it."

"Oh, give it a rest, Brenda," said Mrs. Dario, from her spot on the leg extension machine. "You're not Arnold Schwarzenegger."

"You're darn right I'm not." Mrs. Sanchez put her hand on her hip. "But I could be Linda Hamilton."

Mrs. Dario fake-coughed. "Linda Hamilton's grandma," she said.

"How about we compromise," Guy suggested. "Let's set the pin at ten pounds, and you can see how you like it?"

"Fine." Mrs. Sanchez pulled the pin out herself and stuck it into the stack. She grabbed the handle and executed three perfect biceps curls in a row. "See? No problem."

Hannah grinned. She loved watching Mrs. Sanchez stand up for herself.

"Try going slower," said Guy, "and see if that makes it harder." He kept his sights set on her form, like he was making sure she wouldn't hurt herself. "There, good job," he said, as Mrs. Sanchez slowed down.

"That does make it a teensy bit more challenging," Mrs. Sanchez admitted, sweat beading her forehead.

"What about me?" Mrs. Dario asked.

Guy adjusted the oblique abdominal machine. "It's almost set up for you."

Hannah looked back down at the desk and picked up the

battery pack. After a minute or two of struggling, she decided that sadists had designed the hard plastic packaging because she was completely unable to open it. She needed scissors. Guy wouldn't mind her borrowing some, would he? She didn't want to disturb him with his clients, so she went ahead and opened the top drawer and peered inside, but all she found was a motley assortment of paperclips.

"Is there something I can help you with?" Guy called from across the room.

Hannah jerked her chin up. "Scissors?" she squeaked. "I can't open the batteries."

"Right-hand drawer," Guy said, before returning his attention to Mrs. Dario.

Hannah pulled the drawer open and found scissors and a first-aid kit. "Thanks," she replied.

"This one looks like fun." Mrs. Dario sat in a machine and extended her leg, causing the weights to clank together.

"Be careful!" Mrs. Sanchez cautioned.

"I'm never careful," Mrs. Dario sassed back.

"The oblique machine's ready for you," said Guy, waving her toward it.

"Oh, goody!" Mrs. Dario took a seat. "This one's my favorite, because you get to spin around."

"If you're spinning around, that means he's not giving you enough weight." Mrs. Sanchez paused between reps.

"I give people the amount of weight I think they can handle," Guy said, in a tone that Hannah thought was incredibly patient, especially since the two women were particularly feisty today.

Mrs. Dario spun in the chair. "This is the perfect amount of weight. Good job."

"I haven't put the pin in yet." Guy stopped her chair from spinning.

Hannah chuckled as she sliced open the battery package.

"Please hold still while I set it up," said Guy. Hannah looked over and saw him put the pin into the lightest setting before releasing the chair. "Now try," he told Mrs. Dario.

"Oof!" Mrs. Dario squeezed her eyes shut. "Now I feel it. I can't remember the last time I felt my ab muscles like that."

"You're doing great, Elena," said Mrs. Sanchez. "Keep at it."

"Thanks." Mrs. Dario spun back and forth in the chair.

"So, Guy," Mrs. Sanchez said, "yesterday you promised you'd tell us all about your old girlfriend."

Hannah's ears perked as she climbed up on the stepstool. She was curious about Guy's past dating history, too. She unscrewed the smoke detector and popped out the old battery.

"I don't remember promising that," said Guy.

"Oh but you did," said Mrs. Dario.

Guy looked sideways at Hannah and got her eye, like he needed moral support. Hannah giggled, and pushed in the new battery, causing the smoke detector to let out a roaring beep. "Sorry!" she called.

Guy looked back at his clients. "Those are enough reps on your right side, Mrs. Sanchez. Let's switch to your left."

"You read my mind." Mrs. Sanchez did a few shoulder rolls before gripping the handle with her left hand and pulling down on the cable. "Now back to your old girlfriend. Start talking."

"Tamara," Guy blurted, "her name was Tamara."

"Was she pretty?" Mrs. Dario asked.

"She was drop-dead gorgeous, and made sure everyone knew it."

Hannah puffed her cheeks for a second before frowning. *Of course Guy's old girlfriend was a knockout.* She climbed down from the stepstool.

"I should have known Tamara wasn't right for me from the beginning," Guy continued, "but I was too dumb to realize it. Every picture she sent me involved her making a duck face."

"What's that?" Mrs. Sanchez asked.

"You know, Brenda. Like this." Mrs. Dario pursed her lips and made a smooching noise.

"Eww." Mrs. Sanchez wrinkled her nose. "I hate pictures like that. What did she do for a living?"

"She was a makeup artist for some of the richest socialites in Manhattan," said Guy.

"That's a sad face." Mrs. Dario poked him. "Are you okay?"

"I'm fine," said Guy. "Let's move you to a different exercise." Guy switched her to the biceps cables that Mrs. Sanchez had been working on earlier. He set the pin to the lightest setting and demonstrated the form. "Look straight ahead so you don't hurt your neck, and curl your arm like this."

"Okey-dokey." Mrs. Dario took the handle.

Hannah put the used battery back in the bag. Then she returned the scissors to his desk drawer. Only instead of opening the right drawer, she opened the left one by accident. Instead of seeing a first-aid kit, she saw... *more vintage postcards?*

Hannah's eyes were glued to the pictures. Not just any postcards, these were exactly like the ones that used to be in the lobby when she was five years old.

The same type that she'd found in that box on New Year's Day.

Precisely like the ones she'd mailed off to Connecticut with the jar of sand dollars.

What the heck?

Hannah slammed the drawer shut, feeling guilty, like she had invaded Guy's privacy. She opened the right drawer and put the scissors away next to the first-aid kit. Then she picked up the extra batteries and dragged the stepstool over to the other side of the room where the second smoke detector waited for her.

"Impressive work, Mrs. Dario," said Guy. "It's probably time to switch to your other arm for those biceps curls."

"Finally." Mrs. Dario shook out her hand and laughed. "My right arm feels like cooked noodles."

Why did Guy have those postcards in his desk? Hannah wondered. The business side of her brain perked up. If there was a box of them somewhere, maybe they could start selling them in the gift shop again... Vintage Americana was hot. This could be an unexplored revenue stream, assuming she could figure out where the postcards had come from, of course.

Guy removed some cleaning wipes from a container and wiped the machines down. "Wow, would you get a load of the time? We only have five minutes left. Let's do some neck and shoulder rolls, and finish with our stretches. Get the tension out."

"It's going to take more than a few shoulder rolls to do that for me." Mrs. Sanchez kneaded the back of her neck. "It's a good thing we have those spa appointments later."

"You are going to be *so* happy that I talked you into the chocolate-coffee body scrub," said Mrs. Dario. "It's divine."

"I'm only doing it because the masseuse said it would be too hard on my tissues to do two days of massage in a row." Mrs. Sanchez sat on the exercise mat Guy pulled out for her. "How's it going over there, Hannah? Is the smoke alarm going to scare us witless?"

"Any second now." Hannah stepped onto the stool and grabbed the detector's case to unscrew it. "Brace yourself." She pulled it from the ceiling and plopped in the new batteries. As soon as she put the case back into place, the alarm chirped loudly.

"You tested my hearing, too." Mrs. Dario pointed to her ears. "Still works great."

"Except when I remind you that dairy makes you gassy," said Mrs. Sanchez.

"Ehh?" Mrs. Dario cupped her ear. "I didn't hear you."

Hannah stepped off the ladder just in time to see Guy look

over and wink at her, making her smile. *Did he used to wink at Tamara like that?* Tamara, the big-city knockout who would probably run rings around Hannah when it came to sophistication. The whole concept of a woman like Tamara out there, toying with Guy's heart, made Hannah feel like a country bumpkin. Still, she was curious.

On her walk back to the lobby, Hannah googled *Tamara. Makeup artist. New York City*, and found a highly stylized Instagram account with over twenty thousand followers. Guy was right. Tamara was gorgeous. Jealousy pricked Hannah's heart. Not only did she have wavy blonde hair that fell to her waist, Tamara also had sparkling brown eyes, an amazing figure, and a designer wardrobe with labels so famous that even Hannah recognized them. And she rocked high heels, too—in every picture! Hannah only managed them for important events like work interviews and conferences. Still, Hannah could see what Guy meant about the duck face. Tamara pouted in every pose.

Hannah scrolled through Tamara's feed, searching for any mention of Guy, but found nothing.

"How's it going?" Guy asked, sneaking up behind her.

"What?" Hannah covered her phone with her hand. "I mean, nothing." She put the phone in her pocket. Had Guy seen what she was looking at? Hannah wasn't sure. "I mean... Sorry, I was distracted and I'm not making sense."

"I'll say." He handed her the stepstool. "You forgot this."

"Oh, whoops. I didn't mean to clutter up your space. My apologies."

"No biggie. Is this your first night in Strawberry Cottage?"

Hannah nodded. "Mary has a friend from design school helping her collect a sofa bed and recliner in his truck that they found on Facebook Marketplace. Apparently the furniture smells like cigarettes, but since it was all free, the price was right." She looked down at the stone path, wishing that she hadn't mentioned money.

"It sounds like you'll be busy then, moving in and getting settled. Could I bring you dinner?"

"What?" Hannah looked up. "That's unnecessary."

"It would be my pleasure. It's easier to cook for five people than it is to cook for one."

"Five people? But it's just Mary, Gran, and me."

Guy grinned sheepishly. "Plus, I have to make some for Lark. I'm convinced that if she eats more anti-inflammatory foods like vegetables, it'll help get her tendonitis under control."

"Oh. That's really nice of you." *Suspiciously nice...* That confirmed it. Guy must have a thing for Mary. Hannah needed to drop the news that her sister was already taken ASAP. "Mary's boyfriend, Aidan—he's about to propose, we think— never cooks for her."

"Maybe he needs lessons," Guy said diplomatically.

"Could be." Hannah searched Guy's face for any sign of disappointment at hearing that Mary had a serious boyfriend, but all she saw were his blue eyes gazing back at her with an intensity that gave her butterflies. "I pick Gran up at six tonight from her friend Patti's house, but we'll be here after that."

Guy smiled warmly. "I'll see you then." He walked down the path to the studio.

So Guy wasn't interested in Mary after all? He was helping them just to be nice? *Or,* her heart whispered, *because he might like me?* No, that wasn't it. The very thought made her feel foolish, especially after she had a second go at stalking Tamara's Instagram. There was no way Hannah could compete with cheekbones like that. Tamara looked like an advertisement for buccal fat removal.

After she had put the stepstool away in the broom closet, she realized that she'd forgotten to ask Guy about where he'd found the postcards. She asked Herman and Will if they'd seen boxes of vintage postcards lying around, and they both had said no. She went back and searched the broom closet, the break room, the storage shed, and the closet where they kept gift shop merchandise, but nope—she couldn't find any sign of them. The only postcards she'd seen in recent memory that looked like those in Guy's desk were the ones she'd found on New Year's Day. So how did Guy have them in his possession? She really needed to ask him the next time she saw him.

In the meantime, it made for interesting conversation to share with her grandma on the drive back from the senior center. Ferdinand slept in his carrier in the back seat, occasionally purring. Hannah thought Cheryl would appreciate the postcards being a blast from the past, but all her grandma saw was a mystery.

"Let me get this straight," Cheryl said, as she stared at the dashboard. Her spine curved in such a pronounced way that she could no longer look through the windshield. "You found an ornately carved box in Strawberry Cottage on New Year's Day, figured it must have belonged to a guest who came two decades ago, mailed it off to his address in Connecticut, and then you saw that exact same postcard in Guy's desk?"

"Not the same postcard. At least, I don't think so." Hannah adjusted the heating vents, so they'd blow away from her grandma's face. "Probably it was a copy."

"But it could have been the same one, right?"

"I suppose..."

"Did you look at the back?"

"Of the ones in Guy's desk?" Hannah asked. "No, I didn't. I'm not a snoop."

"It's not snooping if it's detective work. It's investigating."

"I think you've been watching too much *Law and Order*."

"Actually, I prefer cozy mystery shows over true crime. You know that."

Hannah rolled her eyes. "I find it highly unrealistic that

Guy would have somehow acquired the postcard I mailed to Connecticut."

But Cheryl wouldn't let it go. "What did those postcards say? Do you remember?"

"Something about love making people foolish but still believing in happily ever afters. A man named Joe signed it. Does that ring a bell?"

"You expect me to remember a guest named Joe from twenty years ago?"

"Ah, no. Sorry, that was a dumb question," said Hannah.

"No need to apologize. But that definitely adds to the mystery."

"There *is* no mystery."

"Look," said Cheryl. "I just spent four and a half hours watching a *Murder She Wrote* marathon. There's definitely a mystery."

"I thought you said you never watched television at the senior center?"

"I don't," said Cheryl. "Unless Angela Lansbury's involved."

Hannah sighed. Ever since her osteoporosis had become severe, Cheryl hadn't been able to get out much. Maybe it wasn't the worst thing in the world to let her grandma have a bit of fun over this. "Okay," she relented. "Maybe there is a mystery. How are you going to solve it?"

"The Mystery of the Vintage Postcards." Cheryl clapped her hands together. "Don't worry, Hannah. I'm on the case."

Hannah rolled her eyes again.

"I saw that, young lady!"

"Am I going to be able to afford your rates?" Hannah asked.

"You can pay me in cat kibble. I need to keep Ferdinand happy."

Hannah slowed to a stop for a red light. "It's a deal."

"The first thing I need to figure out is more about Guy. I

haven't met him yet, but from hearing Mary yammer on about him, I'm expecting Daniel Craig with a soft spot for rats."

"I wouldn't say Guy has Hollywood good looks," Hannah clarified. *Except, of course, he did.* "But what do you think about me flat-out asking him where he found the postcards?"

"Because then you'd have to admit to snooping in his desk."

"I thought you said it wasn't snooping if it was detective work," said Hannah.

"It's not." Cheryl gingerly repositioned herself in the passenger seat. "That's why, later this evening, you're going to go back to the wellness studio, open Guy's desk, and see what's written on the back of those postcards."

"I'm not going to do that!"

"You have to. Something smells off about the whole situation."

"That's being a bit dramatic," said Hannah. "Don't you think?"

"No, I don't. If Guy had a personal connection to Seaside Resort, why didn't he tell that to you during his job interview, or the past three months that he's worked here?"

"I don't think he has a personal connection to Seaside Resort. I think he found leftover postcards somewhere."

"But that doesn't make sense," said Cheryl. "We got rid of that stock ages ago, once Blanchet Maison bought the property. They wouldn't allow us to sell anything official without their logo."

"Oh." There went her idea of making money on the old cards. "Why didn't you tell me that in the first place?"

"Didn't I?" Cheryl scratched her ear. "Sorry. I thought I had."

"Wait..." Hannah pondered it. "Is that why you think that the cards I saw in Guy's desk were the same ones I found in Strawberry Cottage?"

"It seems logical to me."

"But I sent those to Connecticut." Hannah turned into the drive for the resort, looking up as she always did at the old sign that hung above the entrance. The wood support holding it up was rotting, and she'd asked Nick repeatedly to fix it but he "hadn't got to it yet."

"How about we do this?" Cheryl tugged at her seatbelt. "After you introduce us, I'll ask Guy if he's ever been to Sand Dollar Cove before or knows someone who has. I'll find out the truth in no time. Old ladies like me get away with being nosy."

"You're the detective." Hannah shrugged. "Sounds like a plan." A ridiculous plan, but if her grandmother wanted to live out her lady detective fantasies, Hannah wasn't going to stop her.

She parked the car in a wheelchair accessible spot and hung Cheryl's disabled persons placard on the rearview mirror. Hannah would come back down and move her car later to free up the space. Seaside Resort just barely had enough parking spots to meet federal laws under the Americans with Disabilities Act, and it was one of the things she wanted to change, if she ever got the chance to redesign the parking lot. She didn't think hitting the minimum was good enough when it came to welcoming guests with disabilities. There should be more ADA spots, the pavement should be smoother, and the lighting needed to be brighter, too. But redesigning the parking lot had always been a low priority for the resort, since they could barely keep up with cottage maintenance.

"I feel like I'm headed to work." Cheryl undid her seat belt.

Hannah opened the rear door and lifted out Ferdinand's carrier. "Seaside Resort is glad you're on the case."

"And not only is this an active investigation, but I get to stay in the cottage with the best view." Cheryl smiled. "Did you hear that, Ferdinand? We're going to be living in style."

It warmed Hannah's heart to see her grandma happy and enthused. "Hang tight. I'll get out your wheelchair."

The path up to Strawberry Cottage was steep, and by the three quarters mark, Hannah was out of breath from pushing Cheryl. She tried to reserve a little bit of energy in her tank to get the wheelchair over the two steps leading up to the porch that she knew was ahead. But when they arrived at Strawberry Cottage, she was surprised to find Guy already waiting for them.

"Hi, Hannah." Guy waved at her and then stepped off the porch to shake hands with Cheryl. "Guy Barret, nice to meet you."

"It's nice to meet you, too. My name's Cheryl. I feel like I already know you since the girls talk about you all the time."

"They do, do they?" Guy stood straight and looked at Hannah.

"Not all the time," Hannah spluttered, her cheeks blooming hot. "Gran, you're exaggerating."

"The way Hannah and Mary tell it, you protected us from rats, helped remove the nasty old carpet, and fed them dinner, too."

"Well, speaking of dinner." Guy pointed to the porch. "I brought food."

"You did?" Cheryl's eyes lit up. "That's awfully nice of you. I've already eaten, but Hannah hasn't, and Mary should be here any moment. I'm sure both my girls are hungry. They need feeding three times a day or they become hangry."

"Gran!" Hannah protested.

"See what I mean?" Cheryl shot Guy a look. "Hangry."

"Come on, Gran." Hannah spun the wheelchair around so that the back wheels faced the porch. "Let's get you upstairs."

"Hang on." Guy reached for the handles. "Let me help."

"I got it." Hannah didn't budge. "It's only two steps."

"Two steps, yes," said Guy. "But lifting wheelchairs can be risky. The strongest person should be in back taking the heaviest load. That's safer for you, and your grandmother."

"He's right," said Cheryl. "Don't be a martyr, Hannah. I worry about you girls wrestling me around without help."

"Fine." Hannah released the handles and moved to the front of the wheelchair. Bending down, she gripped the frame.

"On the count of three," said Guy. "One. Two. Three." He pulled the chair up onto the porch and pushed Cheryl around so she was facing the door.

"Prepare to have low expectations," Hannah warned her grandmother. "Mary hasn't worked her magic yet."

"I realize that," said Cheryl. "She texted me twenty minutes ago saying that she and her friend were on their way with our new furniture."

"Which might need to be aired out a bunch because of cigarette smoke." Hannah took out the key and opened the door. "Here we are. Home sweet home."

"Home sweet home," Cheryl echoed.

Strawberry Cottage was a shell of its former self. The kitchenette and bamboo table were still there, as well as the tiny bathroom, but the rest of the room was empty save for a suitcase Hannah had brought over that morning, and Ferdinand's litter box. Wallpaper peeled from cracking plaster, and the bare wood floor had rough edges from where they'd ripped up the carpet nails. The only good thing Hannah could say about the space was that it was rodent-free. She'd checked that fact over her lunch break.

Hannah pushed Cheryl inside, and waited until Guy had entered too before she closed the door behind them, so that Ferdinand wouldn't escape. "Thanks for bringing dinner," she told him. "That was kind of you."

"I should have realized there wasn't a microwave," he said, frowning. "Sorry about that."

"The stove still works, and there's a couple of pots and pans in the cupboards." Hannah walked over to the kitchenette and took them out.

"Revere Ware lasts forever," said Cheryl as Ferdinand jumped off her lap. "You can't go wrong with copper bottoms."

"That'll work," said Guy. "I brought roasted butternut squash soup and a fresh green salad." He went to the sink and washed his hands, drying them on one of the fluffy towels that housekeeping had left.

"Have you been here before?" Cheryl asked. "To Washington State, I mean? Or do you have family who lives here?"

"No, ma'am." Guy washed the pot before pouring soup into it. "Unless you count flying through SeaTac Airport on the way to Hawaii. All my family lives in New York."

"They've never been here either?" Cheryl winked at Hannah behind Guy's back.

"Not that I know of." Guy opened a drawer and fished out a long metal spoon. "Wow. There's hardly any silverware in here. I see three forks, two spoons, and a knife. If I'd known that, I wouldn't have brought soup."

"It's okay," said Hannah. "I'll drink mine in a mug."

"That works for Mary, too," said Cheryl. "But Guy, I find it fascinating that you moved all the way out to the West Coast having never visited here before." She rolled her wheelchair closer. "That showed a lot of gumption on your part to pick up and move someplace new, especially considering you were leaving an exciting place like New York."

"Fleeing was more like it." Guy stirred the soup. "I couldn't handle one more day of city living."

Hannah rustled around in the cabinets. Following Guy's example, she washed the dishes she found before setting the table. "New York sounds pretty exciting to me. I've always wanted to visit the East Coast."

"I haven't been," said Cheryl. "But I had a hankering to see Vermont after watching *White Christmas*."

"I just rewatched *White Christmas* after I read a book about Rosemary Clooney," said Guy.

"Neat," said Cheryl. "Visiting one of those other New England states would be fun, too. Like New Hampshire or Connecticut."

"That would be nice." Hannah found paper towels and folded them into quarters, so they'd look like napkins.

"Have you spent any time in Connecticut?" Cheryl asked Guy.

Wow, thought Hannah. *Gran's really going for it.*

"Some." Guy turned up the electric stove. "I used to go to summer camp there."

"Ooh!" Cheryl clapped her hands. "I went to summer camp once, when I was about ten years old or so. I found the most interesting things in the arts and crafts barn. A sculpture made of macaroni noodles... A bag of peacock feathers... Strips of leather to make into bookmarks... I don't know where they got all that stuff!" She scooted closer to Guy. "Did you ever find anything interesting at summer camp?"

"Yes, actually." Guy stirred the soup with a firm hand. "The camp I attended had a taxidermy collection. Nobody could officially call themselves a Camp Quercus regular until they'd kissed the stuffed gazelle in the dining room."

"Yuck!" Hannah exclaimed, watching him cook. "I mean, kissing taxidermy. Your soup smells delicious."

"It sure does," said Cheryl. "Almost as good as that Salisbury steak I ate at the senior center." Her phone buzzed. "That's Mary. She and her friend just pulled up in the parking lot."

Guy looked at Hannah. "Do you mind stirring the soup? I'll go help with the furniture."

"That would be awesome," Hannah said. "If you don't mind." She'd been worried how they'd get the couch and recliner up to the cottage.

"It'll be a snap with the dolly." Guy looked at Cheryl. "Could you please tell Mary I'll be right there?"

"Absolutely." Gran turned over her phone and slowly moved her knobbly hands as she typed.

Guy rapped the spoon on the side of the pot to get the excess off and rested it in a bowl. "Just keep stirring now and then so it doesn't scorch."

"Will do," said Hannah. As soon as he'd left the cottage, she looked at Cheryl. "Well?" she asked. "What do you think, Detective Turner?"

"That I need more information," said Cheryl. "But that's where you come in."

"Wait, what?"

"Were you listening to me back in the car? I need my trusty assistant to break into the wellness studio at midnight and find those postcards." Ferdinand yowled in the corner. "Not you, cat." Cheryl pointed at Hannah. "You."

THIRTEEN

"What the hell are we doing?" Mary asked. "I don't want to be arrested."

"We're not going to be arrested." Hannah took her hand out of her pocket. "I have keys."

"But Gran said—"

"I know what she said, but this isn't technically a break-in. As an employee, I have every right to be here." It was just past midnight, and Hannah and Mary stood outside the wellness studio. "The sooner we get this over with, the sooner Gran will let this postcard thing go." Hannah unlocked the door and held it open for her sister. "Honestly, I wish I'd never mentioned them to her in the first place."

"It's dark in there." Mary didn't budge. "You lead the way."

"Fine." Hannah crossed the threshold and clicked on the lights. "If anyone asks, we're here to get bandages."

Mary limped forward dramatically. "Because I twisted my ankle, and it really hurts, and I might need crutches, too."

"Your Hollywood days are really paying off."

"Oscar-worthy, don't you think?" Mary beamed and walked normally again. "So, where's Guy's desk?"

"Over here." Hannah led the way to the corner. "The post-cards are in here," she said, as she opened the left-hand drawer.

"Bubblemint?" Mary gasped. "I thought Guy was more of a Polar Ice type of man."

"What?" Hannah looked inside the drawer. Instead of post-cards, all she saw were gum wrappers. She slammed it shut. "I must have mixed up which drawer they were in." She quickly opened another.

"Who keeps this much hydration powder?" Mary picked up a packet from a box in the drawer. "Do you think he'll notice if one is missing? I've always wanted to try this stuff."

"Put it back," Hannah chided. "We're not thieves." She opened the main drawer that held paperclips, and then the drawer with the first-aid kit and scissors. But there was no sign of the postcards anywhere. "They're gone!" she muttered.

"He must have taken them home with him," said Mary. "Or maybe you saw brochures and got confused."

"No, they were definitely postcards. I bet Gran giving him the third degree made him nervous." Hannah looked at her sister. For the first time she began to wonder if her grandma had been right. *Could it be true? Did Guy have Joe's postcards?*

"If you tell that to Gran, she'll get wound up again," said Mary.

"First, let's be one hundred percent certain the postcards aren't here." Hannah looked around the room. "Check every corner. Maybe he moved them to the weights rack, or something."

Mary walked over to the linens. "Ooh! Sweat towels rolled into neat little bundles. Fancy."

"What's never made sense to me about Guy is why would a Dartmouth grad who speaks multiple languages want to work here, as a personal trainer?"

"You heard what he said." Mary helped herself to a cup of

water and added pilfered hydration powder, much to Hannah's chagrin. "He wanted to escape big-city living."

Hannah peered behind every weight machine. "Okay, but why take a job that pays okay, but has almost no room for advancement?"

"I could ask the same thing about you."

"Huh?" Hannah turned to face her sister.

"Why are you here, in Sand Dollar Cove," Mary asked. "Instead of Seattle, or Portland, or... I don't know, New York City for that matter?"

"What are you talking about?"

"Someplace with more opportunity for you to progress in hotel management."

"But I'm going to become general manager. I mean, I *might* become general manager."

"Of a run-down resort in a small town in the middle of nowhere."

"This isn't the middle of nowhere," Hannah protested. "This is the Washington Coast. Sand Dollar Cove was once a major tourist destination."

Mary tilted her head to the side. "That's stretching it a bit, don't you think?"

"We were the Riviera of the West."

"In promotional brochures maybe, but never in reality." Mary came over to Hannah and sat down on a weights bench in front of her. "Once I have my interior design degree... Once I marry Aidan..." Mary stretched out her arms. "My life will be perfect. I want yours to be perfect, too."

"I don't know what you mean."

"You could be running a Hilton, or a Hyatt, or the Ritz. Hell, you could work at the flagship Blanchet Maison on Park Avenue someday. Wouldn't that be amazing?"

"No, it wouldn't." Hannah shivered. "I couldn't leave Gran." *I couldn't leave Sand Dollar Cove.*

"Nobody's talking about leaving Gran. She could move with us. We could move someplace together."

"You want to leave our home?"

"What home?" Mary put down her water. "I love Sand Dollar Cove, but in case you didn't notice, we're living like vagabonds right now."

Hannah felt goosebumps prick across her arms. She should have brought her coat with her. The only thing that would make things better right now was the comfort of her dad's down coat. "But this is where Dad grew up," she protested. "This is where I remember him."

Mary reached forward and brushed her fingertips against Hannah's arm. "You can remember Dad anywhere you go. I wish I could. I don't have any memories of him at all."

"I'm sorry about that, truly sorry. And it's not like I have tons of Dad memories. I had barely turned five years old when he died. But the memories that I do have are important to me, and I don't want them to fade away. Dad used to carry me in a backpack when he mowed the lawn. He and I would pick flowers for Mom. We'd search for shells on the beach." Hannah's gaze drifted up to the ceiling. "I'd step up on his toes and we'd dance around the living room." She could still hear Max singing.

"Do you think Dad had depression?" Mary asked in a near whisper. "Do you think he drove himself off of Blackfish Point on purpose?"

Hannah shook her head. "No, I don't." She squeezed her eyes shut so she wouldn't cry and then opened them again, clearheaded. "I've thought about it a lot. I don't remember much from when I was little, but I do remember Dad singing and whistling cheery tunes. That's something a hopeful person does. And mowing the grass—that's something a responsible person does. Right? I think Dad was a person who believed that good things happen to people who work hard—because look at how hard he worked. Don't forget about his education, either. That's something we both know about him. The University of Washington isn't an easy college to get into, and the school of engineering is even more challenging. So Dad must have been the type of person who believed that by working hard, we make our own luck. Our own happiness. He must have really believed in the American dream."

"But what if he stopped believing in it?" Mary asked. "What if he experienced trauma working overseas, or saw so many bad things in Afghanistan that he wasn't able to process his emotions? What if he sank into a depression that nobody knew about but him?"

Hannah sat down on the bench next to Mary. "Then he hid it from me, that's for sure."

"You were a little girl. How would you have noticed?"

It was a fair point, but Hannah wasn't dissuaded. She'd spent her whole life creating an image of her father that she'd inferred from tiny details. "If Dad was depressed, he hid it from Gran, too. She's never mentioned seeing signs of him being depressed."

That image of holding Max's hand in the lobby in front of the postcards popped up in her memory bank again. Kelly was next to them, cradling baby Mary. They were waiting to pick up Cheryl to go out to dinner. It was her last memory of her father.

"Dad took us out to dinner a week before he died. He was happy. I remember him being happy." Her eyes filled with unshed tears. "I think Dad loved his work. He must have been proud that his life was making a difference. I don't believe he would have killed himself."

Mary rested her hand on Hannah's knee. "Do you think Dad would want you to be chained to this place forever?"

"I'm not chained. I want to be here."

"You can go anywhere in the world, Hannah. You can take

any job that you want. You don't have to work at Seaside Resort forever."

"But I want to." Hannah hugged herself, trying to warm up. "The only place I've ever wanted to be is right here." She stood resolutely. "Now, let's look for those postcards."

"Why should we?" Mary rose, too.

"Because Gran wants—"

"To invent a mystery where there isn't one." Mary grabbed Hannah by both shoulders and looked at her sharply. "The only mystery here is why you're trying to make up something sinister about Guy that was probably innocent."

"That's not—"

"What a normal, trusting person would do. You're right, it's not."

"What are you saying?" Hannah jerked away from Mary's grasp. "I trust people just fine."

Mary held out her palm. "Yeah, like five people total in the entire world." She counted them out one by one on her fingers. "Me, Gran, Herman just barely, Jasmine, and probably Lark."

"You forgot Nancy and Patti." Hannah lifted her chin.

"My point is, here you have this totally amazing, incredibly handsome man showing up every few nights with homemade food, and instead of doing the reasonable thing, which would be to ask him out, you're inventing excuses not to. Because you have trust issues."

"I don't have trust issues." Hannah marched to the desk and opened the left-hand drawer one more time to double-check, but all she saw was gum litter. "Okay," she mumbled. "Let's say I do have a little bit of difficulty when it comes to trusting people." She closed the drawer gently. "What do I do about it?"

"Well, for starters, let's lock this place up and go to bed. After that, I don't know." Mary picked up her cup. "Maybe try having a little more faith?"

"That's the most generic, unhelpful advice ever." Hannah

opened the door and faced the cold night air. The foghorn crooned in the darkness, guiding vessels through the mist. Mary came up behind her, making Hannah jump.

"Sorry," her sister apologized. "I didn't mean to spook you."

The cold made Hannah's teeth chatter. "What should we tell Gran about the postcards?"

"That Guy is a handsome, charming man, who seemingly adores you, and that you made a mistake. You don't know what you saw in that drawer."

"But—"

"Have faith in *my* judgment this time, okay?" Mary held up seven fingers. "I'm one of the people you trust, right?"

Hannah nodded.

"Well then," said Mary. "I'm telling you to let it go and give Guy a chance."

Hannah took a cleansing breath of cold air and expelled it in a puff of steam. "Okay," she answered reluctantly. "I'll try."

FOURTEEN

Four days later, Hannah held her computer close to her side as she stood outside the Vista Room that was next to The Summer Wind. Used for weddings and large gatherings, the space doubled as a conference room. Today however, the only person in the room was Herman, who sat in the corner, facing the view, talking on his phone.

Seeing that Herman was engaged in a private conversation, Hannah turned to go, so she wouldn't intrude. She was a few minutes early for her presentation, after all. But when she accidentally overheard what Herman was saying, she lingered.

"Don't you worry one bit, ma'am. I'm keeping a close watch on your guy. He's doing great so far, and hasn't given me any cause for concern. You'd be proud."

Your Guy? What was that about? Hannah stepped into the shadows by the front door so that she'd remain unseen.

"I appreciate the financial compensation, but it really isn't necessary," Herman continued. "Your guy's an asset to this place, and I'm glad to have him around."

Hannah's heart squeezed like it was being choked. *Had someone paid Herman to look out for Guy?* A darker thought occurred to her. She knew this competition for the general manager was rigged, but what if it wasn't rigged in her favor?

Stop it, she told herself. Ever since her conversation with Mary, she'd been trying to work on her trust issues. But instead of walking away, Hannah leaned forward, so she could hear better.

"That's no-bunnies business but mine," said Herman. He laughed at his own joke. "You better believe it. Yes, I'll talk to you later. Bye."

Hannah stepped to the right, into the sunshine, and leaned against the wall. Closing her eyes, she tried to steel her nerves, but all she felt was the rollicking ache of betrayal. Seaside Resort was supposed to be her past, present and future. Could she have nothing hopeful in her life? Not even the fulfillment of knowing she'd worked so hard to achieve something?

"Are you okay?" Guy asked. "You look pale."

Hannah opened her eyes to find Guy standing in front of her wearing black pants and a royal-blue shirt that accented his eyes. He was calm, poised, and steady. Everything Hannah didn't feel right now. "I'm fine," she said. "I was just taking a breather."

"Good to hear. If I didn't know any better, I would have thought you were nervous about our presentations."

"I'm not." Hannah's palm sweated so much, she worried she'd ruin her computer. "I'm fully prepared. Get ready to be blown away."

"I was about to say the same to you."

"I'll do great so long as there aren't any rodents involved."

Guy chuckled. "Please tell Herman I'll be right there." He took out his phone. "I just have a quick phone call to make."

"Okay, but you know how he feels about punctuality. Our meeting is supposed to start in five minutes."

"Just one more reason for him to choose you. But don't

worry, I'll be quick." Guy rushed off around the back of the building.

Hannah's phone buzzed with a text from Mary.

Guess what! Mary wrote. *Aidan says he wants to talk about something important with me when he gets home.*

You know what that means, Hannah replied. *Hopefully he took notes when he called me the other day.*

He called you???

Shoot. Had she forgotten to tell Mary about Aidan's call? Hannah had been so stressed lately that she couldn't remember. *All I'll say is that it was a good thing you told me exactly what type of engagement ring you prefer,* Hannah replied.

Mary texted a diamond emoji. *Bling, bling!*

Btw. What are we doing for Gran for Mother's Day? Hannah texted, thinking of her never-ending mental to-do list.

Paris. Rome. Tokyo. You choose!

Ha. I wish. Hannah sighed. *Breakfast in bed, and what else?*

Breakfast in her recliner, you mean.

Yes.

How about new slippers? That's in the budget, and her old ones are ratty.

Good plan, Hannah texted. *I'll order some from Amazon.* The online retailer was a lifesaver since the nearest Walmart was one hour away.

I'll do it, Mary replied. *You might pick out something ugly.*

Thanks a lot! Hannah wrote.

You're welcome.

Hannah wasn't sure if Mary had picked up on her annoyed tone or not, but she didn't have time to analyze. She put her phone away and headed into the Vista Room. When she opened the door, Guy glanced her way and smiled. A ripple of delight washed over her, seeing his friendly expression, but then it became muddied with suspicion. She wished she had never seen those postcards, because they made her so confused. Hannah put her computer on the conference table.

"Just the person I wanted to see," said Herman. "Hannah, you've got to see this." He took out his wallet and unfolded the billfold, before carefully removing a small picture. "I'm dog-sitting for one of my poker buddies. Here's a Polaroid. Isn't he something? That was Nancy's favorite pair of slippers, by the way. Well, the left one, that is."

Hannah looked at the photo and tried to make sense of what she was seeing. Pink fabric and fluff surrounded a cute brown puppy with soulful eyes.

Herman put the Polaroid away. "I thought those slippers were ridiculous, but Nancy loved them. Tell me though, what type of sixty-one-year-old woman wears bunny slippers?"

"Huh?" Hannah asked. She heard "slippers," and she thought of her text exchange with Mary. Her brain wasn't following Herman's one-sided conversation.

"Exactly." Herman nodded. "This beagle did her a service. The only problem is my friend's wife keeps calling every day to check up on him, as if Nancy and I aren't capable of caring for a dog." Herman grunted. "Nancy says it's because they don't have kids or grandkids to worry about. This is their 'fur-baby,' or whatever." Herman made air quotes. "But enough about my dog drama. Let's see your presentations."

Suddenly, Herman's mysterious phone call made sense. Was *that* what it had been about? Massacred bunny slippers? If so, maybe Hannah still had a chance to win this promotion. She should have been relieved, but all she felt was annoyance. Her nerves were at breaking point.

"Who wants to go first?" Herman asked. "Maybe we should flip a coin again."

"I'll go first." Hannah opened her computer. "Guy went first last time." She plugged it into the projector.

"Sounds fair to me," said Guy.

Hannah's presentation contained graphs, projected data, customer reviews, and photos. She spoke with authority and made a serious case for how historically accurate cosmetic improvements, combined with cost-effective marketing on social media, could increase revenue. "Mid-century modern appeal is hotter than ever," she said. "Our ultimate goal should be to offer a Seaside Resort experience for every price point, from cottages with premier views, to the family-friendly dormitory I suggest building where the storage shed currently resides. We could double our occupancy, improve our reputation, but also respect the environment at the same time. Let's make Seaside Resort a top destination for everyone who lives in the Pacific Northwest." Hannah clicked off her presentation and sat down.

Guy clapped. "Great job."

"Thanks." Hannah smiled modestly.

"Attagirl," Herman said, patting Hannah on the back. "Those pictures you shared were really pretty." He pointed at Guy and pulled an imaginary trigger. "You're up."

"Great. Um... Hannah, would you mind if I borrowed your computer? If not, I'll run back."

"Sure," Hannah offered. "Go right ahead. It's a company computer, after all." *Nothing belonged to her*. Except for her car, and she was still making payments on that.

"Thanks." Guy plugged in his thumb drive and waited anxiously until his presentation popped up. Unlike Hannah, his presentation was packed with clever infographics. Guy zeroed in on the potential for part of Seaside Resort to be a rehab facility for physical trauma.

"Don't get me wrong," he said. "I'm not saying we should become a convalescent hospital. But I do see the potential for us to be a place of healing and rejuvenation. Imagine the cachet we'd have if Seahawks came here to recuperate from injuries, or if Hollywood stars came to get in shape and prepare for their next starring role. I'd like to have a least one physical therapist on staff to provide services to guests that could also bill to insurance. I predict that our senior citizen guests would use this component as well. So many people put off dealing with chronic pain until it becomes unbearable. Let's give them the opportunity to find real solutions so that they leave their vacation in better shape than when they arrived."

He nodded at Hannah. "While my vision of Seaside Resort might not be as inclusive as Hannah's, it takes us into a different realm of prestige, revenue sources, and possibilities." Guy closed his presentation, ejected the thumb drive, and sat down.

"Well, well, well." Herman clapped. "That sure was something, wasn't it, Hannah?"

"Yeah." Hannah clapped twice. "Very interesting." Her lips pressed together into a Mona Lisa smile that hopefully gave no indication of what she was really thinking, which was that she was screwed. Guy was serious competition. Her hopes for getting that promotion grew ever dimmer.

"Thanks for letting me borrow your computer," Guy said.

"No problem."

"Today's May 9th," said Herman. "I don't need to submit my final decision until Friday, May 24th."

"Is that the deadline from Blanchet Maison?" Hannah asked.

"No, they wanted my decision ages ago. But what are they going to do? Fire me?" Herman scoffed. "I swear those franchise executives live to harass us. You should see my inbox. It's full of spam from the Local Flavors team. Delete. Delete. Delete." He pounded the table with his index finger. "Telling them on the 24th is plenty of time. I'll submit my recommendation, and the suits running the Local Flavors portfolio will rubber-stamp it, especially now that I can prove I considered two candidates. It shouldn't be too complicated. That'll give me a couple of weeks to train Hannah before I retire on June 10th. The following day Nancy and I are leaving for Vegas." Herman leaned back in his chair and laced his fingers behind his head. "Boy, am I looking forward to those buffets. I heard you can even get prime rib."

"What if they reject your choice?" Guy asked.

Herman widened his eyes. "They wouldn't dare. That's not how this arrangement works."

"Why?" Guy asked. "Blanchet Maison is a billion-dollar corporation. Choosing the next general manager is a big decision. Why are they giving you so much power?"

Herman leaned back in his chair. "Because I've been working here since 1977 and running the place for most of that time. Nobody knows more about Seaside Resort than me."

Hannah coughed gently, catching their attention. "And also because the Local Flavors structure allows us to operate as independent contractors under the umbrella of the brand," said Hannah. "Except for a link from the national website, and help with HR and accounting, they leave us to our own devices."

"Don't forget about them making us brag about Mr. Winter Olympics." Herman pantomimed cross-country skiing and shooting a rifle.

"That's right." Hannah chuckled. "I take back what I said about Blanchet Maison being hands-off. They made us post a picture of Gabe Blanchet in his Team USA Biathlon uniform for thirty years."

Herman nodded. "I finally took it down after the last audit. It's in the storage shed so we can pop it back up for the next one."

Guy leaned forward. "So if corporate doesn't do anything for us, why not be our own hotel again?"

"Because someone would have to buy it back from Blanchet Maison, and who could afford to do that?" Hannah asked.

"They leech off of us," said Herman. "They're New York vampires."

"Blanchet Maison won't even retweet something from our Twitter account, or like a post we tag them in on through Instagram," said Hannah, feeling riled up. "It's like we're invisible unless they want to suck money from us."

"That must be frustrating." Guy put the thumb drive in his pocket. "You work hard on our social media feeds, and it shows."

"Thanks," said Hannah.

"They'd be better if we had a Seahawk staying here." Herman knocked on the conference table. "That's one helluva goal, Guy."

"It's one that's achievable." Guy sat straight. "It'll just take the right approach."

"I'm sure Hannah will accomplish it, too, especially with you here helping." Herman gave him a thumbs up. "Well, the next step is to run both of your pointer presentations past my panel of experts."

"Your panel of what?" Hannah asked.

"Longtime employees," said Herman. "And Nancy. That way I can also show corporate that I used a committee approach."

"But then everyone will know I didn't get the job," Guy exclaimed.

"Why should you care about that?" Hannah asked. "I thought you didn't want the promotion?"

"I don't. But I don't want to look like a loser."

"Don't worry about that." Herman chuckled. "I'm going to show the presentations without names attached. That way, people can decide based on content. What did the lady from HR call it? A duck blind, or something? Anyhow, once I strip the names off the PFDs, it'll be fair and square."

"Oh," said Guy. "Okay. I only know a few people in town, but I don't want them to think I'm a failure. I'll make sure my name isn't on the PDF file of my slides before I send it to you."

"Thanks." Herman stood. "I appreciate that. We're done here for now." He pushed in his chair. "Oh, say, Hannah, I walked by Strawberry Cottage the other day and it looks like you, Cheryl, and Mary are all settled in."

"We are. Thanks." Hannah unplugged her computer from the projector. "But I realize this is only temporary. I've put in applications for two apartments already, and Mary is looking at a third one tomorrow."

"That's good," said Herman. "In the meantime, you need to get rid of those pots you have on the porch."

"My tomato plants?"

"I don't care what's growing in them—they look tacky."

"But there are strawberries, too," said Hannah. "I mean... okay. I'm so sorry. I'll get rid of them right away."

"Strawberry plants are fitting." Guy stood too, and looked directly at Herman. "Don't you think?"

"Maybe, but none of the other cottages have plants growing in front of them like that," said Herman.

"That could be an idea worth considering," said Guy. "Farm-to-table is huge right now."

"That's a good point." Herman slapped Guy on the back. "But for now, dump 'em. Those pots look cheap. Where'd you find them in the first place? The Goodwill?"

"Yes." Hannah's cheeks turned pink again. "I'm so sorry. I'll remove them right away."

"That's my Hannah." Herman squeezed her shoulder. "I better go. Nancy and I are looking at an RV she found on Craigslist today. Retirement's only thirty-three days away!" Smiling, he charged out of the Vista Room, letting the door swing shut with a thump behind him.

"I'm sorry," said Guy.

"Why are you apologizing?" Hannah clutched her laptop under her arm.

"Because that was unfair."

"Which part? The part where he patronized me, or the part where he shamed me for thrifting?"

"He didn't shame you," said Guy.

"Of course he did, which is rich, considering..." She shook her head and walked to the door.

"Considering what?" Guy followed her.

Hannah spun on her heel to face him. "Considering Gran worked here for fifty years with no healthcare and barely any wage increases. She started at minimum wage and only bumped up a couple dollars higher than that, yet she was the most reliable staff member on the property. The only two days of work she missed were my dad's memorial service and a court appearance when the judge granted her custody of Mary and me. That's it. So excuse me if her garden grows in second-hand pottery." Hannah covered her face with her hand for a few seconds before letting it slip away. "Sorry. I didn't mean that outburst."

"I think you did. I wish there was something I could say that would help. It sounds like Blanchet Maison really screwed her over."

"I didn't mean to say anything negative about working here. This is one of the best employers in town, and I have no complaints." Hannah lifted her chin. "Zero. Especially now, given our emergency housing situation. I'll text Mary. I bet she can give the plants away on her Buy Nothing group within a few hours."

"Wait," said Guy. "I'll take them. I have a balcony at my apartment. I can plant-sit for you until you're in a permanent place, and then I'll give them back."

"What if our next home doesn't have a place for plants?"

"Then I'll keep them. I've always wanted to grow tomatoes. I was thinking about buying some anyway."

"Okay." Hannah pulled a lock of hair behind her ear. "Great. Thanks. I... ah... just need to explain to Gran, and then you can take them."

"I'll take good care of them for her. I promise."

"I thought you said you'd never grown tomatoes before?"

"That's true, but I'll do my best. Maybe you could give me some pointers?" Guy tilted his head to the side and grinned. "I'm not asking you to make a... what did Herman call it? A Point Power presentation for me, but..."

Hannah laughed. "Come over before you go home tonight and I'll help you load them into your car and give you watering instructions."

"Will do."

"Your presentation was good. Nice job."

"Thanks. I enjoyed yours as well."

"Now it's the same old, same old," said Hannah as she opened the door. "Wealthier, more powerful people than us, deciding our fates."

"Ah... right."

Hannah realized too late that she'd put her foot in her mouth. "Sorry, I forgot you went to Dartmouth. Ignore what I just said."

"Not everyone who goes to Dartmouth is rich. Half the brothers in my fraternity house had part-time jobs, and almost everyone had some type of financial aid."

"Oh."

"That's not to say that wealth and privilege don't help some people access college."

Hannah sighed, knowing how true that was. "Did you catch when Herman called our work PFDs?" she asked, feeling a bit wicked. "If the promotion doesn't work out, at least we can use our presentations as personal flotation devices."

"Yeah." Guy fished the thumb drive out of his pocket. "This PFD is a lifesaver."

FIFTEEN

As soon as she left the Vista Room, Hannah headed to the lodge, where she was due for a shift at the front desk. With each step, her mind raced. It wasn't about the tomato plants. For the first time, Hannah considered the possibility that Herman's plan might not work, and Blanchet Maison might give the promotion to someone else instead of her. Even Guy seemed like a possibility. He had that Ivy League diploma, after all. Plus, he was smart, charming, forward-thinking, and—darn it! *So good-looking.* She could absolutely see him leading Seaside Resort into the next era. But if Hannah didn't get the promotion, what did that mean for her career? She didn't want to be assistant manager forever. She was ready for the next step. But leave Seaside Resort? That was unthinkable! Still, she *had* to consider it. She had to claw her way higher, or else the Turner women would be stuck in financial insecurity forever, and Hannah refused to allow that to happen.

Hannah opened the back door to the lodge and entered through the administration office. She left her computer on her desk and walked through the hall to the lobby.

"Hi, Will," she said as she took her spot beside him. It was mid-morning, and they still had an hour before final checkout. "Has it been busy?"

Will shook his head. "Not really, which is a bummer."

Hannah made a face. "Yikes. Prepare to be slammed, huh?"

"Yup. Everyone's going to check out at once." He stepped out from behind the desk and helped himself to a cup of coffee. "How'd your presentation go? Jasmine said something about you trying to convince Herman that we should add more EV charging stations to the parking lot. Then Lark mentioned she saw a glimpse of your PowerPoint as she was bringing fresh linens. Do you think Herman will go for it?"

"It's hard to say."

"I hope he approves. The more charging stations the better. We should add solar panels while we're at it."

"Exactly. With the amount of solar exposure we have, our roofs would be perfect for panels." Hannah smiled. It felt good knowing that Will agreed with her. Hopefully, he was one of the trusted employees Herman sought for feedback.

"There might be a tax credit to help pay for those upgrades," said Will. "At the very least, it would be great PR for our website." Will set down his coffee and opened his textbook. "I'm taking a class about renewable energy right now for one of my science credits."

"If I'd known that, I would have asked for your help with my presentation." Hannah grinned. The phone rang, and she answered it. A guest wanted assistance making reservations at The Summer Wind. After logging that into the system, Hannah took out one of the complimentary maps they gave guests and spread it out in front of her.

She'd inspected it a thousand times before, but never with the intention of looking for other places on the Olympic Peninsula where she might want to seek employment.

Lake Chelan in Eastern Washington and Coeur d'Alene in Idaho had hospitality jobs that intrigued her, but they would mean ripping Cheryl away from her community to start over, or else leaving her here with Mary, and then they'd have two households to pay for when they could barely afford one. Hannah sighed, not liking either option. Seattle, Spokane, Tacoma, and Olympia had potential opportunities. But Hannah didn't like the idea of living in a big city. Here in Sand Dollar Cove, everyone knew everyone. Then there was Olympic National Park. Lake Crescent Lodge, Lake Quinault Lodge, Sol Duc Hot Springs Resort, and Kalaloch Lodge all had potential. Or, outside of the national park, there were also casinos and hotels. Nothing would feel like home like Seaside Resort did, but there were opportunities for her, although limited. Perhaps it was time to brush off her resume.

"Hannah," said a raspy voice. "Glad I found you. I've got great news."

Looking up from the map, Hannah saw Nick wearing a flannel and cargo pants, along with a tool belt slung around his waist. He chewed on a toothpick and spoke without removing it from his mouth. Nick was talented that way.

"What's up?" Hannah still hadn't forgiven him for leaving her and Mary to deal with the rat-infested mattress on their own.

"One of my crabbing buddies mentioned his brother moved here from Aberdeen last year."

"Fascinating." Hannah's brain jumped to alert. Aberdeen was a depressed sawmill town where her mother lived, drowning in drugs and alcohol. The last time Hannah had seen Kelly was two years ago, when she and Mary had driven to Aberdeen to deliver Christmas presents to their mom. Kelly had taken the presents, and had also helped herself to Hannah's credit cards. By the time they'd driven home, Kelly had racked up over $2,000 in charges. The bank issued a fraud hold, thank goodness, so Hannah wasn't out of any money. But she did face the humiliation of explaining to the fraud investigator that her own mother was to blame. Hannah knew that addiction was a disease, and on some level she had compassion for Kelly, but not much.

"Ken," said Nick. "That's my friend's brother's name. He's the apartment manager at a complex on the edge of town, and there's a one-bedroom for rent on the ground floor."

"Really?" Hannah folded the map and pushed it away.

"No stairs." Nick grinned. "And plenty of handicap parking. I asked."

"It's called accessible parking now," Will interrupted.

"That's right," said Hannah. "And accessible parking is important for Gran."

"I was thinking that, too," said Nick. "I told my friend Brad about Cheryl's hunchback."

Hannah bristled. But she was too desperate for a housing lead to risk a confrontation. "Did your friend say how much the rent was?"

"One thousand four hundred dollars a month, utilities included."

"Yes!" Hannah shot her arms up in the air like she was cheering at a football game.

"I knew you'd be excited." Nick beamed. "I've known Cheryl for twenty years. It kills me seeing you guys struggle." He fished a crumpled paper from one of his front pockets and handed it to her. "This is the number to call. Tell him I sent you. No, wait! Tell him Brad sent you. That's my crabbing buddy. Brad is Ken's brother."

"Brad..." The name rang a bell. Hannah looked at Nick's scrawling handwriting and then up at him. "Brad from the Sand Dollar Inn?"

Nick nodded. "That's him. The spot along their shoreline is some of the best places to drop pots."

"It's true," said Will. "My dad crabs there, too."

"Anyhow," Nick continued. "Fourteen hundred dollars a

month for a good-sized one-bedroom. That's what Brad said Ken has available. I told Brad to tell Ken that you'd be the perfect tenants."

Hannah smiled. *Small-town connections for the win.* "Thank you so much," she said. "I thought you were coming to talk to me about the rusty hinge on the sign over the driveway, but this is so much better. I'll call Ken right away."

"Do that. And good luck." Nick tipped an imaginary hat to her and walked away.

Hannah just barely had time to call Ken and schedule an appointment to look at the apartment the following morning when the checkout rush began. For the next hour and a half, she checked out one guest after another. By eleven, the line of guests became so long that Hannah and Will barely had time to breathe, let alone chat about the future.

"I hope your stay this time was just as enjoyable as your last visit," Hannah said as she assisted Mr. and Mrs. Sanchez.

"It was incredible." Mrs. Sanchez deposited her keycard into the receptacle. "I'd say it was even better than last time, since we brought the Darios with us. Have they checked out yet?"

"Not yet." Hannah clicked the print button and waited for the receipt to print out.

"I'm not surprised." Mrs. Sanchez chuckled. "I love Elena, but she does tend to run a few minutes late."

"I'm here. I'm here!" called a voice from the back of the line. Mrs. Dario waved. "And I heard what you said about running late, Brenda. I'd rather be five minutes late than fifteen minutes early."

Mrs. Sanchez winked at Hannah. "That's why when we go to New York, I'm setting her watch back ten minutes when she's not looking."

"Split the difference," Hannah whispered. "Smart." In her peripheral vision she saw Guy enter the lobby and approach

Mrs. Dario at the end of the line. He presented her with two soup cans, and she hugged him. Hannah took Mrs. Sanchez's receipt out of the printer and gave it to her. "Thanks for staying with us. I hope you come back soon."

"Vicente and I are already talking about dates for next summer." Mrs. Sanchez put the receipt in her purse. She stepped out of the line and walked up to Guy to say goodbye.

Hannah moved on to helping the next customer, trying to ignore her pang of jealousy at how well Guy connected with guests.

What would happen if she didn't get the job? Would she stay put, living in the sweet new apartment they would hope-fully get tomorrow? Or would she spread her wings and search for a way to expand her career someplace else?

All day long, Hannah weighed the possibilities, even though the thought of leaving Sand Dollar Cove terrified her. When she updated the budget for landscaping costs, she pictured what it might be like to move to Seattle. When she ate a sandwich on the beach during a quick lunch break, she gazed at the ocean and pondered what life might be like in the arid climate of Lake Chelan. But it was on her evening drive to pick Cheryl up from the senior center that she solidified her thinking.

This decision wasn't just about her being too chicken to leave town; it was also about Sand Dollar Cove being her grand-mother's home. Cheryl had lived here since 1961. She was nineteen years old when her family moved here from Nevada. Hannah and Mary could pack up and start over without too much heartbreak, but for Cheryl, moving away from her community would be devastating.

Hannah parked the car in front of the Sand Dollar Cove Senior Center and took Cheryl's disabled persons placard out of her glove compartment and put it on the dash. There was a wheelchair-friendly ramp from the sidewalk to the front door.

Once a roller rink, the senior center was now a popular hub

for retirees on a fixed income. For the bargain price of $200 a month, Cheryl got unlimited access to the facility, and three meals a day, Monday through Friday. She could also take home a box of pantry goods for the weekend. Besides Keith, the director, there was also a social worker who came a few times a month to connect seniors with services, a nutritionist for the diabetics, and a mobile health clinic that parked in front once a month. Without the senior center, Cheryl would be stuck at home all day with nothing to do but watch TV. She couldn't turn her head to look behind her, which meant she could no longer drive.

Opening the door to the center, Hannah smelled the delicious aroma of chicken-fried steak. She walked past card tables spread out with puzzles and craft projects to the dining room, where Cheryl sat at a table with her friends, Don and Patti. All three laughed as Don told a story.

"And so I said, 'Gary, if you're serious about improving your marriage, maybe you should try turning your hearing aid on once in a while!'"

"Did he take your advice?" Cheryl asked.

Don shook his head. "Nope. Gary said to me: 'Don, this off switch is the only thing standing between me and divorce. I don't want to mess with things now.'"

Cheryl and Patti both laughed even harder, and Hannah chuckled, too. She sat at the empty seat at the table.

"Who said you could sit here?" Patti asked. "I demand to see your senior citizens' discount card."

"She showed it to you a minute ago and you've already forgotten," said Cheryl.

"Har, har," said Patti. "It's my husband who has dementia, not me." She opened her arms wide. "What, no hug for your Aunt Patti?"

"My apologies." Hannah jumped up and embraced her. She'd known Patti since she was little. Don, however, was a recent addition to Cheryl's circle of friends. They'd only met last year when Don moved to Sand Dollar Cove after his wife died of cancer.

"I'm almost done with my green beans, and then we can go," said Cheryl. "Sorry I'm not ready. I've been talking too much, I guess."

"It's my fault," said Don. "I won't shut up, and then she's bound by social conventions to respond."

"That's right." Cheryl giggled. "You're a real blabbermouth."

"We're just glad to have some male company at our table." Patti discreetly pointed to a table in the corner full of women. "The Diabetes Sisters want you for their table, but we fight them off."

"I've got a mean right hook." Cheryl punched her arm and then picked up her fork to scoop up the last bite of beans.

"I am grateful for your protection," said Don. "The one and only time I sat with them, they kept asking me about my blood sugar." He shuddered. "None of them believed me when I shared about my fear of needles."

"They think they're hot stuff because of the attention they get from the nutritionist and their special meals." Patti sliced into her meat. "But look who's eating chicken-fried steak, and who's suffering through tilapia."

"It's true," said Cheryl. "This is where the cool kids sit."

Hannah's stomach rumbled. She hadn't eaten dinner yet, and the meal looked good. The chicken-fried steak, that is, not the fish. Hopefully Mary was cooking a box of macaroni and cheese for them to eat when she got home.

"Don't let me rush you," Hannah said. "But I'll get your chair set up, so it'll be ready."

"I'll be fine with my walker." Cheryl blotted her mouth with a napkin.

"I know," said Hannah. "But once we get to Seaside Resort, that path up to Strawberry Cottage is steep."

"I said I'll be fine," said Cheryl, in an unusually stern tone. She looked quickly at Don. "I worked on my feet my whole life. A little walk will do me good."

"That's the spirit," said Don.

"Okay then," said Hannah. "I'll go put your chair in the car." She didn't want to correct her grandma in front of her friends, but there was no way that it was safe for Cheryl to walk all the way up from the Seaside Resort parking lot to the cottage. Sure, she could manage the walk from here to the car, especially since she was parked in one of the accessible spots, but once they reached the resort, Hannah would have to insist on the wheelchair.

"Here, let me help you with that," said Keith as Hannah lifted the collapsed chair. "It's heavier than it looks."

"It sure is," said Hannah, grateful for the help. "I probably should have opened it up and rolled it."

Keith was in his mid-thirties and had worked at the senior center for several years, first as one of the community social workers, and then as the full-time director. Casually dressed in jeans and a long-sleeved Henley, Keith wore wire-rimmed glasses that gave him a studious look. Hannah was wary of him. She hadn't forgotten the stern talking-to he'd given her the morning after the flood, as if she'd negligently put her grandma in danger. Still, the hotel vouchers Keith had provided had helped, Hannah was forced to admit.

"Cheryl said the three of you are living at the resort." Keith held the door open as they carried the chair outside.

"That's right. Only temporarily, though. I've got a great lead on an apartment I'm looking at tomorrow." Hannah took out her keys. "Let me open the trunk."

Keith carried the chair the rest of the way by himself and loaded it into the back of Hannah's Civic. "The way Cheryl tells it, you're not just staying at Seaside Resort, you're living in the very best room."

"Hardly. It has the best view, that's true, but right now there's a hodgepodge of used furniture my sister found in a Buy Nothing group. It's safe, though," she added, worried about what Keith might think. "Gran has a roof over her head, a working bathroom, and a kitchenette."

"That's great." Keith closed the trunk.

Hannah almost didn't hear what he said next. She was thinking about how she'd tell her grandma about Herman insisting on giving her plants away.

"I didn't want to say anything that might get Cheryl's hopes up, but I might have a lead for you on a housing situation if that rental you're looking at tomorrow doesn't work out."

"What?" Hannah looked at him. "Really?"

"It's a four-bedroom house, three thousand square feet, with a hot tub, by the golf course."

"Wow. That sounds spectacular, but it's probably out of our price range."

"You said fourteen hundred a month, right?"

"Yeah, but no way would a house like that rent for so little." Keith's dad had been her pre-Calculus teacher in high school. Why was he so bad at basic math?

"This place might rent for less than that."

"How?"

Keith glanced back at the senior center for a moment before returning his eyes to her. "It wouldn't be the entire house. It would be a shared housing situation."

Oh gosh. Keith wasn't offering for them to move in with him, was he? Because there was no way that would happen.

"You know how we have a dietitian for our clients with diabetes?" he asked.

Hannah nodded. "Yeah. Gran's mentioned that."

"Well, Brittany, that's her name. Brittany just went through a messy divorce." His ears turned red. "He was a real loser, if you ask me, and I think she could do way better."

Better like Keith, Hannah figured, with an internal sigh of relief. She could see where this was going now.

"I don't want to share confidential details, but suffice to say Brittany kept the house, and now that she faces paying the mortgage on her own, it's a challenge. I told her I knew the perfect renters for her that could help with that. There's a ground-floor bedroom that would be just right for Cheryl."

"You've seen the inside of her house, I take it?"

Keith's ears burned even redder. "Yes. Quite a few times, actually."

"Is Brittany really on board with the shared housing idea, or did you talk her into it on our behalf?"

"No. She likes the idea, too. Originally she was considering renting out rooms through Airbnb, but the thought of a steady stream of strangers coming into her home made her nervous."

"I can imagine."

Keith pulled a piece of paper out of his pocket. "This is her number, if you're interested."

"Is she allergic to cats?" Hannah asked, thinking of Ferdinand.

"No, she loves cats."

"Well, great then. Thanks. At this point, I'm exploring all options."

"The housing market is brutal right now."

"It's not making it easy for renters, that's for sure."

"As I said, I won't mention the idea of renting from Brittany to Cheryl because I don't want to get her hopes up," said Keith. "And also because the seniors love to gossip. Brittany and I can't stand next to each other without them naming our future children."

"Ha! Mum's the word." Hannah walked back to the building and opened the door, as Keith followed her.

Inside the senior center, Don was pulling out Cheryl's chair for her and helping transfer her to her walker.

"See you tomorrow, dollface," Don said, as he waved goodbye.

"Get ready for me to beat you at gin rummy," said Cheryl. "It'll be a death match."

Hannah thought about Keith's suggestions as she helped her grandma to the car. Was shared housing an idea worth considering? It had only been a week and a half of searching for a new apartment. They weren't ready to give up on finding their own place yet, were they? Hannah bit the inside of her cheek on purpose before releasing the pressure. She'd talk about this with Mary, that's what she'd do. Mary would have a strong opinion on it one way or another. Her sister might be younger than her, but she deserved an equal vote.

"Why are you so quiet?" Cheryl asked ten minutes later, when they were on the drive home.

"It's been a long day," Hannah answered, not wanting to worry her.

"How did your presentation go with Herman?"

"Well, I think."

"Good, but watch your back. Herman's a chauvinistic pig."

"Gran!" Hannah took her eyes off the road and looked right into her grandmother's eyes, shocked that she'd say something so negative about her former boss.

"What?" Cheryl braced herself against the dashboard. She was so hunched over that car rides were difficult. "At least I didn't say asshole."

"Herman does let male employees get away with things that I think should be dealt with." Hannah thought about Nick's shoddy work leading the maintenance department. "But I've known Herman almost my whole life. I'm hoping that familiarity gives me an edge."

"You mean nepotism?"

"Well, yeah. Kind of. Although I'm not related to Herman, so I'm not sure the word applies."

"But the principle still stands. I'm telling you, I've known Herman even longer, and if it comes down to nepotism or the old boys' club, he'll pick the old boys' club every time."

Did that mean Guy? Was Guy part of the old boys' club? Hannah pulled through the gates of the resort, slowing her speed to five miles per hour. Wild roses, budding but not yet blooming, grew along both sides of the road. "Where does that leave me, in terms of my career?" she asked. "I'll never be part of the old boys' club."

"I don't know," said Cheryl. "But I'd hate to see you stuck at a low-paying job your whole life, like I was. You've got the brains and the degree to do whatever you want."

"But this is what I want." Hannah parked the car. "I love Seaside Resort. It's my second home. I want to shepherd it into the future."

Cheryl turned her neck to look at Hannah and grimaced from the pain of moving. "My advice is, don't let Herman get in your way."

"You mean knock him off? Hire a hit man? I'm not sure that's in the budget."

"No, silly. Herman's a numbskull, but he doesn't deserve to die. I mean, go over his head. Contact someone at Blanchet Maison and convince them, not Herman, why you are the perfect person for the job."

"Herman would go ballistic if I did that. And I don't think it's needed. Herman's trying to *help* me get the promotion, not torpedo me."

"Consider it a tool of last resort."

"I don't want to have to break the rules."

"Bend them," Cheryl corrected.

"Bend them, then. I want to win that promotion fair and square, because I'm the right person for the job."

Cheryl patted Hannah's hand. "Sweetie, one thing I've learned playing cards is that if the deck is stacked against you there is no way to win."

Worry pierced her heart. "Do you think the deck is stacked against me here?"

Cheryl paused a moment before answering. "I can't say for sure. But take me as an example. Yes, I only had a high school diploma, but I'm a fast learner. Herman has his associate's degree from the community college. That's not much more education than me. So how come he rose through the ranks to general manager, and I tapped out as head of housekeeping?"

Computer skills? Hannah wanted to say. Her grandma could barely work the remote control. But then again, Herman wasn't so slick with technology either. "Who put Herman in charge in the first place?" she asked instead.

"That would be the former owner of Seaside Resort, a man by the name of Oscar Lexter. He's the one who started Herman's poker group, back in the day."

"Wow. Did you know Oscar?"

"He hired me. Pinched my butt every time I walked past him."

"That's sexual harassment!"

"No kidding." Cheryl sighed. "I'm pretty sure he was screwing the architect, too. Not that she didn't deserve the commission. As for me, I was a widowed mom and didn't have many options, so I stuck with the job so I could provide a stable life for your dad." She squeezed Hannah's hand. "He'd be proud of you, Miss College Graduate."

"Thanks."

"Never forget that you're smarter than Herman. You're worth two of him put together."

"Gran, about Herman. There's something I need to tell you... It's about your plants."

Oh boy, Hannah thought, *Here goes...*

SIXTEEN

"Hannah? Are you alright in there?" Mary asked.

The only privacy Strawberry Cottage afforded was the bathroom, but even that was limited. "I'm fine." Hannah washed her hands and dried them on the towel. She'd just barely gotten home after retrieving Cheryl from the senior center.

"Someone knocked, and I think it's Guy," said Mary. "But I won't let him in yet if you're having bathroom drama."

Hannah opened the bathroom door. "I'm one hundred percent drama-free."

Cheryl snorted. "The Turner family has *never* been drama-free." She rose unsteadily to her feet. "Time to put on my detective cap again."

"Gran," Hannah said quickly. "Let's drop this postcard thing, okay? Those were probably brochures, and I misinterpreted what I saw."

"That's right," said Mary. "It makes the most sense."

"I'll be the judge of that." Cheryl shuffled to the entryway and opened the door for Guy. "Hello, there. Are you here to rescue my plants?"

Guy stood on the porch holding a reusable shopping bag of something that smelled delicious, even from where Hannah was standing on the other side of the room. "It remains to be seen if I save your plants or kill them. I have no idea if my thumbs are green or black." He lifted the bag. "But I do come bearing a lentil, beet, and goat cheese salad."

"That sounds fancy." Cheryl opened the door wider. "Come on in."

"Hi, Guy." Mary smiled girlishly. "Nice to see you again, as always."

"Thanks for bringing food." Hannah walked to the kitchenette and took out some plates and silverware.

"It's the least I could do, since you're bestowing upon me your upcoming tomato harvest." Guy took out several containers from the bag and set them on the bamboo table.

"Don't plan on making salsa just yet," said Cheryl, and she crept back to her recliner. "It all depends on how much sunshine we get this summer."

"Lark warned me that tomatoes can be finicky," said Guy.

"You're friends with Lark?" Cheryl asked. "She was my favorite trainee."

"Yeah. She's my neighbor." Guy folded the bag and looked around the freshly decorated cottage. "Wow. This place looks incredible."

"You haven't seen the inside since Mary fixed it up?" Cheryl asked.

"No, ma'am, I haven't." Guy peered down at the floor. "Is this that floor stencil you were telling me about, Mary? You tried to describe it to me, but I couldn't quite picture what it would look like."

"It looks like an expensive rug," said Cheryl, "but doesn't trip me up. Mary's a master of things like this. That girl could bedazzle a turd."

"Gran!" Hannah cringed as she undid a container lid.

"Don't gross Guy out. He's not used to your humor." But then she bragged about her sister, too. "I thought it was a waste of time when Mary was working on it, but I have to admit it brightens up the place. She saved leftover paint from going to the dump, too."

"Ecology should always be a part of home design." Mary smiled happily.

The floor wasn't the only transformation. Mary had removed peeling wallpaper and freshened the walls with crisp white paint. Hannah had sprinkled the used pink recliner and sofa bed with baking soda, let it sit for a few hours, and vacuumed all the upholstery to rid it of the stale scent of cigarettes. Patti had given them an embroidered tablecloth for the kitchenette table, and a flowered teakettle sat on the stove. Except for the storage boxes in the corner, the whole cottage had a homey feel, even if it was no longer the glamorous place it had once been.

"This place is as pretty as a postcard," Cheryl said, looking Guy dead in the eye. "Don't you think?"

"Yeah." Guy nodded genially. "It sure is."

"Seaside Resort used to sell postcards," Cheryl continued. "Twenty or thirty years ago, but I haven't seen one of those cards in ages. Have you?" She looked at Guy.

"Guy's only worked here a few months," Mary said, coming to Guy's rescue.

"That's right," he said apologetically. "I'm not very familiar with the souvenir merchandise."

Hannah knew she needed to act fast to stop Cheryl from giving Guy the third degree. "Have some food, Gran," she said, bringing a container of salad and a fork over to her grandma.

"That looks yummy, but I already ate at the senior center," said Cheryl.

"Leafy green vegetables?" Guy asked.

"No." Cheryl picked up the fork. "Chicken-fried steak. I guess a few bites of salad wouldn't hurt."

Ferdinand zipped up against Guy's pant leg, slinked next to the fabric, and then raced behind the couch in a blur of black fur.

"Where do you all sleep?" Guy asked. "I don't see any beds."

"I sleep in my recliner," said Cheryl. "The girls share the hide-a-bed."

"It won't be forever," said Hannah. "I have a strong lead on an apartment I'm looking at tomorrow."

"Yeah." Mary held out her left hand and gazed at her finger-tips. "And my boyfriend Aidan is coming home in a few weeks and is about to propose."

"You're not intending on getting married right away, are you?" Hannah asked, worried that Mary might become so consumed by wedding planning that she'd let her coursework slide and not finish her degree. She'd always been a dreamer like that.

"I don't know." Mary lowered her hand. "Aidan still lives at home, technically, even though as a traveling nurse he's rarely in town. So I guess we'll need to figure out housing and the wedding date together. But that should be easy. Aidan's been saving for a down payment. Maybe we'll buy a house and you two can move in with us."

"Move in with lovebirds?" Cheryl wrinkled her nose. "No thank you." She looked at Guy. "This salad is delicious, by the way. Thank you so much for bringing it."

Hearing Cheryl mention dinner made Hannah hungry. She wasn't sure if she should start eating now or after Guy left. "Have you already eaten?" she asked him.

"Yes. I remembered that Strawberry Cottage was low on silverware and figured I should eat at home, so I didn't have to scoop salad with a spoon."

"Would you mind taking my plate, Mary?" Cheryl asked. "I need to use the little girl's room." She pushed on the recliner arm with her free hand and struggled to her feet.

"Here, Gran. I'll help." Hannah pushed the wheelchair over.

"Where's my walker?" Gran asked. "The wheelchair won't fit in the bathroom."

"It's in the car." Hannah pushed the wheelchair out of the way. "I'll go get it."

"No rush," said Cheryl. "I can still walk."

But seeing Gran shuffle forward made Hannah nervous. She picked up her purse and hunted for her car keys. "I'll go grab the walker for you so it'll be ready if you need it later."

"I'll come with you," said Guy. "I'll bring the first load of plants." He opened the door for Hannah.

"Take your time." Cheryl was halfway to the bathroom. "I don't really need that thing, anyway."

Hannah locked eyes with Mary and sent her a secret message to keep watch over Cheryl. Mary nodded as if to say she heard that message loud and clear.

Outside on the porch, Guy was inspecting the plants. The pots didn't match, but the eclectic esthetic worked well, in a whimsical way. Strawberry crowns spilled over the edges of their containers, and the tomatoes grew neatly corralled in wire cages. "These will be perfect for my balcony." He lifted the heaviest one. "I just hope I can keep them alive."

"You'll do fine, so long as you water them." Hannah picked up a pot in each arm and headed to the parking lot.

"Is your grandmother seeing a physical therapist for her osteoporosis?" Guy asked.

"No. Is that a thing?"

"Physical therapy for osteoporosis? Yeah. Physical therapists see osteoporosis patients all the time. They work on weight-bearing exercises to increase stability and improve quality of life. I don't want to stick my nose where it doesn't belong, but Cheryl seems like she's unsteady on her feet."

"She is." Hannah shuddered. "One wrong step and she could break a hip. Gran's never mentioned physical therapy before."

"What did her doctor advise?" Guy paused a moment, as he readjusted his grip on the enormous tomato plant. The tomato cage blocked his face and made it difficult for Hannah to read his expression.

"I don't know. Gran never tells us much about her doctor's appointments."

"She doesn't let you go back with her to the exam room?"

"No. The only reason I know her doctor's name is because of the medical paperwork that comes to the house. Gran never liked to go to the doctor to begin with, but eventually her back got so bad that she had to go. She's on medication, but she complains about the side effects so much that I'm not sure she's reliable about taking it."

"Oh boy. Well, physical therapy could still help, otherwise it becomes a vicious circle."

"What do you mean?"

"The more she sits, the weaker her muscles become. Increased atrophy contributes to instability, which will make her want to sit even more. If she gets to where she can't walk to the bathroom or rise from her chair, that would decrease her quality of life."

"You're right." Hannah set down the two tomato plants, even though they weren't at the parking lot yet. She wiped sweat off her forehead with the back of her hand. In retrospect, she wished she had only picked up one plant, because now she was melting into a sweaty mess. But the conversation about Cheryl worried her. She knew Cheryl needed help, but her grandmother was too proud to accept it. "Mary and I have talked to Gran about moving more, but she always says that after fifty years of working on her feet, she's earned the right to sit down."

"There are exercises she could do sitting that I'm sure a physical therapist could teach her, and Medicare should cover the appointments." Guy held onto his enormous pot with one arm, swooped down to pick up one of Hannah's, wedged it under his elbow, and put both hands back on the larger pot, impressing Hannah with his nimbleness.

"You don't have to do that," Hannah protested. "I can carry both of them."

"It's no big deal."

Hannah picked up her remaining pot and kept walking to the parking lot, which was in sight.

"There are two physical therapy clinics in Sand Dollar Cove," Guy said, as he followed her. "But one of them focuses on hands, so really there's only one choice, unless you drive further into the county."

"How do you know so much about this?"

"I'm a personal trainer. It's a related field." Guy stopped behind his SUV, set down one pot, and opened the back. He pushed his two pots into the back of the cargo area and then took the pot that Hannah held and stowed it, too. But instead of closing the hatch after that, as she expected, Guy sat on the edge of his car like he was waiting for her to join him.

Hannah thought about walking straight to her car to retrieve the walker, but the opportunity to hang out with Guy was too tempting to pass up. She sat down next to him, her feet dangling. "You know," she said, "it just occurred to me that since you're a personal trainer, Gran might listen to you more than me about her health. Would you mind asking my grandma if the doctor has suggested physical therapy? She might be more receptive hearing it from you." *Even though she thinks you're a postcard thief.* "Gran doesn't like Mary or I worrying about her health. But maybe if you lead with your personal trainer background, that would convince her. Would you try?"

"Absolutely. I hate seeing people in pain."

"Thanks." Hannah exhaled a deep breath. "This might be the first time I've sat still all day."

"It's been a busy day."

"Sure has. Busy enough that even the parking lot looks inviting."

"I've always thought that the landscaping around the parking lot could use some improvement," said Guy.

"Same. It's the first thing guests see. The rugosa roses are beautiful, but they only bloom in summer. There should be something else here to make people feel like they've arrived."

"You mean, something besides that creaky sign hanging over the driveway?"

Hannah looked over her shoulder at it. "Ugh! Nick still hasn't fixed that thing. It's a safety hazard."

"Hopefully it doesn't fall on someone."

"Yeah. And that sign is only the tip of the iceberg. These empty planters look horrible. We should tear out the weeds and install native plants. Maybe an Oregon grape, or some camas lilies."

"I don't know what those are, but they sound pretty. What does Herman say about it?"

Hannah knit her eyebrows together before responding. "He said there's no room in the landscaping budget for improvements, which is true, because the landscaping budget hasn't been increased in three years, not even for inflation. But he said if I could come up with a way to improve things for free, without using any extra labor resources, I could."

"That sounds like a cop-out answer." Guy leaned back on his hands, and his right arm brushed behind her slightly, making Hannah's heart skip.

"I know," said Hannah, trying to ignore Guy's proximity. "It was also a violation of labor laws because I was working hourly at the time of that conversation. Now I'm on salary, but back then, I wasn't. Managers can't ask employees to work for free. That's against the law."

"Doesn't Blanchet Maison ever come to check up on things?"

"They send a team out to audit us every three years." Hannah stretched out her legs. "It's a nightmare. There's a binder of rules we need to follow to be part of the Local Flavors division, and if we miss one little thing, like housekeeping puts the toiletries on the left side instead of the right side of the sink, they'll ding us."

"Wouldn't it be better to be in the habit of following the binder all along so that the audit goes more smoothly?"

"Do *you* follow your binder?" Hannah asked.

"What binder?"

"You don't know where your Blanchet Maison Local Flavors binder is?"

"Nobody ever gave me one. Herman handed me the keys to the wellness center and said to have at it."

"The previous trainer should have left it for you." Hannah pulled her feet up and leaned against the window.

"The binder was missing by the time I arrived."

"But at least the broken treadmill was gone."

"Broken treadmill?" Guy asked.

"A guest spilled beer all over it, and fried the electrical components."

"Beer in the wellness studio?" Guy palmed his forehead. "Oh, jeez."

"It gets worse. Nick couldn't fix the treadmill."

"Of course he couldn't. Nick couldn't fix a sandwich."

Hannah chuckled. "Nick's smarter than he acts. But he's lazy. Herman miraculously approved the purchase of a new treadmill, finally, but then when it arrived, there was nobody to set it up because Roxanne had already quit. I would have done it myself, but it was too heavy and the old, broken treadmill was still there."

"But that's dangerous. Why didn't maintenance move it out of there?"

"I asked Nick several times, but he never got around to it until 'broken treadmill' showed up six times on our Yelp reviews and I convinced Herman to put pressure on Nick to remove it." Hannah rested her feet on the tailgate and hugged her knees. "Thankfully nobody got hurt."

"Remind me why Nick still works here again?"

"Don't you know?"

Guy inched closer. "No, I honestly don't."

"He's one of Herman's poker buddies. I still think you should have said yes when Herman invited you. That was your engraved invitation to their inner circle."

"Maybe I don't want to be part of their inner circle."

"Then you're even smarter than I thought."

"You think I'm smart?" Guy grinned.

"Of course you're smart, you went to Dartmouth, didn't you?" She looked at him closely. "Although I don't understand why you took a fancy degree like that and became a personal trainer."

Guy's grin disappeared. "Something doesn't add up, right? That's what you're thinking."

"I didn't say that."

"But you thought it." Guy's blue eyes peered at her so intently that it was like he could see straight into her soul. "I had a huge fight with my parents," he whispered. "A massive blowup. I said things that couldn't be unsaid, and so did they."

Whoa! Hannah was shocked. But Guy's admission made sense. "Gosh. I'm sorry." She leaned a little closer. "What was the fight about?"

"Me not being what they wanted. Them not believing in me, ever, no matter how hard I tried, or what I did."

"That's awful. Gran always believes in Mary and me. I could tell her I was going to climb Mount Olympus on my lunch break, and she'd remind me to double-knot my hiking boots."

"You hike?"

"No. But Gran would encourage me if I said I did."

Guy smiled. "She sounds like an excellent parent."

Hannah nodded. "My dad was a great parent too, when he was alive."

"What happened to him?" Quickly, he added: "You don't have to tell me if it's too hard to talk about."

Hannah swept a lock of hair away from her eyes. "He was a private contractor working in Afghanistan. I have pictures of the schools and hospitals he helped build. Or at least I did... The photo albums got all wet." Her heart tugged with sadness. "Thank goodness most of them are backed up on digital."

"That's a relief. But I'm sad to hear that he died in Afghanistan."

Hannah could have let the misunderstanding go, but she knew she needed to correct it. Even if her father died of suicide like the insurance company declared, there was no reason to be ashamed of mental illness. "He didn't die overseas," she said simply. "According to the reports, his truck ran off the road near Blackfish Point. The vehicle ripped into pieces and his body was never found. I was five years old at the time. Some people think he died from depression, but I don't know about that. My dad loved me and Mary, and he was excited to be home on a visit and he was proud of the work he did overseas. He was a hero, no matter how he died."

Hannah's gaze wandered off into the distance as emotions washed over her like waves. "My mom couldn't handle it. She became an alcoholic and almost killed us in a drunk-driving accident. That's when we went to live with Gran. But sometimes I wonder what it would be like if my dad was still alive. If he'd been able to be the father that I know he wanted to be." She stared off without seeing, and lapsed into silence.

"Children deserve good fathers," Guy said after a while. "That's one thing I know for certain."

Hannah nodded. "Oh wow," she said. "The sun's down. Gran's probably wondering where we are." Hannah hopped out of the SUV. "I need to get her walker."

"And I was going to talk to her, delicately, about going to physical therapy." Guy shut the hatch. A minute or two later, when they were walking up the path to the cottages, he asked her a gentle question. "What was your dad's name?"

"Max Turner. Mary looks a bit like him with her blonde hair and brown eyes. Dad took that contractor job because he dreamt of making the world a better place for girls like Mary and me. Building schools so they could get an education."

"Education's important to your family."

"It is, because it's hard to come by. Although at first Mary didn't care about college that much. When she graduated from high school, she drove down to Los Angeles, hoping to become an actress."

"I take it that didn't work out how she would have liked."

"No, unfortunately for her it didn't. But I'm glad for me and Gran because I love having Mary here."

"I like Mary, too. But you're more interesting to talk to."

"I am?" A thrill of delight tickled Hannah's ego.

"Sure, you are." Guy stopped walking and smiled at her mischievously. "You're like a walking encyclopedia of Seaside Resort history. How could I not flock to you like a moth to a flame?"

Was Guy flirting with her? Hannah couldn't tell.

"You make me sound like the Funk & Wagnalls encyclopedias we have in the resort library," she said, taking a step closer.

"You're not *that* ancient."

"I don't have gold lettering on my spine, either," said Hannah.

Guy raised his eyebrows. "That sounds like a wild frat party waiting to happen."

"A frat party where people dress up like encyclopedias?"

"It would be easier that dressing up like Wikipedia."

Hannah laughed. "I suppose you're right."

"Here. Let me get that." Guy took the walker from her. His right hand swung next to hers, but didn't touch. They walked up the sidewalk to Strawberry Cottage in companionable silence, as the solar path lanterns turned on one by one. Neither of them spoke until they reached the porch. "I'll speak with your grandmother about you-know-what," Guy said.

"Thank you." Hannah looked up at him, his face dimly lit by twilight. He smiled and her heart filled with happiness. "I appreciate it."

"My pleasure." Guy set down Cheryl's walker so the wheels touched the ground. "I'll do the talking," he said. "I'll have her convinced of the wonders of PT in no time."

SEVENTEEN

"You should ask Guy out," Mary said, as they worked together to collapse the hide-a-bed the next morning.

"Don't be ridiculous." Hannah picked up a seat cushion and placed it on the couch.

"I'm serious." Mary added another cushion. "I saw the way he was looking at you last night. I think he likes you."

"He's my co-worker."

"So?" Mary put on the final cushion. "Lots of people date their co-workers."

"By the end of summer, I might be his boss."

"But he's so nice."

The toilet flushed in the background. Mary looked over her shoulder to where Cheryl was in the bathroom, door shut. "You saw how great he was with Gran last night. If Guy hadn't asked her about physical therapy, we never would have known that her doctor had been encouraging her to go to PT for years."

"I feel awful," said Hannah. "I wish I had known that the doctor had submitted that referral a long time ago, but that Gran had put it off because she was worried about transportation."

"It's not our fault." Mary artfully arranged the blanket she'd made over the back of the second-hand sofa bed, hiding a tear in the upholstery. "Gran never lets us go back with her to the exam room, so we didn't know what the doctor had recommended until Guy asked."

Hannah sat on the couch. "Still, I feel like I failed her."

"You're not responsible for the whole world. Gran's a grown woman who's capable of making her own decisions." Mary opened the top dresser drawer and took out her makeup bag. The rest of their salvaged belongings were in boxes piled in the corner. Mary walked to the kitchenette and opened a cabinet where she'd hung a mirror, and dabbed foundation onto her already flawless skin. "Back to what I was saying about Guy, maybe you could invite him to the movies. There's a new one playing in town that opens tomorrow night. One of the baristas told me it was good."

"We're looking at another apartment tomorrow night, remember? Fingers crossed that the one I'm viewing this morning works out, but if not..." Hannah collected her shoes from their spot next to the couch, and put them on. "You said you scheduled it with work so you'd have the night off."

"Oh. That's right. The ancient apartment building across from the laundromat."

"It's not ancient. It's from the 1960s. That's the same age as Strawberry Cottage."

Mary raised her perfectly arched eyebrows. "Like I said. Ancient."

"Who's ancient?" The bathroom door opened, and Cheryl emerged, wearing her bathrobe. "You weren't talking about me, were you?"

"Of course not." Hannah opened the closet so that Cheryl could select an outfit. "We were talking about the apartments we're checking out tomorrow night." She looked back at Mary. "There's another option we can consider if we get desperate.

Keith told me about rooms for rent in a shared house he knows about."

"*My* Keith?" Cheryl pushed her walker closer to the closet.

"I didn't realize you'd called dibs on him," said Mary.

"Patti called dibs, which I think is unfair since she's married." Cheryl parked her walker and grabbed the sleeve of a blouse. She raised her arm as far as it would go but couldn't take the hanger off the rod. Just as Hannah was about to help her, Cheryl jerked the fabric and pulled it off the hanger. Hannah stepped back, knowing that her grandma wouldn't want help unless it was absolutely necessary. Proud and resourceful, Cheryl used the same trick to retrieve a pair of slacks. She stashed both garments on the seat of her walker and shuffled to the recliner.

"Do *you* want to call dibs on Keith?" Mary asked Hannah.

"On Keith?" Hannah recoiled. "No way."

"Why not?" Cheryl sat down. "Keith is a catch. He owns his own condo and has a pension plan with the city."

"How do you know about his retirement plan?" Hannah asked.

"Because that's one of the five major topics of conversation at the center." Cheryl untied her bathrobe and unbuttoned her nightshirt. Hannah and Mary turned around to give her privacy. "Retirement, grandkids, health problems, the food, and who's banging who."

"Gran!" Hannah exclaimed. "That can't be true."

"Don gets around," she grumbled. "But he goes for flexible women, so I'm out."

"That sounds like another reason to do physical therapy." Mary zipped up her makeup bag. "You used to be flexible."

"I sure was," said Cheryl. "Not that it did me much good."

Hannah filled the sink with soapy water to wash the cereal bowls. She couldn't remember Cheryl ever dating. Her grandpa had died in the Vietnam War. Cheryl left for Seattle when she was twenty-three years old and came back home at twenty-five with a new last name and one-year-old Max. Luckily, she'd found work at Seaside Resort right away. It had helped that it was the late 1960s and Sand Dollar Cove was booming. There was plenty of work to be found and Cheryl even got away with bringing Max with her when many places frowned on the idea.

"Hey Hannah," said Cheryl. "I think you should call dibs on Keith. I'd love to see you have some fun once in a while."

"I think he's seeing someone," Hannah answered, which seemed kinder than saying she wasn't interested in dating him for a laundry list of reasons, including his autocratic nature and being related to her pre-Calculus teacher.

"Brittany? That's just a rumor. The diabetes club would love that, wouldn't they? They'd lord it over the rest of us if Keith and Brittany were together." Cheryl made a clucking sound with her tongue. "I can only imagine the drama. Would you like me to put a good word in for you with Keith?"

"No, thank you."

"I think Hannah should date Guy instead," said Mary.

"I don't know about that," said Cheryl. "We never figured out that postcard business."

"I was thinking about that some more," said Hannah. In fact, she'd dreamt about it all night. "Maybe I was so stressed out that I mistook a Seaside Resort brochure for a vintage postcard."

"You have been under a lot of stress lately," said Mary.

"Yeah, and last night Guy told me that the main reason he'd moved out here was because he'd gotten in a big fight with his parents and wanted a fresh start. That makes sense, right?"

"I'm not sure Miss Marple or Jessica Fletcher would agree," said Cheryl. "But... I guess it makes sense. Men that good-looking aren't usually mail thieves. Has he asked you out?"

"No, of course not." Hannah plunged the bowls into the soapy water. "We're colleagues, nothing more."

"I don't know about that," said Mary. "I think there might be a spark. He listened to you drone on and on about that book you were reading, even though it sounded boring as hell."

"The life and times of Marion Davies isn't boring." Hannah rinsed a bowl and set it on a towel to air-dry. She'd spent her own time perusing the celebrity memoir section at the library, before she'd figured out the inter-library loan program. "You didn't find the part about diamond bracelets interesting? How her showgirl friends would go out with rich guys from Wall Street and come back with diamonds on their wrists?"

"I still don't know who Marie Davins is," said Mary.

"*Marion Davies*," Hannah corrected. "I thought you'd know about her from living in LA. She was an actress who was most famous for being William Randolph Hearst's mistress."

"His name sounds familiar, but I can't quite place him." Mary brushed her hair.

"Hearst," said Hannah. "The newspaper tycoon?"

"How could anyone make money publishing newspapers?" Mary asked. "I thought they were going bankrupt."

"Now, they are struggling," said Cheryl. "But back when I was your age, people actually read things instead of getting their news from TikTok."

"I don't get my news from TikTok." Mary buckled the ankle straps of her wedge shoes.

"Careful, Gran." Hannah drained the sink. "You're sounding like Herman."

"Heaven forbid," Cheryl harrumphed. "Okay, you two can turn around. I'm decent." She eased herself into her recliner so she could slip on her shoes. Ferdinand jumped onto her lap.

"I'll drop you off at the senior center on my way to campus." Mary unfolded the wheelchair and rolled it to the recliner. She looked back at Hannah. "Unless you want me to ditch school and go with you to look at that apartment you're seeing today?"

"No need." Hannah collected Cheryl's walker and purse. "I can manage."

"If it looks good, take it on the spot," said Mary. "I trust you."

"So do I," said Cheryl. "Although it's been fun bragging to my friends about living in the lap of luxury."

"Lap of something." Hannah picked Ferdinand off Cheryl's lap and moved him to the couch. "I'll go load the car."

"Could you get my messenger bag, too?" Mary asked.

"Sure." Hannah slung it over her shoulder along with her own purse.

"Thanks, girls." Cheryl slowly lowered herself into the wheelchair. "I don't know what I'd do without you."

"The feeling's mutual," said Mary.

Hannah opened the front door so they could exit. As she watched them pass by, she felt her heart squeeze with panic. How could she consider applying for a job outside of Sand Dollar Cove? Sure, a job in Seattle might pay better, but she couldn't leave Cheryl and Mary behind. How would they manage? The three of them were a team. Take one person away from the equation and they'd all fail. What would happen when Mary tied the knot with Aidan? Intuitively, Hannah knew they couldn't afford to become co-dependent, but she had no idea how to change the equation.

First things first, though. She needed to find someplace permanent for them to live. Thank goodness for Nick giving them this tip on an apartment. Sometimes it was all about who you knew.

Hannah arrived at the property twenty minutes later, and was pleased to see that the outside of the building was in good condition. Even better, the ground-floor units were close to the parking lot. It would only be a few steps from the car to the front door. That would be perfect for her grandma.

Hannah collected her purse and her folder of documentation. If this apartment worked out, she'd be ready to apply for it that morning, like Mary had said. The sooner the process got rolling, the better. Her credit was good, because she always made her student loan payments on time, and she had sufficient funds to cover first and last month's rent. She didn't know how she'd manage it, but this time Hannah would find a way to afford renter's insurance, just in case.

The manager's office was on the end unit with a sign in the window. Walking down the sidewalk, Hannah admired the brightly colored geraniums planted along the path. The flowers weren't fancy, but they showed that the complex was well kept. She slid the folder under her arm and knocked on the door.

It swung open twenty seconds later, revealing a middle-aged man. He wore an open Hawaiian shirt over a stained white T-shirt, and tube socks with Crocs. "Right on time. Good for you."

"Thanks," said Hannah. "You must be Ken. Nice to meet you. I'm Hannah Turner." She held out her hand and looked him in the eye.

"Good to meet you too. Brad's told me all about you. His friend Nick says you're the best tenants a landlord could ask for."

"That's right. I pay my rent on time, I keep my porch clean, and I never play loud music."

"The last name 'Turner' sounds familiar. Are you from Aberdeen?"

"No." Hannah shook her head. Did Ken know her mom? That wasn't a connection she wanted to use in this situation, or ever. "I've lived here all my life."

"An old-timer. Interesting. Sand Dollar Cove doesn't have many of those. This place is swimming with retirees, most of them from Google or Microsoft." He waved her inside. "Let me get the master key and I'll show you the place."

"Great. I'll wait out here. The sun's coming out, and we haven't seen it for a while."

"Ain't that the truth." Ken came out a moment later, shaking the keys. "When I moved here from Aberdeen last year, I had no idea it would be so cold and windy."

"The good days make up for it, though," Hannah said, unwilling to let anyone slight her hometown, especially someone from Aberdeen. She followed Ken to the apartment and tried to contain her enthusiasm when she walked inside. Everything about the apartment was perfect!

"The laminate floors are brand-new. The kitchen has a dishwasher, garbage disposal, and microwave, and there's a stacking washer and dryer over here in the closet." Ken opened the door to show her. "Technically, this is a one-bedroom, but this little alcove over here could work well as an office."

Or a second bedroom, Hannah thought. *All you'd need to do would be to hang a curtain to separate the space.* "What about a refrigerator?" Hannah asked.

"You'll have to provide your own."

That wasn't such a big deal. Perhaps they could buy a small one on sale at Walmart. "Okay," Hannah said. "We can manage that. I'll take it." She waved her folder. "I have all the info right here to fill out the application and put down the deposit."

"Hold your horses, little lady. Things have changed a bit since we spoke on the phone."

"Hold my what?"

"Figure of speech." Ken shrugged. "I have six other people interested in this place. Originally the rent was fourteen hundred a month, but given the market, the landlord has asked me to adjust that."

"Adjust it to what?" Hannah tried not to panic. She'd done the numbers. They could go up to $1,600 but no higher.

"That's the thing." Ken scratched behind his ear. "I'm not sure. What I'm telling people is to write out a bid."

"Like... what type of bid?"

"How much rent you're willing to pay each month. How much cash you're offering upfront. I probably shouldn't be telling you this, but one of the prospective tenants said they'd pay six months on signing."

"Eight thousand four hundred dollars," she whispered, not meaning to speak the number out loud.

"Actually, nine thousand. That couple was willing to pay fifteen hundred dollars a month instead of fourteen hundred. And you need to have perfect credit."

"I see. Uh... okay. I'll go home and talk with my sister and grandmother and will drive over our bid tonight."

"Wait a second." Ken scrunched up his nose. "Is it just you and your sister living here, or you and your grandmother, or what?"

"All three of us would be here. We have three sources of income, so we'll be able to submit the top bid, no problem." She would bluff if she had to.

"Oh jeez. Brad didn't mention that there were three of you. I'm sorry to bring you all out this way for nothing, but this apartment has a maximum occupancy of two individuals. Since it's a one-bedroom and all."

"But there's plenty of room." Hannah pointed to the alcove. "That's practically a second bedroom right there."

"Not according to the city. It's something to do with the septic system. Like I said, sorry. I can keep your number on hand if a two-bedroom comes up."

"How much do those go for?" Hannah asked, trying not to drown in disappointment.

"Eighteen hundred a month at the moment, but those prices will probably go up soon, too."

Hannah thought of half a dozen curse words she wanted to say, but took a deep breath instead. She couldn't afford to tick Ken off, not if they ended up being able to afford a two-bedroom someday. "Thanks for your time," she said, as she marched to the door. Hannah hurried out to her car without saying goodbye.

As Hannah drove away, she tried not to cry. How in the hell had it become so difficult to be a renter? If only they had the house that Cheryl had inherited from her parents. The one that Hannah's dad had grown up in. But Cheryl had sold it to pay for Max to go to college. Then she'd spent the rest in court fees to secure custody of Hannah and Mary.

The sense of security Hannah had felt for eighteen years, ever since she'd moved in with Cheryl, was slipping away. It was up to her to bring that safe feeling back. This apartment didn't work out, but maybe the next one would. Hannah willed that to be true. Tonight, she'd take another hard look at their budget. She'd find a way out of this mess somehow. She had to. Her sister and grandmother were depending on her.

EIGHTEEN

"The only useful thing in here is the carpet cleaner," said Hannah. It was Friday afternoon and she and Guy stood in front of the storage shed. She picked through her key ring to find the right one. "The rest of this stuff is junk that Herman won't let me throw away."

"Thanks for coming out to unlock the shed for me," said Guy. "I really want to find that binder."

"It's weird that the previous trainer didn't leave it someplace safe. Roxanne was a Type A personality and usually pretty organized."

"I did find a lifetime supply of hydration packets. Luckily, they had a long expiration date because I add one of them to my water bottle every time I go on a long run."

So *that's* where those hydration packets she'd found in his desk had come from. "At least they aren't going to waste." Hannah tried a key in the door, but it wouldn't budge. "Lark used to date her, you know."

"Really? She never mentioned that."

"It was only for a few months, and I think Lark's better off without her, even though she was crushed when Roxanne left for Seattle. Once I was in the break room and I overheard Roxanne nag Lark about belly fat and eating too much sugar."

"That's horrible. There's no excuse for body shaming like that."

"I agree."

"The joke's on Roxanne now, because Lark's doing great. She was strutting around the lobby this morning wearing old jeans from high school that she'd found in the back of her closet." Hannah tried another key in the lock. "She told me she feels a hundred times better since you started cooking for her."

"Never underestimate the power of vegetables. Lean into vegetables and they'll turn your health around."

"Bam!" Hannah unlocked the door. "That's the power of beets right there. I found the right key."

"I'm going to need the power of carrots if I hope to be able to see anything." Guy poked his head into the shed. "It's dark in here."

"There's a light switch somewhere." Hannah opened the door wider, letting in a little more outside light.

Guy pulled a chain hanging from the ceiling, illuminating the shed in a bright glow. "Game on. Thanks again for the help."

"No problem. Herman asked me to find the old stereo system from the lobby. He wants to take it home with him when he retires. I'm not sure we actually still have it since it's not worth anything, but I promised I'd look."

"I'm surprised Herman wants a used stereo. He strikes me as the type of man who still owns the system he bought in high school."

Hannah chuckled. "You're right. He does, and it's a vast source of contention. Nancy complains about the giant speakers in their living room every time I come over. She has houseplants sitting on top of them, but they still look hideous."

Hannah took a step forward at the same time as Guy, and

they almost bumped into each other. "I'm sorry," Guy said, taking a step back. "I didn't mean to crowd you."

"It's okay." Hannah twisted a strand of hair behind her ear. "It's a tight space." *Too tight.* Being this close to Guy caused her nerves to flutter. Did he feel that, too? Their flirty conversation last night had left her reeling. Mary had messed with her head, too, what with her saying that Hannah should ask Guy out. That was a terrible idea. Wasn't it? Hannah bit her bottom lip and looked up at Guy. What would it be like to feel his brawny arms around her? If she slid her hands up across his chest, would he pull her in for a kiss? Hannah shivered, imagining that delicious delight.

"Are you cold?" Guy unzipped his fleece. "You can have my jacket."

"Thanks, but I'll warm up once I get moving." Hannah looked away. Unfortunately, she'd been right in her assessment of the shed. Most of the stuff was junk. There were old mirrors with ostentatious gilt frames, stacks of outdated bathroom tiles, a couple of broken dressers, and a few pieces of machinery. A pressure washer stood next to a carpet cleaner and some sort of flooring device. There were dozens of paint cans that Mary had recently combed through for her refurbishment of Strawberry Cottage. The tins were so old that the labels were difficult to read.

"If I was a binder, where would I be?" Guy asked as he inspected a pile. "Hey, I think this might be a sewing machine. Would that interest Mary?"

"It probably would. She can't sew clothes, but she can sew a straight line." Hannah scooted over to the opposite side of the shed because the nearness to Guy was distracting her. "She's great at making curtains, but that's it."

"What about costumes? Didn't you say Mary wanted to be an actress?"

Hannah nodded. "She did. That's how come I know she

can't sew clothes. In high school she had to make her own Cinderella costume for *Into the Woods*, and ran into so much trouble that my grandma's friend Patti had to do it for her. Aunt Patti is a whiz with a needle."

"That's too bad that Mary's dream of becoming an actress fell through." Guy pushed the sewing machine to the side and sorted through old picture frames. "Not being able to work at the profession that calls to you is horrible."

"I wouldn't know. I've never felt called to any profession except for keeping Seaside Resort going." Hannah paused for a moment and analyzed what she had just said. Did she feel called to stay at Seaside Resort? Like she alone was in charge of its well-being? *Absolutely*. That's what made the thought of leaving so difficult.

"Any luck?" Guy asked, a few minutes later.

"No. This feels like a poorly planned Easter egg hunt. I wish I could move half of this stuff to the dumpster, maybe more."

"Why don't you?"

"Herman. He has it in his head that there's valuable stuff in here."

"Like this beauty?" Guy picked up a large black and brown box.

"The stereo! You found it!" Hannah hopped over piles of junk to come see. "Wow. I wonder if it still works?"

"Maybe. It looks like all it has is an AM and FM radio."

"High tech from 1984."

Guy laughed. "Would you mind holding this?" he asked, as he handed it to her. "I think I see something else useful."

Hannah held onto the stereo and watched Guy crouch down next to two pieces of rubber that looked like cannonballs. "What are those things?"

Guy heaved one up in each hand. "Kettlebells. Yes! Finally, something interesting." Guy hauled them outside into the sunlight and Hannah followed with the stereo. "This was a lucky find. I can definitely incorporate kettlebells into my training programs."

Hannah put down the stereo. Really, she should head back to work, but now she was curious. She followed Guy back into the shed to the spot where he'd discovered the fitness equipment. Lying next to where the kettlebells had been were five bags of what appeared to be folded blue sheets, along with a box of rock-climbing hardware.

"Are these what I think they are?" Guy asked.

"Sheets?"

Guy knelt down and opened a bag. "Not sheets," he said, inspecting the blue fabric. "Aerial silks. And the anchor hardware to go with them."

"Aerial what?"

"Silks. Or aerial hammocks. That's what it says on the package. You can use them for strength and stretching exercises. Some people call it aerial yoga. The best part is using them for inversions—poses that flip you upside down and release pressure from your neck, shoulders and spine." Guy counted the hammocks and hardware. "It looks like Roxanne purchased enough gear to run a class with five people." He looked up at Hannah. "What happened? Did her program ever get going?"

"Not that I know of," Hannah said with a shrug. "But now that we've found kettlebells and the silk sheet things, maybe the binder's here, too." She knelt next to Guy and blew dust from the lid of a cardboard box before lifting it off and setting it on the ground. More dust billowed up, causing her to sneeze.

"Are you okay?"

"I'll be fine in a moment," Hannah said while wheezing. Dust burned her eyes, and she shut them tightly.

"Here. Let me help," said Guy. Hannah felt something cool and silky wipe dirt off her face. When she opened her eyes, she saw Guy holding a corner of silk and looking at her with concern. "Better?" he asked.

She nodded. "Thanks."

"One more spot." Guy gently brushed off her cheek. Feeling his touch made her wish more than ever that they might lean closer. Close enough to kiss. Close enough for their lips to seal together, and for Hannah to feel those strong arms wrap around her. For a half-second, Guy had a look in his eyes that made Hannah think he might want that too, but then he put the silk down and peered into the box.

"What's inside?" Hannah asked.

"It looks like monogrammed stationery." He picked up an envelope. "Who's Oscar Lexter?"

"The man who hired Gran." Hannah looked into the box. There were envelopes, notecards, and sheets of paper, all with the same name embossed on top. "Oscar hired Herman, too. Gran said the guy was a total jerk and used to sexually harass her and all the housekeeping staff."

"That's awful!"

"I know, right?" Hannah was just about to uncover the second box when a flash of light shining into her face caught her attention. She jerked to the right to see where it came from. Was it a flashlight? No, she realized. Light was reflecting off glass wedged next to the boxes. It was the framed picture of Gabe Blanchet in his Team USA Biathlon uniform that Blanchet Maison insisted be hung in the hotel lobby. Hannah would recognize that punchable face anywhere. But Gabe wasn't the only Blanchet in the frame. There were three ovals with the names listed beneath each photo:

Guido Blanchet I.

Guido "Gabriel" Blanchet II.

Guido "Gabe" Blanchet III.

"It's just a picture," Guy said in a stilted tone.

"Yeah. At first, I thought it was a flashlight angled at my

face." Hannah pointed to each photo. "Guido came over from Italy and founded Blanchet Maison. Gabriel is the one who died last year. He's the one who was in charge when they bought Seaside Resort. Gabe is the total idiot who runs the business now. He's the Olympics star. Then there's also his son, Guido the fourth, who's not pictured."

"The one you said was in the Twitter disaster?"

Hannah nodded. "Yup." She put the frame aside and opened the next box. This one was full of matchbooks. They all had the Seaside Resort logo on the front, and on the back, each one had the name of a different location. Seagull Perch, The Summer Wind, Pirate's Paradise, Beachcomber's Bride, Strawberry Cottage... Hannah enjoyed sorting through them, but they were more things that belonged in the garbage. Seaside Resort had been smoke-free since 2004.

"My granddad used to smoke," Guy said, as he picked up a matchbook.

"Used to? Did he quit?"

"Cigarettes, yes, before I was born, but he smoked cigars until the day he died."

"I've never liked the scent of cigars."

"Me neither." Guy flipped over the back of the matchbook and looked at the Seaside Resort logo. "But I'd give anything to walk into his apartment and smell one of his cigars one more time."

"I'm sorry for your loss," said Hannah. "It sounds like you two were close."

"We were." Guy put the matchbook back in the box. "I spent every vacation with him. Every school holiday. Every Christmas." Guy smiled fleetingly. "He's the one who calmed my parents down when I announced I was a vegetarian."

"I don't understand why they'd be angry. Lots of people don't eat meat."

"My dad was a hunter."

"Oh. That's right. I remember you mentioning that."

"And my mom wears fur."

"Really? In this day and age? You mean like UGG boots with sheepskin lining, or are we talking full-length mink coats?"

"Mink, fox, chinchilla, ermine, fisher... You name it and she has a dead animal hanging in her closet."

"What about Dalmatian?"

Guy burst out laughing. "You got me there. She draws the line at dogs."

"Fur coats don't even make sense anymore, what with all the high-tech fabrics they have now. I'd much rather be in Gortex and fleece than an animal hide. Plus, how do you wash them? What if you're wearing one and get sweaty, and then you can't toss it into the washing machine to get the funk out?"

"You bring up a lot of good points."

"I can see if you inherited a fur coat, and had memories attached to it from a loved one and so you wore it from time to time. That would be different. But I don't understand buying a new fur coat on purpose these days. And I say that as someone who loves to eat meat." Hannah reached for another box and opened the lid. "This one has outdated maps."

"How do you know they're old?"

Hannah unfurled a map and pointed to Main Street. "The T Bone Bluff's bandstand and the roller rink aren't here anymore."

"There was a roller rink? I bet that was fun."

"It was. It was a popular place to hang out on the weekend in middle school. Jasmine and I had this whole roller-skating routine we did to a Katy Perry song wearing matching low-rise jeans and—" Too late, Hannah realized she'd said too much. No way did she want Guy picturing her roller-skating in circles like an idiot.

"What?"

"Never mind."

"Which song?"

"It's not important." Already the tune of "Teenage Dream" was humming in her mind. She looked at the tiny illustrations on the map. "The roller rink is the senior center now, and the bandstand is a public parking lot."

"That bandstand must have been a fun place for dates, don't you think?" Guy asked with a hopeful look that made Hannah's pulse beat faster. "Not as much fun as synchronized roller-skating, but dinner, dancing, and live music must have been fun, too?"

"I don't know if you would have liked the steak dinner very much."

"True." Guy chuckled. "I could have made do with a baked potato and Caesar salad, though." He tilted his head toward her. "With the right company, of course. Someone smart, beautiful, and easy to talk to."

"The right company is everything." Hannah's gaze drifted to his lips for a second, and she looked back into his blue eyes.

"What do you think it was like back then at the T Bone Bluff? Crowded? Packed with celebrities?"

"Yes, and yes."

"Those must have been amazing nights," Guy said, wistfully.

"Twirling around the dance floor, listening to live music."

"With the woman of your dreams in your arms." Guy leaned forward, resting his elbow on one the boxes. "Hannah, would you ever—"

Hannah's phone rang from deep in her pocket. She wished she could quiet it in time for Guy to finish asking her whatever it was he was going to ask her. *Out on a date, hopefully?* But it was too late, the moment was gone. "Hang on a sec," she said, as she whipped out her phone. She recognized the number from the front desk. "It's Will," she said. "I'll be quick."

"Hannah!" Will shrieked. "There's an emergency!"

"What?" Hannah asked.

"An emergency!"

Hannah jumped to her feet. "What happened?"

"The sign fell in the parking lot." Will spoke with a panicked edge to his voice. "Nobody can leave the resort."

"What's going on?" Guy asked.

"The sign collapsed," Hannah explained. "People in the parking lot are trapped."

"Damn Nick and that rusted hinge," Guy muttered.

"Call maintenance," Hannah told Will as she leapt over piles of junk to race out the door. "And tell them I'm on my way!"

NINETEEN

The elegantly scripted sign that read SEASIDE RESORT and had hung over the entrance to the parking lot for five decades had fallen down, blocking the driveway. One look at it, and Hannah saw that one of the rusty hinges holding it in place had finally snapped into two pieces. *This was Nick's fault!* Hannah's temper burned red-hot. *He should have fixed it ages ago!*

Outside of the resort, a line of cars backed up along the state highway as drivers rubbernecked to inspect the disaster. At least the sign hadn't fallen on a guest and killed them. But knowing that did nothing to allay Hannah's concern, especially since the way it had fallen, it now trapped guests in the parking lot.

Hannah jogged over to the sign to see if she could drag it out of the way. She attempted to push the sign out from the center of the road, but it swung back into place. She tried yanking it with all her strength, but it wouldn't come off the hook. This job required an extension ladder.

"Let me help," Guy called, running down the path to help her.

Hannah felt a moment of relief seeing him race to her aid.

But what could Guy do without a ladder? "Lifting it isn't the problem." She pointed to the hook. "That corner up there is attached to the post."

"I'll try it, anyway. Sometimes the brute force method works."

While Guy jostled the sign back and forth, Hannah texted Nick. *911. Sign fell and is blocking entrance to the parking lot. Help needed ASAP.*

Nick replied seconds later. *It's my day off. Shane's on the schedule.*

Shane? Nick's son-in-law? He was even more of a screw-off than Nick. In fact, Hannah was positive Shane turned up to work stoned, half the time. She looked back at the sign to see if Guy had made any progress.

"This sign is toast," he said, stretching his shoulders. "I tried to move it out of the way, but it wouldn't budge."

"Maybe if we work together," Hannah suggested.

"Good idea."

Now there was a minivan parked at the exit, waiting to leave. The driver had stepped out of his car and was taking pictures.

"Great. Just great," Hannah muttered. "Those guests are probably seconds away from posting a negative review on Yelp."

"Lovely scenery, great food, and service," Guy said in a deep voice. "But run-down exterior is unsafe. Can I give it no stars? Will not return!"

"Exactly!"

"You work your charm on the guests," said Guy. "I'll go see if I can find a ladder."

"Charm the guests? Isn't that *your* specialty?"

"Are you saying you think I'm charming?"

"No comment."

"I'll take that as a yes." Guy grinned. "But I've seen you work your magic. You can be charming, too."

"I don't know if charm is in my tool set, but good old-fash-ioned customer service is."

"I'll run up to the maintenance building and be back as quick as I can."

Hannah watched as Guy took off at full speed, and then she hurried to the minivan. "Mr. Leary," she said, as she lurched to a stop. "I am so sorry for this inconvenience. Sometimes those ocean breezes do a number on us."

"That sign could have killed someone." Mr. Leary snapped another picture. "What if my wife and son had been standing under it?"

"Mrs. Leary and Jason?" Hannah asked. "Did the three of you already eat breakfast? I can offer you a complimentary meal at The Summer Wind to compensate you for this delay."

"No, thanks," the man barked. "We've had breakfast."

"What if I credit you back fifty dollars to your payment on record? How about that?"

"Fifty lousy dollars? For something that could have killed us?"

Hannah widened her stance. "You were nowhere near that sign when it fell." Her phone vibrated in her pocket with a text from Guy.

Bad news. Nick took the extension ladder home with him to paint his neighbor's house. I told him to bring it back ASAP, and he cussed me out.

Hannah plastered a fake smile on her face. She needed to calm Mr. Leary down because she didn't know how long it would be before she could move the sign. "I'll credit you seventy-five dollars," she said. "That's as high as I'm allowed to go."

"Fine." Mr. Leary continued photographing the wreckage.

Hannah took a deep breath and lifted her chin. No ladder.

No Nick. No Shane. Guy was still at the maintenance building. It was up to her to solve this problem all by herself.

She approached the spindly wooden fence next to the metal pole that held the sign, knowing what needed to be done.

"Hannah!" Guy shouted from across the parking lot. "What are you doing?"

"What I've done since I was seven years old," she hollered back. "I'm climbing all over Seaside Resort." Courage flowed through her with force. Hannah put her right foot on the fence next to the pole. Bracing her hands on the top, she pushed herself up, and then walked across the edge like a balance beam until she could grab onto the metal pole.

"Careful," Guy called. "That looks risky."

Risky? Hannah appreciated his concern for her safety, but no way would she allow the broken sign to reflect negatively on the resort.

Wedging her feet and legs around the pole, Hannah scooted up the metal, inch by inch. She didn't know if she could still manage it, but somehow, she did. Every core muscle burned with exertion. Sweat dribbled down her forehead, running into her eyes. Her arms felt like limp noodles. But somehow, Hannah reached the top. "Okay," she called. "You lift the sign, and I'll unhook it."

"Wow!" Guy exclaimed. "That was incredible."

"Less praise. More help," Hannah grunted. Holding on with just her legs and one hand was challenging.

"On the count of three."

"Okay," Hannah gasped. She looked down for a second. "Oh, no. I'm getting dizzy."

"Don't look down," Guy said in a calm voice. "I'm counting now. One. Two. Three!" Guy lifted the sign and began to wiggle the hinge on the hook.

Hannah was just barely able to guide the hook over the loop

before her feet slid downward and she clung back to the pole for dear life.

As soon as Guy could move the sign out of the way, he rushed to spot her.

Down in the parking lot, the Leary family applauded. "She's like our cat Whiskers!" Jason declared, holding onto his mom's hand.

Hannah slid down the pole like a firefighter. When she reached the fence, she climbed off, and jumped to the ground. She waved to the Leary family as they loaded back into their van and drove away.

"That was seriously impressive." Guy grinned at her. "The kid was right; you climbed that pole like a cat scaling a tree. I didn't know you could do that."

Hannah shrugged. "No big deal. But Nick should be reprimanded over this. Mr. Leary is right. That sign could have killed someone, and I have documentation proving that I submitted a maintenance request to fix that rusty hook three times."

"I have screenshots of my text interaction with him just now. Rude doesn't begin to describe it." Guy took out his phone. "I'll forward them to you."

"Holy moly!" she said a few seconds later, after she'd read the screenshots. "That's unacceptable."

"I know, right?"

"I appreciate that Nick gave me a lead on an apartment, even though it didn't work out, but that's no excuse for a history of incompetence."

"I wonder if Shane will ever get here."

"I doubt he'll show up."

"The entire building and maintenance crew needs a reckoning," said Guy. "I asked Nick to replace a broken lock in the men's locker room last week, and haven't seen him since."

"Typical." Hannah muttered. "I'm building a case for termination as soon as Herman retires."

"Herman won't like that."

"But it won't be his decision anymore. Once he retires, he won't be able to protect Nick any longer." Hannah picked up her jacket. "You agree with me that Nick needs to go, right?"

"Absolutely. Shane, too." Guy took a couple of pictures of the sign and broken hinges and pocketed his phone.

"Okay, then. Whoever gets that promotion will have a nice thick file of documentation to forward to Blanchet Maison's HR department along with the termination papers."

"*You're* going to get the promotion," said Guy. "That job was made for you."

"We'll see," Hannah said in a pinched tone. "I appreciate your support."

Guy took something out of his pocket. "Before I forget, I brought this for you."

"A magazine article?" Hannah read the headline out loud. "'*Foods to Prevent Osteoporosis.*'"

"It's on calcium-rich vegetables. Cooked spinach, kale, and collard greens."

Hannah pointed to a picture of an emerald-green leaf. "What's this one?"

"Collard greens. They're more popular on the East Coast, but you can find them in the frozen vegetable section, if you look in the upper-right corner. I'm not a nutritionist, but I follow food news. You can also add calcium to your diet with figs, canned salmon, fortified orange juice, and other foods, too. Those would be good for your grandmother to eat, but also for you and Mary too, just in case."

"You mean so I don't end up like Gran."

"I don't want to worry you, but my understanding is that osteoporosis could be hereditary."

Hannah nodded. "I know." They began a slow walk up the

path to the resort. "Gran eats most of her meals at the senior center, but I can ask Keith what's on the menu."

"Keith? Who's Keith, and why is he cooking for you?"

Did Hannah detect a note of jealousy in Guy's tone? "Keith's the senior center director, and he doesn't cook for any of us. The senior center has its own cafeteria." She folded the article and put it in her jacket pocket. "Thank you for this."

"No problem. You know, weight-bearing exercises would be good for you, too, not just your grandmother." He palmed his forehead. "That sounded patronizing. I'm sorry."

"No, you're right. And encouraging people to exercise is your job, after all. I wish I could make myself run or something, but I can't deal with another form of stress right now."

"Exercise doesn't have to be stressful. It could be a stress reliever. Now's the time for you to build bone density while you're still young."

"Did you or did you not see my impressive feat of strength, climbing up to take down that sign just now?"

Guy grinned. "I did, and it makes me think you might like aerial yoga."

"You mean with the silk sheets?" Hannah's cheeks turned hot. She didn't require a mirror to know that she was blushing.

"Yes, exactly," Guy said, apparently ignoring her embarrassment. "It's like a mixture of tree climbing and floating in a hammock. You'd love it. It's wonderfully stress-relieving."

"I don't know about that," said Hannah. "Exercising with a hammock sounds kind of weird."

"It is weird, but it's also fun." They were at the main lodge now, but neither made a move to go inside.

Probably Guy had a training client, Hannah figured, but that didn't explain why he was letting this conversation linger instead of heading directly to the wellness studio. Could it be that he wanted to spend time with her outside of work? A thrilling thought occurred to her. *Was this Guy's way of asking her out on a date?*

"I'll get a couple of hammocks set up in the wellness room," Guy continued. "And you can try them out and see for yourself. What's your schedule like tomorrow?"

"I have the morning shift, and I'm off at four."

"Perfect. My last client is at three. Swing by right after work before you've eaten dinner, so you won't get nauseous."

"Nauseous? What are you signing me up for?"

"So that's a yes, then?" Guy asked, his voice flexed with excitement. "You'll come?"

"Yes. Sure. But I'm still curious about the nausea thing."

"Sometimes people get queasy hanging upside down. But I don't think you'll have that problem, not after seeing you scale that gate."

"Well, okay. Let's hope you're right."

"It'll be fun. You'll see. I bet you love it."

"Hanging yoga?"

"Aerial yoga," Guy clarified. "And don't worry. I'll install the hammock anchors myself. If I let Nick or Shane do it, we might fall down."

Hannah chuckled. "If you asked Nick or Shane for help, it would never get done."

"Maybe afterward we could watch a Marion Davies movie?"

"Where? At Strawberry Cottage?"

"With your grandma and Mary?" Guy raised his eyebrows.

"Uh... yeah... I guess."

"Well... sure. Mary definitely needs an education in old Hollywood."

"Even though she lived there for eighteen months." Hannah's excitement over the plan diminished knowing that Cheryl and Mary were coming too. "Do you think you could really find a Marion Davies movie?"

"I have a few leads." Guy raked his fingers through his sandy-blond hair. "Actually, I haven't started searching yet. But I'll drive all the way to Seattle and back to find one if I have to."

"That's noble of you."

He grinned boyishly. "I have to do something heroic after you put me to shame with that stunt in the parking lot."

"Great. A movie sounds fun. More fun than my plans for tonight, which involve looking at more apartments we can't afford."

"I hope something comes through for you."

"Me too." Hannah hugged herself. "But at least now I have something to look forward to. What I really need, besides a new apartment, is stress relief, and yoga sounds perfect." She dropped her arms and smiled. "The opportunity to torture Mary with black-and-white movies is an added bonus."

"Torturing your sister is relaxing?"

"I take it you don't have a sister."

Guy shook his head.

"Well, you can't have mine. I'm the only one who gets to torture her. Unless you wanted to invite her to come to yoga, too?" she asked, testing him.

"I was thinking just you and me for yoga, but... I guess... if you wanted your sister—"

"No," she interrupted. "Just the two of us is fine."

"Great."

"Great," she echoed. Maybe this *was* a date. She made it all the way to the privacy of the staff restroom before she cheered out loud.

TWENTY

"That definitely sounds like a date," said Mary, as they drove to the apartment they were looking at. It was Friday evening, and they'd left Cheryl home at Strawberry Cottage watching TV with Ferdinand on her lap.

"I'm not entirely sure about that." Hannah instantly regretted letting Mary know about her plans with Guy tomorrow. She was nervous enough as it was. Every time she thought of Guy, her heart quickened. But she and Guy were just co-workers. He was way out of her league.

"You're doing a cool and unusual activity together, and then watching a movie. How is that not a date?"

"Because you and Gran are coming, too."

"To aerial yoga?"

"No, silly, to the movie. Or rather, Guy is coming to Strawberry Cottage with a DVD."

"Wait a second." Mary drove faster than Hannah would have liked through the residential neighborhood they were exploring. "How did Guy word it? Did he say: 'How about we watch a movie with you, your sister, and your grandma?' Or what?"

Hannah thought back to the conversation that morning. "Uh... I think originally he just mentioned the movie, and I was the one who mentioned you and Gran."

"What a dummy."

"Who, me?"

"Yes, you. Guy was asking you out, and you invited your little sister and grandma along."

"I did not. I mean... did I?" A torrent of emotions hit Hannah at once. Excitement, nervousness, hope, and fear swirled around her like a hurricane. "I don't think Guy likes me like that."

"Well, *I* think he does. When we were moving the tomato plants, he asked me what your favorite foods were."

"What did you tell him?"

"Deli sandwiches."

"Good. I love sandwiches. Especially if there are dill pickles on them. Did you tell him about the pickles?"

"No, I did not talk to Guy about pickles." Mary braked hard as a pedestrian came out of nowhere, and the seat belts bit into their shoulders.

"Watch the speed limit, okay?"

"I always watch the speed limit." Mary put on her sunglasses. "I love suggestions."

"It's not a suggestion. The speed limit's there for a reason."

"Can't you take a joke? Lighten up."

Hannah changed the subject. "What do you know about this apartment we're—"

"I'm not done talking about Guy," Mary interrupted. "Here's the plan. When you come back from yoga, and if you feel like things are going well, give me a signal and I'll take Gran away for the evening and you two can have the cottage to yourselves."

Alone with Guy in Strawberry Cottage? Hannah's heartbeat

fluttered. "What type of signal?" she asked. "And where would you go?"

"We could go watch that new Marvel moving playing."

"Gran would hate that."

"She'd play along. She loves Guy, and I think she's gotten over her detective fantasy. I'd say that I had no interest whatsoever in watching an old movie, and Gran would say she had a hankering for movie theater popcorn, and then we'd roll out of there and give you some privacy."

"We're co-workers. Nothing more." But even as she said it Hannah knew that was no longer true. The earlier crush she'd felt when Guy had first started working at Seaside Resort had grown stronger than ever. He was so kind and attentive, not to mention easy to talk to. No wonder he had a history of holding up the checkout line. When Guy spoke with someone, he fully engaged. He remembered details that other people would have forgotten. Now that she thought back to all her conversations with Guy, she realized that he always showed a genuine interest in her life and what was happening to her.

If she had an afternoon with Guy all to herself, with no work crises to distract them, what would happen? What would they talk about? Guy knew a lot about her, but she knew little about him, aside from his mentioning a blowup fight with his parents. Oh, and him not having any sisters. Did he have a brother? Hannah didn't know.

Guy was a mystery to her in so many ways, and it surprised her how much she wanted to find out more.

"What would the secret signal be?" Hannah asked.

"Compliment me on the new end table I found in the Buy Nothing group."

"But I hate that end table. It's not big enough to hold the lamp you found."

"That end table is gorgeous, and you're too clueless to realize it."

"Fine. I'll lie and say the end table looks great, if, and only if needed."

"I hope you tell me it's great, not just because it'll feel good for you to admit the truth, but also because I like Guy and think he'd be great for you."

"Really?"

Mary pulled in against the curb and parked her car. "Yeah." She patted Hannah's shoulder. "You deserve to have some fun for once. All you do is work and stress out."

"I thought that's what being in your twenties meant," Hannah said, meaning it as a joke. But Mary took her quip to heart.

"Don't be ridiculous. If you work this hard now, what will happen to you when you have a midlife crisis when you're forty? I'll be living my fabulous life with Aidan, and you'll be stuck at home drinking wine and watching reruns of *The Golden Girls*."

"I happen to love *The Golden Girls*. And besides, forty isn't midlife."

"Fifty then, whatever. You'll be one of those women who starts hoarding cats and ordering junk she doesn't need from the television shopping channel. It'll be you and Ferdinand two point oh, plus all of his extended family members buying elastic-waist trousers sold by D-list celebrities."

"You've really thought about my future a lot. Thanks."

"Meanwhile, I'll be jet-setting all over the world with Aidan, and designing homes for the rich and famous." Mary removed her sunglasses and put them away in their case.

"What about kids?"

"I'm not sure about them yet."

"Well, I'll have lots of fur-babies," said Hannah. "Make sure you design a guest suite for me and all my cats."

They both laughed.

"First things first, though," said Mary as she dabbed on fresh lipstick. "We need to get this apartment. It's across the street from the laundromat. That's convenient."

Hannah pulled up the listing on her phone. "They built it in 1961. I asked Gran, but she said she didn't think her dad worked on it."

"He usually did fancier projects."

"That's right. And nothing about this apartment building is fancy. No dishwasher. No garbage disposal. No central air."

"That should scare the posh people from California away," said Mary.

"Hopefully so."

"Are there wall heaters, or something? How does the heat work?"

Hannah scrolled. "Wall heaters, yes."

"Those aren't very efficient."

"No, but..." Hannah let her unfinished sentence dangle in the air. They'd seen half a dozen apartments in the past two weeks, and been priced out of all of them. The clock was ticking. They needed a new place to live soon. They couldn't stay in Strawberry Cottage forever. It would be demolished on July 1st.

"Ugh," Mary said as she looked at the building. "I recognize this place. It's been a dump ever since we were little."

Hannah agreed, but she was trying to remain positive. "I thought original brick was a thing."

"It is." Mary got out of the car and Hannah followed. "It's not the brick I mind," Mary said. "That walkway and railing look rickety. This unit isn't upstairs, is it?"

"Not according to the ad. It said ground floor."

"I hope it's not the one with the broken window. That looks sketchy."

"This is Sand Dollar Cove. We don't have sketchy apartments."

"Yes, we do." Mary pointed at the building. "Right there.

And this is barely Sand Dollar Cove. We're on the edge of town."

"Oh no!" Hannah threw up her hands. "We're on the edge of town. Call the National Guard."

"You know what I mean." Mary scowled. "Do you want to live here?"

No! Hannah's internal alert monitor screamed. *She didn't.* But desperate times... "This wouldn't be my first choice of location because it's so far away from everything, and gas prices are climbing. But I'm willing to give it a chance if you are. Let's at least look inside."

"Okay," Mary said with a shrug.

Five minutes later the apartment manager was showing them the one-bedroom for rent. As first impressions went, Hannah liked the manager, even though she was a newcomer to town. Sloan was a woman in her forties with rainbow-colored hair and a nose ring. She held a mug of tea in one hand as she opened the front door with the other. Sloan carried the scent of orange pekoe with her, and Hannah found the fragrance comforting.

But once she entered the apartment, Hannah couldn't smell anything but mildew.

"Whoa," Mary exclaimed. "What's the odor?"

"Would you believe me if I said the briny sea air?" Sloan asked.

Mary shook her head. "No, we wouldn't."

Hannah looked down at the beige carpet, which appeared to be in good condition. "How old is this carpet?" she asked.

"Brand spanking new," said Sloan. "Which is why I need to ask you to remove your shoes."

Hannah stepped out of her flats. "Did they replace the carpet pad, too?"

"They did." Sloan removed her clogs. "I watched them do it myself."

"Where's the smell coming from then?" Mary asked.

"Well... you know..." Sloan directed them to the tiny kitchenette. "Did you see this vintage tile? It's one of the special features I love about this place. They don't make Harvest Gold like they used to. The apartment comes with a refrigerator, too. Some places make you supply your own."

Hannah eyeballed the dinosaur appliance, suspicious that there might be spoiled food inside, from 1961. "Is it alright if I look inside?"

"Go right ahead." Sloan waved her forward. "I cleaned it out after the last tenant myself."

Hannah opened the refrigerator and smelled the pungent scent of bleach. "You did a great job." She peeked inside the crisper. "This fridge sparkles."

"I do love the yellow color," said Mary. "Vintage is hot right now."

"And it matches the linoleum," Sloan pointed out.

Hannah closed the fridge and looked back toward the living space. Where was the smell coming from? The window, which was thankfully intact, had vinyl blinds, not fabric drapes. Could there be mildew on the slab underneath the matting and carpet?

"The bedroom is really big," said Sloan, "and so is the bathroom. I know you said you needed an apartment that would be good for someone dealing with mobility issues, and I think you'll be impressed. There's plenty of room to maneuver a wheelchair in here. I saw that myself when—" She covered her mouth. "Forget I said that."

"There was a wheelchair in here?" Mary asked. "Why?"

Hannah wanted to know too, but she was trying not to ruin their chances for the apartment. The smell could be a deal breaker, but maybe they could root out what was causing it and fix the problem without too much fuss.

"Did I say wheelchair?" Sloan asked. "I meant gurney."

"Like for the paramedics?" Mary asked.

"Yes, but... Would you look at the gigantic bedroom?" Sloan held her arms out wide, encompassing the space. "There's room for a queen-size bed and bunk beds. It's a great size for three people."

"It *is* quite large." Hannah opened the sliding closet doors and gagged. The musty smell was so strong she could hardly breathe.

"Yuck." Mary pinched her nose. "What's in that closet? I can smell it from here."

"Nothing." Hannah pivoted on the ball of her right foot. "The closet's empty, but it reeks so bad that any clothes we put in here would pick up the odor."

"Febreze might help," Sloan said. "I already tried cedar and sage, but that didn't do much."

"Why does this place stink?" Mary asked, point-blank.

Sloan sighed. "The people who lived here before were hoarders. They stuffed the whole place top to bottom with garbage. It was an older couple. The husband had a bad leg and the wife could hardly see. I was afraid they'd die in here. It was awful. Finally, the state got involved, and a social worker came. The wife died a few months later—not in the apartment, though. Nobody died in the apartment. When the paramedics rolled her out on that gurney, she was still alive."

"What a sad situation," said Hannah, feeling horrible.

"The landlord has replaced the carpet and repainted every-thing with an anti-odor paint. I disinfected everything. You saw the refrigerator, it's as good as new."

"New in 1960, maybe," Mary muttered.

"Perhaps we could bleach the walls, too," said Hannah. "That might help. How much was the rent again?"

"No way." Mary gripped her purse straps. "We're not inter-ested. Thanks, anyway."

"Fourteen-fifty a month with only a first and last month's deposit," said Sloan. "That's a bargain in this market."

It *was* a bargain, Hannah knew that to be true. But Mary was right; the stench was horrible. It would cling to them like a bad credit score.

"Thank you for your time," she told Sloan. "Unfortunately, this isn't the right place for us."

"I was afraid you'd say that. What if I knock off fifty dollars a month? I have the authority to do that."

Hannah looked at Mary, considering the proposal, but Mary shook her head.

"Thanks, anyway," said Hannah. They put their shoes back on, said goodbye to Sloan, and headed to the car.

"I can't believe you were actually considering that dump," said Mary once they were safely inside her sedan.

"I didn't want to consider it, but we're running out of options. Strawberry Cottage will be torn down soon. We need to find a new place to live, pronto."

"I know, but can you imagine how living in a place like that would destroy our lives?" Mary turned on the car.

"Aren't you being a tad dramatic?"

"No, I'm not. When I come home from work, my clothes reek of coffee beans. That's not so bad. People love the scent of coffee." Mary smelled her sleeve. "But get a whiff of this." She held out her arm for inspection.

"I can smell my own arm, thank you very much." Hannah buried her nose in her sweater. "Bleh! Mildew, just like that apartment. That was fast. We'll need to wash these as soon as we get home."

"Where? We don't have a washing machine, and I wasn't planning on going to the laundromat until Sunday when I have the morning off."

"We'll just have to bag up our clothes and stuff them in the trunk, I guess."

Mary pulled a lock of her blonde hair in front of her nose. "I need a shower, too. Maybe two showers."

"Stop complaining and start driving. I'm ready for Friday night to be over." Hannah leaned back against the headrest. What a miserable start to the weekend. Stress flooded around her, filling up the space. She was neck-deep in it. What was she going to do? Where would they live?

"I have an idea," Mary said, as she turned left onto the main road that headed toward town. "What if we buy an RV? We could park it at the state park."

"You can only stay there for two weeks before you have to move."

"Maybe we could park it on the side of the road and stay there until someone told us to leave?"

"Like drifters?"

"No, not like drifters," said Mary. "We could be van life people. I could start an Instagram account dedicated to it, plus a TikTok. We could be influencers."

"You've spent way too much time on social media. How would Gran live in an RV?"

"The same way she lives now. Very carefully."

"She needs her recliner to sleep. We would need a truck to pull a trailer, or a huge down payment to purchase the RV."

"Not necessarily. I see old junker ones on Craigslist all the time. Maybe I could fix it up?"

"No," said Hannah. "If it were just the two of us, I'd think about it, but not with Gran. That wouldn't be good for her. She needs stable housing, not a house on wheels."

"What if I can find a plot of land where we could permanently park? Then would you consider it?"

"If there was plumbing, and electricity and proper sewage disposal, yes. But those types of plots are expensive. There are tourists who want those spots. We can't compete with tourist dollars."

"I guess we'll keep looking then. Or I could take out loans to cover my last tuition payment."

"No," Hannah said, more sharply than she intended. "I don't want you sunk by loans. They'd drag you down."

"At least I'm graduating this June, and then I won't be such a burden to you. I'll plan a super-cheap wedding. Aidan and I could elope."

"You're not a burden. I love you."

"But I'm ruining everything. We wouldn't be in this situation if it weren't for my tuition payments."

"You didn't cause that pipe to break," said Hannah. "It's not your fault our rental flooded." She saw Mary's tears, and couldn't bear to see her sister cry. "It's going to be okay," Hannah promised.

"I just wish I could help more," said Mary.

"You're helping plenty." Hannah rubbed her sister's back. "I'm glad you're on my side. I don't know what I'd do without you."

"Really?" Mary glanced over at her for a moment, before looking back at the road ahead.

"Really," said Hannah. "Even though you brought home the ugliest end table ever."

Mary chuckled and wiped her cheeks with the back of her hand. "I really think Guy likes you. I hope you can be brave enough to give him a chance."

"Me, brave?" It wasn't an adjective Hannah usually used to describe herself.

"Yes, you," said Mary. "My smart, beautiful sister who deserves all the good things. You're always brave for me and Gran. It's time to show some courage for yourself."

Hannah didn't answer, and the two of them lapsed into silence. *Was Mary right?* Had she been a coward when it came to her love life? Hannah pressed her forehead against the window and stared into the dark forest. It was easier for her to be cautious than it was to take risks, especially when a man like Guy was involved. *Or a job change. Or moving away from Sand Dollar Cove...* Hannah was allergic to risky behavior.

No, that wasn't exactly true. She'd climbed the pole in the parking lot and removed the wooden sign. Why was it easier to be brave where the resort was concerned? Because it held a piece of her heart, that's why. That's also what made it so difficult to leave.

"Slow down," she said, when she noticed Mary's leaden foot on the pedal.

"I will in a moment. I just want to get past this spot."

Hannah turned to see what Mary saw from the driver's side window, and her heart floated in her chest. They were driving by Blackfish Point, where Max had died. Stress splashed against her so hard she could barely breathe. "I always drive faster here, too," she whispered.

When they reached the parking lot of Seaside Resort ten minutes later, Hannah was glad knowing that Strawberry Cottage waited for them like a life raft. But she was terrified knowing that it was only a temporary solution.

TWENTY-ONE

"Guy?" Hannah called. "Are you there?" All she could see was a cocoon of silk floating in the air. It was Saturday afternoon, and the moment she'd been looking forward to was finally here. Hannah stood in the middle of the wellness studio ready for her evening with Guy. She'd thought a lot about her conversation with Mary last night and was feeling bolder—at least when it came to Guy. She didn't know if there was a future between them beyond friendship, but she was eager to find out.

Guy slid his feet out of the hammock, grabbed the fabric, and backflipped to the ground. "Hi," he said. He wore slim-fitting black stretch pants that showed off thick thigh muscles, and when his shirt had slid around just now, she'd caught a peek of taught abs.

"Whoa..." Hannah said, still gazing at his midsection. She felt like the temperature had risen ten degrees. But then she caught herself staring and tried to recover. "I don't have to do flips, do I?"

"Not unless you want to." Guy's blue eyes twinkled back at her, like he'd caught her ogling and enjoyed the attention.

"Come on in. I installed the hammocks inside the personal training room. More privacy that way."

"Privacy?"

"That way, guests using the weights or machines won't bother us."

"That makes sense," said Hannah, realizing that Guy was talking about exercise. But what had *her* mind been thinking about? Taking risks. Being brave. Stepping closer and sliding her palms up to his shoulders. Pulling his lips toward hers for a kiss. Guy's toned physique pressed against her. Hannah felt her cheeks grow hot. "That trick you did was really cool," she said, trying to regain control over herself. "I know I *said* I don't want to do backflips, but, goals, right?"

"If there's one thing I know about you it's that you're goal-oriented. That's something I appreciate."

Hearing the compliment made her grin. "Goals are important to everyone," she said modestly.

"But sticking to them is a real skill." He closed the door behind them. "I'm going to lock this, not to be creepy, but to keep guests from wandering in and startling us when we might be upside down."

"Good thinking." Hannah brushed her hand against the silky-soft hammocks. "These things are probably a liability lawsuit waiting to happen."

"We'd need guests to sign hold-harmless waivers if we got an aerial program going. Did Roxanne ever suggest that when she bought the hammocks?"

Hannah shook her head. "I have no idea. The health and wellness budget goes to Herman, not me."

"That's right." Guy chuckled. "I bet if Herman saw 'five hammocks' on the reimbursement list, he would have approved that no questions asked, not realizing what type of hammocks he was buying."

"Exactly."

"I like Herman, but you're definitely the right person to take Seaside Resort into the next era."

"Thanks." Hannah smiled and looked down at her sneakers.

"About your shoes, though."

"What's wrong with them?" Hannah asked, feeling embarrassed.

"Nothing. But this is yoga. Bare feet or grip socks. Also, you're not wearing any jewelry, are you? Jewelry and zippers can snag the fabric. I should have mentioned that earlier."

"I'll take off my watch. That's the only thing." Hannah removed her shoes and placed her watch on a weights bench. She wore tight black leggings, and a loose-fitting tank top over a black sports bra. Her chestnut-brown hair was swept back into a ponytail.

"Are you ready to get started?" he asked.

"Ready as I'll ever be."

"Great. Let's step in front of the hammocks. Reach behind you and grab five handfuls of fabric. Bunch them up, and then sit back into your bucket seat." He showed her how to climb into the hammock and sit in a comfortable position.

"That doesn't look too hard." Hannah adjusted the silk behind her and sat down. "There! I did it."

"Nice!"

"Are my feet supposed to dangle like this?"

"Yes. If they could touch the ground, the hammock would be too low and you could hit your head. But let's take it slow. No need for inversions yet. Starting off, it's important to feel comfortable. Each hammock can hold two thousand pounds. Trust that the fabric will support you."

"Trust that a giant handkerchief will support me?"

"You use silk handkerchiefs?"

"No. Never. I should have said scarf. Wait. Scarf is the

wrong word, too. I should have said cocoon. I feel like a silk-worm, or maybe some sort of weird caterpillar."

"That's a lot of description. Our goal right now is to focus on breath and quiet the mind."

"I'm not sure that's possible for me."

"I've seen you accomplish big things," said Guy. "I know you can do it." He led her in a few minutes of guided breath work and her nervous chatter finally stopped. "Okay," he said, when she had finally settled. "Grab the fabric with your right hand and push out, then move your left leg to the other side like you're sitting astride a horse." He demonstrated the posture by facing her so she could see what he was doing.

Hannah struggled at first to move into position, but eventually got saddled up. "Is my back supposed to be rounded like this? I feel like Gran."

"Reach up behind you and pull on the fabric. That'll straighten you out."

Hannah made the adjustment. "Much better. If only it were that easy to help Gran."

"So true. But right now, we're focused on helping you."

"Helping me?" Hannah asked. "To do what?"

"To relax. I know you can do it if you try."

Hannah scooted up in her seat. "Maybe," she said doubtfully.

"I believe in you. Let's go back to those deep breaths. In through your nose, two, three, four, five, and now out through your mouth in a big whoosh."

Hannah followed along and felt tension melt away. The tightness in her forehead eased and her jawline relaxed. This was as close to floating as a person could feel on land.

"Great." Guy stretched his arms up, leaned over, and touched his left ankle. "Let's do a side bend."

"Look at me," said Hannah. "I'm bendy."

"So bendy."

After they balanced it out on the right side, he had them get out of the hammocks and use them to stretch one leg at a time.

"I'm really starting to get the hang of this," Hannah said, leaning forward into half-splits.

"You are. Aerial sounds intimidating, but the hammock is basically another type of exercise prop, like a weight, or mat."

"When do I get to do something harder, like one of those cool flips you were doing when I arrived?"

"You're always up for a challenge." Guy grinned. "That's another thing I like about you."

"That makes me sound adventurous, and I'm not."

"Are you sure about that? Wanting to take control of an aging resort like this and bring it into a new era is pretty brave."

"Seaside Resort is just a bit stuck, that's all," Hannah said. "I want to help it get unstuck so it can move forward."

"Speaking of moving forward, are you ready to try an inversion?" Guy asked.

"Ready as I'll ever be."

"Okay, go-getter," he said, putting both feet on the ground. "Let's turn your world upside down."

Hannah planted her feet. "Let's do it."

"This is called a rope wrap. Watch me first, and then I'll lead you through it. I stand in front of the fabric with the silk behind me. Then I reach back, with my thumbs pointed forward, and grab the fabric right where it hits my hipbones. The next step is to lean back, allowing the fabric to hold me." Guy pivoted backward until he was upside down. "My legs are out wide at first, but it's easier to put my soles together." He pressed his feet inward. "I can put my hands on the ground, or I can reach behind me for a pectoral stretch."

The blood rushed to his head, and Guy's cheeks turned red.

"How do you not pass out?" Hannah asked.

"You get used to it. But the first time might make you

queasy." Guy reached for the fabric and pulled himself upright. "Ready to try?"

Hannah nodded. "I sure am."

They went through the steps together until both of them were upside down in their hammocks.

To Hannah, it felt like her head might explode. "I have to think about breathing," she said. "This is hard."

"One breath at a time," he murmured. "You got this."

"It feels like my eyeballs are going to pop."

"That's normal. It'll be easier in a second. What else do you feel?"

"The vertebrae in my spine. It's like they're stretching out one by one."

"That's right."

"And my neck feels longer."

"Some people actually measure taller after aerial."

"I can see why." Hannah closed her eyes and breathed slowly. "I can't think of anything else when I'm upside down. Just breathing."

"And that's okay. It's good to not think about things for a while. Just breathe, Hannah. All you have to do is breathe."

After another minute had passed, Guy led Hannah out of the inversion and taught her how to wrap the silk around her shoulders like a backpack, lean forward, and let the blood rush back to her feet.

"That was amazing," said Hannah. "I want to try the flip next."

"Of course you do." Guy smiled. "Okay, then. Hop back into your bucket seat."

"Five bunches of fabric and then I sit down, right?"

"You got it." Guy climbed into his hammock and grabbed the fabric like a rope behind his head. "Angle your thumbs down, like this, and then lean backward, holding onto the silk, until you flip, and land your feet on the floor. But don't try it until I can watch you, okay?"

Guy flipped out of the hammock and stood behind Hannah while she tried.

"I'm not sure my arms will be strong enough," she said, as she tipped back. But then, in one fluid movement, she'd somersaulted backward, safely to the ground. "I did it!"

"You sure did." Guy grinned and then smiled even wider when she smiled back at him.

"This is fun." Hannah grabbed an edge of the fabric and fluttered it. "I can't remember the last time..." She looked down, not finishing her sentence.

"The last time what?"

She looked up at him. "The last time I had fun. Or did something that was just for me. All I do is work and worry, and it's been like that for ages."

"Life shouldn't be only about work and worry. But I know the feeling. The last time I had fun was the night I visited Strawberry Cottage and picked up the tomato plants. I sure enjoyed talking with you, your grandma, and sister." He held onto his hammock and pulled it taut. "But especially you."

"You just liked finding someone weird enough to know who Marion Davies was."

"I wouldn't say you're weird." He took a step closer. "Wickedly smart is more like it." His gaze met hers with a softness that calmed her.

"That would make you wickedly smart too, because you talked about old Hollywood like you'd read a dozen books about the subject."

"I would never admit to reading that many celebrity memoirs." His eyes drifted to her lips for just a moment. "But I would admit to wanting to spend more time with you."

Hannah swallowed. "I bet you say that to all your aerial students."

"I do, because the only person I've done this with is you."

Hannah wanted to kiss him. She wanted him to curl his arms around her and pull her into an embrace that would make both their hearts stop from pure delight. She wanted to whisper his name—no, murmur it. Hannah wanted all of that and more. But even as she longed to be closer to him, nervousness held her back. "What's next?" she asked, taking a step to the side.

Guy cleared his throat. "Let's try tree pose, since I know you're not afraid of heights."

"Tree pose?"

"Up in the hammock. I bet you'll get it right away." He bunched the fabric together and stepped on the silk. "This can be a lot of pressure on the bottom of your foot, so spread out the fabric, but make sure it doesn't cover your heel or toes. Then grab hold of the silk and pull yourself up to standing." With one effortless move, Guy was off the ground and floating in the air, balanced on his right foot.

Hannah did likewise, and Guy showed her how to adjust her shoulders so that she locked into position. "You can rest your left foot on your shin or thigh," he said. "Just be careful to avoid your knee."

"I think I got it," she said, with only a slight wobble.

"Let's move to the other foot," Guy said. He kept a close watch on Hannah's footwork as she carefully transferred her weight from one foot to the other. Then he demonstrated how to descend safely from tree pose. "Let's sit back in our bucket seats," he said.

Hannah didn't say anything until she was in her hammock and facing him. "I'm getting better at trusting that the silk will hold me," she said, holding onto the fabric.

"You are." Guy floated in his hammock for a minute, not saying anything. "Hannah, I wanted to tell you something."

"What?"

"It's about my granddad, and why I came here."

"Oh." Hannah became as still as a statue in her hammock, trying to make it stop swaying.

"He was a brilliant man. Smart at business. Great at remembering names. A lover of fast cars and beautiful women—at least, that's what he told people." Guy laughed. "The truth was he was more likely to be home with my grandma—when she was still alive—watching old black-and-white movies and eating Chex Mix. He loved things that were salty."

Hannah, who had never had the chance to meet either of her grandfathers, listened closely, wondering why Guy was telling her this. It seemed like a weird thing to bring up, especially now.

"When I went to Dartmouth my granddad would send huge care packages to my frat house every month," Guy continued. "I think he thought the Sigma Nus would let a vegetarian like me starve. Instead, we all had to figure out what to do with ten pounds of Florida oranges, or Oregon pears, or whatever happened to be the fruit of the month." Guy leaned his head against the side of his hammock chair. "Granddad was kind like that, always looking out for me."

"He sounds really thoughtful, like you."

"Thanks." Guy looked down at the ground. "Being compared to my granddad is the best compliment anyone could give me." He looked up at Hannah again. "We had the type of relationship where we'd talk to each other on the phone at least every other day. Once I moved back to New York, I'd eat dinner with him a few times a week. He wouldn't let me cook for him, though." Guy grinned. "All Granddad ate was meat and potatoes."

"Like a true American," Hannah said wryly.

"Yup." Guy pushed his foot against the floor and his hammock swayed. "But he was in fairly good health for someone who was ninety-one. When he died, it was a huge shock."

"That must have been hard for you to lose him." Hannah couldn't imagine how she'd feel when Cheryl passed. She tried to never think of it.

"Yes." Guy nodded. "I felt a heaviness like I had never known before. I guess you could say I was stuck, just like Seaside Resort is stuck, unable to move forward."

"What got you unstuck?" Hannah asked softly.

"Following his last bit of advice for me. 'Head West, young man. Live your own life. Search for joy and healing.'" Guy said nothing for a moment. His hammock swung gently. "If it weren't for my granddad's encouragement, I'd be holed up in my Manhattan apartment right now, eating takeout. Instead, I'm here with you, Hannah, and I'd give anything to be here with you right now."

"You would?" Hannah felt butterflies in her stomach. Maybe Mary was right. Maybe she did have a chance with Guy after all.

"I'm so happy I met you, Hannah," Guy's blue eyes looked at her intently. "Sand Dollar Cove is beautiful, but you make it perfect."

Hope was here, in this room, swirling around them soft as silk. Hannah could feel it. She trusted it. She was ready to take the risk. Their relationship was on the verge of moving from friendship to something more, and Hannah was up for the challenge.

She took a deep breath before speaking. "I wanted to tell you something, too. Thank you for this. Nobody has done something this thoughtful for me in ages. And also..." Hannah felt like she might explode from all the adrenaline coursing through her. Before she could stop to think, before her brain could tell her she shouldn't move one more inch, Hannah did what her heart wanted. She hopped out of her hammock and stood next to Guy, resting her hand on his arm, their bodies inches apart. "I'm really glad you came to Seaside Resort. You make this place better. And..." Her thumb brushed against his biceps and she couldn't *believe* how solid it was. "Um..." She was so close that there was no turning back now. "I'm really glad that I've gotten the chance to know you better."

"Me too." Guy slid out of his hammock and placed his hand on her opposite arm, connecting them in a semi-embrace. "Meeting you is the best thing that's happened to me in forever."

Everything felt like it was moving in slow motion, like they were moving through honey. Hannah lifted her face, inch by inch. She slid her hand up his arm and caught hold behind his shoulder. Her body warmed degree by degree as the space between them disappeared. Then Guy was moving, too. His palm traveled to the small of her back and clasped her against him.

Yes! Her heart cried. *This risk is worth it!* When their lips locked together the feeling was sweet as honey, soft as silk, and as beautiful as a Pacific Northwest sunrise. Guy's hands roamed up Hannah's back. Energy ignited, like fireworks sparking all around them. Hannah entwined her arms behind him, pulling them closer together. Guy gathered a lock of Hannah's hair in one hand.

This was what hope felt like. This was joy. This was the happiness that Hannah hadn't tasted in longer than she could remember, perhaps ever, because she couldn't picture a time when her heart had felt so full. With Guy's arms wrapped around her, Hannah felt empowered to believe in a future where anything was possible. She was safe in Guy's arms. Protected. He watched out for her and cared about her well-being. He'd earned Hannah's affection through his words and actions. The broken part of her soul, the part that had felt abandoned ever since her parents left her, stitched together with every kiss.

Bam. Bam. Bam.

"What's in this room?" a child whined. "Mom, I want to go in there."

"Oh no." Guy let out an exasperated sigh, and rested his forehead against Hannah's, cupping the back of her head. "I better go deal with that. Kids—"

"Aren't supposed to be in the wellness studio," Hannah finished for him.

"Right. Someone could get hurt. I'll go talk to them and be right back."

"I'll be here, hanging out." Hannah kissed him on the cheek and darted over to her hammock. "But not upside down. Not without supervision. I don't want to get hurt."

As she said the words, unease pricked her joyful feeling like a balloon popping. *I don't want to get hurt.* The elation she'd felt a moment ago hissed away under a litany of what ifs. What if this didn't work out? What if Hannah got hurt? What if she hurt so bad, she couldn't stop hurting? Nobody Hannah loved stayed around for long. And the ones who did, were let down by Hannah's inability to properly care for them.

Hannah looked down at the scar on her forearm. Her fingertip traced the silvery line, and her nerve endings tingled in a heebie-jeebies sort of way. She hadn't been able to protect Mary the day that Kelly had almost killed them. Her litany of what ifs grew longer. What if she had hidden her mother's keys? What if she had dumped Kelly's rum down the sink? What if she had refused to get in the Corvette? She could have picked up Mary and run to a neighbor's house and begged them to call Cheryl. But Hannah hadn't done any of that. She had trusted Kelly. Trusted her mom to keep them safe. And look what had happened!

But even as her fears compounded, Hannah heard her sister's advice. *Have a little faith in people,* Mary had told her.

Guy wasn't Kelly, or Rob, or Nick, or an angsty Yelp reviewer. Guy was Guy.

If I do get hurt, this will be worth it, she told herself as she climbed back into the hammock. The silk cocooned her with the fragile strength of a million butterflies. Guy was worth being brave for—no, *she* was worth being brave for. Hannah was ready to take a risk in order to be happy.

TWENTY-TWO

Did that really happen? Back there with Guy? An hour later, Hannah still couldn't believe it. The last time she'd made out like a teenager had been when she was, well, a teenager. But Rob had never kissed her like that. Now Hannah and Guy stood on the porch of Strawberry Cottage, gazing at the ocean, listening to the foghorn croon in the distance. Hannah's back was against Guy's broad chest, and his arms wrapped around the front of her, holding her safe like a seat belt. The small cooler filled with food Guy had brought rested on the deck where Cheryl's tomato plants used to be.

"Wow," said Guy. "The water's so blue tonight. It looks like opals."

Hannah turned her head and looked up at him. "I thought opals were white."

"Some are. Others are turquoise. My mom's friends with the owner of an opal mine in Brazil."

"How'd she meet him? Or her?"

"I don't know for sure. My parents know lots of people. Not all of them are worth knowing, at least not in my opinion. I'll tell you about my folks someday, but not now. Right now, I want to do this." Guy spun Hannah around to face him so their hearts pressed together. He cupped her chin and sealed their lips together with a kiss so tender that Hannah's heart flip-flopped, just like it had done back in the wellness studio.

Was this what people meant by being swept off their feet? Guy was handsome and charming, sure; anyone could see that. But he was also so much more. *Kind. Thoughtful. Attentive. Gentle.* Hannah felt supported whenever she was near him, which was a big deal because Hannah was used to supporting everybody else, not the other way around. Yet here she was, her hands exploring the ropy muscles in his back, and feeling sheltered—absolutely sheltered—in his arms.

She crushed her lips against his. When Guy pulled her closer, Hannah's heartbeat raced. His hands slid across her backside and she lifted to her toes.

"Hannah," Guy moaned. "What are you doing to me?"

"Should I stop?" she teased, before nipping at his bottom lip.

"No. Never."

Never. That was the right word. Hannah never wanted to stop kissing Guy either. Now that she'd done it—now that she'd taken the risk—Hannah wanted to reap every sweet reward risk-taking had to offer.

Her tongue touched his and she thought about the future. A future where Guy made her dinner at his apartment—and breakfast, hopefully. Hannah slipped her hands under his shirt and her fingers felt the bare skin above his waistband. Her risk-taking self would take him back to Rhododendron Lane, only this time she'd bring a picnic, and a bottle of wine. She arched her back and Guy leaned forward, deepening the kiss. Risky Hannah would do things she'd always wanted to do—call in sick, stay out late, dive into the Pacific wearing nothing but lace. In every fantasy, Guy was by her side making the risk worthwhile. Just like he was here now, the heat from his body warming hers, their arms intertwined so tightly they were bound together.

A few minutes later they both pulled away, equally out of breath.

"I guess we better go inside," Hannah said.

Guy rested his chin on her head. "I suppose you're right."

Reluctantly, Hannah opened the front door. Cheryl was in her recliner watching commercials, and Mary sat on the sofa "reading" a book. It was upside down.

"Hi, Hannah," Mary said in a high-pitched voice. "Did you see the new end table I found at the thrift shop?"

Hannah took one look at the hideous thing and laughed. "It's beautiful, Mary, you've really outdone yourself this time."

Mary popped a bookmark in between pages and beamed. "I was *hoping* you would say that." Ferdinand jumped off her lap.

"So was I." Cheryl turned off the TV. "Hi, Guy, nice to see you again. Sorry I can't stay, Mary promised to take me to the McDonald's drive-thru for dinner."

"McDonald's?" Guy lifted the cooler. "But I brought sandwiches."

"Great." Cheryl rose laboriously to her feet and held onto her walker. "We'll take a couple for the road. I mainly want to order a milkshake and heckle the drive-thru attendant."

"Who's the attendant?" Hannah asked, wondering where this was going.

"Brittany's son, Jeremy," said Cheryl. "Can you believe it? Brittany the dietitian from the senior center. Jeremy got a job at Mickey Dee's to spite her, and everyone's talking about it." Cheryl shuffled toward her wheelchair. "Wait until the Diabetes Sisters hear I ordered a strawberry milkshake with extra whipped cream. They're going to be so jealous."

"Gran," Hannah chided. "That's not very nice."

"*They're* not very nice," said Cheryl. "They're always

lording it over us, with the special attention they get from Brittany."

"Brittany." Mary picked up her purse. "That name sounds familiar."

"She's the landlord with the shared housing opportunity that Keith told me about," said Hannah. "When you're in the drive-thru, size up the teenager and see if he's someone you think we could stand living with."

"I don't know if I'd want to live with Brittany," said Cheryl. "She'd probably lecture us about blood sugar levels."

"That picture!" Guy suddenly exclaimed, looking at the wall. "Where did it come from?"

"Huh?" Hannah turned her head so that she could see what Guy was referring to. Mary traded so many decor items with her Buy Nothing group, that she was constantly swapping one thing for another.

"I found it at the thrift store." Mary picked it off the wall. "Cool, huh?"

Guy leaned across her so he could get a closer look. "It looks like a Frank Sinatra concert."

"Winner winner, chicken dinner!" Mary cried. "Er... uh... fake-chicken dinner."

"That was a popular poster back in the day," said Cheryl. "They sold it at the T Bone Bluff Bandstand."

"And there's ole Blue Eyes, standing in front of the orchestra." Guy pointed at the glass. "You can see the audience, too, out in front, sipping drinks."

"Those were glamorous times." Hannah loved how Guy took such an active interest in Sand Dollar Cove's past. He was really working hard to immerse himself.

"Oh, wow." Guy's attention was glued to the picture like he was attracted by an electromagnet. "The audience..."

Hannah walked over and looked closer at the image to see

what intrigued him so much. "Whoa," she said, pointing to a familiar face. "That looks like Lark, selling cigarettes."

"What?" Cheryl asked.

"You're right," said Mary. "That totally looks like Lark."

"It can't be," said Guy. "Lark told me her mom used to work at the Lumberjack."

"They all said that," said Cheryl.

"I wish I could find out more about this picture," Guy murmured, still staring at it. "I wish I could step inside the frame and ask those people questions."

"About what?" Hannah asked.

Guy's ears turned red. "Life in general, I guess. Most of the people in this picture lived in the same era as my granddad. I'm always curious about what life was like when he was younger."

"I love a man who appreciates the past," said Gran. "Come on, Mary. Let's get going before the ice cream machine breaks again."

"Don't forget your sandwiches." Looking away from the photo, Guy walked into the kitchenette and set a few containers on the bamboo table. "Here. You can take this cooler. I'm sorry I forgot napkins."

"That's okay," said Cheryl, settling into her wheelchair. "We can get some with our milkshakes. Has anyone seen my coat?"

Hannah looked around the apartment before remembering where she'd last seen the garment. "I think we forgot to bring it home from the senior center."

"Oh," said Cheryl. "Darn. I guess I'll be fine in a sweater."

"But it's cold out there." Hannah walked to the corner where she stored her clothes. "Here, take Dad's coat."

"That ratty thing?" Mary frowned. "Where's the new one I bought you?"

"Uh, in a box, I think." The truth was, Hannah wasn't sure.

"Max's coat will be just fine," said Cheryl. "And I'm

honored that you're lending it to me."

Hannah helped her into it, while Guy handed the cooler to Mary.

"I'll help you and your grandma out to the car," he said.

"Thanks." Mary took out her keys. "I appreciate it." She shot Hannah a conspiratorial look. "Sorry we're missing the Hearst Castle Film Festival, but honestly, it sounded kind of boring."

"Old Hollywood is not boring," said Hannah. "I thought you of all people would at least appreciate the set design."

"I would if it were in color." Mary opened the door. "Do you know why Instagram became so popular?"

"Because people are self-absorbed and love to take pictures of themselves?" Hannah asked.

"No, dummy," said Mary. "Because it's not in black and white."

"I'm ready to roll out of here in style." Cheryl sat in her wheelchair wearing her wraparound sunglasses from her cataract surgery last year.

"That's my cue." Guy opened the front door and then wheeled Cheryl through it.

"Let me help with the step." Hannah rushed after them.

"I got it." Mary blocked Hannah's exit at the door. "Go brush your hair," her sister whispered. "Your ponytail's lopsided."

"It is?" Hannah reached for the elastic. "Dang. I guess that's from hanging upside down."

"Change your shirt while you're at it," Mary continued to whisper. "You don't smell that great, either."

Hannah clenched her arms to her sides. "Will do."

As soon as someone safely shut the door, she grabbed a clean T-shirt and raced to the bathroom. Mary was right, her hair needed help. She washed her face and applied fresh mascara. By the time there was a knock at the front door, she was brushed, flossed, and fluttery with excitement. "Coming," Hannah called, as she raced through the cottage, ready to jump into Guy's arms. "You could have just come in," Hannah said, as she swung the door wide.

"Really?" said Herman, standing on the porch. "That doesn't seem safe. What if I'd been a psycho killer?"

"In Sand Dollar Cove?" Hannah asked, feeling put out that Herman was here, interrupting her date.

"You never know," said Herman. "I could have been a deranged kitesurfer. Mind if I...?" He gestured into the cottage.

"Ah... sure," said Hannah. What else could she say? She didn't own the place.

"I have news." Herman walked toward the couch, but when he saw the sandwiches sitting on the kitchenette table, he took a seat there, instead. "These look delicious." Herman picked up a parchment paper-wrapped sandwich and inspected it from all angles. "Wow. Whoever made this really outdid themselves. Is this Jasmine's work? I haven't seen this on the menu at The Summer Wind."

"No, that would be me," said Guy, with a note of annoyance. "Hi, Herman, how are you doing?"

More like, what are you doing here? Hannah wanted to know.

Herman put down the sandwich and frowned. "You should give Jasmine the recipe for this. I bet it would be popular on the lunch menu." Wiping his hands together to shake off crumbs, Herman stood and walked back to the couch. "I'm glad you're both here. This will save time." Herman sat down. "Take a seat," he instructed.

Hannah sat next to him on the couch and Guy took Cheryl's recliner.

"This sounds important," said Hannah. *Important enough to crash her date.* As soon as she thought that, her nerves leapt with excitement. "Is this about the promotion?"

"Unfortunately so," Herman said, wearing a dour expression. "There's no easy way to say this, Hannah..."

Hannah's heart had already sunk. She didn't need to hear what Herman said next to know that it was bad news.

"What?" Guy asked, since Herman still hadn't finished his sentence.

"Neither of you got the job," said Herman. "Blanchet Maison turned you both down for the position of general manager. Turned you down early, too, I might add, thanks to that damn reorg."

"What?" Hannah's fists clenched. "Why?" She could understand Guy not getting the job, but her?

"They said they wanted someone with experience at other properties to take over, to give fresh input." Herman grimaced with annoyance. "The person they chose has worked at Blanchet Maison properties in California and Texas."

Hannah couldn't breathe. For one hot moment it felt like the wind had been knocked out of her completely.

Guy rushed over and knelt at her feet. "This isn't fair," he said, squeezing her hand. "You deserve the job."

"I think so, too." Herman shrugged. "But there's not much to be done. Nancy said she'd help you with your resume if you want to explore other options."

"Thanks," Hannah said, feeling numb. "I'm not sure what I want to do yet."

But she *was* sure. What was it her grandma had said about a tool of last resort? Hannah would go over Herman's head and contact the bigwigs in New York if she had to.

"We're going to fix this," said Guy. "I'm going to fix this."

"What can you do about it?" Herman asked. "It's pretty clear nobody from corporate cares one iota about any of us." He rose to his feet. "I'm glad I'm retiring so I don't have to put up with their cockamamie bullcrap any longer." He patted Hannah on the back. "Sorry, my girl. I was rooting for you."

Hannah nodded numbly and watched Herman go. She didn't utter a peep until he'd seen himself out. Then Hannah, who never cried, burst into tears.

"Oh, Hannah," said Guy, as he encircled her with his arms. "Don't cry. We'll make this right."

"How?" Hannah demanded. "What they said about me is true. I don't have experience outside of this property."

"Which is what makes you so knowledgeable about Seaside Resort. You're the expert on how this place works, not some transplant from corporate."

"But... but..." Hannah sputtered, feeling the words get stuck in her throat. "I'm being selfish. They turned you down, too, and I'd rather see you in charge than an outsider."

"That's nice of you to say, but it doesn't change the fact that they screwed you over."

A fresh torrent of tears overtook her. "I hate Blanchet Maison," Hannah cried. "I hate everything about them. I gave them all I had, and they took advantage of me. They've been taking advantage of my family for decades."

Guy's face blanched white. "Hannah, I need to tell you something."

"What?" Hannah reached for a tissue.

"It's about my—"

"Can you believe how awful they are?" Hannah interrupted, not able to contain her ire. "If I saw Biathlon Man or Bunny Boy, I'd punch them both in the face."

"You'd seriously punch them?"

"No, not really." Hannah clenched her fists. "I'm not a violent person. But I'd call them nepo babies, at the very least. If it wasn't for nepotism, they'd be nowhere."

"I don't disagree with you."

"I'd tell those nepo babies to crawl back into their trust funds and never come out."

"Yeah, uh..."

"They don't have any idea what the real world is like, and I have zero respect for either one of them."

"Zero respect." Guy pushed hair off his forehead. "Wow."

"I'm sorry." Hannah looked at Guy. "I interrupted you, and it sounded like you were about to say something important."

"That's right." Guy blinked three times in a row and then he took a deep breath before continuing. "It's about that picture on the wall. I'm still thinking about it because it's a bit mysterious, don't you think?"

"Mysterious? How?" More importantly, why was Guy bringing the picture up now?

"Maybe mysterious is the wrong word. I should have said intriguing. I meant it when I said that I wish I could jump into that picture and ask people questions. I don't know who was in the audience, but Sinatra was there and, well, this is about Sinatra. Kind of." Guy scratched his head. "Or about people who go to Sinatra concerts. That is to say—"

Hannah's phone buzzed on the end table. "Hang on a sec." She leapt across the room to retrieve it. "That might be about the promotion." But when she looked at the screen, she saw that it was Mary calling, which was weird, since Mary knew she was on a date. Hannah accepted the call. "Hello?"

"Don't freak out," said Mary. "But there's been an accident."

"An accident?" Panic shot through her. "Are you okay? Is Gran okay?"

Across the room, Guy jumped to his feet.

"Everyone's okay," said Mary. "It was a coffee accident. Tea, actually. A leftover turmeric latte in my car."

"What?" Hannah asked, not understanding.

"I'm sorry, Hannah," Mary said, her voice shaking. "It's about your coat. Can you come down here to the parking lot and bring a blanket or something to keep Gran warm?"

"I'll be right there." Hannah ended the call and looked at

Guy. "My coat," she said, so startled that she didn't realize she was crying again.

"I heard." He picked up the blanket on the back of Cheryl's recliner. "Maybe it's not so bad. I bet it could be dry-cleaned."

"You can't dry-clean down," said Hannah. "There are natural oils in the feathers that keep it fluffy. It needs to be washed with a special detergent and—" Why was she explaining this to him? Didn't he know anything about winter garments? Hannah wasn't thinking straight. She couldn't, because her heart had broken into a million pieces the moment Herman had told her she'd been passed for the promotion. And now this. "Not Dad's coat," she cried.

"Let's not worry until we see what we're dealing with." Guy grabbed the afghan that was on the back of the sofa bed and threw it around Hannah's shoulders like a cape. "It's important for you to stay warm, too." He offered her the tissue box. "Take a few of these for the road."

"Thanks." Hannah blew her nose and attempted to dry her tears. "You must think I'm stupid—"

"I would never think that."

"I know it's just a coat."

"It's not just a coat." He repositioned the afghan so she'd be warmer. "Let's go figure this out together. Okay?"

Hannah gulped and nodded. She concentrated so hard on stopping her tears that she was unable to speak.

They left the cottage and walked down the steep path to the parking lot in silence. Hannah wiped her eyes and blew her nose a few times, clinging to the afghan so it wouldn't fall down. Guy carried the second blanket for Cheryl. When they reached Mary's car, they found Cheryl in her wheelchair, and Mary flapping the coat back and forth, flicking off yellow liquid the color of puke.

"It was my fault," said Cheryl. "Don't blame Mary."

"No, it was my fault." Mary stopped flapping and faced

Hannah. "I'm the one who left my drink in my car last night and then forgot about it."

"I said it was my fault and I meant it," said Cheryl. "I complained about it smelling like a dead animal, and instead of waiting for Mary to move it I picked it up myself to hand it to her, not realizing the lid was loose. And then—"

"But it was *my* fault that the lid wasn't on there properly," said Mary. "Otherwise—"

"Let's stop playing the blame game and make sure everyone is warm." Guy knelt in front of Cheryl and tucked the blanket around her. "Better?"

Cheryl shivered. "Much. Thank you."

Seeing her grandmother shiver snapped Hannah back to attention. "It's just a coat," she said, trying to mean it more certainly this time. "The important thing is that everyone is safe." When she looked over at Mary she saw tears roll down her sister's cheeks. "Why are *you* crying? You hated that thing."

"I know," Mary sniffed. "But *you* love it, and *you're* crying, and oh my gosh, Hannah, I'm so sorry to do this to you."

"You didn't do anything to me. I'm not crying because of the coat." She was, kind of, but she also wasn't. "I'm upset because I got passed over for the promotion."

"What do you mean, you didn't get the promotion?" Mary exclaimed.

"Those bastards!" Gran shouted. "When I get out of this chair I'm going to march to New York and flush Blanchet's face in the toilet, where it belongs."

"Which one?" Mary asked. "I thought there were two or three of them."

"Two of them now," Hannah clarified. "A father and a son."

"I'm so sorry." Mary threw her arms around her. "That totally sucks."

Hannah appreciated her sister's sympathy, but now that she was this close to the coat, she was getting barf-y vibes. "Gross," she said, pulling away. "It smells like a skunk died in the down. Are you sure coffee did that?"

"Not coffee, a turmeric latte made with whole milk that must have soured in the car overnight," Mary corrected. "I already told you."

"What would you like to do?" Guy asked Hannah. "Maybe we could bring the coat over to housekeeping and ask them to put it in the washing machine?"

"That's a great idea," said Cheryl. "Because the sooner you get the gunk out, the better. Turmeric stains. But the washing machines here are industrial strength, and would destroy the coat altogether." She looked up at Guy innocently. "Does your apartment have a washer and dryer? Maybe you and Hannah could go have your film festival at your place, and save her coat at the same time?"

"That's a great idea," said Guy. "Hannah, what do you say?"

A laundry emergency wasn't what Hannah had in mind when she'd thought about visiting Guy's apartment for the first time, but she was too numb to think of an alternative. If she couldn't have the promotion, at least she might still have the coat. "That would be great," she said as Guy took her hand. "Thank you." She looked up at him. "When we drive over there you can finish telling me what you wanted me to know about Sinatra."

"What?" Guy held tightly to her hand. "Oh, never mind about that. I was just going to say that his daughter wrote a memoir."

Hannah rested her head against Guy's shoulder. "I love that you read."

"Too bad he doesn't read anything interesting," Mary quipped.

Hannah ignored her and squeezed Guy's hand. "I think a daughter's memoir about her father sounds fascinating."

TWENTY-THREE

"So it's really dead," Mary said the next morning as she and Hannah stood on the porch of Strawberry Cottage. Hannah held a tray of food from The Summer Wind and Mary held a bouquet and present.

"Yeah." Hannah knelt by the still-wet bundle of torn fabric and mildewy down. "The coat was so old that even though we washed it on the gentle cycle, the fabric wasn't strong enough for the agitator."

"Maybe it needed a high-efficiency model or something? I had one of those at my apartment in LA."

Hannah nodded. "Maybe." She felt as heavy as the wet down. "At least I had a nice time with Guy last night." The evening had been so ruined that all they'd done was cuddle on the couch and watch the movie, but that had been nice. Comforting. Cozy. Perfect, really. What should have been one of the worst nights of Hannah's life had turned out not so bad. Guy had such a calming effect on her that her whole world felt steady when he was near. "Now let's wish Gran a happy Mother's Day."

"I'll get the door," Mary said, as she unlocked the handle.

One look and it was clear to see that Cheryl was pretending to be asleep. But as soon as Mary pretended to wake her up, she popped her eyes open. "Breakfast in bed? You girls spoil me."

"Blueberry pancakes with extra whipped cream, and a side of Canadian bacon." Hannah placed the tray on her grandma's lap.

"Happy Mother's Day!" Mary placed a bouquet on the end table next to her along with the gift-wrapped slippers.

"Those pancakes look delicious." Gran picked up the mug. "And coffee, too."

"With real cream," said Hannah. "Jasmine made the pancakes especially for you and would not let me pay for them until I insisted."

"Oh, that girl." Gran beamed. "Not only is she the best chef The Summer Wind ever had, but she's a sweetheart. Wait! I take that back... Sven Nilsen was the best chef we had, but only on a scale of hotness—no offense to Jasmine. But, wow!" Gran smacked her lips. "That man could make bacon sizzle all by himself."

"I want to hear more about Sven," said Mary, as she pulled up one of the dinette chairs to sit next to Cheryl.

"He only worked here for six months in 1975 before they caught him with a guest in Triton's Cottage, entertaining her with his trident." Cheryl sliced into her pancakes. "Oscar was furious. Fired him on the spot."

"That was before Herman's time, right?" Hannah tidied up the hide-a-bed. Her pride still stung from not getting the promotion, and it felt like she was drowning in worries. But focusing on the tasks at hand—making Mother's Day special for Gran, and collapsing the hide-a-bed—helped calm her fraying nerves.

"That's correct." Cheryl sipped her coffee before continuing. "Herman didn't come onto the scene until 1977. Back then, Oscar was in charge, but he mainly spent his time schmoozing celebrity guests and harassing housemaids." She frowned. "I think with Sven, the real problem was that Oscar's wife Iris had a thing for him, too. We all did." She patted her heart. "To this day when I see Swedish meatballs, I think of him."

"Speaking of Swedish meatballs," said Mary, turning toward Hannah. "Have you heard from Guy?"

"What does Guy have to do with meatballs?" Hannah pushed the hide-a-bed mattress back into the couch. "He's a vegetarian."

"We're talking about hunky men," said Mary. "It fits."

"No," Hannah said, more sharply than she intended. "I haven't heard from Guy since last night. What about you? Any news from Aidan?"

"Yes!" Mary clapped her hands together. "He comes home three weeks from today. He said he can't wait to see me and take me someplace private." She danced in her chair. "You know what that means!"

"But I haven't given him my blessing yet for him to propose to you," said Cheryl. Both girls glared at her. "Kidding," she said, with a laugh. "This isn't the nineteen-hundreds."

"Speaking of blessings, Guy's going to meet me later to help me give the coat a proper sendoff," said Hannah.

"You mean, like in a dumpster?" Mary asked.

"No." Hannah tugged her collar. "It was Guy's idea. He said we should have a bonfire on the beach like a funeral pyre. That way I can have closure."

"I think that's a great idea." Cheryl speared her bacon with her fork.

"Cremation, burial, whatever." Mary went over to the corner where they stored their clothes. "I think it's a great idea, too, and I have something for you to wear for the special occasion."

"You do?" Hannah asked.

"Ta da!" Mary whipped around and held the brand-new puffer coat she had bought Hannah last year. It was bright purple—a color Hannah would never have chosen for herself, but in perfect condition. "Look what I found."

Hannah accepted the coat from Mary and put it on. "Fits like it was made for me," she said.

"You're welcome." Mary beamed. "Maybe now you'll finally wear it."

"I will." Hannah hugged her. "Did I ever tell you you're my favorite sister?"

"I'm your only sister."

"It was a tough competition." What would life be without a sibling? Hannah pulled away from the hug and looked at Gran. "Has it been hard being an only child?" she asked.

"What?" Gran put her fork down.

"Not just now, but when you were younger and moved here from Nevada. That must have been so difficult," said Hannah.

"Yeah. Even transferring to a new school would have been hard." Mary patted Hannah's back. "We might have been three grades apart, but I always knew you were across the playground ready to support me if I fell off the monkey bars."

"I had my parents," said Cheryl. "And then your grandpa and your dad…" She sighed. "And then, I had you two."

"I'm sorry," said Hannah, realizing too late that she'd brought up sad memories on what should have been a happy day. "I wanted Mother's Day to be happy, and here I go revisiting the past."

"It's okay," said Cheryl. "Mother's Day always makes me think about the past. My mom, and yours, too. Have you girls called Kelly?"

"Mom?" Hannah squeaked. "Why would we do that?"

"Because it's Mother's Day," said Cheryl. "And no matter how many rotten things she did to you, she still gave you life."

"And she almost ended it, too," said Hannah.

"She's paid her debt to society," said Cheryl. "All I'm saying is maybe give her a call."

"Mom *has* been texting me recently," said Mary. "I don't know how to respond. She says she wants to talk about money."

"Don't you dare give her a penny." Hannah pointed at her sister. "Not one cent, no matter what her sob story is. She'll spend it on drugs."

"But food or warm clothes," Cheryl added. "You could give her those."

"We've got enough problems without adding Mom's to the pile." Hannah stood and took the tray from Gran since she had finished eating. She washed the dishes quickly.

"What are you girls up to today?" Cheryl asked.

"I have a shift at the coffee stand this morning," said Mary.

"And I have some emails to write before I meet Guy." Hannah dried the plate. "Then I'm due at the front desk at eleven." She'd taken more risks in the past twelve hours than she'd taken in the past twelve years. There was no point in stopping now. "I'm going to comb through the Blanchet Maison website until I find the name of an executive who might be able to help me. Then I'm going to write to them and explain that they made a mistake in not hiring me."

"That's my girl," said Cheryl. "Advocate for yourself, or nobody else will."

Hannah sat down with her computer and started working. She quickly found the email and phone number for Nate Webber, COO of Blanchet Maison. Hannah looked at her watch. What time was it in New York City? Weren't they three hours ahead? It would be rude to call on Mother's Day, but sending an email would be fine.

After fortifying herself with one of Guy's leftover sandwiches, Hannah wrote her heart out. She explained why she was the best person to lead Seaside Resort. It seemed liked she'd already expressed this a million times before. Why did she keep having to prove herself? It was like being in love with a company that didn't love her back. That was the truth of it.

Hannah loved Seaside Resort. She cared about its future. She didn't care one lick for Blanchet Maison, but she adored Strawberry Cottage, the view outside her window, and the people who worked here.

As soon as she finished her email Hannah hit send. She closed her computer with a satisfying click. "See you this evening," she told Cheryl and Mary, before heading out to the beach with the stinky coat.

Guy had arranged to meet at 9 a.m. down by the bonfire pits, but Hannah got there ten minutes early. She used the time to gather driftwood and create the perfect A-frame shape for a fire. Driftwood made the best fires. Hannah had loved watching sea salt cause the flames to bloom different colors ever since she was a little girl and Max had showed her the phenomenon. It seemed fitting to be here, in front of the logs, ready to light the flames one more time next to his coat.

Hannah went to the metal box the resort kept to store matches and a first-aid kit. She took out a matchbox, a fire starter, and some tinder the last person had cut, and went back to the pit. It was five past nine now, but Guy was probably running late. She sat in the sand waiting for him to arrive.

Wind whipped her hair across her cheek, but the sound of waves crashing against the shoreline soothed her. Cold seeped through her jeans, but the sand was a soft place to sit. As the minutes ticked by and Guy still hadn't arrived, she wondered if maybe she'd gotten the time wrong, so she checked her phone to see if he'd texted her. There was nothing.

It was now twenty past, and Hannah knew that driftwood fires sometimes needed extra time to get going, so she leaned forward and lit the fire starter. Guy would be there any minute. Flames licked up the starter and hit the tinder. A few minutes later, the fire burst to life. But at half past, Guy still wasn't there, so Hannah texted him.

The bonfire's going strong. Did I get the time wrong?

Guy didn't answer.

That seemed odd, but Hannah figured he might be driving and unable to answer. She waited another ten minutes for him to show up before she tried calling him. His number went straight to voicemail.

"Hi Guy, this is Hannah. I'm down here by the beach. Maybe you meant nine at night and not nine in the morning? Okay, well... I'll see you at work." She hung up and checked her email. When her eyes saw a message from Nate Webber in her inbox, she felt a jolt of adrenaline—until she realized that it was a company-wide email and not sent specifically to her.

Apparently, Guido "Gabe" Blanchet III, aka the former Biathlon star, had been rushed to the hospital last night with an undisclosed medical condition.

The financial markets are still closed since it's Sunday, Mr. Webber wrote, *but we expect this news to impact stock prices tomorrow morning. Rest assured we have a plan in place to steady the ship and keep shareholders happy. Please join me in sending our sincerest wishes to the Blanchet family that Gabe makes a swift and immediate recovery.*

Hannah swiped out of her email. It figured that a corporate bigwig like Mr. Webber would think of stock prices first, and a family in crisis second.

As for her, it was time to think of herself. The fire roared now, and she had a difficult job to finish.

Hannah picked up her father's coat and hugged it one last time, even though it was soaking wet.

"Dad," she said, speaking into the wind. "I want you to know that I love you, and that a part of you will always be with me, with or without this coat." Her voice fought against a lump that was forming in her throat, but she soldiered on. "I've spent my whole life trying to be responsible, like you. Now I'm trying to be brave like you, too. Part of that means taking risks and expanding the circle of people I trust."

An unwelcome thought occurred to her. Had her father had issues trusting people? If he had been depressed, nobody had known it. He had never confided struggles with mental health with anyone. Was it that the insurance company was wrong, and his death hadn't been by suicide, or was it because he truly had suffered from depression and didn't trust anyone enough to share that information? She would never know the truth, and that realization added to her sorrow.

Hannah gave Max's coat a final hug. "I love you, Dad, no matter what you went through, and I want you to know that you can trust me to take care of our family."

She threw the coat on the roaring fire and watched the flames sizzle from the added moisture. The fire sputtered, struggling against the weight of wet down. It needed help, but Hannah knew what to do. She took her new coat off and fanned the flames, using her purple coat to bring the bonfire back to life. Only when it raged again did she put her coat back on and zip it up. She stuffed her hands into the pockets and gazed into the flames. This coat from Mary was wonderfully warm—stylish, too. It was a coat a grown woman wore; an adult who was fully capable of taking care of herself, no matter what horrible situation life threw at her. This coat fit Hannah to a T.

TWENTY-FOUR

Hannah stood at the front desk, waiting for the onslaught of guests who would arrive at 4 p.m. Her success for the day, besides saying goodbye to the coat, was that she had emailed Brittany and made an appointment for later tonight to find out more about the shared housing situation. The only catch was, she still hadn't heard from Guy. Hopefully the appointment at Brittany's would be done before nine o'clock, because Hannah had reasoned that Guy must have meant 9 p.m. on the beach instead of 9 a.m. The time mix-up might have been her fault. When her phone buzzed and she saw that it was Guy calling, she answered it before the second ring.

"Hi, Guy. Did I get the time wrong for the beach?"

"No, you didn't. I'm sorry, I should have called earlier. A family emergency took me out of town. I'm at the airport now. My plane just landed and is taxiing to the gate."

"Oh no! I'm so sorry," Hannah waited for Guy to elaborate with more details, but he didn't. "Is there anything I can to do help?"

"Yes, actually. Could you cancel my training clients for the rest of the week? I don't know when I'll be back. I'm sorry for the lost revenue."

"Don't worry about it. The last thing I care about these days is making Blanchet Maison more money. Focus on your family —that's what's important."

Will showed up at his spot at the front desk and Hannah was relieved to see him. She pointed to her phone. "I'm going to take this outside," she whispered. He waved his approval and she darted out the door.

"It's so good to hear your voice," Guy said. "I miss you already."

"I miss you too. Are you tired? Were you able to sleep on the plane?"

"A little. My dad's in the hospital. That's the emergency."

"Oh no!"

"The doctors are with him now. At first they said heart attack, but now they are saying it's a stroke."

"That's serious."

"I know. I'm trying not to think of it. Instead, I spent the whole plane ride thinking of you. I'm going to help you get that general manager job."

"Thanks, but don't worry about me. Your family needs you more than I do."

"I can focus on more than one thing," Guy said. "Unless you're around. Then I can only focus on you."

Hannah giggled. "That's the cheesiest line I've heard in a while."

"I didn't sleep much last night, so cheesy lines are all I have to work with."

"Were you stuck in the back row next to the bathrooms since you booked the flight at the last minute?" Before he could answer she added: "What airline are you flying, Alaska? That's my favorite."

"Um... It's, uh, one of those airlines nobody's heard of."

"Oooh. I hope you brought your own snacks in case they tried to sell you twelve-dollar peanuts."

"Snacks are always a smart idea. Listen, there are so many things I want to tell you, and I tried to explain yesterday, but... You know I told you I'm an only child, right?"

"Yeah, like Gran. That must make it especially difficult in a family emergency."

"How so?"

"Because you don't have a sibling to help you. Mary always helps me. No matter what. Do you have someone in your family like that?"

"Not anymore," he replied hoarsely. "Not since my granddad passed away."

"But you have your mom though, right? I bet she's grateful that you're coming."

"She is. At least, I think she is. When I spoke to her last night, the doctor had given her a sedative because she was so upset. Whatever they gave her made her loopy."

"I don't like to take any medicine unless I absolutely have to," Hannah said, thinking of Kelly and her chemical dependence issues.

"Same. Look, I wish I had more time but I'm at the gate now. I need to go, but I wanted you to know, the main reason I came to Sand Dollar Cove was because of my granddad, but the reason I stayed was because of you. Seaside Resort wouldn't be what it is without you. It's been a great place to work. I finally feel like I can breathe again. And I hope that yesterday was only the beginning for us, no matter what the future holds for your career or mine."

"Me too," said Hannah. "I'll see you when you get back."

"Yeah. I'll see you when I come home."

Home. There was that word again.

It seemed like a far-off dream, but later that evening it felt like it was within reach. Hannah, Mary, and Cheryl were sitting around Brittany's kitchen table about to sign papers for their lease. Their housing drama was almost over. Hannah just hoped it was a happy ending, and not the start of more chaos.

"Okay, so I've never done this before, but I'm hoping it's a good thing for all of us," said Brittany. A curly-haired woman in her mid-forties, Brittany wore a tank top, joggers, and flip-flops. Her nose ring twinkled in the light. For a nutritionist, she was a lot more mellow than Hannah had expected. Yes, there was a bowl of fruit on the counter, but there was also a box of snack-sized chips on top of the refrigerator. "So to confirm, rent will be fourteen hundred a month for two bedrooms, the upstairs bathroom, and exclusive use of the living room. Jeremy and I will each have our own rooms and bathroom, as well as the family room. You ladies will have the right side of the refrigerator and we'll have the left. Ditto with the pantry."

"We should establish a cleaning checklist ahead of time," said Cheryl. "The kitchen should have a baseline that we are all responsible for keeping to."

"That's a good idea," said Brittany.

"For the laundry room, too." Cheryl leaned forward slightly, resting her elbows on the table. "If there's one thing I'm an expert at, it's housekeeping."

"That's true," said Mary. "Growing up, I lived in fear of leaving crumbs on the counter."

"Mary!" Hannah shot her sister a look. "She's joking," Hannah told Brittany. "I promise."

"No, she's not," said Cheryl. "I'm part wicked witch. Where'd you think I got this hunchback?" She cackled, and they all laughed with her.

"Keith said you had a sense of humor," said Brittany. "That's always handy when you live with a teenager. But to be totally honest, this will help me out financially quite a lot. I'm no longer receiving alimony from my ex-husband, and I've been squeaking by trying to make the mortgage payments. Now I'll be able to keep my house, no problem, and also set some money aside for emergencies."

"And we'll be living with a view like that." Mary pointed to the canal outside. "Gorgeous. My future in-laws live next door down."

"The DeLacks? Ah..." Brittany's mouth gaped open.

"What?" Mary asked.

"Nothing." Brittany clamped her mouth shut.

"It's okay," said Cheryl. "We want to know what she's getting into."

"*I* know what I'm getting into," said Mary. "Aidan is great, but his parents are a bit prickly."

"The DeLacks don't like anyone," said Brittany. "It's not just you. Stewart lectured me about letting my grass go dormant last summer."

"But that saves water," said Hannah. "Lots of homeowners do that."

"Not Stewart and Heather DeLack." Brittany rolled her eyes. "Another time I heard Stewart berate Aidan for accidentally driving over the sprinkler head. If his son had still been a teenager, I might have given him a pass on that, but this was only a few months ago, before he left for the Midwest."

"Poor Aidan," said Mary. "I know that his traveling nurse jobs pay well, but I've always wondered if the distance from his parents was also a reason for not taking a local position. He's never come out and said so, though."

"Stewart and Heather are really hard on him," said Brittany. "They're perfectionists."

"Mary can be a bit of a perfectionist, too," Hannah said, thinking of the ridiculous amount of time her sister had spent on that floor stencil in Strawberry Cottage. "Especially when it comes to decorating. Maybe Heather will admire that quality about her?"

"I wish." Mary winced. "But Heather goes for the 'coastal grandma' esthetic, and that's not really my style."

Brittany nodded. "The one time she invited me inside I thought her house was the set of a Diane Keaton movie."

"I will channel coastal grandma if my future clients absolutely insist upon it," said Mary. "But no, that's not my first choice for decorating. I love the boho chic vibe you've gone with, though. This is much closer to my taste."

"It's gorgeous," said Cheryl. "Pretty and homey at the same time."

"And I can't get over the waterfront access." Hannah looked forward to borrowing Brittany's kayak and exploring the canal system that had at one time promised to make Sand Dollar Cove the Riviera of the West. "Thank you for taking a chance on us," she told Brittany.

"I'm so glad Keith recommended you." Brittany smiled. "Reducing the financial pressure I've been under is the best Mother's Day gift I could ask for."

"We can relate," said Cheryl. "A new place is all I wanted for Mother's Day." She looked at Hannah and Mary. "Besides that lovely breakfast tray you girls brought me this morning, and my new slippers."

"I didn't get breakfast in bed." Brittany frowned. "Teenagers... Anyhow, I know your first choice would have been to not bother with roommates, just like our goal was—and is—to have our own place, but maybe this will be a happy medium."

Jeremy, a tall, gangly teenage boy with a mop of brown hair shuffled into the kitchen. "Hey," he said, before opening the refrigerator, drinking milk straight from the carton, and putting it away. "I'm off to work. See ya later."

"Use a glass next time," said Brittany. "And drive safe."

"We'll be like the Golden Girls," said Cheryl, once Jeremy had left. "With one notable exception."

"I'll put down masking tape in the refrigerator so he doesn't accidentally contaminate your food," said Brittany. "Or wolf down all of it in the middle of the night."

"I had a teenage boy once," said Cheryl. "They're lovable bottomless pits."

"So true." Brittany signed her name on the contract. "Okay, that's my signature." She handed the pen to Hannah. "Last chance to back out of this experiment."

"I'm all in." Hannah signed her name and passed the pen to Mary.

"Wait until I tell my design school friends that I have a golf course view from one window, and a canal view from the other." Mary scribbled her name with an extra flourish.

"The views are great," said Cheryl, as she picked up her pen. "But what I'm looking forward to is what the diabetes group says when they find out about this arrangement."

"Oh, jeez." Brittany winced. "They love to gossip."

"They're going to be *so* jealous." Cheryl signed the contract and slid it back to Brittany.

"You heard what happened when they found out I was dating Keith, right?" Brittany asked.

"No," said Cheryl. "What?"

Brittany pulled a lock of hair behind her ear. "Someone tracked down a decade's worth of high school yearbooks to find out what years we graduated and how much older I am than him."

"That's nosy, even for Sand Dollar Cove," said Hannah.

"We're only eight years apart," said Brittany. "It's not such a big deal."

"The main thing is if you like each other," said Mary.

"Exactly." Brittany nodded. "And we do. Keith and I both like working with the community and we both love having jobs that deal with math. He has to balance the senior center budget, and I'm tracking calories and blood sugar levels. I also crunch numbers to balance the grocery bill."

"It's good that you and Keith found each other." Hannah took her checkbook out of her purse. "I'll write out the check for first and last month's rent."

"Great. And you three can move in the first week of June. I'll have the storage boxes moved out of the downstairs bedroom by then."

"That'll give me time to find furniture for Hannah's and my bedroom," said Mary. "The recliner and TV can go in Gran's room, and the couch and end table can be in the living room."

"Where will you put the picture of the T Bone Bluff and Frank Sinatra?" Hannah asked, thinking of Guy.

"I'm not sure yet." Mary looked through the kitchen to the living room. "Maybe by the fireplace."

"I remember the T Bone Bluff." Brittany crossed her legs and dangled a flip-flop off her toes. "My parents always let me order a Shirley Temple, and they'd tell the waitress to bring extra cherries."

"You had to be a certain height to work at the T Bone Bluff," said Cheryl. "I was two inches too short, not that my father would have allowed me to work there, anyway."

"Why not?" Mary asked.

"Yeah," said Hannah. "And what does height have to do with being a waitress?"

"The owner hired girls with a certain look." Cheryl cupped her hands. "Big tits, legs for days, and behinds with the right amount of wiggle."

"*That's* what the T Bone Bluff was like?" Hannah asked. "A glorified Hooters? This whole time I thought it was a fancy steakhouse with a bandstand attached."

"You say steakhouse. I say meat locker." Cheryl shrugged. "Even if I had been tall enough for those uniforms, the owner would never have hired me because he knew my father."

"My great-grandpa was a builder," Hannah explained.

"That's right." Cheryl nodded. "Oscar Lexter brought him in from Las Vegas because he knew he did top-notch work."

"Fascinating." Brittany uncrossed her legs. "You know, now that I think about it, I remember my mom telling my dad to put his eyes back in his head when we'd go to the T Bone. At the time I didn't know what that meant—I thought he needed to wear his glasses."

Hannah wanted the conversation to continue because she knew Guy was curious about the T Bone Bluff and its connection to his grandfather, but she was also preoccupied by the email from Nate Webber and wanted to call him back right away. Now that the papers for the house share were signed, she was already thinking about work again.

"We should probably get going." Hannah handed Brittany the check. "It's late, and we have plans to make."

"There will be plenty of time to gab around the kitchen table like we're the Golden Girls later," said Brittany. "I'm really excited."

"Excited enough to stock the freezer with cheesecake?" Cheryl asked.

"Absolutely," said Brittany. "Just don't tell my clients."

"I have dibs on being Blanche," said Mary.

"Why do *you* get to be Blanche?" Hannah asked.

"Because she's the hot one, obviously." Mary straightened the napkin holder and the salt and pepper shaker in the middle of the table, before she stood. "You can be Dorothy. You've already got the stoic, bitter vibe going."

"I do not." Hannah put her hands on her hips.

"Picture it," said Cheryl. "This one time in Sand Dollar Cove." Rising unsteadily to her feet, she braced herself on her walker.

"Yes?" Hannah asked. "What comes next?"

"I don't know," said Cheryl. "I'll tell you the next time we have cheesecake."

"I guess this makes me Rose Nylund." Brittany stood. "Which I'm totally okay with because I adored Betty White."

"You know," said Mary, as she slung her purse strap over her shoulder. "When I first heard about this shared housing idea, I wasn't so sure, but now I think it might be better than having our own place."

"You say that now," said Brittany. "But wait until Jeremy uses up all the hot water while taking the longest shower known to humankind."

"I learned to never complain about my teenage son shower-ing." Cheryl walked slowly across the floor toward the front door. "It was better than the alternative."

"Yuck." Mary wrinkled her nose. "Dad didn't shower?"

"Not until he discovered girls, he didn't." Cheryl chuckled. "And then I had a whole new set of parenting dilemmas to deal with."

"See, you really are Sophia Petrillo," said Brittany. "I'll be glad to have an experienced parent in the house to offer me advice."

"What about you, Hannah?" Mary asked. "What do you think about all of this?"

Hannah gazed in wonder at the empty living room that was soon to be their own. "I'm just relieved that we'll be in a safe place that we can afford." She clasped her hands together like she was praying. "Thank you, Brittany. Thanks again for taking a chance on us."

"Thanks for taking a chance on *me*," said Brittany. "And Jeremy, who lest there be any confusion, will be the squeaky wheel in our Golden Girls reunion. Or the smelly wheel. Possibly the crabby one? It depends on the day. Every day he's like a different kid."

"We'll duct-tape our milk cartons shut and everything will be fine," said Cheryl.

Everyone laughed and said goodbye. Hannah drove home, barely listening to Mary's chatter about how she was going to arrange the furniture in the upstairs bedroom to maximize the morning light and catch the evening breeze. Not that Hannah didn't care about her new room with Mary, or the logistical details about how they would physically move all their worldly possessions to their new place. It was just that Hannah couldn't concentrate on anything at the moment. Her mind jumped from the *Golden Girls*, to her lost promotion, to Guy kissing her yesterday, to the email from the COO of Blanchet Maison, and to the T Bone Bluff, where thirty years ago it was considered perfectly acceptable to hire women based solely on their breast size. Hannah was glad the place was under new ownership.

But as she drove into the parking lot of Seaside Resort, past the fallen sign that was pushed neatly over to the side, she wondered how she'd feel if they bulldozed the resort to make room for something different. The new general manager might suggest such a thing. If they tore down the cottages, they could put up a high-rise that would boast five hundred rooms instead of fifty. Forget about historic architecture. Nobody seemed to care about who Kara Lee Paul was but her. *And Guy.* Guy had asked about architectural significance. Where was he now? Hannah wished she could check her phone and see if he'd texted her, but she couldn't, since she was driving. If only she could call him again, once she got home, and hear his voice. But no; it was late in New York, and Guy needed to concentrate on his father's health. She didn't want to disturb that.

Hannah parked her car in the lot, a few spots away from where Lark was climbing into her hatchback.

"Hi, Turner women." Lark waved.

"Hi, Lark." Hannah stepped out of her car. "Any fun plans tonight?"

"Not unless you count watering Guy's tomato plants. He texted me just now and said he was out of town for a family emergency."

"That's right," said Hannah. "Thanks for doing that for him." *Guy had texted Lark?* Hannah felt jittery with excitement. Maybe he'd texted her, too. As soon as it was polite to do so, she looked at her phone. Her hope deflated when she didn't see any further messages from Guy. He had texted Lark, but not her? Hannah felt saddened at first, but then she took the initiative.

I found out some interesting tidbits about the T Bone Bluff, she texted, hoping that would garner a response. Then she felt like a royal jerk for bothering him with local gossip, when he was probably in the hospital right now sitting beside his father's bed. *I can tell you about it later,* she added. *I hope your father's improving.*

Hannah put her phone away before she made another poor decision. It was late. She wouldn't bother Guy again because she didn't want to appear too needy.

"Are you okay?" Mary asked, as she opened the trunk to remove Cheryl's wheelchair. "You've got a weird look on your face."

"Weird, how?" Hannah removed Cheryl's walker as well while the trunk was still open.

"Like you're disappointed. Is that it? I know a shared housing situation isn't what we wanted, but—"

"I think it'll be great," said Hannah. She didn't want her sister to fret.

"Is this about not getting the promotion, then?"

Hannah nodded.

"I thought you said there's still a chance." Mary locked Cheryl's wheelchair into position.

"There is," said Hannah. "Barely."

But there wasn't, was there? Hannah couldn't afford to lose her job now, not when they'd finally found stable housing. No, she would have to chug along. Stick it out. Keep going. Her career was stuck in neutral, but at least the engine still worked. Who needed hopes and dreams when she had a family to support? Not her.

She helped bring Cheryl's walker up the path to Strawberry Cottage as Mary pushed the wheelchair. Their nights of being resort guests were coming to a close, and that was a good thing. But instead of feeling happy, Hannah's emotions rumbled with unease. Her career had stalled and Guy was gone. No wonder her worries spun in circles.

TWENTY-FIVE

"Whoa!" Jasmine ran into the lobby Monday morning, still wearing her apron. "Did you hear the news about the turmoil at corporate?"

"What turmoil?" Lark asked, as she turned off the vacuum cleaner.

Hannah was curious, too. The last thing she'd seen was the company-wide email from Nate Webber yesterday morning about Gabe Blanchet being in the hospital.

"Old man Blanchet's in the hospital," said Jasmine.

"I thought everyone knew that." Hannah arranged a stack of maps in the guest information display. "There was that email."

"Yeah, but now they are saying it's a stroke," said Jasmine. "At least, that's what's being mentioned in the private chef group for Blanchet Maison employees I'm in."

"Stroke?" Hannah's ears perked up. *Like Guy's father?*

"Holy Toledo!" Herman ran in through the double front doors. "Nancy just heard about Blanchet being sick on the radio. Stock prices are already plummeting!"

"It's a stroke," Jasmine said. "They're not announcing it yet, but that's what the chef at the flagship in New York City is saying."

Hannah rushed to her desktop computer and looked up the national news. The first headline she saw said: *Blanchet Maison in Steady Hands as Son Takes the Helm*.

Hannah leaned closer to read the subhead.

Dr. Guido Blanchet IV assures shareholders that company is secure while his father, "Gabe" Blanchet III recovers from unspecified health condition. Promises focus on employee well-being.

In the back of her mind, a tiny bell rang. *Unspecified health condition?*

"When did Gabe Blanchet become ill again?" she asked.

"Saturday night," said Jasmine.

"That's what the email said," Herman confirmed.

The bell rang again in Hannah's brain.

"Why are they being so hush-hush?" Lark added. "Maybe he had a botched facelift."

"It's a stroke," Jasmine said. "I already told you."

"Do we know anything about Guido IV?" Hannah asked. Her focus had always been on Seaside Resort, with an occasional glance outward at the other Local Flavors properties. Wall Street gossip didn't interest her. But a son rushing off to help his ailing father? *Once again, that bell rang.*

"Yeah, don't you remember?" Jasmine pulled out her phone. "It's hilarious. Last year the guy went viral after using a bunny filter by accident." She held out the screen.

"Panicked Rabbit?" Lark asked. "That was him?"

The *guy* went viral... Hannah's pulse picked up again.

"I remember it distinctly," said Jasmine. "Apparently he showed up to a Blanchet board meeting on Zoom with the bunny filter still on."

"What in tarnation is a bunny filter?" Herman asked.

"It changed his appearance, so he looked like a rabbit," Lark explained.

"The thing is, he's a physical therapist," said Jasmine. "That was his explanation, at least. He'd been meeting with a young patient right before and didn't realize the filter was still engaged."

A physical therapist. Hannah felt like she might faint. *Guy was knowledgeable about physical therapy.*

"He's been off-grid since Panicked Rabbit," said Jasmine. "Completely AWOL."

"I love that gif," said Lark. "It's hysterical."

"I remember people sharing it in the chef's group." Jasmine tied her apron strings. "Well, I better get going." She waved goodbye. "See you later."

"Yeah. See you," Hannah said in a faint voice. She looked at Herman. "Can you handle the front desk? I'm not feeling so well."

"But I never cover the front desk," said Herman. "I don't know where the guest register is anymore."

"It's on the computer." Hannah opened up the screen. "Here you go."

"I don't know—" Herman protested.

"I gotta go or I'll puke," Hannah exclaimed.

Herman jumped back. "In that case." He squirted hand sanitizer into his palms and rubbed vigorously.

Hannah ran as quickly as she could to Strawberry Cottage. Mary was at school, and Cheryl was at the senior center, so she had the place to herself. Using her phone, Hannah searched for everything she could find about Guido Blanchet IV. There wasn't much. All the tabloid shots from last year showed a man shielding his face and wearing a mask. It was impossible to get a clear look at him. Gabe and Marla's pictures were all over the web in one glamorous photo after another, including extensive documentation about Gabe's Olympian prowess. But except for a few early photographs of Guido IV as an adorable brown-haired child, they didn't seem too keen on showing him off. When Hannah checked Wikipedia, there was one measly sentence about Guido IV graduating from Dartmouth.

Dartmouth!

Hannah leaned back on the couch, the room spinning. She was hungry, not nauseous. That was it. When was the last time she'd eaten? Had she accidentally skipped breakfast? Hannah got up and found a banana on the counter. As she peeled it, she tucked the pieces of information away like shoeboxes sliding into place on a shelf.

Guy went to Dartmouth.

Guy rushed home to New York when his father fell ill on Saturday night.

Hannah ate the banana and looked over at the wall, where the vintage print of Frank Sinatra singing at the T Bone Bluff hung. That picture had fascinated Guy. Was it really because he'd read a celebrity memoir, or was it something more? Hannah scratched her chin. Didn't Gabriel Blanchet II purchase Seaside Resort right about then? Back in the early 1980s?

Tossing the banana peel into the wastebasket, Hannah googled Guy's name. She'd searched for it before, prior to hiring him as the wellness instructor. Back then, she had found nothing, but she had primarily been looking for social media, and inappropriate posts that might reflect poorly on the resort.

It was the same now. Hannah couldn't find one mention of Guy Barret on the web. That was weird. Who got this far into life without one phantom post following them online forever?

On a whim, she tried searching again. This time for the name Guido Barret.

Bingo!

The first article that pulled up was from a fraternity website.

The Delta Beta chapter of Sigma Nu is proud to initiate Guido Barret Blanchet IV to our ranks. Pledge name: Guy.

Hannah palmed her forehead, unable to process. Next, she searched for Guy Blanchet. Immediately a website called Wellness in Action came up. Hannah couldn't find any mention of Guy on the site until she searched through the gallery of past photos, and found an archived one of him standing next to a patient riding a recumbent bike.

That was him, alright. Her Guy Barret, only with brown hair.

No, not hers. And his name wasn't Guy Barret, it was Guido Blanchet IV, and he was a liar.

A key turned in the lock and the front door swung open. "Hey, you," said Mary. "What are you doing home at this hour? I thought you had to work."

"Guy's a liar!"

"What?" Mary dropped her keys on the end table. "Slow down, I can't understand you."

"I've been tricked!" Hannah jumped to her feet. "We've all been tricked." She ripped the frame off the wall and shoved the picture in Mary's face. "And what the hell is this about? Why was Guy so intrigued by this stupid picture? I'm tired of being jerked around!"

"It's not a stupid picture. It's a classic piece of Sand Dollar Cove Americana." Mary took the photo away and set it on the ground next to where Ferdinand was sleeping in a spot of sunshine. "You're not making any sense, sis. Slow down and try again."

Hannah sank back onto the couch. She didn't know where

to begin, but she started with the news that sliced her heart. "Guy lied to me. He's not who he said he was."

"He's not? Who is he then?"

"Guido Blanchet IV, heir to the hotel chain."

"Shut the front door."

"You already did."

"No, I mean, you can't be serious."

"But I am." Hannah explained what she'd learned, and showed Mary the things she'd found on the internet.

"He's been a prince in disguise this whole time?" Mary asked.

"I wouldn't call him a prince."

Mary held up her hand and counted on her fingers one by one. "Did he or did he not, one, save all of us from rats. Two, help us make this place habitable. Three, convince Gran to go to physical therapy. Four, bring us homemade food every time we saw him. And five, make out with you like Romeo on the porch over there, and don't deny it because I watched the whole thing."

"Eew." Hannah wrinkled her nose. "Creeper."

"But it's true, right?" Mary asked. "Guy's a prince, no matter which family he comes from. And he's crazy about you, too!"

Hannah let Mary's words sink in. What she said about Guy was true. She hated that he'd lied to her, but all of his deeds had been full of integrity. Warmth, too. Especially those scorching-hot kisses.

"I can't date a liar," Hannah declared.

"So tell him that," said Mary. "In person. To his face. Fly to New York and tell him—I dare you."

"With what money?"

"Charge it. My emergency credit card has a pretty high limit."

"Mine does too, but I'm not going to charge a last-minute

flight to New York," said Hannah. "That would be so irresponsible."

"Would it?"

"Yes!"

"Would it really, though?" Mary grabbed Hannah by the shoulders. "Take a risk, Hannah. Stick up for yourself. Fly to New York, not only to tell Guy that you caught him lying but also so that you can march into corporate headquarters and tell them you won't put up with their BS any longer. *You're* the right person to run Seaside Resort. *You*, and nobody else."

"Maybe..." Hannah said, feeling uncertain. Her gaze drifted down to the picture that had hung above the couch. "It would better if there was a way I could have the upper hand."

"I don't think love's about getting the upper hand."

"No, but it should be about equal footing." Hannah studied the picture of the Sinatra concert. "Guy was fascinated by that photo. He said it was mysterious, and he mentioned his granddad. Why?" Her mind spun like a top.

"Maybe Guy likes Sinatra, I don't know."

"No, it's something more than that." Hannah concentrated, trying to remember the bits and pieces that Guy had shared. "Guy said he wished he could step through the frame and ask people questions."

"Like Mary Poppins without the cool umbrella?"

"I guess. But what questions would he have asked?"

"Something about his grandfather?" Mary suggested. "What else do you know about him?"

"I know that Guy's granddad told him to head out West. Guy's Guido number four. That means his grandfather was Guido number two, the one they called Gabriel—the one who bought Seaside Resort from Oscar Lexter."

"I didn't follow any of that," said Mary. "There's too many Guidos."

"Not really." Hannah counted them off. "Guido the first

leaves Italy. Gabriel buys Seaside Resort. Gabe is in the Olympics—he's Guy's father, and is the one who's in the hospital right now. Then Guido the fourth is actually Guy." She tapped the photograph. "This vintage picture is an important clue to the story."

"Let's find out more about it then. I'm all for equality in relationships."

"But how? The library doesn't have records. They razed the T Bone Bluff's bandstand years ago. Where else can I find intel?"

"By stepping into the picture frame." Mary looked at it closely. "These people are young in the photo, but I bet they're old now. What we need is a group of people who love to gossip about the past."

The two sisters locked eyes and smiled.

"The senior center," they both said at the same time.

Mary picked up her keys. "Let's hit the road and find out who remembers something about that Sinatra concert."

TWENTY-SIX

Two days later a considerably wiser and more knowledgeable Hannah arrived at the flagship Blanchet Maison hotel on Park Avenue. The red-eye from SeaTac to JFK had been brutal, but Hannah had been so exhausted that she'd managed to get a solid night's sleep for the first time in days. She wore black slacks, high heels she'd borrowed from Mary that didn't look *that* cheap, a blouse, and her trusty Ralph Lauren blazer that she'd commandeered from the lost and found. Plus she'd put on winged eyeliner and red lipstick in the tiny airplane bathroom, which was a big departure from her normal look, but which added a touch of sophistication that made Hannah feel more comfortable now that skyscrapers surrounded her.

She hadn't told Guy what she had discovered about his grandfather. She'd keep *him* in the dark for once, and it felt good. He had no idea she was coming to town.

The taxi pulled right up to the revolving glass doors of the lobby, and a tall man wearing red livery opened her car door. "Welcome to Blanchet Maison," he said. "Can I help you with your bags?"

Hannah clutched her briefcase protectively. The secrets it contained had been hard won.

"There's one bag back here," said the driver as he popped the trunk.

"I'll take that," said the bellhop.

"Careful with the handle," said Hannah, as she stepped out of the car. "It'll fall off if you—"

Bam! The ancient Samsonite fell to the ground.

"I'm so sorry, miss. My sincerest apologies." The bellhop picked up the suitcase and carried it with both arms.

"It's okay." Hannah hooked her purse over her shoulder. "There's nothing valuable in there." She held onto her briefcase with white knuckles and put on a brave face. It didn't matter if she wore red lipstick or not. She was still the same person she always was, Hannah Turner from Sand Dollar Cove, dressed in second-hand clothes and carrying barely enough cash to tip the bellhop. But she *would* tip well. She'd be generous. Hannah knew how hard the service staff worked, because she was one of them.

"Right this way, miss." A doorman shepherded her into the lobby. "We hope you'll enjoy your stay."

Hannah's high heels clicked across the marble floor. Hundreds of twinkling lights from an enormous crystal chandelier glowed overhead. Murals depicting French landmarks adorned the walls. The air was rich with the scent of a spicy fragrance. Hannah couldn't tell what it was for certain, but assumed it might be Sandalwood and Ivy, the signature Blanchet Maison fragrance used in the toiletries line only available at the luxury properties. She'd never smelled it before, but had read about it in marketing materials.

"Miss Turner," called a voice. "We weren't expecting you until later, but welcome." A concierge rushed to greet her. "My name's Deshan."

"Thanks, Deshan. Nice to meet you." Hannah shook his

hand. "But please, call me Hannah. I'm grateful to you for allowing me to cash in my employee credits like this."

"Ten years of earning points and you've never used them." He clucked his tongue. "Such self-control. I blow mine every year as soon as I accumulate them. Jamaica... Hawaii... Paris... I've been everywhere."

"You probably earn more points than I do since I'm with Local Flavors. It took all I had to book two nights here with an alley view."

"Don't worry about that." Deshan winked. "We employees need to stick together, am I right? I upgraded you to a junior suite, on the house."

"You did? Thank you so much!"

"Of course." Deshan pulled out a tablet. "If you follow me to my desk, I'll get you checked in without waiting in line."

"I don't need special treatment. I can wait in line with the guests."

"Don't be ridiculous." Deshan stepped behind the concierge counter. "As far as I'm concerned, you're our highest-priority guest at the moment."

"I thought we were your highest-priority guests," said a familiar voice. "That's what you told us yesterday."

Hannah turned and saw two faces that her brain struggled to identify at first because, like her, they didn't belong here. "Mrs. Dario and Mrs. Sanchez? What are you doing here?"

"Seeing the shows and living in the lap of luxury," said Mrs. Dario, with a huge smile on her face. "Is that you, Hannah, or are you a doppelgänger for this spunky gal we know from back home in Washington?"

"It's me." Hannah put her briefcase on the desk to give her arm a break from carrying it.

"I can take that for you," said the bellhop, who was still lurking behind her.

"No, thanks." Hannah picked it up again.

"I hope you get a good room," said Mrs. Sanchez. "When we first checked in, we were paying six hundred and fifty dollars a night for a view of a brick wall."

"But now we have a private suite with a view of Central Park," Mrs. Dario added. "It almost makes me forgive Mr. Moneybags for all those push-ups he made us—"

"Hush, Elena. You're blabbing."

"Oh." Mrs. Dario slapped her hand across her mouth. "You're right," she mumbled between her fingers.

"We'd better get going." Mrs. Sanchez grabbed her friend by the elbow and dragged her away. "See you later, Hannah. Glad you came."

Guy had told *them* the truth about his identity, but not her? Hannah's irritation simmered.

"I booked you into the Dauphine Suite." Deshan handed Hannah a packet. "Here's your room key, and my business card with my personal cell phone number. Call me if you need anything during your stay."

"Thank you so much, Deshan. This is above and beyond."

"My pleasure. I'll escort you to your suite right now in the VIP elevator."

"Thanks."

Ten minutes later, Hannah had kicked off her uncomfortable shoes and was padding across marble. She opened the balcony doors of her suite and took in the jaw-dropping view of Central Park.

It was time to put her plan into action.

She'd been stringing Guy along for days, not letting on that she knew his secrets.

Now she was ready to drop her bombshell.

Hannah held her phone out as far as it could go and took a wide-angled selfie that included her face, a glimpse of Central Park, and the Blanchet Maison logo on the velvet curtains behind her. It took several tries to get a photo she liked. One where she wore an expression that showed she meant business.

She attached the picture to a text and wrote the words she was desperate to say.

I'm tired of being lied to. Let's talk.

Then she sat on the hotel bed and waited.

TWENTY-SEVEN

Staring at her phone, Hannah read the text one more time. It wasn't from the sender she expected.

Dear Ms. Turner, please call me as soon as you can. — Sincerely, Nate Webber.

It was ten minutes after she'd sent the picture to Guy, and he still hadn't responded. And now this? She hit the call button, but Guy's number went to voice mail again. Taking a deep breath, she called Nate Webber next.

"Hi, Mr. Webber. This is Hannah Turner, calling you back."

"Hi, Ms. Turner. You can call me Nate. I'm glad I finally reached you."

Call him Nate? "Thank you. I've tried emailing you before, but never heard back."

"Sorry about that. It's been a rough few days. But I'm glad we're speaking now. Without beating around the bush, Hannah, I'd like to offer you the job of general manager of Seaside

Resort. Multiple sources have told me you're the perfect person for the position."

A thousand fireworks exploded around her. Confetti rained from the sky. A ticker tape parade cheered in the background. Or rather, Hannah accidentally bumped into a crystal lamp, next to the bed, and almost knocked it to the ground.

"You want me to be the general manager?" Hannah asked in a tone that was surprisingly calm. "I was previously told that Blanchet Maison had decided on an outside candidate."

"Yes, and that was an oversight on our part that has been rectified. Hannah, we'd like you to start as general manager on June eleventh. That's immediately after the current manager retires, correct?"

"That's right. Herman retires on June tenth."

"Great. In the meantime, we're flying you here to New York for two weeks of training, and also so we can get your input on the inner workings of the Local Flavors properties."

He didn't know she was in New York? Guy must not have told him yet. "Thank you, but I'm already in New York."

"You are? I didn't know that."

Hannah listened, but couldn't tell if his surprise was genuine or not.

"I am. I'm staying at the Blanchet Maison, in fact, waiting to speak with Guy." There. She'd said it. Truth bomb *ignite*.

"I'm sure that will be an enormous comfort for him. Guy has spoken highly of you. He's putting his parents on the medevac flight to the convalescent hospital in Nice right now."

Whoa!

"That must be difficult for him." Hannah tapped her toe on the ground. She didn't want to do anything that would jeopardize her promotion, but she had to know the truth. "About my new job, can I please ask you why the decision changed in my favor?"

"Ah... that's a tricky question. I should probably wait for

legal to be here for this one."

"Am I only getting this job because I know Guy?"

"No. I can tell you that without consulting legal for sure. From what I've been told, you were our top candidate from the very beginning. That's all I can say right now."

"I see. Well, I look forward to leading Seaside Resort into the future. I care passionately about its success, and will do everything within my power to help it earn revenue and increase in prestige."

"I'm sure you will, Hannah. Let's be sure to meet in person while you're in town. My secretary will get ahold of you shortly."

"Thank you, sir." Hannah said goodbye and hung up. Did that really just happen? She finally got the job? And she had *always* been the top candidate for the job? Meaning someone had swooped in and taken her off the list? Who would do such a thing?

And poor Guy, sending his parents off on a medevac flight. For a half-second, she felt sorry for him, until she remembered that he'd been lying to her for months. Still, she knew what it was like to lose a father. She wouldn't wish that pain on anyone, even a trickster like Guy.

Not just a trickster, her heart whispered. *A kind, gentle man that you were falling in love with.* Her eyes blurred with tears, but she blinked them away. Why had Guy done that? Made her fall for him despite all his lies? It wasn't fair. None of this was fair.

Since Hannah apparently had time to kill, she fired up her computer and searched for the most recent news about Blanchet Maison. According to the *Wall Street Journal*, Guy was already making his mark. With his father's shares under his control, Guy had an eighty percent voice on the board. Industry analysts said that Guy seemed less concerned with answering to the remaining twenty percent of shareholders than he was over ensuring that the Blanchet Maison brand signaled a quality experience for guests *and* employees. He'd already put the brakes on the reorg which—Hannah gasped—had apparently included a plot to sell off the Local Flavors division!

It shocked Hannah when she read that. Blanchet Maison was going to sell Seaside Resort? To whom? She'd had no idea that plot was in the works. Herman must not have known either, or he would surely have said something. Maybe now with Guy in charge, the company would be different. His father was better at being a figurehead than a corporate leader. She'd trust Gabe's advice on biathlon training, but not about anything else. But could she trust Guy? Hannah wasn't sure anymore.

She went outside to the balcony, leaned on the railings, and soaked up the view, falling deeper and deeper into thought. It was difficult unpacking her emotions. She longed for stability, craving it deep in her bones. But she also wanted kindness, support, and love. Guy was all those things, and so much more. She went back into the suite, turned her computer back on and clicked over to the funny video of him showing up at a Zoom meeting with the bunny filter engaged. Wall Street had mocked him, but the whole thing made her smile, knowing that Guy had gone above and beyond to help make his pediatric patient more comfortable during a Telehealth appointment. That was so like Guy. He always put the needs and feelings of other people first.

"Hannah!" Guy's voice called from the suite's main door. "Are you in there?"

Hannah flinched, pushing her computer onto the bed and crossing the room to open the door. Guy stood in front of her, wearing a suit and tie—more handsome than ever, but his left eyebrow twitched like he was nervous.

"Hi, Guy." She rolled her shoulders back. "Or should I say, hello, Dr. Guido Barret Blanchet the fourth?"

"You knew?" Guy gulped. "For how long?"

"Only since Monday afternoon. Why'd you lie to me? I feel

like an idiot."

"I didn't mean to trick you." He extended his arms like he wanted to hug her, but then dropped them when she didn't do likewise. "Hannah, I was lost," he said. "Totally and utterly lost until I found you. I came to Seaside Resort because I was broken, and one of the last things my granddad told me was that it was a place of healing. He was right." Guy held up his hands, palms up. "Hannah, I've missed you so much these past few days. I was intending to tell you everything. The whole truth about my name and my family—and also about how much I'm falling for you. But then my dad..."

"How is your father?" Hannah asked, not taking his outstretched hands.

"He's gone."

Hannah's eyes opened wide. "Oh no! I'm so sorry."

"Not *gone* gone," Guy said quickly. "At least, I hope not. He and my mom are on a medevac flight to France right now." Guy loosened his tie. "Can I come inside to talk?"

"Of course." Hannah opened the door wider so he could enter. "You own the place." She crossed the room and sat on the velvet couch. Then, feeling bad for coming over so harshly when he was in the middle of a family crisis, she softened her tone. "I'm sorry your dad's health is so delicate right now. That must be awful for all of you."

Guy sat next to her on the couch. "My mom can't deal with hospitals. That's why she found a special treatment center in Nice that will take my dad."

"Like your idea for Seaside Resort. A place where the rich and famous would come to do rehab."

"Yeah." Guy hung his head. "Pipe dreams."

"That have a lot of potential." It broke her heart to see how much he was hurting. Hannah placed her hand gently on his arm. "I've missed you, Guy, or Guido, or whatever your name is. I've been worried about you, despite everything else."

"You have?" He raised his head. "And it's Guy. Just plain Guy is fine. That's all I've ever wanted to be."

"And all I've ever wanted to be is a person who could take care of herself and her family." Hannah held onto his arm. "But no matter how hard I've tried it's felt like the cards have been stacked against me."

"I think because they were, at least at Blanchet Maison they were. All my parents care about is money and power."

"But your grandfather was different. He believed in dreamers." Hannah withdrew her hand.

"Yes. That's right. But how did you know that about him?"

Hannah walked to the window and knelt down next to the chair she'd been sitting in. She picked up her briefcase and pulled out a frame. "Because of this." She showed him the photo that had hung on the wall at Strawberry Cottage.

"Frank Sinatra's concert?"

"This wasn't an ordinary concert."

"It wasn't?"

Hannah shook her head. "No. This was a private concert for investors from Chicago, Nevada, New York, and Florida. Other places, too." Hannah pointed to a table. "Like Kansas City."

"I don't understand."

"Mobsters. Remember how originally Sand Dollar Cove was supposed to be a gambling town? They built it on the understanding that Washington State would legalize gambling. When that didn't happen, the whole thing collapsed like a house of cards. Oscar Lexter, the previous owner of Seaside Resort, and his cronies flew in unhappy investors for a weekend of luxury, trying to prevent them from pulling out, but it was too late. Most people abandoned the idea and moved elsewhere, taking their money with them."

"How'd you find out about this?"

"From the cleaning ladies, dishwashers, and dry cleaners.

They knew everything that happened in this town, and now that they're retired, they're happy to spill all the details if you ask them."

"I still don't understand." Guy scratched his head. "It's like you're giving me puzzle pieces I don't know how to put together."

"Mary and I went to the senior center and passed this photo around until we knew everything. The seniors we spoke to might not have been directly in the picture, but some of them were behind the scenes, preparing food or waiting tables when Sinatra came to town."

"Oh!"

"The only person we haven't heard from yet is her." Hannah tapped on the picture of the woman selling cigarettes who looked like Lark. "This is Karen, Lark's mom. She lives in Florida."

"But Lark said her mom didn't work at the T Bone Bluff. I asked her."

"Gran thinks Karen might have been too ashamed to admit it. T Bone Bluff waitresses had a reputation, if you know what I mean. Which makes this vignette even more interesting." She pointed at the profile of a man who was staring directly at Karen's chest. "I think that's your grandfather."

"What? No. That can't be. I examined this photo before, and didn't spot him." Guy picked up the frame and stared at it closely. "I'll be damned," he said, looking at the grainy image. "That's Granddad's nose. And chin! And I think those are the cufflinks he gave me for graduation." Guy looked at Hannah. "But what was my granddad doing in a room full of mobsters?"

"I don't know, but investment money has to come from somewhere."

"I need to call Lark. I need to speak with her mom."

"I'm sure that can be arranged." They were sitting on the

couch again. "What's the story with my promotion?" Hannah asked, changing the subject.

"Nate called you?"

Hannah nodded. "Just before you arrived."

"Finally." Guy hunched forward, resting his hands on his knees. He had purple splotches under his eyes, and although at first Hannah had been blinded by his familiar good looks, now she realized how worn down he was. His face bore a grayish tinge, like he hadn't slept in ages. "I'm sorry you got dragged into that mess."

"What mess? Me not getting the promotion? Am I only getting it because I'm your... friend?" she added weakly.

"No," Guy said in a sharp tone that wasn't like him. "They took it away from you because of me. That was my father's doing. He was trying to force me to come back to New York. He's wanted me to take an active role in the company for years, and couldn't stand that I had started over in Sand Dollar Cove. So he opted for slash-and-burn. Sell off the Local Flavors division. Change up the staff. Ruin the whole resort just to control me."

"What?"

"And the thing is, I do care about the company. I've always been proud of what my granddad and great-granddad built. But I knew early on that I couldn't work for my father. He's bullied me my whole life. So I chose a different path, and—"

"Became a physical therapist," said Hannah.

"That's right. A career that I'm passionate about and enjoy. But if I did take over the company... I mean, if I do, permanently, then I have ideas for how I'd like to make the whole organization better."

"Like the ideas you shared in your presentations to Herman?"

"Yeah."

"Those were good ideas."

"You think?"

Hannah nodded. "Wonderful ideas." She yearned to forgive him. She longed to wrap her arms around him and hold him tight. Hannah could see how much he was hurting, and she couldn't bear it. But she also couldn't bear having been lied to. "I still don't understand your deceit." She folded her hands in her lap. "Why did you lie to me?"

He looked at her with blue eyes that were full of pain. "I can explain everything, but I need to show you something first. Will you come to my dad's office with me? It's only a few floors up."

"Okay." Hannah stood, glad that the walk there would give her time to think. Seeing Guy in person had tempered her fury. But it felt like their relationship had gone into reverse. They were right back to being co-workers again, only worse. Guy was her boss.

"Follow me," Guy said as he led the way out into the hall-way, up the private elevator, through another hallway, and to the presidential suite.

The space was immaculately decorated, and Hannah tried to memorize what she saw so she could report back to Mary. Black-and-white photographs of Blanchet Maison properties all over the world graced one wall, and life-sized pictures of Gabe at the Olympics dominated the other. Hannah felt like an inter-loper. The only thing she recognized was the jar of white sand and sand dollars on the desk.

"That's from Strawberry Cottage," she exclaimed, walking over to it. "I sent this to Connecticut." She whipped around to face him. "That's where you got the postcards! I didn't misinter-pret seeing them." Darn Mary and her gaslighting, making Hannah think she'd invented it all.

"No, you didn't. I wasn't sure if you saw them in my desk that day, but I took them home to my apartment just in case."

"How is Joe from Connecticut related to you?"

"Joe was a nickname my granddad sometimes used when he was trying to sound more American," Guy explained. "But his parents didn't like it, so he usually went by Gabriel."

"Oh," said Hannah. "Interesting."

"You sent the box to the address of my granddad's vacation house, and then the household manager sent it to me. I still can't figure out what it's all about. That's part of why I came to Sand Dollar Cove, to find out who my granddad wrote that note to."

"At least now you know how he got the Sinatra autograph." Hannah picked up the jar and looked inside. "He was at the investors' meeting."

"Would you like to sit down?" Guy offered.

"Sure." Hannah took the jar with her and sat on the leather sofa.

"Then there was the box that came with it." Guy opened a desk drawer and took out the ornately carved wooden box that Hannah had originally found with the jar. She recognized the carved rhododendron on top. "My granddad sent me a note on the day he died. I've kept it in the box the jar came in." Guy placed the box in Hannah's hands. "I haven't shared these things with anyone until now."

Hannah traced the flower on the top and then lifted the box's lid. Inside was a cream-colored notecard. "Is it okay if I read it?"

Guy nodded. "Go right ahead. I have it memorized."

Hannah opened the notecard and read it what it said.

Dear Guy,

I will explain all of this in person. But the main thing I want you to know is that I am so proud to be your grandfather, and I love you with all my heart. If you ever find yourself hurting, Seaside Resort is waiting for you. It healed my heart and it can heal yours too.

Always yours,

Granddad

"What does this mean?" she asked. "How did Seaside Resort heal his heart?"

"I don't know." Guy sat down beside her.

"Let's look in the jar again." Hannah peered through the glass. "Maybe there are clues."

"I've inspected it a million times, and all I see are sand dollars and some old postcards."

Hannah unscrewed the lid. "Postcards they sold in the gift shop when I was little." She took out a sand dollar and scooped her finger inside. "I thought there might be something in the cavity, but there's nothing." She examined the other three sand dollars too, and found nothing.

The notecard was there, but she'd already read it in January. Hannah glanced at it again to jog her memory.

Dearest One,

They say love makes people do foolish things. Perhaps that's why I've held onto this for all these years. Love has made me keep it. Love has made me hide it. Love is prompting me to bring it back to you. I still believe in our happily ever after. Together we can return this to the sea.

Always yours,

Joe

"No idea who 'dearest one' was?" Hannah asked. "Is that what he called your grandma, maybe?"

"Not that I know of."

"Oh. Awkward..." Hannah continued her inspection by moving on to the postcards. She carefully removed them from the jar. "It's weird that they're stuck together, don't you think?"

"I figured they were sold that way."

"Not that I know of." Hannah ran her fingernail along the edge. "Like I said, I remember seeing similar ones in the gift shop when I was younger and used to come with Gran to work."

"I've always thought that was so strange, but didn't want to say anything. What did you do while she was working? Who watched you?"

"I watched myself." Hannah turned the cards over and looked at the autograph again. "Mary, too. We'd climb trees or fly kites at the beach. It wasn't that bad if the weather was good, but when it stormed, we hung out in the laundry room and folded towels."

"Did they pay you?" Guy asked.

"Of course not. Why would they pay us?"

"Because that's child labor. That's against the law."

"True." Hannah wiggled the corner of the cardstock. "Sometimes we grow up thinking things are normal, but then we look back as an adult and we recognize how messed up they were."

"Like me, moving from one hotel to another and never getting the chance to make friends, or simply breathe."

"Was that what your life was like?" Hannah rested the cards on her lap.

"Yes. It was." He tugged at his hair. "Look, if you're going to understand why I pretended to be someone different, then I need to be upfront about everything. My parents liked the idea of me. A son. An heir. But neither of them likes children, and I don't think they ever liked me in particular. I was raised by nannies and tutors. Then they sent me to boarding school for high school, where I had a really hard time making friends, because I'd never learned how."

"That's awful, Guy. I'm so sorry. Even when my mom was whacked out on drugs, I knew she loved me. As much as she was capable of, that is."

"I think my parents love me too, but liking me is different. With my granddad, I always knew that he loved me and liked me at the same time. He'd be excited to see me. He'd ask—no, demand—that I come visit, every winter for two entire months in a row. Those are some of my happiest childhood memories, spending Christmases with Granddad." Guy looked up at the wall plastered with yet another Gabe Blanchet Olympics picture and cringed. "I was never good enough for my parents. They didn't care about my talents or what I was interested in. When I told them I was going to grad school to become a physical therapist, they freaked out."

"But you're great at helping people. You're kind and patient. The best listener I know. If it weren't for you, Gran wouldn't have started treatment."

"Thanks. I appreciate you saying that." Guy sighed. "My parents didn't see it that way. Being a surgeon would have been acceptable to them, but not a physical therapist. What they really wanted me to do was take a larger role in the family business. My dad wanted someone to boss around." His shoulders sagged. "And here I am. They got their wish in the worst possible way."

"It's going to be okay." Hannah squeezed his hand. "You've got the skills to do this." Feeling Guy's hand within her own felt wonderful.

He looked into her eyes. "Really? One of the main reasons I used a fake name when I came to Seaside Resort was that I didn't know what I was good for. Especially after the Twitter humiliation and that stupid Panicked Rabbit gif."

"It's not stupid. It was cute. You were trying to help a young patient."

"My parents didn't see it that way. My dad accused me of

doing it on purpose because I was an idiot. He said my whole
life was a sham, and that the only thing good about me was my
last name. That's why I needed to become Guy Barret, to prove
to myself that I could make it on my own without the Blanchet
name."

"You don't need to prove anything to anyone." Hannah
squeezed his fingers. "You're your own person, Guy, more than
anyone I know. You've made your own way through life. You've
followed the career you really wanted, and you're great at what
you do. Plus, you're a superb cook. If anyone can heal this
company, it's you."

"You really think so?"

"I know so." Hannah smiled shyly. "And I'm not just saying
that because you're my boss, in case you're wondering. As far as
I'm concerned, I'm now *your* boss, because Guy Barret is still on
the payroll. As the soon-to-be general manager of Seaside
Resort, I get to tell you what to do."

Guy chuckled. "Is that so?"

"I'd tell you to kiss me, but that would be sexual
harassment."

"What if I asked to kiss you?" Guy said with a hopeful look
in his eyes. "What would you say?"

"I'd say you better be serious, Guy Barret, because I've been
dreaming of kissing you for days."

Guy cupped her face and pressed their lips together. A
thrill of joy overpowered her like sunshine. Hannah's lips
parted and her tongue tasted sweetness. He slid his arms down
her back and pulled her closer. Heat bound them together like
balm. Entwined around one another, their kisses melted
together until time passed and Hannah had no concept of how
long they'd been on that couch, or even what day it was.

"Hannah," Guy whispered, when they finally parted for air.
"I think I'm falling in love with you."

"That's a relief." Her thumb traced his jawline. "Because I'm falling in love with you, too."

Guy pulled her closer, so she was sitting on his lap, and then shook when a crash of glass sounded against the floor.

"Oh no!" Hannah looked down in horror. "I'm so sorry."

"It's just a jar. Are you hurt?" Guy scooted her away from the broken pieces. "We'll get more sand when we return home."

"At least the postcards are safe." Hannah reached down and picked them up. "No," she said dejectedly. "They must have gotten damaged between us. The corner's torn."

Guy looked to see what she meant. "There are probably more like these somewhere."

"Not with Sinatra's autograph."

"No, but—"

Wait. "Is this handwriting?" Hannah passed the cards to Guy.

"What? Really?" Guy began to pry the stuck-together cards apart. "I've always been so careful with them, but..." He ripped them apart.

"There's writing on the back!" Hannah exclaimed.

"In my granddad's handwriting!" Guy read the note aloud.

Eleanor,

It has come to my attention while reviewing Gabe's physical for the Olympic Games, that he is blood type AB. As I recall from your hysterectomy, you are blood type B. I myself am type O and want to know what the hell is going on? Who is Gabe's father? It's certainly not me. Contact my attorney with your reply. I don't want to speak to you. The lawyers can reach me in Sand Dollar Cove.

—Gabriel

TWENTY-EIGHT

Guy's face had gone completely white. "They had incompatible blood types?" He raked his fingers through his hair and pulled it up by the roots. "Granddad's not really my grandfather?"

"And you're not actually a Blanchet," Hannah whispered, afraid to say it too loudly.

"I don't know what to say. My whole life is a fraud."

"No!" Hannah grabbed Guy's arms and pulled them down. "Don't say that." She hugged him tightly. "Your grandfather loved you, with words and actions. You just told me all about that. He wanted to spend time with you. He welcomed you home, for two months every year, right? Even though he knew you weren't biologically his."

Tears flooded Guy's eyes, and the sight of them broke Hannah's heart. "He gave me a fifty percent stake in the company, too," Guy said.

"Because he wanted *you*," Hannah said. "Your grandfather loved you."

"So why'd he wait so long to tell me the truth, then? And why'd he never actually tell me?"

"Maybe he was waiting for your father to," Hannah suggested. "Or maybe your dad doesn't even know."

"There's no way to find that out now, since my dad can't talk at the moment," Guy said grimly.

Hannah reached down and looked at the postcard. "Your grandfather wrote this, but he never sent it. What does that tell you?"

"That my granddad wanted an Olympian in the family? I don't know."

"Maybe. I never met your grandfather, but you did. Do you think that's it? Was this about glory?"

Guy took the postcard from her and sighed. "No. It was about honor and forgiveness. I'm sure my granddad thought he was doing the right thing by coming home to his wife and son."

Hannah plucked the second postcard off the ground, the one with Sinatra's autograph. It didn't have any message on the back, but there was a red smudge. No, not a smudge. Hannah blinked several times to make sure she saw clearly. "Lipstick!" She tapped her finger on the mark. "This is a kiss mark, on the back of the other postcard."

"What?" Guy looked at it closely. "Son of a gun."

Hannah drew her finger in the air as she thought, like she was pulling puzzle pieces together. "Okay, so... Your grandfather realizes that your dad isn't his. He's heartbroken. Furious, probably. He drives or maybe flies out to the other side of the country where some of his hotel cronies are having a big party and trying to keep—or discover—new investors." Hannah bent down to look at the T Bone Bluff picture again. "He goes to the Sinatra concert. He has a grand old time. Maybe he even gets lucky."

"Gets lucky? How many old movies have you watched?"

"Enough. But never enough." Hannah continued with her thoughts. "Your grandfather falls in love, either with his fling or with Seaside Resort. He buys it from Oscar Lexter because he's a dreamer. Everyone else is giving up on Sand Dollar Cove, but Gabriel sees its future potential, even without casino revenue. Then he flies home to your dad and grandmother, and puts it all behind him, because the end result is he gets the best grandson of all time, and he also gets to hold onto his memory of the time in Sand Dollar Cove."

Guy took the frame from her. "Would anyone at the senior center be able to confirm that hypothesis?"

Hannah shook her head sadly. "I don't think so. Mary and I tapped out that knowledge base while we were there." She looked at the photo. "But Lark's mom might have more info. She might even be behind that lipstick kiss."

"My granddad did say that love helped heal his heart. Where does her mom live, again?"

"Florida, I think. Not too far from one of the Local Flavors properties. The Key Strokes Inn. It has a rhythm and blues theme."

"Feel like getting on an airplane again?"

"With you?" Hannah leaned her head on his shoulder. "Absolutely."

Everything happened fast after that. Luckily her meeting with Nate hadn't been scheduled yet, because Hannah barely had time to rush to retrieve her suitcase. Before she knew it, she was in a limo being whisked away to the airport. She and Guy hopped on the first flight to Florida, flying first-class commercial, because it was better for the environment than using the corporate jet.

"What if this is a wild-goose chase?" Guy asked, kicking up the footrest of his seat.

"Then at least we've visited the Key Strokes Inn and gotten an inside look at how they operate." Hannah paged through the giant binder Guy had given her about the reorg he was untangling. "I can't believe they wanted to sell off the Local Flavors division. Without those properties, Blanchet Maison would be just another soulless hotel chain."

"They're assets. Not liabilities."

"Exactly!" Hannah bit her lip. "At least, Seaside Resort is. I don't know about the other locations." She sipped her champagne cocktail and nibbled on a chocolate strawberry. "Does the Key Strokes Inn know you're coming?"

"That *I'm* coming, or that *we're* coming?"

"Yes." Hannah grinned. "Both." The alcohol was hitting her bloodstream now, and she was a wee bit tipsy.

Guy grinned. "I asked Deshan to make the reservations under Mr. and Mrs. Barret Turner."

"You did not!" Hannah giggled. "That's brilliant."

"But there are two beds in our room." Guy's voice deepened. "I didn't want to make any assumptions."

"I think it's safe to assume that's one bed too many," Hannah whispered, her pulse racing.

"Oh, really?" Guy picked up her hand and kissed each fingertip.

Hannah felt bolts of electricity shoot all the way to her toes. She didn't know how to handle energy like that, not here, in the middle of a crowded airplane. "I bet the people at the front desk will think that Mr. and Mrs. Barret Turner are an unhappily married couple, to require separate beds," she said, trying to temper the tingles she felt as Guy's lips brushed against each digit.

"You're right." Guy dropped her hand and put up the giant seat divider between them. "I need my space. You're crowding me."

"I've felt that way too, ever since we were fake-married," Hannah said over the wall.

"It's a good thing we're not married then." Guy put the divider away and took her hand again. "At least for now," he whispered before kissing her tenderly on the lips.

The tingles Hannah felt were more like explosions now. She leaned into him and kissed him back as eagerly as she could, being mindful of the people in the aisle next to them who were probably watching. Her hand rested on his chest, and his heartbeat pulsed through her fingertips, uniting them together in a single rhythm. His jawline was scratchy from the stubble poking through. Her cheeks brushed against it, but she didn't mind one bit until a funny thought occurred to her.

"Hey," she said, pulling away and scrutinizing him. "Your beard's dark." She brushed her fingers through his blond hair, remembering the picture of the young brown-haired boy called Guido Blanchet IV that she'd seen on the internet. "What's your natural hair color, anyway?"

"Brown." He grinned sheepishly. "I dyed it when I changed my name to come out West."

"You did? Why?"

"On the off chance that someone would recognize me from that stupid Panicked Rabbit gif."

"I would never have recognized you without the bunny ears."

"It gets worse. I had an allergic reaction to the peroxide. It gave me hives every time I used it."

"You're a physical therapist, not a salon worker. Maybe you used the wrong brand?"

"Could be."

"What made you go into physical therapy in the first place?"

Guy kneaded his shoulder. "A hockey injury when I was fourteen and at boarding school. The physical therapist who worked with me made a big impression."

"Was he kind, like you?" Hannah asked.

"She was a fifty-five-year-old German woman with meaty hands and a stern attitude."

"Oh. That's not what I expected you to say."

Guy chuckled. "But yes, she was kind, in a way. She took a broken teenager like me who was hurt and depressed and helped me move my shoulder again. She taught me that healing people was more than cutting them open or dispensing pills. If it weren't for her, I'd never have become a Doctor of Physical Therapy."

"Dr. Blanchet," Hannah said, liking the sound of it.

Guy kissed her cheek.

Hannah laughed. "Well, I guess your brown hair will make it easier to pass as Barret Turner." She patted him on the shoulder. "You know, I like sharing my last name with you. I could get used to that, in fact."

There. She'd said it. But hadn't Guy said something similar just a moment ago? She could picture a future with him as easily as sunshine could burn off fog.

"What do you think your dad would have thought of me?" Guy asked. "It seems like I should know that, since I'm borrowing his last name and head over heels for his daughter."

Hannah rested her head on Guy's shoulder. "He would have loved you because you're so kind to his mom, his daughters, and everyone you come across." Hannah chuckled. "I don't think he would have understood you being a vegetarian, though. My dad loved a good steak."

"I like cauliflower steak. Does that count?"

"No. It doesn't."

Guy laughed. "My dad never thought so, either." He took a deep breath and his tone became serious. "My parents should arrive in Nice in a few hours. I don't know what to tell them about what I've learned, or if my father will be alert enough to hear it."

"You don't need to tell them anything until you find out more, right? Would the truth change anything?"

"For me, yes. One hundred percent yes. But for them..." Guy sighed. "They do what they want and don't necessarily care about my feelings. So no, I guess it wouldn't change how they operate."

"Narcissistic parents are something I'm familiar with. My dad was wonderful, but my mom was, and is, only concerned about herself. She says she's sober now, but she's claimed that before and it hasn't been true." Hannah lifted her head and looked at him. "But I've always had Gran and Mary to balance that, and you know what I've learned?"

"What?"

"As awful as my mother's neglect has been, it's made me appreciate my grandma and sister all the more." She ran her palm down his arm and held his hand. "If there's anyone deserving of kindness, love, and compassion, it's you."

"Thank you." Guy squeezed her hand. "What I really want is roots. Deep roots. Living in a place where I belong that's full of community."

"You're going to get that, too." Hannah swept a lock of blond hair off his forehead. "One thing I've noticed about you is that you build community wherever you go."

"I don't know what you mean."

"Don't you? You remember people's names. You put them at ease. Feed them. You teach them things. Why, just this afternoon when I arrived at the hotel, I ran into Mrs. Sanchez and Mrs. Dario. They went on and on about how wonderful their new room was."

"I'm the one who should rave about Mrs. Dario and Mrs. Sanchez. They both treat me like family, Mrs. Dario especially. It really lifted my spirits when I ran into them in the lobby and realized they'd come to New York to see the shows."

"That's what I mean about your kindness being returned." Hannah picked up the binder that had slid down onto the floor. "I think that consultant wanted to reorganize the company in the wrong way. Maybe the flagship hotels should stay the same, but what if you took the Local Flavors properties and moved forward with your ideas about turning them into rehab centers or places of healing?"

"I thought you said it was wrong to turn Seaside Resort into a place that only the rich and famous could afford."

"I did. And I stand by that." Hannah flipped to the back of the binder where there was a small section about the Blanchet Maison foundation. "Perhaps instead of investing in art museums and opera houses, your family's foundation could invest in people. Like..." Pain squeezed her heart as she thought of her own life. "What about week-long vacations for families dealing with the loss of a parent? Or special rates for grandparents raising grandchildren on their own? That could happen side by side with Seahawks players coming to rehab their shoulders."

"What about your dormitory for dirtbag climbers?" Guy asked.

Hannah laughed. "That could be there, too." She closed the binder and stuffed it under the seat. "Dream big, Barret Turner. The world is your oyster."

"It certainly feels that way." Guy tilted his head and kissed her on the sensitive spot behind her ear, then trailed kisses down to the nape of her neck. "Hannah Turner, you've flipped my world upside down."

"I could say the same about you. And we're not even in a hammock."

TWENTY-NINE

"My mom said their flight to Nice was ghastly, but they made it," said Guy. "My dad is at the convalescent hospital being cared for by staff, and my mom is at the local Blanchet Maison in the Dauphine Suite."

"That's good that they are settled." Hannah stood at the edge of a lagoon in front of a NO SWIMMING: BEWARE OF ALLIGATORS sign. It was Thursday morning, and they were due to meet Karen for lunch soon. Hannah had been surreptitiously evaluating the property and chatting with the housekeeping staff ever since she and Guy had enjoyed a leisurely breakfast in bed. "Has your father woken up from the sedation yet?"

"No. Not yet." Guy's voice wobbled. "The doctors there said that brains are fragile and these things take time."

"Oh Guy. I'm sorry this is happening." Hannah hugged him tightly, and he rested his forehead against hers.

"At least they're in France now, like my mom wanted."

"Yes. Although that seems weird to me that your mom would have your dad travel when his health is so shaky."

"That's my mom for you."

"Oh. Did you tell her that you were at the Key Strokes Inn?"

"Yes, and she asked me why I was visiting, in her words, 'that dump.' Then, when I explained I was there with my girlfriend, she said she was late for her esthetician appointment and had to go."

"Esthetician appointment? When your dad is fighting for his life? Wait!" Hannah's eyebrows shot up, and she felt a bubble of glee. "Did you say girlfriend?"

"Yes, I did." Guy trailed kisses all the way from her forehead to her ear. "Are you okay with that?"

"Yes." Hannah blushed. "Although I also like the term 'general manager of Seaside Resort.' Speaking of which, you'll never guess what I discovered while you were on the phone with your mom. They run an under-the-table operation here where they let the locals buy memberships to the hotel gym and pool."

"What? How are they getting away with that?"

"It's cash only. Probably with no insurance or hold-harmless contracts. I don't know where the money is going, but the concept itself is brilliant—if you do it properly." She linked her arm through his elbow and pulled him away from an alligator that was snapping at the surface of the lagoon. "We should visit all the Local Flavors properties undercover. Or... Well, it would be nice to do that, but you have your work, and I take over from Herman in a couple of weeks."

"Sneaky, spy operations could definitely be in our future," said Guy. "Or we could send Mary. I bet she wouldn't miss one detail."

"Especially if it involved outdated wallpaper." Hannah squeezed his biceps. "How are you doing? Are you okay?"

"I'm great."

"I thought you might be nervous about meeting Karen."

"Not so much nervous as curious." Guy led them up the path to the restaurant, the Bluesy Bayou. "We still don't know if

Karen was involved with my granddad or not. She might not even recall seeing him at that Sinatra concert."

"Did you text Lark about this?"

Guy nodded. "I did. I told her you and I were in Florida near where her mom lived, and that we were taking her out to lunch to ask her advice about raising tomato plants."

"And she bought that excuse?"

"No." Guy laughed. "Lark said that was the dumbest thing she'd ever heard, so I told her the truth. I said I thought it was possible that Karen had known my granddad, and I wanted to ask her a few questions."

"Did you explain who your granddad was?"

"Not yet. But I'll need to soon. It's not fair to keep lying. I'm ready to be myself again."

Hannah rested her head on his shoulder. "You were always yourself, no matter what color you dyed your hair."

"Yes. I suppose so."

Ten minutes later, Hannah and Guy sat at a beachside table with their toes dug into the sand, drinking iced tea from mason jars. A pianist played love songs from the 1980s that reminded Hannah of elevator music, but the restaurant patrons didn't seem to mind. When Hannah looked up, she saw Karen walking toward them. The resemblance to Lark was uncanny, although Karen had long hair and didn't have any colorful tattoos. She wore a floral sundress with sparkly sandals, and her tanned skin was leathered from sun. Hannah couldn't remember how old she was—late sixties, perhaps? Karen was nimble on her feet and appeared to be in good shape.

"You must be Karen." Guy stood and held out his hand. "I'm Guy, Lark's next-door neighbor."

"The king of vegetables. She's told me all about you." Karen shook his hand and then hugged Hannah. "I can't believe it's you, kiddo. The last time we saw each other, you were swinging from a tree branch."

"She still does that occasionally." Guy grinned.

"Guilty as charged." Hannah hugged Karen. "Lark's going to be so bummed that she missed this."

"We'll have to take a picture and send it to her." Karen sat down. "So she'll be extra jealous and finally agree to move here where I can see her more often."

The three of them chatted about the weather and Lark's newest tattoo until the waiter came and took their orders. Then Guy got down to business.

"Karen," he said. "I haven't been completely honest with you, or Lark."

"You don't say." Karen sipped her iced tea and looked at him coolly.

"My name's not Guy Barret, it's Guy Blanchet."

"You don't look like a Blanchet."

"I don't?" Guy asked.

Karen leaned back in her chair and studied him. "Your hair's wrong. But I can spot a bad dye job from across the room. No, it's the shape of your eyes, and your nose, and your mouth. Your height, too."

"I've been told I look like my father," said Guy.

Karen raised her eyebrows and gulped her tea. "You do," she said as she put the glass down.

"How do you know what the Blanchets look like?" Hannah asked. "Did you meet Gabriel when he came out to buy Seaside Resort?"

"I haven't thought about him in years." Karen fanned herself with her napkin. "Or days... Or minutes..."

Guy folded his hands on the table. "Lark said you never worked at the T Bone Bluff, but we have a picture of you there talking to my granddad."

Karen fiddled with the clasp of her necklace. "Only fast girls worked at the T Bone. That's what they called them back then. 'Fast' or 'loose.' I wasn't either, but I needed the money.

Especially with a baby girl at home to pay for. Lark was in diapers, and her dad had left us. So yeah, I worked at the T Bone. I put on fishnets and flirted for tips. But as soon as I could afford it, I switched over to a job at the Lumberjack. The tips weren't as good, but nobody pinched my ass."

Guy winced. "My granddad didn't pinch your ass, did he?"

Karen laughed. "Of course not. Until I asked him to, that is." She finished her iced tea in five big gulps. "Could I get something stronger? Can we Long Island this thing?"

"Sure," said Hannah.

"My granddad was married when he met you," Guy blurted. "What exactly was your relationship with him?"

Karen's expression froze, and then she shielded her face with her hands as if she couldn't believe she was finally being asked about this. "We were in love. Two perfect months of bliss." She pulled down her fingertips. "I knew he was married, but I didn't care. I'd never had a man treat me so nice. He brought me flowers every time he saw me. He paid for Lark's babysitter. Hell, he paid for everything. Even my groceries. When he saw the hole in the roof of our trailer, he bought us a brand-new double-wide to replace it. He wanted to buy me a house, but I said no. Sand Dollar Cove was bigger back then, but it was still small enough that people talked. I didn't want to be known as a kept woman."

"Why didn't my granddad get a divorce then, and marry you?"

Hannah leaned forward and lowered her voice. "We know about his wife cheating on him. We realize that Guy's not his biological grandson."

Karen squeezed Guy's hand for a moment, then pulled away. "That was really tough news for Joe—that's how I knew him, as Joe, not Gabriel—to grapple with. You weren't born yet, but your father was months away from heading to the Olympics. Joe was so proud of him, and everything he'd accomplished. That's why he went back to Eleanor. He loved his family even more than he loved me."

The waiter came, and Hannah ordered three stiff drinks for all of them. Guy said nothing. He appeared to be having a hard time forming words. But once the waiter left, he found his voice again. "Did you ever hear from my granddad after he went back home?"

"Only once," said Karen. "And that's what ruined our lives." She looked directly at Hannah. "*All* of our lives."

"Huh?" Hannah was confused. "What do you mean?"

"I don't even know how to begin." Karen's tan face became ashen. "This is about you, too, Hannah, and your father."

"Dad?" Hannah gasped. "Max Turner?"

Karen nodded.

Guy put his arm around the back of Hannah's chair, and his reassuring presence steadied her.

"What about my dad?" Hannah asked.

"It was 1984, and Eleanor had just died."

"My grandma," said Guy.

"Yes." Karen nodded. "A couple of weeks after the funeral, Joe flew out to Washington to come see me. And—"

"Wait." Hannah interrupted. Icicles crept down her spine that the Florida sunshine couldn't melt. "My dad died in 1984. His truck careened off the highway into the Pacific Ocean and he drowned."

"I know." Karen crouched forward, wringing her hands. "I was there."

Hannah looked at Guy. "What is she saying? What's this about?"

"I don't know," Guy whispered. He pulled her toward him in a firm side hug. "But I'm here. Let's give her a chance to finish."

Hannah whipped her gaze back to Karen. "Tell me," she demanded.

"Eleanor died. Joe flew to Washington to see me." Karen blurted the words in a rush. "He picked me up at my brand-new trailer that he'd bought me. It was beautiful. Top-of-the-line. Heat, air conditioning, and also a dishwasher. It changed my life. Lark's, too. When I finally sold it, I used the money to buy my condo here in Florida. If it weren't for your grandpa, I never would have been able to retire."

"I don't care about the trailer," Hannah snapped. "Tell me what this has got to do with my dad."

Tears splashed down Karen's cheeks. "Joe picked me up at the trailer. We were driving to Strawberry Cottage. Lark was at school. I suggested we stop at Blackfish Point to see the view. It was my favorite place. But it had rained that morning. Joe was driving too fast, and he wasn't used to our slick country roads. Your dad's truck came around a corner just as Joe leaned over to kiss me, and—"

A sob ripe with twenty years of anguish exploded from Hannah's heart. She roared with the pain of a thousand sleep-less nights. "No!" Hannah cried out. "No!" She sprang up from the table so fast that her chair toppled over. She wouldn't wait to hear what Karen said next. She couldn't bear it. All these years of sorrow. All the hardship she'd endured from Max's death being ruled a suicide. Losing her dad. Losing her mother to drugs and alcohol. Losing everything. And for what? So some rich prick could ruin her life without consequence?

"Hannah, I'm so sorry," Karen cried.

"Don't talk to me. Don't you dare talk to me!" In her rush to get away, Hannah almost tripped over the fallen chair. But she picked herself up just in time and escaped to the beach.

THIRTY

Hannah sat on the sand, surrounded by happy tourists. Little girls built sandcastles. Teenage boys leapt into the waves. Lovers walked hand in hand against a crashing Atlantic shoreline. Everything seemed wrong to Hannah. Nothing about this was right. The sun was too hot, the sand too gritty, and the people too scantily dressed. She missed the icy winds of Sand Dollar Cove. She longed for the kites and tire tracks that signaled home. She'd give anything to hear the foghorn croon in the distance like a lullaby. *That* was home to her. *That* was the beach. Not this fantasy wonderland of suntan lotion and bikini bottoms. Where were the Dungeness crabs? Where were the sea lions? Where were the beachcombers bundled up in fleeces and wool hats? She needed the Pacific Ocean to steady her. The Pacific... Her father's final resting place.

Hannah buried her head in her hands and cried until she was senseless. She was too distraught to notice the tourists spring away, like she was a drop of dish soap in a sink of oily water.

"What can I do?" she heard a voice ask. "How can I ease your pain?" Turning, she saw Guy, his face blotchy with tears.

"My family destroyed your life. How can I fix even a tiny part of that?"

"It's not your fault." She dug her feet into the sand. "Lying to me was your fault, but none of the rest of it was." She looked back at the water. "Besides, Gabriel wasn't biologically related to you."

"But he was the closest thing to a good parent that I had." Guy sat next to her, but kept his distance. "I hero-worshiped him my whole life."

"It's good to have heroes."

Her dad had never failed her. Even after all these years with people whispering about how he'd died, Hannah had never doubted her father's courage. Even when sometimes she allowed herself to believe that yes, maybe his death was suicide, that didn't change his hero status in her book.

"But Gabriel failed me," Guy said. "My granddad wasn't the good person he pretended to be. He lied to me, and he's probably guilty of organized crime, in the early days."

"And manslaughter," Hannah said bitterly.

"And manslaughter." Guy hung his head. "You must hate me."

"I don't hate you."

"You must hate my family, then."

"Yes, for being assholes. How could I not?"

Guy gulped. "I don't know. I just wish I knew how we could keep that from becoming a giant wedge between us."

"Why does it have to come between us?" She looked at him. "Why should we let them ruin what we have?"

"But... wouldn't it?"

Hannah shook her head. "Not necessarily. I'm not going to let them take something else from me. I can't stand lying, though, or omissions of truth."

"Neither can I. These past three months of pretending to be who I wasn't—that's not who I am."

Hannah made bunny fingers and hopped them over to Guy's knee. "I know who you are, Mr. Panicked Rabbit, and it's nothing sinister. You're someone who goes to great lengths to put other people at ease."

Guy covered her hand with his. "I can't forgive Gabriel for what he did to your family, but part of me will always love him because he was my granddad. Can you understand that?"

"That's the wedge between us you mentioned?"

Guy nodded.

Hannah traced the silver scar along her wrist. She finally allowed herself to picture the memories that she usually held back. *Her broken arm poking out at an odd angle. Her body crumpled around Mary's tiny one in the passenger seat. White-hot pain searing like fire. Flashing lights and sirens. The fire-fighters prying open the Corvette.* Two accidents shaped her life forever; not just the one at Blackfish Point. Not just the one with her dad.

"Sometimes the people we love make awful choices," she said, thinking of her mom. "But we can't let their choices ruin our lives. So no, I don't think it will be a wedge between us because I won't let it become one. Will you?"

Guy shook his head. "No. I won't let my family come between us ever again."

When she looked into Guy's tear-filled eyes, Hannah considered how much his family had ruined his life, too. Sure, he'd been given wealth, privilege, and an Ivy League education, but he didn't have the riches Hannah had grown up with. He didn't have Gran or Mary. He didn't have Herman teaching her to parallel-park, or Nancy helping her with her college applications. He didn't have Jasmine making her gourmet sand-wiches, or Keith helping find her family a safe place to live. And as much as her soul longed to return to Sand Dollar Cove and dip her toes into the icy Pacific, she knew that the sweetest homecoming of all would be the one when Guy was by her side.

"What are we going to do next?" she asked.

"First, we're going to burn these postcards." Guy unscrewed the lid to the jar. "I'm done with this." He dumped out the sand. "I'm done with all of it." He threw the sand dollars out toward the waves. "Then I'm going to call up the CEO of the insurance company and clear your father's name. After that, you're going to throw Herman a retirement party and take over the resort. And then..." Guy's voice cracked and he lapsed into silence.

"Then what?"

"Then I'll make *you* dinner for once, because you deserve to be taken care of, too."

"That sounds good."

"You haven't tasted my cooking yet."

Guy smiled as he pulled a matchbook from his pocket and handed it to her. "Would you like to do the honors?"

Hannah looked at the matchbook with a tiny picture of Seaside Resort. "I'm horrible with cardboard matches," she admitted. "I'm better with wooden ones."

"I'll teach you a trick." Guy took the matchbook back and ripped off a match. Then he folded the matchbook backwards and slid the match through the cover. A flame burst to life. "My granddad taught me that," he whispered as he watched the fire glow. He let the flame climb up the cardboard stick until it almost burned his fingertips, and then dropped it into the sand. "You try." Guy passed her the matches.

She ripped off a stick from the book and pulled it through the matchbook cover like Guy had showed her. The tiny flame burst into light. "There," she said with satisfaction. "You were right. That wasn't hard at all." Guy held out the postcard and together they watched Gabriel's handwriting disappear.

Hannah stared into the flames, letting it all sink in. She finally had closure about Max's death, and the comfort of knowing that he had died in a state of happiness instead of depression. It was as if, for the first time since she was a little girl being carried in his arms, Hannah could breathe freely. She could let out the giant breath she'd been holding for years. Hannah was ready to put the past behind her and live her best life possible, not only for herself, but for Max, too. Every minute she spent in joyful living was a moment that her father's memory was still alive. He would probably love the fact that she was sitting here on the beach, next to a good man who loved her, finally ready to live her life fearlessly.

Hannah scooted closer to Guy and linked her arm through his. She laced their fingers together into one firm grip. *Do you see me, Dad?* her heart whispered. *Do you see me?* She watched as the embers changed to ashes. The ghosts of the past no longer haunted her. Max's spirit was free, and so was she. Her heart could see him, too.

EPILOGUE
FRIDAY, MAY 31ST

"This is it!" Mary shot her palms in the air and danced around Strawberry Cottage. "Who's excited?"

"We're all excited," said Cheryl. "There's never been a private party for the staff in the Vista Room before. Too bad it's for Herman's retirement and not something more exciting, like Hannah's promotion. I just hope Jasmine gets to put her feet up and enjoy herself for once, instead of spending all day over a hot stove."

"It's being catered, so that the kitchen staff can come, too," said Hannah.

"Catered?" Cheryl asked. "By whom?"

"The culinary team at Grays Harbor State," said Mary. "Basically, we're eating dorm food. But that's not what we're excited about, right?" She stopped tap-dancing and looked both of them in the eye.

"Uh..." Hannah blinked as she stalled for time. She had no idea what Mary was talking about. "We're excited about Guy finally telling the staff that his last name isn't Barret?" she asked.

"Or about our move to Brittany's house next week?" Cheryl suggested.

"No, sillies." Mary flashed her left hand. "We're excited that Aidan's coming home this evening. Three days early. And he's going to propose!"

"Oh gosh, sis. That's right." Hannah rubbed hand lotion onto her elbows. "I'm sorry. These past few weeks have been a lot to process."

"I'll say." Gran rose unsteadily from her recliner and braced herself against her walker. "I still can't believe the chief executive officer of Washington National Insurance called me to personally apologize for inaccurately ruling Max's death a suicide. They said the check should arrive in our accounts in five business days—with interest!"

"That'll be life-changing," said Hannah. "For all of us. I just hope Mom doesn't blow her share on beer." She looked at her watch. "Shoot. We need to walk over to The Summer Wind, or we'll be late. Gran, are you sure you don't want your wheelchair?"

"Take it with us for backup, but the physical therapist said I should walk one thousand steps a day." Gran lifted her wrist. "She gave me a Fitbit."

"Cool," said Mary. "Those are fun."

"Right now, it says 873, so I still need to get my steps in. My goal is 1,200 steps, because I'm an overachiever."

"That seems to run in the family." Hannah took in a panoramic view of Strawberry Cottage. "You know, Mary, I don't say it enough, but you outdid yourself with this place."

"I told you she could bedazzle a turd," said Cheryl.

"More like turn a dump into a home." Hannah hugged her sister. "I'm going to miss Strawberry Cottage, but not as much as I'm going to miss you when you get married and Aidan takes you away."

"I won't go far," Mary promised. "Unless he gets a traveling nurse job someplace exciting, like Chicago."

"What about LA?" Cheryl asked. "Ever get a hankering to go back to acting?"

Mary vigorously shook her head. "No, thank you. Eighteen months of being a starving actress was enough for me."

"I'm glad you came home and are getting your degree," said Cheryl. "A woman's education can never be taken away from her."

A knock at the front door interrupted their conversation.

"That might be Aidan!" Mary exclaimed. She ran to the door and threw it open.

Guy stood there waiting for them, holding a basket covered with a tea towel.

"Hi, Mary. I brought you all home-baked blueberry muffins for breakfast tomorrow."

"Of course you did," Mary said, sounding disappointed.

"Do you not like blueberry? I'm sorry about that. Next time I'll bring—"

"I love blueberries. I just love Aidan more. I thought you were him." Mary stepped aside so that Guy could enter the cottage. "You didn't see him in the parking lot, did you?"

"If I passed him I wouldn't know, since I've never met him before." Guy put the basket on the kitchen table and Hannah hugged him from behind.

She stood on her tiptoes and whispered into his ear. "I happen to adore your baked goods."

"Oh you do, do you?" Guy spun around and allowed Hannah to pin him against the counter. "I'm a beginner baker, so be nice."

Hannah nibbled his earlobe. "Did you add crumble topping?"

"Yes, with extra brown sugar. I became very sticky in the process."

Hannah cupped his face and crushed her lips against his.

"Would you two cut it out?" Mary asked. "There is such a

thing as a romance being *too* sweet."

"How are my tomato plants doing?" Cheryl asked, changing the subject.

"Still alive," said Guy, as he stroked Hannah's hair.

"I rotated them this morning because they keep bending toward the sun," said Hannah.

"As soon as I can manage stairs again, I'm inviting myself over to see your apartment," said Cheryl.

"You mean *Guy's* apartment," said Mary. "Hannah still lives with us. Technically."

"And you still live with us too, *technically*," Cheryl replied. "But who knows what will happen now that Aidan's coming back to town? It might just be me, Brittany, and that boy of hers, living in the McMansion."

"And Keith popping over for visits," said Hannah. "I bet he'll be part of the equation."

"Good grief," Gran muttered. "The Diabetes Sisters will love that."

Hannah checked the time. "We'd better scoot if we're going to make it to Herman's retirement party on schedule. You know Nancy expects promptness."

"That she does." Cheryl walked to the front door. "Would you look at that? Now my Fitbit says 892." She shuffled forward and backward as Hannah and Mary collected their purses. "Yes!" Cheryl cheered. "I hit nine hundred!"

"Well done," said Guy.

"I'm putting our coats in the wheelchair in case it's cold when we walk home." Hannah put the purple coat on top, so it would be safe. She was about to ask Guy if he'd mind walking next to Cheryl to keep an eye on her, but he was already standing right by her grandma's side, ready to catch Cheryl if she stumbled. "Lock the door behind us, will you?" Hannah asked Mary.

"You got it." Mary had her key in her hand.

The Pacific Ocean greeted Hannah when she rolled the wheelchair out onto the porch. She took the deepest breath her lungs would allow, and let it out one beat at a time. The calm she felt was incredible. Meeting the love of her life was one thing, but realizing how much Guy cared for Cheryl and Mary made her happiness complete. If there was one thing she'd learned from Guy, their families, and Sand Dollar Cove, it was that joy was even sweeter when it rose over stress like a kite on a breeze.

When they reached The Summer Wind and the Vista Room, the deck was packed with friends. Michael Bublé crooned over the sound system. Will and his girlfriend chatted with Jasmine and her boyfriend. Nancy wore a flowing dress that reminded Hannah of peach sherbet. Herman, Nick, Shane, and friends from his poker club held steins of beer. Lark was there, too. Hannah was grateful that their friendship had been able to remain intact despite the intense conversation they had shared after Hannah and Guy had returned from Florida and revealed what they'd learned about Karen's role in Max's death.

But the person Hannah was always most excited to see was Guy, who was arranging a chair for Cheryl to sit down. His slacks were the same color as the sand, and his darkening blond hair matched his shiny leather shoes. They locked eyes over the crowd and smiled. When "It's A Beautiful Day" began, Hannah parked the wheelchair and ran up the steps onto the deck, straight into Guy's waiting arms.

"Are you happy?" he asked after twirling her around.

She nodded. "You bet." Her heart flooded with warmth. The kindest, gentlest, most supportive man in the world was by her side. "And you? Are you happy, Guy?"

"Deliriously so." He nodded. "Your gran was just telling me that there's an open position at her physical therapy clinic, and I was thinking, once you have time to hire my replacement, I might—"

"Do the job that you were called to do?" she asked.

"That's right. For one day a week, at least. That's all I can manage while also running the company remotely. It might get kind of complicated."

"We'll figure it out together."

"We will?"

She nodded. "Heck, I might even learn to cook tempeh or nutloaf for you."

"That, I'd pay to see."

Hannah smiled. "You're not alone anymore, Guy Barret, or Guy Blanchet, or whatever you want to call yourself."

"And neither are you, Hannah Turner." He kissed her lightly on the cheek since so many people were watching.

Hannah smiled knowing that the Turner name meant something in this town. It had always meant something. Only now the shadows from the past were gone. The truth had set Max's story free. The torch her father had passed her, the torch she had always carried, lit her path. Hannah's beacon of hope and responsibility glowed as bright as ever.

"This is everything I ever wanted and so much more," she confessed. She held onto his arm as she gazed out at the water. The foghorn sang in the distance.

"Me too, my love." He kissed her hair. "I'm finally home."

But a few seconds later, their quiet revelry was interrupted.

"Hannah? Is that you?" called a voice. "Do you know where I can find Mary?"

Hannah turned around to see who was speaking to her. When she saw who it was, her heart crunched like a potato chip. Aidan DeLack stood on the deck's steps, holding a woman's hand. And the woman was visibly pregnant.

"Aidan..." Hannah sputtered. "What? Who...?" She had difficulty stringing words together.

"This is my wife, Lara." Aidan lifted her left hand and showed off Lara's wedding ring. Atop it sat her engagement ring. *A gigantic pear-shaped bling machine.* "Thanks for the advice on what setting to buy. It would have been too awkward to ask your sister."

"You... your... Huh? I don't understand." Hannah's voice shook.

"I'll find Mary," Guy whispered. "Let's go someplace quiet so she won't be publicly humiliated."

But it was too late.

"Aidan!" Mary cried from the other side of the deck. She skipped past partygoers until she was seconds away from leaping into his arms. At the last moment, she caught sight of Lara and froze. "Who's this?" she asked.

"Lara, my wife. Mary—I can explain," said Aidan.

Mary yelped like a wounded animal. "Your wife?"

"Mary," Hannah said in a steady tone. "It's going to be okay." Her power of speech had returned to her with an extra dose of venom. "Guy, would you please take Lara over to the buffet and help her get a plate of food, since she's eating for two? Aidan's coming with Mary and me to my new office. I'll call you if I need the aerial silks. They might come in handy if I decide to tie the bastard up." She folded her arms and lifted her chin.

How dare Aidan come to Seaside Resort and hurt Mary like this? She wouldn't let Aidan break Mary's heart without making him squirm.

Hannah grabbed her purple coat and put it on like battle armor. She drank in the heady scent of the ocean like it was an elixir. As she marched Aidan toward the lodge, she felt the strength of her own power. This conversation would be difficult, but she was up to the challenge. Hannah knew that she was capable of brave things. She took risks. She moved forward. And above all else, she protected her sister. Aidan had better watch out.

A LETTER FROM JENNIFER

Thank you from the bottom of my heart for choosing to spend time with Hannah, Guy, and all of my characters in Sand Dollar Cove. I hope you feel like you've taken a fun trip to Washington State and can feel the cool breeze kiss your cheeks. Sand Dollar Cove is a fictitious place, but it was inspired by the real town of Ocean Shores, Washington, where the wind almost always blows and you can drive right up to the beach.

Did you enjoy the twists and turns that Hannah and Guy explored? Stay tuned, because there are lots more secrets for Mary to discover. You can keep up with all of my latest releases by subscribing to my newsletter. Your email will never be shared and you can unsubscribe at any time.

www.bookouture.com/jennifer-bardsley

Another fun way to stay up to date on the latest happenings in Sand Dollar Cove is to follow me on social media. I also have a private, VIP reader group on Facebook called Jennifer Bardsley's Book Sneakers that I would love for you to join.

Finally, I'd like to say a huge thank you to all of you wonderful readers who take a quick moment and leave a review on Amazon and Goodreads. I value your input tremendously, and your thoughts help other readers find my books.

I hope to see you again in Sand Dollar Cove really soon. Hannah and Guy's love story is in full bloom, but Mary deserves a happy ending too, don't you think?

KEEP IN TOUCH WITH JENNIFER

www.jenniferbardsley.com

facebook.com/JenniferBardsleyAuthor
x.com/JennBardsley
instagram.com/jenniferbardsleyauthor
tiktok.com/@jenniferbardsley

ACKNOWLEDGMENTS

Thank you to my agent, Liza Fleissig, my editor, Lucy Frederick, my critique partner, Penelope Wright, my copyeditor, Jenny Page, my proofreader, Liz Hurst, and the wonderful team at Bookouture for bringing the world of Sand Dollar Cove to light. Thank you especially to my readers, who have traveled with me from one little town in the Pacific Northwest to the next. I appreciate you tremendously, and hope that if you ever get the chance to visit Washington State, my books help you remember to bring layers, sturdy walking shoes, and a highly competent raincoat.

PUBLISHING TEAM

Turning a manuscript into a book requires the efforts of many people. The publishing team at Bookouture would like to acknowledge everyone who contributed to this publication.

Commercial
Lauren Morrissette
Jil Thielen
Imogen Allport

Cover design
Emma Graves

Data and analysis
Mark Alder
Mohamed Bussuri

Editorial
Lucy Frederick
Imogen Allport

Copyeditor
Jenny Page

Proofreader
Liz Hurst

Marketing
Alex Crow
Melanie Price
Occy Carr
Cíara Rosney

Operations and distribution
Marina Valles
Stephanie Straub

Production
Hannah Snetsinger
Mandy Kullar
Jen Shannon

Publicity
Kim Nash
Noelle Holten
Myrto Kalavrezou
Jess Readett
Sarah Hardy

Rights and contracts
Peta Nightingale
Richard King
Saidah Graham